STONESKIN'S REVENGE

a tale of Calvin McIntosh

TOM DEITZ

AVON BOOKS NEW YORK

STONESKIN'S REVENGE is an original publication of Avon Books. This work has never before appeared in book form. This work is a novel. Any similarity to actual persons or events is purely coincidental.

AVON BOOKS
A division of
The Hearst Corporation
105 Madison Avenue
New York, New York 10016

First Avon Books Printing: March 1991

AVON TRADEMARK REG. U.S. PAT. OFF. AND IN OTHER COUNTRIES, MARCA REGISTRADA, HECHO EN U.S.A.

Printed in the U.S.A.

RA 10 9 8 7 6 5 4 3 2 1

ACKNOWLEDGMENTS

thanks to:

Boo Alexander
Gilbert Head
Adele Leone
Betty Marchinton
Larry Marchinton
Paul Matthews
Mike McLeod
Chris Miller
Chris Myllo
Klon Newell
Vickie Sharp
Jean Starr
Brad Strickland
Sharon Webb

and to

Buck Marchinton,
natural history consultant *par excellence:*
a special note of appreciation
for finding time in Hell Quarter to answer all
those stupid questions,
for being my eyes and ears in far-off places,
and
for being a friend when it was an awful lot of
trouble to be one

Oh Lord, my name is Calvin, an' Indian blood run through
   my veins.
Yeah, my name is Calvin Fargo, an' Cherokee blood be
   pulsin' in my veins.
I've had some wild adventures; seen an awful lot o'
   wond'rous things.

Well, I got a friend in Georgia; David Kevin Sullivan be
   that boy's name.
Got me a good, good friend in Georgia; David Sullivan
   be his Christian name.
Dave saw some lights one evenin'; an' ever since he ain't
   been quite the same.

Well, you know my buddy David? One day he went an'
   got the Second Sight.
Yeah, you know my buddy David? He fooled around an'
   got the Second Sight.
He saw the Faeries ridin'—an' that gave him one mighty
   fright.

Werepossum Blues
words: Calvin McIntosh
music: Darrell Buchanan

Prologue I: Song-Called

(Jackson County, Georgia— Monday, June 16—between midnight and sunrise)

That there was fog in Jackson County in the close, still hours before dawn was not, of itself, remarkable. Granted, it *was* almost summer, but that did not mean nights could not bring with them a hint of chill, especially in shady places like the wooded hollows off Lebanon Road ten miles south of Jefferson—*especially* when middle Georgia was always humid anyway, present clear sky and moonlight notwithstanding.

But something about *this* fog was different. It had appeared too abruptly, for one thing: easing up from the Middle Oconee in thick white tendrils like the wraiths of the legendary uktena-serpents of the *Ani-Yunwiya,* who had wrested this land from the *Ani-Kusa* and held it and farmed it and hunted it until the white men came with their endless lies and their empty promises and their worthless treaties. The Ani-Yunwiya—the Principal People—the *Cherokee,* as they were called in a tongue not their own—had long since departed, though: marched west in the van of Winfield Scott's muskets. Yet their legacy still lingered, not merely in the pot shards and arrowheads that seeded the nearby riverbottoms, but in the very names of the waters that drained field and forest alike: Oconee, and—more remotely—the smaller stream that fed it: Bloody Creek, where the Ani-Yunwiya and the Ani-Kusa had fought one of their most sanguineous battles.

Both were at peace tonight, however, drowsing beneath a skim of white that grew denser and deeper and crept up the oak-snarled ridges with unseemly haste, as if it hurried to meet some urgent summons.

Perhaps it did.

It brushed granite boulders and enwrapped them, fingered red maples and clung to their trunks and dragged more of its heavy white mass up behind, then hooked other trees, other stones, and flowed deeper into the woods and across the first of the fossilized logging roads. A little farther on it snared a meadow: clover between stands of oak and hickory and loblolly pines. Two apple trees and three chestnuts grew there as late-season enticement for the whitetails that would be hunted in the fall from the tree stand looming above the mist like the crows' nest of some becalmed vessel. Three teenage campers slept in it and whimpered when their dreams went suddenly grim and chill, while a fourth was abroad and furtive. *His* song floated through the nighted woods, low and *a cappella,* in a tongue of the Ani-Yunwiya that was too *strong* to be deadened by fog. Perhaps it was his singing which drew it.

Or maybe it came at the prompting of another who had sensed the boy's need from a World away and responded by the only means it could, for where the white was thickest a deer appeared. It too was white—and not remotely mortal—but it smelled its humbler kindred about and summoned a yearling buck with the barks and grunts that were its language here in the Lying World. They traveled together for a while, and then came whistling death from the singer's arrow and thanks for a life from a lucky hunter—but that was all according to the Law, and *Awi-Usdi,* the Little Deer, approved it.

The ground felt the blood, too; knew it seeping warm

into the loam and clay as it drank it down. And the fog shrank back from that sudden heat, back through the trees, back over the campers and the red Mustang that had brought them, back down the hollows to the Middle Oconee River.

And back to Bloody Creek.

But it did not slide silent into the waters there. It lingered, cold and waiting, coiled around the mortarless piled stones of a long-abandoned bridge abutment—bound, perhaps, by something that was not quite done with the secrecy it afforded. And then that something moaned as if in pain, there where the fog had curdled longest, and then the mist abated.

But in its wake, a thing moved in the land for the first time in countless ages. And that thing too was singing . . .

Prologue II: Wheels Within Wheels

(Walhala, Galunlati—high summer—early morning)

Hyuntikwala Usunhi—Uki, as he was sometimes called in the Lying World—sat cross-legged on the southern spoke of his Power Wheel and stared at the amorphous, fist-sized crystal he had fixed precisely at the juncture of the four radiating strips of dark gravel that marked the cardinal directions and stretched ten arm spans back to the rim, where they terminated in lightning-blasted trees of diverse colors, not all of them natural. The circle of sand beneath those spokes was most times white as salt—as perfectly white as Uki's own hairless skin (though he was not an albino)—but Nunda Igehi's first hot, pulsing light now tinged both with a wash of the red that was Power Color of the East. There was no wind, and it would not have disturbed a grain had there been any; but the odors of cedar and laurel—plants of vigilance—floated delicately across the clearing from where they both guarded and framed this Place of Power.

And still Uki sat unmoving.

He was naked except for a white doeskin loincloth that

bore beaded patterns of lightning bolts, and for the twin golden uktena-bracelets that coiled around his muscular biceps. His black hair hung unbound down wide shoulders to brush the ground. His right index finger still oozed blood from where he had pricked it to awaken the crystal.

And longer yet he lingered.

It was probably not wise to use the *ulunsuti* so, he told himself, not prudent to empower it as often as he lately had to spy between the Worlds, great need or no. Those who minded the World Walls might become capricious and show him things that were not—or reveal pasts or futures in the guise of the present and so confound him. Time was not a constant thing between the Worlds: this much Edahi, his mortal apprentice, had taught him; as Uki had instructed the lad in turn about many other things he hoped would do him good in the Lying World. But *that* bit of knowledge confused far more than it clarified.

Adawehiyu, they called to him: *very great magician.* But what did anyone know? All magic gave you was awareness of the immensity of your ignorance.

Well, not *all*.

Magic had gained Uki sovereignty over the weather here in Walhala.

Magic had given him allies in the Lying World for the first time in almost two hundred cycles of the sun and in so doing had shaken him from his ancient insularity and reawakened his curiosity, which was itself magic of a kind.

And lately it had shown him an illness in Nunda Igehi, and given him a means to effect its cure—if the efforts of certain mortal friends succeeded.

It was to check on them that he had come here with the ulunsuti.

He continued to stare at it, feeling the sun hot across his shoulders, his eyes burning with weariness as he sought to conjure the image of Edahi as Uki last had seen him: tall and straight and strong, with hair like raw stone-that-burns, and the twinkling eyes that had so entranced his half-sisters, the Serpent Women.

But he still saw nothing except glassy haze and the septum of red light that bifurcated the crystal.

And then, abruptly, images . . .

. . . *morning sunlight glints off the pitted chrome and Candyapple Red enamel of a '66 Mustang hardtop that looks as if it needs new paint far more than the frequent waxing that is obvious surrogate. One fender is blue and has been for nearly a year, and it carries the mud and dust of half-a-dozen north Georgia counties across its dented flanks. Its interior is seat-deep in road-trip detritus: maps, candy wrappers, foam plastic burger boxes from the Winder McDonald's, a burgundy T-shirt emblazoned with the sigil of the Enotah County 'Possums, bits of legal paper bearing scrawls in four adolescent hands. And the trunk . . . though closed, that has been lately pillaged of backpacks and coolers and less likely gear. The only noteworthy object there now is a recurve bow of laminated wood, its countless layers shimmering like a rainbow.*

The car sits in an oil-stained driveway just shy of the terminus of a dead-end street in a suburb east of Atlanta. A brick ranch house rises before it, its lawn unmown, the paint on the front door peeling. The nearer side yard is enclosed by a high chainlink fence wire-laced to angle-iron posts anchored ten feet apart. It secures a brace of beagles used for rabbit hunting. Woods rise behind it, shielding any view of civilization in that quarter. It is the last house on the block, the only brick house on its side of the street.

Sudden cries shatter the suburban calm: teenagers—nervous and harried and alarmed. A girl stumbles from the forest. Her hair is red and she drags a knapsack with one hand while clutching a small animal to her breast with the other. (Uki starts at this.) She dashes to the fence and pauses there, terrified, gazing back at the sky above the treetops. Two boys follow: one blond, one dark-haired, also with knapsacks. Between them they assist a third, who is staggering. He too is blond, but here is a strangeness to his features that is not entirely human, for he is one of the Nunnihe who live on the other side of the Lying World from Galunlati. Uki knows all three boys but does not bother to name them. It is sufficient that they are friends.

He wonders what has happened to them, though, for their faces are all haggard with fatigue and dread, and like the girl, they aim apprehensive glances at the sky. The Nunnihe boy screams as they approach the fence.

Birds slide into view above the treetops: vast raptors gliding quick and low. They are black and larger than any eagles, though that is what they most resemble.

The shorter boy, the blond, yells frantic orders, abandons his charge, and scrambles over the back fence, then pounds through the dog lot and vaults the street-side fence. His cut-off jeans rip as he crosses. The beagles are too taken aback to react.

He reaches the car, fumbles in his pocket but finds no keys, then snags his spare pair from under the hood. A moment later he is in the seat, gunning the engine. He backs up, then finds first—and floors the accelerator. Tires squeal, and he aims the Mustang toward the fence. Metal shrieks, the fence collapses, and beagles disperse in terror.

The car hurtles on, smashes the back fence as well, and grinds to a noisy halt atop it. The boy leaps out, the girl takes his place behind the wheel, and the boy helps his dark-haired friend with his screaming Nunnihe companion. A door slams, and the birds descend.

There are six of them, and they attack the car, but seem to be repulsed by the metal. As the Mustang roars into the street, one falls to the pavement and flops about gracelessly. Though already large as a man, it shimmers and blurs, and suddenly takes on the form of a tall, slim warrior in black.

From the shadows by the woods brown eyes can abide such sights no longer. Their owner vents a panicked, yodeling cry and bolts for deeper cover.

But the bird-man does not hear. He regains his equilibrium, shifts shape once more, and wings skyward.

The car speeds away, but in the backseat the Nunnihe boy screams louder still and starts to writhe. His friends watch, concerned, and then the boy in front sets fire to paper and thrusts something into its heart. The blond boy finds himself handed the small animal. Uki's name is

*shrieked aloud, but is cut off. Flame fills the Mustang for
an instant, and then the backseat is empty, though the car
continues on . . .*

For a moment longer Uki watched, a scowl of concern
furrowing his snowy brow, but then he muttered certain
words and cast his vision south. What he saw there troubled him even more: the Nunnihe boy and the blond boy
had succeeded, were here in Galunlati, but far away, which
he had not expected. And Edahi was with them, though
not in his own form. Uki could spare no time to seek
them, but he could certainly send word.

He stood, scanned the sky, and uttered a long, high-
pitched screech.

An instant later an eagle appeared, floating down from
the hot, cloudless heavens to land lightly on the northern
spoke. *"Siyu,"* it rasped gravely. "Greetings, Hyuntikwala Usunhi."

"Siyu, adawehiyu," Uki responded formally. "Greetings unto *Awahili*, Lord of Eagles."

"You have need of me?"

"I do."

And with that Uki delivered unto Awahili certain messages, and took from a pouch at his waist what looked like
two milk-white arrowheads—or maybe they were sharks'
teeth. These he placed in another pouch, which he looped
around his feathered colleague's neck.

"Your message will be delivered," Awahili assured him,
and rose once more into the sky. The sand showed no
mark of his passing; not a single grain had been shifted
by his feathers.

Uki sat down again, though it was not to spy on the
present this time, but to cast his eye to the future a day—
and a World—away.

At first the ulunsuti remained clear, the septum pulsing
dully as Uki sought anew to pierce the World Walls—and
then, abruptly, it darkened. It was as if the Barriers Between had grown solid and opaque when he tried to gaze
upon the results of Awahili's messages, as if someone had
thrown up endless clouds of sand to veil his sight.

He tried harder . . .

Harder—his mind a blank except for that single desire. The septum flared within its crystal housing, writhing like red flame under torture, still revealing nothing.

Which was not good, when he desperately needed to know how Edahi and his companions fared.

There was but one thing more he could try, though it would cost him dear—yet there was no help for it.

Sighing, Uki reached into a second pouch and drew out a thin, finger-long sliver of black obsidian. His face did not twitch a muscle when he slid that sliver across the flesh of his palm, nor when he pressed his hand atop the ulunsuti and let it have its fill.

Long that crystal drank, and long the septum guttered like a torch thrust against a wall of oak planks.

And long the veils of sand and dust resisted, but at last they grew thin enough to show Uki what had raised them.

"No!" he whispered to the surrounding silence. Such a thing should not even *be* in the Lying World! No one there would know what to do with it.

He could not go there himself, for his responsibility to Walhala had to take priority.

But maybe he could still send a warning.

PART I

SIGNS AND PORTENTS

Chapter I: Watched Pot

(five miles south of Whidden, Georgia— Tuesday, June 17—noonish)

"Oh, go *ahead*, I reckon," the waitress grumbled in the lazy local drawl that seemed to grow slower the closer to the coast one got—exactly like the maze of rivers Calvin and his friends had traversed on their trip up I-95 from Cumberland Island that morning. She was perhaps sixteen—probably this year's crop of high-school juniors—and passably pretty, if a bit chubby. Understandable, given the fare her place of employment specialized in, which was fresh, deep-fried seafood. "I'll have to watch you, though an' you can only talk until somebody needs somethin'. An' it's *gotta* be collect," she added with an air of tired finality that was depressingly at odds with her youth and did not bode well for a remarkable future.

Still leaning against the white-enameled cinder-block wall by the kitchen entrance where he had accosted the girl maybe a minute before, Calvin McIntosh puffed his cheeks thoughtfully and nodded his acquiescence, too tired to flash the dazzling white grin, the twinkle of brown eye that would have had most women eating out of his hand before now—never mind that he was barely twenty and didn't look even that. "I just need to let somebody know I'm okay," he reiterated as neutrally as he could. "Anything else is gravy—or this bein' the kind of place it is, maybe tartar sauce."

His attempt at humor went right over the frizzy blond head, but left a confused frown and a grunt in its wake. His own black brows lowered in turn. Recalcitrance was *not* what he needed, not when he was tired as hell and had two days of absence to explain to his girlfriend up in Carolina—days when, as far as she knew, he'd literally fallen off the face of the earth . . . which in a way he had. He wondered if the waitress's attitude was due to impatience (though he and his friends were the only customers at the moment), fear of reprisal for violation of "the rules," or—as he caught his reflection in the round surveillance mirror in the corner—his appearance.

That last was a *real* possibility.

It was not that he was dirty, really—though he hadn't had a proper bath in three days and had sweated through his black T-shirt on the ride up from the island (five people in an un-airconditioned '66 Mustang for a couple of hours in the middle of June guaranteed that); and there was still a bit of sand clinging to his jeans from where he'd got them wet at Cumberland's beach. But neither of those breaches of decorum was likely to raise eyebrows in a county as rural as this, especially in what was obviously *not* a four-star establishment.

What *might* give a teenage girl pause, though, was the haunted look on his face, the wildness in his eyes, that made his coppery skin and shoulder-long, jet-black hair seem positively alien when set against the present rather antiseptic enamel-and-vinyl surroundings. Up where he was most lately from, the combination practically screamed *Cherokee Indian*—which he was. He didn't know what it proclaimed in backwoods south Georgia, but had learned from a year on the Appalachian Trail that a good first impression was important. And that was an uphill battle when you were part of an exotic minority to start with, never mind the complication of looking as scuzzy as he currently did.

"Phone's up in th' office," the girl announced after another round of scowling consideration. "But keep it short, I ain't supposed to let customers use it." She spun around with a flourish and sashayed toward the bank of plate-glass windows that comprised most of the entrance wall of Whidden's Steak-and-Seafood. Her rapid pace indicated that she didn't care whether he followed or not.

Calvin marched dutifully behind, sparing a glance to the booth in the right rear corner where his companions were still puzzling over menus. The blond boy—his name was David Sullivan, and he was very probably Calvin's best friend—whispered something to his septuagenarian uncle that produced a sharp cackle and a wiggle of white goatee. But then Dave noticed him and nodded his okay when Calvin pointed toward the half-wall of rough-cut pine that partly screened the office from the dining room at large.

" 'Member, keep it quick," the waitress reminded him as she ushered him into a tiny white cubicle that was dominated by a gray metal desk, an unmatching file cabinet, and a trash can stuffed full of defunct menus. A pile of *Bon Appetites* accented one of the desk's front corners. The other supported an untidy stack of *The Willacoochee Witness*—and the phone.

The girl stationed herself in the open doorway and continued to glare at him as Calvin picked up the receiver. He ignored her and punched in zero, followed by a certain number in the wilds of the Great Smoky Mountains near Sylva, North Carolina, then informed the sleepy-sounding operator that he was calling collect and who he was.

The phone rang thrice, whereupon an answering machine clicked on: "You have reached Sandy Fairfax. I'm sorry but I can't—" and then: *"Hello?"* The voice that interrupted was musical, soft, with a hint of mountain twang.

"Collect call from Calvin. Will you accept?"

"Yes, oh yes!" And then, with another click, he was through.

"Sandy?" he ventured tentatively, then: "It's me—finally."

"Calvin! Are you all right—is *everybody* all right?"

"Fine as *can* be, e'cept for bein' tired and burned out. I could sleep for a week. We—"

"So where *are* you? Where've you *been?*"

Calvin frowned in perplexity at the hint of irritation coloring the much more obvious relief. "Didn't you get my message? I left one on your machine last night."

"Oops! Yeah, you're right—though I'm not sure I'd consider 'Am in Crawfordville, Georgia, and safe . . . mission mostly accomplished . . . headin' south . . . will call again' much of a message. Not when you've heard absolutely zilch for almost two days!"

Calvin rolled his eyes in resignation. Though she was obviously making an effort to hide it, Sandy sounded more than a little pissed. Still, he supposed she had a right to blow off a little steam, given that he hadn't exactly sent her hourly reports about what had happened to him and his friends since they'd vacated her cabin Sunday evening—not that he always could have, since they didn't have phones most places he'd been, never had and never would. But maybe he could have made a better effort . . .

"I can't talk long even now," he apologized. "I'm in a restaurant near some place called Whidden, Georgia—that's north of Brunswick and south of about everything else, I reckon—but walls have ears, if you get my drift."

"So," Sandy sighed after a pause, "yes or no: did you save the World?" Wistfulness seemed to have replaced her earlier irritation.

"More than one actually," Calvin chuckled wryly. "But, yeah—or it got done, anyway, though *not* the way we planned. Things went okay as far as Stone Mountain, in the sense that we accomplished what we set out to. But Dave and me got separated from everybody else right after we rescued Finno and had to make an on-the-fly switch to—" He paused and glanced over his shoulder to see the waitress totally absorbed with her nails, which was probably fortunate.

"Uh . . . let's just say it was that *other* place I go to

sometimes,'' Calvin finished mysteriously. ''And then I wound up havin' to go on *another* errand there, which I pulled off barely in time. And after that I had to boogie back here. I caught up with Uncle Dale last night—that was up in Crawfordville, where I called you from—but we didn't touch base with Dave again until this mornin'. Things more or less came to a head near Cumberland Island—that's where Alec and Liz wound up—but I only caught the tail end of the action. There was some semi-divine intervention at the end, but I'd probably better leave it at that for the time being. I—''

He paused once more, gazing out the window to watch a bronze Chevy Caprice with WILLACOOCHEE COUNTY SHERIFF'S DEPARTMENT blazoned on its side ease into the parking lot. The driver glanced his way and continued staring as he executed a leisurely U-turn and headed out again. Calvin wondered if the guy could actually see him through mirror shades, tinted glass, and a plate-glass window.

''Calvin?''

''Sorry. Cop car just cruised by and I thought the guy was lookin' at me. Just my old paranoia kickin' in, I guess. You know how I am about bein' unobtrusive.''

''That not real easy with your looks.''

''*That's* why I like to avoid towns,'' Calvin countered gleefully, ''especially small ones. In the woods *nobody'll* notice you, if you're careful. Trouble is, folks've got rules and regulations all over every tree and vine, even in the parks, and when you're a little bit different, they tend to get *real* antsy, so it's best not to let 'em see you in the first place.''

''Which makes *you* paranoid, but we've had this conversation before.''

''Good point,'' Calvin conceded. ''Not the stuff to go over when you're in a rush. Oh . . . thanks, by the way.''

''For what?''

''For alertin' Dave's uncle to what was goin' on. He saved *all* our asses. Brought food, spare clothes, a bunch of campin' gear, just in case. Even brought Dave's bow, which I think he's gonna lend me, since I lost mine.''

"Calvin, no! That bow was made in Galunlati!"

"Tell me about it!"

"You got any money?" Sandy wondered suddenly.

"Just a fifty Uncle Dale slipped me on the sly."

"Need more?"

"Not at the moment."

"Well, feel free to ask if you do; I'm in the phone book."
A pause while Sandy cleared her throat, then: "So what're
y'all gonna do?"

He hesitated. This was it, then: the hard part, the lead-in
to the question he'd been dreading. "Well," Calvin began
finally, "I reckon *they're* gonna ride back with Dale . . ."

"What about *you?* When're *you* comin' home?"

Calvin took a deep breath. *"That's* . . . a real good
question. I—" He cleared his throat in turn, and tried once
more. "It's like . . . well, it's like stuff's just gotten *too*
weird, Sandy. And there's a lot of things I need to think
long and hard about. And . . . and I'd like to puzzle on
'em by myself for a while before I spring 'em on you and
see what they do to the old Unified Field Theory of Cos-
mology. Shoot, I'm afraid I'll *forget* 'em if I don't go over
'em again real soon, 'cause they're the kind of things folks
don't *want* to remember 'cause they're irrational."

"So you're saying . . . ?"

"That I'm gonna hang around down here a couple of
days and try to get my head straight. Otherwise, it'll be a
seven-hour drive back to MacTyrie with the rest of the
folks, durin' which I won't be able to concentrate worth
crap, and then there'd be debriefin' with Dave's friends,
and that'd eat up Wednesday, and then Gary's gettin' married on Saturday, and I can't get out of that, seein' as how
I'm a groomsman, only the hoo-ha with *that* starts in on
Friday—that's when the rehearsal dinner and bachelor party
are—and I'll be up to my ass in all that stuff from then till
sometime Sunday. That *might* give me half a day, and I
need more than that—which means I won't make it back
to your house until Sunday at the soonest, I guess," he
concluded lamely. "Sorry, but I've just *gotta* have a couple of days alone."

There it was; he'd said it, and he felt like a heel because

he knew he really ought to hightail it straight back to Sylva and give Sandy the low-down on what had been going on, then recuperate there. But he simply couldn't face another trip, not yet, not with so much weirdness in his head he felt like it was gonna explode.

"These . . . *things* you keep referring to," Sandy ventured finally, and Calvin could sense her trying to conceal her hurt. "Do they have to do with . . . ?"

He started to reply, then realized that a straight answer would make him sound like an absolute loon to the glowering door-warden, who was now giving him quite an alarming scowl and pointing meaningfully at her watch. His eyes quested vainly, came to rest on a pile of eleventh-grade textbooks atop the filing cabinet. "It's got to do with . . . with geography and astronomy and mythology and biology," he managed at last. "And with lycanthropy—a *lot* with that. I—"

"I understand," Sandy broke in simply. And he knew she did.

"Thanks," Calvin sighed. "You know I'll level with you when I can."

"I could come get you, then go to the wedding and meet these folks you're always talking about . . ."

"Hmmm," he mused thoughtfully. "Not a bad idea. Tell you what, I'll try to find a pay phone and check back with you later in the day when I can talk freely. Deal?"

"Deal. Have fun on your Vision Quest."

"It's not a—"

A warning cough from the waitress drew his attention, and he glanced up to see her striding toward him, a look of grim determination laying the groundwork for future wrinkles across her forehead.

"Gotta go," he finished quickly. "I'll call when I c—" And then the girl touched the transparent button atop the phone and cut him off.

"Bitch," he mouthed before he could stop himself. So much for good impressions, though apparently she didn't notice. Girl had to make a living, too, he supposed; and it really was kind of sorry of him to upset her routine like he had. Still, he wondered what Little-Miss-Evil-Eye would say if he told her that this World wasn't the only one: not by a bloody long shot.

More to the point, he wondered what she'd say if she knew she'd kept vigil not only over a Cherokee Indian, but also over one who just happened to be an apprentice shaman.

He grinned as he trotted over to rejoin his friends. He didn't quite believe it either.

Chapter II:
Inconveniences
(five miles south of Whidden, Georgia—oneish)

The sun was straight overhead in a cloudless sky and his shadow a puddle of black on the parking lot pavement beneath him when Calvin saw Dave's brake lights flash on as he slowed what he called the Mustang-of-Death at the entrance to the main highway. He heard a final shouted "Bye," and then the car passed from view behind a stand of scruffy magnolias, though the tired bellow of its exhaust persisted a moment longer.

And Calvin found himself alone outside an unremarkable restaurant in a south Georgia county he had never set foot in until that morning. It was hot, and there was no breeze; nothing to dispel the sharp tang of the nearby marshes or the sulfur-sweet smell of one of Union Camp's papermills a little farther off to the southeast. There was only the parking lot, the scrap of highway, the unpretentious white cinder-block building, the surrounding loom of pine woods—and himself and his thoughts.

His thoughts . . .

Where did he begin? With the nature of reality maybe?

With the world as it *really* was? But if he got off on that now, it would lead him . . .

Nowhere, Calvin decided, and turned away from both restaurant and road, hoisting a borrowed blue nylon backpack across his shoulders beside the rather special bow Dave's uncle had been thoughtful enough to bring along when he'd joined them. He had not gone three strides, however, before the pack straps began to chafe across his collarbones and tug at his unbound hair. He grunted and paused to resettle them, wishing there was more in it than a change of borrowed clothes, a small assortment of camping gear, a handmade Rakestraw hunting knife (also one of Dale's lendings), and some rapidly mellowing McDonald's biscuits. Comfortable at last, he fished in his pockets and produced a rubber band, with which he secured the bulk of his mane at the nape of his neck. Maybe that wouldn't attract too much attention: lots of twenty-year-old south Georgia boys had black hair. Some of 'em even wore ponytails. But, Calvin reckoned wryly, that was about all he had in common with the local lads. He took a deep breath and marched, with deliberate precision, into the forest.

An hour later Calvin had begun to suspect that the overland route was a bad idea, at least as far as speeding his quest for a pay phone. An hour along open highway would probably have put him in Whidden itself, had he any intention of going there, which he did not. Instead, he'd spent most of his time threading his way through close-grown groves of live oaks, circumnavigating spiky clumps of saw-toothed palmettos, peering through endless tendrils of Spanish moss, and beating off armies of gnats. It was hotter than ever, too, because there was no wind. And sticky. Still, he took some solace from the coolness of the ground under his now-bare feet, and the caress of sunlight across his muscular torso. For a time he'd considered stripping naked and navigating the woods the way Kanati had made him—but that would probably have been pushing his luck and local tolerance a little *too* far. Calvin did not want to make waves; not even a ripple. Complete invisibility was his (so-far-unattainable) goal, but he'd settle for being unobtrusive.

And then he came abruptly to the edge of the forest. Before him was a narrow ditch full of rancid-smelling black water and cattails, then a yard-wide strip of sand, beyond which a two-lane road widened into four—he supposed in anticipation of entering the yet-unseen metropolis of Whidden, which a white-and-green sign now promised to be a mile away. Could have fooled him, he thought wryly. The only signs of civilization were the road, the odd beer can among the browning stems, and the distant whoosh of a semi. There were more woods across the highway: still the ubiquitous pines. And a Magic Market.

"That do it for ya?" The voice was old, tired; the soft, coastal drawl clipped by impatience.

But, Calvin reflected sympathetically, it *was* the middle of the afternoon and the sunburned geezer behind the convenience store's checkout counter had apparently been on duty since, as he so colorfully put it, "God's tomcat went out to take a whizz" (which Calvin reckoned as about 5 A.M.). Add the fact that the place was ungodly hot as a result of an air-conditioner failure ("third 'un this month," the fossil had confided, staring hopefully at the ceiling fan backup) and the poor old soul probably had a right to be irritable—especially as Calvin had been taking his own sweet time making up his mind what he wanted.

Trouble was, he only had fifty bucks to fiddle with, which he needed to stretch as far as possible. No checks, no credit cards (never *had* had them, though), and—at the moment—not even a wallet to store the single wrinkled bill in.

The clerk cleared his throat, and Calvin started, realizing he'd been staring blankly at the shelves of cigarettes behind the man's peeling pate.

"Mister?"

Calvin blinked again, refocused on the clerk, then on the array of items ranged across the counter: a plastic quart bottle of reconstituted orange juice, a Snickers bar because he needed an energy jolt, a small jar of Folger's coffee (too expensive, but it'd beat the headache he'd get when his morning caffeine fix wore off), a couple of sticks of beef jerky, a vacuum-sealed can of generic peanuts (as much for the can as the contents), a box of matches, a small notebook, a Bic pen, a bar of Ivory soap, and the lone surviving *Savannah Morning News* from the rack by the door. This last was an indulgence, but he'd been out of touch with the rest of the world for the better part of three days and figured it was about time he found out what had been going on while he'd been off doing things so preposterous only about ten people in the world would possibly believe them. *Besides,* Calvin could always use the paper to sleep under, to start fires with, or for any of several other purposes. Besides, one of the minor head-lines—something about a woman being found dead in Jackson County—intrigued him. He'd just been in Jackson County, so it had resonated, and . . .

A third, more pointed, prompting from the cashier, and Calvin finally responded. ''Uh, yeah, reckon that'll do 'er.''

The clerk rang up the purchase and took Calvin's money with a relish that did not last until the returning of the change: two twenties and miscellaneous coins. Calvin dropped the pennies one by one into the cut-off paper cup designated for that purpose by the register. The sign above it read, GOT AN EXTRA? LEAVE ONE. NEED ONE? TAKE ONE.

''Not from around here, are you?''

Already turning to leave, Calvin scowled, wondering what had brought on this abrupt change of demeanor from someone who seconds before had seemed anxious to see his heels. Maybe it was simple relief: the guy had his money now and could afford to relax. Or perhaps he was merely lonely.

Except Calvin didn't think so.

'' 'Fraid not,'' Calvin replied at last, trying to be friendly in spite of a sudden urge to vent some heavy sar-casm, which surprised him. Usually he got on well with strangers; often as not brought up his heritage before they did, just to make them easy. The man was waiting for more too; expectant behind his thick lenses. "I'm from Atlanta, mostly," Calvin volunteered finally. "Grew up there, but my folks're from western Carolina."

"You Cherokee?"

Calvin nodded. "Good guess."

The man shrugged. "Common sense. Ain't no official Creeks no more, or Yuchi—which is what we had 'round here—and you don't look Seminole, if you don't mind me sayin'."

"No problem," Calvin assured him, wondering how Seminole, in fact, looked. He'd never seen one.

"Just passin' through?"

Yep, that was the standard next question; Calvin knew that from experience too. Usually folks were simply curious—Southerners were like that: they didn't much care what you did long as they knew you were doing it. It was sneakiness they couldn't abide—and this far south, there wasn't much bigotry toward Indians. Trouble was, folks tended to confuse Calvin's brand of unobtrusiveness *with* sneakiness.

"Uh, yeah," Calvin acknowledged finally. "Rode down to Cumberland with some friends to do a little . . . research. Never been here before and decided it was pretty neat country, so I figured I'd hang around a spell and get a feel for the territory, maybe do some thinkin'."

"Good place for *that*," the man chuckled. "Lord knows ain't nothin' *else* happens 'round here—'cept hurricanes, and ain't quite season for 'em yet. Had a big blow last night, though—guess you know that—if you 'uz down at Cumberland."

"Yeah," Calvin replied, glancing out the expanses of plate glass that fronted the store to where the parking lot was awash with drifts of Spanish moss and broken twigs, all aglitter in the sun. "I missed the worst of it," Calvin continued, "but some friends of mine were caught right in the middle."

"They come through okay?"

"Well as can be expected." And with that Calvin turned away, suddenly having no desire to continue the conversation, since he knew for a fact that the storm had not been remotely natural.

In the ensuing silence, he abruptly became aware of the ceiling fan.

Something about it made him think of flying. Perhaps it was the low-pitched wop-wop-wop that reminded him of vast wings flapping. Perhaps it was the breezes fanning his cheeks that made him imagine the winds of the high air wafting him along. It was a dream, he thought lazily, one all men shared, no matter what their ethnos: to go where one would, not limited to the land; to rise up or glide down at will; to proceed straight to one's goal; to ride on the back of the wind and see things others could not . . .

"You okay?"

The query startled him from his reverie. He blinked, spun around, puzzled as the colors in the room seemed to shift. "Yeah," he managed, blinking once more. "I'm fine." He hesitated at the door with his hand on the crossbar.

"There a pay phone around here?"

The clerk started, took nearly as long to reply as Calvin had earlier taken to respond to him. " 'Round the corner. Cost you fitty cent."

"Thanks," Calvin called, and stepped outside.

He halted at the edge of the concrete curb to wipe his face and shift the items in the plastic bag to his backpack. He *wished* he'd thought to buy a pair of cheap shades, for the world had gone hard and hot with the glare bouncing off pavement, off metal and plastic, off the white sands of the parking lot behind. He almost went back in, then changed his mind. No sense revving up the conversation again.

He was just turning the corner in quest of the promised phone when the crunch of bicycle tires reached him, almost simultaneously with a whoop of victorious exultation.

Trying not to look as if he'd been startled (which he had, a little) Calvin turned slowly around—and saw two lads, maybe thirteen or fourteen, who had evidently been racing on their ten-speeds. Both were around five-foot four or five; both wore cutoffs, sneakers, and T-shirts; and the blonder one was starting to fill out some. The slighter, dark-haired kid noticed him first, and Calvin saw the boy's gray-green eyes slide dubiously over his unlikely figure—and linger on the bow. There was a minute's mumbled pause, during which the dark kid engaged in some form of heated consultation with his companion, and then began peddling straight toward Calvin, who by this time was once more moving on.

"Hey, mister!" the boy called. "Wait up a minute! Mind if I take a look at that bow?"

Calvin grimaced, but stood his ground, then shrugged reluctant affirmation. After all, had he been in their BKs he'd have acted exactly the same.

"*All right!*" the kid cried, braking to a squeaky halt. "I used to hunt some, before my last dad d—"

"I'm Michael Chadwick," the other boy inserted, coasting up no-hands. "Ole Don Larry here don't have a lot in the way of manners."

"Calvin—Calvin McIntosh."

"Like in the next county over?" Michael wondered.

"I'm Don Scott," the shorter boy volunteered in turn, shoving a tanned hand in front of the one his friend was now extending. "And I do so have manners, I just get real *into* stuff sometimes, and it kinda gets the best of me."

"I know somebody like that," Calvin laughed, shaking hands in turn. "Gets him into a lot of trouble. Me too, sometimes."

But now that introductions were over, Don could not take his eyes off the bow.

With a surreptitious wink at Michael, Calvin unslung the weapon from his back and handed it to the smaller boy.

"Oh, wow," Don whispered reverently as he ran his fingers along the smooth, unlacquered surface.

"*Double* wow," Michael echoed, having finally caught his friend's enthusiasm. "Hey, look at all these different kinds of wood, and stuff. Springy at the tips, I bet—and real stiff-like here at the grip where these lightnin' bolt-things are.''

"Looks handmade," Don noted. "Where'd you get it, anyway?''

"A friend made it," Calvin told him truthfully, not adding that the friend lived in another World. "And another friend lent it to me. It's the only one of its kind anywhere around, now," he added with a touch of wist-fulness.

"What's it made out of?" Don asked. "Never seen *anything* like these green bits."

"Don't know most of 'em," Calvin replied. "Don't think we've got trees like that 'round here."

Don bent the bow appraisingly. "Poundage?"

"No idea, but I'd guess maybe sixty."

"Not *bad*," Don whispered. "More'n I could draw easy."

"More'n you could draw *period!*" Michael inserted, with a punch to his buddy's ribs, which Don countered without much effort.

"Could too!"

"It's all in how you use your body," Calvin explained. "I've had to practice a lot. But I've also had a good teacher."

"So what're you doin' here?" Michael ventured. "I mean you're obviously not from around here, and I hate to be nosy and all, but . . . well, it's not exactly huntin' season, or anything."

"Michael!" Don hissed.

"No problem." Calvin grinned. "I'm just goin' camp-in' for a few days and that"—he inclined his head toward the bow—"is mostly for protection."

"We're goin' campin', too," Michael volunteered. "Tomorrow. That's what we're here for. This is the only place around that sells our kind of hotdogs."

"Local brand," Don appended. "They don't let just anybody stock 'em." He paused, then: "Hey, you wanta come *with* us? Bet you could teach us some stuff."

Calvin scratched his nose thoughtfully. He *would* like some company, as a matter of fact—but not right now;

maybe in a day or so when he got a few things straight. Eventually he shook his head. "Sorry, guys, but I kinda need to do this solo. But I'd welcome suggestions on a good spot to set up for a while. Need somewhere there's game enough to hunt without bein' caught, if you know what I mean. Fresh water, no trouble with trespassin' or anything."

"Know just the place," Don Scott replied immediately. And with that he proceeded to describe a spot a few miles east on the bank of something called Iodine Creek. It was on the fringe of a swamp, but not swampy itself. "It's public land," the boy added, "but nobody goes there much—too hard to get to. There's supposed to be some stills in the swamp, too, and that keeps some folks away."

"And there's *'gators,'*" Michael appended.

"No there's not! Not many, anyway; that's just what we tell the tourists so they'll stay away!"

"And speakin' of which," Michael sighed, "I guess we'd best be movin'. But hey, Calvin, we're gonna be right up the creek a couple of miles from that place I told you about. Why don't you come join us 'round seven or so? Tomorrow, that is."

"Maybe I will," Calvin replied, retrieving his bow. "Maybe I will."

"Carry on," Don called, turning away.

"Nice to 'uv met you," Michael added, and scooted ahead of his friend to be first inside.

And Calvin was once more alone.

Roughly thirty seconds later, he had found the phone. But Sandy was evidently not home, and he had no desire whatever to talk to her machine, though he told the operator to hold a minute longer in case she was outside, as she often was that time of day.

He was still trying to decide whether or not to hang up when the crunch of tires made him glance over his shoulder.

The cop car was back—the same bronze Caprice he'd seen down at the restaurant—and this time it was idling really slow, and the driver was, without a doubt, staring straight at him—and frowning. He stood there for a moment, frozen in anticipation, though his conscience was completely clear. "Damn!" he whispered into the receiver, quite forgetting who was on the other end. "Just can't abide a stranger, I reckon. God, I hate this."

"Sir?"

Calvin ignored both the operator's suggestion of termination and the expectant, post-tone silence on Sandy's line. Something had caught his eye—something much more ominous than slow-cruising Chevys. The Magic Market stood next to an abandoned trailer park, largely overgrown with palmettos and sand, but as he'd been hassling with the operator, he'd been absently scanning the sky. He'd seen a familiar shape there: tapering, swept-back wings, fan-shaped tail, narrow body; seen it swoop and caper until he could confirm its form: a peregrine falcon, scarce in Georgia even along the coast and certainly at this time of year. Still, not *too* remarkable—unless you'd been watching as one dived from a clear sky and swept up an instant later with what looked suspiciously like a very small rattlesnake twisting in its beak.

"Sir? I'll have to charge you if you want to leave a message . . ."

"Huh? Oh . . . sorry. I'll try again later." And with that Calvin hung up and returned his gaze to the sky, seeing no sign of the falcon that was his totem.

An electric-blue Z-28 Camaro roared down the highway, going at least ninety. The Caprice followed it, lights blazing, siren a-wail. Calvin was not there when it returned alone.

Chapter III: The Hunter and the Hunted

(Stone Mountain, Georgia— late afternoon)

Forrest was lost, had been for over a day now, and wasn't very happy about it.

It was pretty silly, too; because he wasn't *that* far from home—*couldn't* have been, because he'd started out from there when he ran away, and he hadn't been gone very long at all before he'd gotten control of himself and begun trying to retrace his trail. Trouble was, he was nearly at the Big Rock by then, and there were so many scents around—oil and gasoline and people by the thousands and grass and trees and asphalt, and all so thickly layered and confused—that he doubted he'd *ever* be able to nose out one that was familiar. And now he was hungry and lonesome and tired, and that made paying attention even harder.

It wasn't as if he hadn't had *reason* for bolting, either: like somebody ramming their moving metal box right through the chainlink fence around the yard where he'd been playing with his friends—and smashing right on through to the other side, almost into the woods. And then

31

there were those great big birds that had been flying around right after—the ones that had changed into men while he was looking right at 'em. *They'd* be enough to make anybody take leave of their senses and run off through the trees. Why, it made Forrest's tail stop wagging every time he thought about 'em.

Fortunately he was calmer now, and trying to figure, as best his canine mind allowed, how to get back home. So far he had narrowed his search to places where there were trees, because there'd been trees around the place he'd fled from. *Unfortunately* there were a *lot* of trees around; though often only in small patches. The only thing he was sure of was that he hadn't crossed the big smooth-stone trail the metal boxes ran on, the one with the strip of grass captive in the middle. He'd have remembered crossing that because the one other time he'd run off he'd wound up there, and Master had just about worn him out with a switch when he found him.

But if he hadn't come upon it *again*, he was a puppy. Just to make sure, though, he poked his tan-and-white nose out of a stand of azaleas at the edge of somebody's yard and trotted up a short, grassy hill. The sun was waiting for him there, reflecting back at him off a familiar hard white surface, and it brought those thick, bitter smells he identified with the metal boxes. *Figured as much,* he grumbled, and turned back.

A short while later he found forest once more, dense with pine and poplar and maple, the underbrush mostly dogwood. For a while he sauntered along, nose to the ground; and as he ran, he gradually worked his way into older suburbs, threading between yards, along fence lines, ever alert for the right sort of cover.

He caught something then: his own spoor undiluted. And he followed it, first uphill through a stand of pines, then through a thicket of blackberry briars, and finally to a veritable wall of woody debris overgrown with kudzu. He searched there until he found the place where he'd burst through in his terror; cautiously retraced his steps back inside . . .

. . . and came into a tiny, grassy clearing completely

encircled by trees—except on the side he'd entered from, where the kudzu made a sort of rampart. There were stones there, too: low, flat slabs of gray granite like Big Rock over to the right—the one with the carving on it—all pushing through the earth like bones wearing through a week-old kill.

And there were more familiar odors: his own—and another that he recalled from long ago. An image swam into his mind: a black-haired boy kneeling before him, scratching his head, bringing him food, wrestling with him, throwing him sticks. And a series of sounds came with it: *Calvin.*

But there were other human smells here as well: three of them—two male and one female, all young. Forrest found where someone had poured colored earth on the ground in a pattern that, when he traced it with his nose, proved to be a circle quartered by a cross. A fire had been built in the middle of it, and there were a *lot* of unfamiliar odors there: oils and blood and resins. There was also a bit of food about—or the wrappers it had come in: candy bars and chips and—and the wild-smelling stuff he'd tasted only once before: deer meat. He nosed up the morsel, swallowed it, though it was sun-dry and someone had burned it and rubbed vegetable stuff all over it. Not as juicy as the rabbits he loved to chase that Master sometimes took him long distances to pursue, but sufficient to a stomach that had not been properly tended for over a day.

Something else caught his attention then: a slab of brown leather. A poke of his nose flopped it open, revealing bits of greenish-white paper with pictures on them. He took it in his mouth, ran a dozen or so yards uphill to the largest of the boulders—and froze.

Something wasn't right. He could not fix on it, but there was definitely a wrongness here. He dropped the leather, raised his head, gazed around, hearing, sniffing, finding nothing to indicate what had made his hair stand suddenly on end.

And then, unbelievably: "Forrest, yo! Forrest! Here, boy!"

It was Master!—jogging out of the woods at the top of
the hill and loping down toward him, his footfalls heavy
on the ground. He was middle-sized for a man, stocky
and dark-skinned, though not in the way most folks around
here were, because his had a coppery cast. His hair *was*
black like theirs, however, and closely cropped. The clink
of metal accompanied him, from the tools that hung from
his waist on another strip of leather. He smelled upset,
and Forrest was ashamed he hadn't noticed his approach.
Why, the wind should have brought him the scent long
ago! But he didn't care now, because he was running and
frolicking, and Master was running too.

"Forrest! Hey, boy!" And then Master was upon him,
kneeling down to reach out and fondle his ears, while
Forrest nearly peed from joy, leapt up to put both front
paws on the man's shoulders, and licked him, tasting sweat
and tobacco.

"Where you *been*, boy?" But Forrest couldn't tell him,
didn't care, he was so happy to be almost home.

"Come here, boy, let me look at you!" the man continued. "Let's get out of these weeds!" And with that
Master picked him up and carried him over to the slab of
rock, where he sat down with Forrest in his lap and began
giving him a good going-over, muttering all the time about
how he'd been afraid he'd lost his favorite beagle, about
how some low-down sorry so-and-sos had smashed down
the dog lot fence with a car, and how he hadn't found out
about it until just a minute ago 'cause he'd had to stay at
the construction site he was working on all night and the
boy he'd paid to check on the hounds hadn't bothered.
Soon as he got the rest of the pack rounded up, he was
gonna call the cops, Master informed Forrest as he examined his ears for ticks (finding five), but he didn't have
much confidence in 'em. Maybe they could at least find
out what kinda car had run through the yard, though, and
use that for a starting place to chase down the culprit. All
he could tell was that it had been a smallish one and had
to have been red, from the paint he'd found all over the
chainlink.

"Hey, what'cha got there?" Master asked abruptly,

freeing one hand to stretch across the stone toward the slab of leather Forrest had just been playing with.

Still securing Forrest with his elbow, Master reached further, practically lying on his back across the boulder when it would have been a lot easier to get up and walk around, though Forrest didn't care about that either, because it meant Master was more interested in him than a bunch of old dead cowhide.

"Got it!" And then: "Well I'll be damned! It's my boy's billfold! Must've been *him* that busted down my fence and left all this shit lyin' 'round here." Forrest felt Master's heart rate increase, then slow back down as he stuffed the leather thing in his shirt pocket. "First off, though," Master added more lightly, "let's take a look at them footsies."

And then Forrest sensed it once more: that strange uneasiness. His hair prickled and danced all across his body. He still couldn't tell what caused it, except that there was some sort of vibration in the ground, almost like the rocks were sliding along each other. He didn't like it, either; not at all. He had to get away, had to warn Master . . .

"Easy, boy!" Master cried as Forrest tried to struggle free, baying loudly in sudden alarm, then changing to the sort of whiny growl that was both fear and warning. "Hey, what's got *into* you?"

But Master held him firm, asking over and over what the matter was when it should be obvious, because something was wrong with the whole *place* here, something he couldn't name because he had no name *for* it.

"*Shit!*" Master hollered all at once, leaping to his feet. He dropped Forrest in the process, who then proceeded to run in circles around the stone, sniffing it suspiciously and whimpering. A sharp, bitter smell reached him from Master—the one that meant he was hurt or scared, but with it Forrest caught another, stranger scent: dry mud and sunbaked rocks and the briefest hint of fresh blood. But Master exhaled suddenly and chuckled, rubbing his hand along his side as if it itched. He picked Forrest up then, and started toward the house. "Boy, *that* 'uz a weird 'un," he whispered. "Got the granddaddy of all great stitches in

my side! Still,'' he added as he increased his pace through
a grove of trees Forrest recognized, "I reckon the *first*
thing I gotta do is give you a bath and take you to the vet.
See if you et anything you shouldn't, or if anything 'sides
ticks took a nibble outta you. *Then* I'm gonna call the
cops.''

They were in sight of home now: a line of fencing
around the familiar low brick house, a long section lying
flat along the ground. Forrest had expected that. But
something wasn't right! Master wasn't walking as surely
as he ought. He was stumbling, and Forrest could feel his
grip growing weaker.

They reached the fence, picked their way across the
flattened part; and Master held onto him with one hand
while he fumbled at the metal thing on the back door with
the other. The door opened, and Master put Forrest down.
He loped onto the linoleum-floored kitchen beyond, then
turned around in alarm, ignoring the yips of his fellow
refugees as they came up to renew their acquaintance.

He was staring at Master. But Master hadn't come inside yet; he was just standing there on the stoop, clutching
his side, then suddenly ripping his shirttail up and staring
at where something was hanging out there, right below his
ribs: something reddish-brown and bloody.

Forrest caught the odor of blood much more strongly,
and with it the thicker scent of viscera—and then the bit-
terness of fear again, which came exactly as Master
screamed.

Chapter IV: Dreams and Visions

(east of Whidden, Georgia— two hours before sunset)

"Thanks again, guys," Calvin whispered. "Thanks a bunch for your lives." He licked his fingers and stared appreciatively at the prickly white remains of the last of the three catfish he'd hooked earlier that day, watched the westering sunlight play off the ribs and vertebrae, and contemplated their pearly beauty as if they were works of art. It was the right thing to do: to ask living things for their lives before pursuing them, and to thank them again when they laid those lives down in his behalf. Sometimes one even covered the blood, but that depended on the prey. The blood of these three fish, along with their innards and their heads, was already well on its way back to the earth— either that, or was food for turtles like the fine-looking grandpa snapper he'd spotted earlier when he'd taken a long cool soak in the creek on whose sandy banks he had made camp.

"Like I said, guys, it's been fun—truly your meat was delicious." And with that Calvin laid the skeletons on the dull inside of a large magnolia leaf, rose from where he'd been sitting cross-legged by the tiny fire on which he'd cooked them, then deposited them back in the tannin-dark waters a foot beyond his bare feet. That done, he reduced the fire to steam and sludge with water from his peanut can, and—satisfied the flames would not incarnate again should he fall to napping—flopped back against the trunk of the vast live oak that over the past few hours had become a sort of surrogate for his rocker on Sandy's porch.

The view wasn't bad either: the creek, maybe thirty feet wide here; the opposite bank a mass of live oaks and red cedars, their branches weighted with Spanish moss that dragged along the lazy water like fraying snake-skins—exactly like this side, except the trees were taller here and a little more widely spaced. It was a symphony of dark green and glossy brown—and of blue sky and metallic-black dragonflies. Vaguely melancholy, maybe; or perhaps that merely reflected Calvin's mood.

He was depressed—or so confused and perplexed he could hardly tell the difference. Three days in various Otherworlds would do it to you—too many things to rationalize all at once, too many snap decisions, too many preposterous things to accept without thinking them through.

And for the past two hours he'd been trying to do exactly that and was making absolutely no progress, which was really starting to annoy him. That was what he was here for, after all. Elsewise he could be in a red Mustang riding up the road with his friends, or better yet, be on a bus on the way to see Sandy.

Instead of getting eaten alive by gnats, which was yet another irritation.

Answers? Ha! He still hardly knew what the *questions* were—except that they had to do with the nature of reality and the rationale behind magic, and how to reconcile the worldview he'd been brought up to believe in with one that was much more irrational. For he, Calvin Fargo McIntosh, was one of the very few people on Earth (as far as he could tell) who knew with absolute conviction that the World men saw was only part of what actually existed.

His friend Dave Sullivan had been the first to learn the

truth, two years ago, when he'd heard music in the night and followed it into the woods to discover that the Irish myths he'd lately begun to explore were based far more on fact than he'd ever suspected. For that night Dave had met the Sidhe—the Faeries—the old gods of Ireland—as they embarked on one of their ceremonial ridings. There'd been a contest of riddles between Dave and one of the Faery lords which had ended with Dave triumphant and possessed of a magic ring that protected him from physical intervention by the Sidhe. But Dave had quickly learned to his sorrow that it was not wise to make a lord of Faerie look foolish . . .

Yeah, that was how it had begun; with Faerie—a land as real as this one, but all unseen, that lay upon this World like wet tissue paper tossed upon a globe.

But there were other Worlds, too: the Lands of Fire, through which Dave had journeyed a year later; and the Realm of the Powersmiths, which bordered—at some distance—a country much closer to Calvin's own heart.

For beyond what the Powersmiths called the Burning Sea lay Galunlati: the Overworld of the Cherokee Indians.

It was invisible, of course, hidden from the sight of men by what Dave called the Walls Between the Worlds, but in most other ways it was more or less like pre-Columbian North America. It had the same trees, for instance (though Galunlati's were bigger and healthier); possessed the same wildlife—plus a few: passenger pigeons and Carolina parakeets and great auks—and creatures that had been extinct longer, like saber-toothed tigers and mastodons and dire wolves. Calvin even had a friend there, an archetypal being called Uki, who was also his patron and a shaman of sorts, and had charge of the weather in the southern quadrant. (Not being a strictly spherical World, Galunlati needed help with things like that, which was one of the notions Calvin had a hard time comprehending.)

The really remarkable thing, though, as far as Calvin was concerned, was that he alone of the Ani-Yunwiya had actually been there in modern times; uniquely among all his tribe, he *knew* that Galunlati was as real, as solid as the earth beneath his body or the bark behind his back.

He had breathed its air and it had sustained him; had drunk its waters, tasted its food, and ventured to this World intact if not unchanged.

But it was *hard,* dammit, to look at the World around you and know there was more than one. But doubly hard it was to accept that the laws by which one lived—the things you took for granted, like what Isaac Newton had worked out, or Einstein, or Steve Hawkings—didn't necessarily hold true everywhere.

Like such basic concepts as what the World was made of.

Science said it was all matter and energy, each shifting back and forth and all bound up in time. But where did that leave the less tangible things like spirit? Was consciousness only the interaction of chemicals and the flow of electrons? Or was there something more? Had there been a spiritual Big Bang as well as a physical one? Had God—for lack of a better word—once embodied all of spirit there was and consciously chosen Second One to fragment himself into an infinity of souls that slowly reconnected across the eons and became ever more conscious in the process, even as matter slowly clumped together into stars and planets? Would the End of the World—that point when all matter had rejoined and collapsed back onto itself—have some kind of analog whereby souls merged more and more and eventually united again into one Over-Spirit that encompassed all knowledge—that, indeed, knew everything that a trillion-trillion-trillion separate consciousnesses had ever seen and felt and understood?

It was too much, too goddamned much.

And that wasn't even considering Power.

That was what the Sidhe called it, and Calvin had picked up the habit from Dave, who knew more about it than anybody he had regular commerce with. Most people would call it magic—or maybe psi, depending on how it manifested. His tribe called it medicine, witchery, many names. But what *was* it? It was immaterial, but it could influence the material—in that way it was like energy. But it was born of sentience—though, apparently, it could also be conferred upon non-sentient objects the same way some substances absorbed water; which implied that all the other elements had to act or react to one another as well. Maybe they did. Maybe matter weighed down spirit. Maybe Power—magic, whatever—was the active principle to spirit's passive one. Maybe there really were only two elements, matter and spirit, and each also had an active and a passive aspect: energy and Power, respectively. Or maybe . . .

Calvin clutched his head, closed his eyes. No, dammit, he was *still* thinking like a white man—natural, given that was the culture he had been born into. Though at least half Cherokee, Calvin's father had renounced his heritage, had tried to live the white dream as a high-steel construction worker in Atlanta. His mother's blood was what he needed now: the World her medicine-man father had shown him before his death had made Calvin take to the road to find himself. He had to think like the Ani-Yunwiya.

The *premise* of Cherokee magic was simple: there were classes of being that, very roughly, aligned with the four elements of air, fire, earth, and water. Four was a Power number: four directions, each with their totem color; the Four Councils Sent From Above. But things that were in more than one category, or that combined elements of more than one category—ah, that's where the fun began.

Which brought him to the uktena.

An abomination, white men might have called it; a monster, though it was a natural part of Galunlati—or as natural as anything there could be. It *looked* like a vast, ruddy serpent patterned white down its back with blotches red as a coral snake's red bands—except that it was hundreds of feet long and had horns. But it had once been a man, before Kanati, the Hunter God of the Ani-Yunwiya, enchanted it, so it was already in two categories right there. And it had horns like some kind of antelope, so there again it combined the characteristics of two classes of being. And its scales were hard as crystal—maybe *were* crystal for all he knew.

Without really being aware of it, Calvin rested his hand on his bare chest and tapped the two-inch-long clear/white triangle that lay, entwined with silver wire and depending from a rawhide cord, between his pecs. Absently, he slipped a finger along the vitreous edge, careful not to push too hard. For, though it *looked* like a shark's tooth, it was a scale of the great uktena he had helped to slay on his first trip to Galunlati, and it did strange things when it tasted blood.

Like change you into an animal.

Calvin knew: for he had himself been transformed that very way—into a 'possum—and had been lost in the 'possum brain until Dave had freed him. Since then he'd shifted shape twice more: both times into a peregrine falcon. He'd been more prepared those other times, but it had still scared him shitless, because he could sense, every minute, the avian consciousness hovering there waiting for him to drop his guard so it could take over. The best way to combat that, he'd discovered, was to make up songs, like the one he'd started jotting down on the yellow pages of the small notebook he'd bought at the Magic Market. "Werepossum Blues," he was calling it: the whole long tale of how he and Dave and their friends had gotten tangled up in the politics of the Sidhe. It had another function, too: one darker and much more serious—but he didn't even like to *think* about that, and *certainly* not now, when he was trying to come to terms with something much more imminent that frightened him to death on the one hand, yet tempted him almost past tolerance with the range of its possibilities on the other.

He had determined, in short, to master his fear of skin-changing. And, he supposed, there was no time like the present to begin.

Sighing, Calvin stood and slipped out of his jeans and skivvies—your duds didn't change with you, and you could find yourself in quite a bind if you chose your new form badly. Fortunately his riverside sanctum was warm and secluded.

Once naked, he lay down again, and took the scale in his left hand, adjusting it so that if he squeezed, the edges and the twin points at the root end would quickly bring blood. Now what did he want to become? It had to be something he was familiar with, something he could imagine. It also had to be something he'd eaten—presumably so one's body would have some sort of pattern to go by. (He'd tasted most wild game—even sampled falcon when he accidentally shot one and was forced to eat his kill by a grim-faced grandfather.) And—so Dave had said—you had to *want* to change. Which might be a problem because he was scared to let himself go. Those other times he'd been practically consumed with a desire to escape a situation—and that fear had helped him overcome his apprehension. But here, now, there was only doubt, wonder, frustration. Only one thing else he knew—something Uki had told him quite casually. It was best to transform into something with roughly your own body mass; that help keep the beast-mind at bay. Let's see, he was about one-sixty, and what kind of critters weighed that much? Not many around here: deer, maybe, or at least big does and mid-sized bucks. Cougar? But he hadn't eaten cougar and didn't want to. Besides, if he turned into one of them he might rouse undue interest because there were not—officially—any cougars in Georgia. 'Gators, maybe? He didn't much like that last notion, either; their thoughts were likely to be too different from his own.

Which left him where he'd started.

Now, where to begin?

Well, the procedure he'd followed before called for him to close his eyes, squeeze the scale until it brought blood, while imagining how it would feel to be the animal desired. The *change* had then come upon him quite abruptly.

But, he wondered suddenly, how would it be if he tried to shift a little at a time, or maybe only *one* part?

Yeah, he'd try that.

Left hand still clutching the scale, he tightened his grip slightly, and felt a jolt of pain as the substance pierced his flesh. A trickle of warmth slid over his palm, cooling rapidly, but he did not look that way. Rather, he was gazing at his other hand, thinking how the bones lay and imagining them stretching, merging, bringing the outer fingers with them as his nails grew thick and long and hard and became a cloven hoof. He could feel something now, a dull throbbing, a sort of grinding in his hand—a warmth flooding up from his other palm, through his arms and chest, and back down to the experimental appendage. There was a tingling as well—but he tried to banish it, though he had begun to feel dizzy. He was sweating all over, too, and more than his hand was now twisting and stretching. There was a truly appalling itch at the base of his spine, and he felt decidedly uncomfortable lying flat on his back. A glance down showed far more body hair than he'd had before (which was almost none), and his penis seemed to have shifted a little higher. And his vision kept blurring and dimming, so that he had trouble focusing on one thing. He also had a headache.

No, it wasn't working—or rather, was working *too* well. He had to stop, *had* to, for already he could sense strange instincts filtering through his thoughts: a desire to flee, to run; an almost insatiable urge to eat his fill of green grass and tender leaves.

His hand was on fire, but the rest of him was too. And it all had to end right *now!* He thought of the things that made him a man, forced himself to run his free hand along his side, over his chest and belly and hips, ignoring the coarse hair, his single desire to once more find a man's shape there.

Abruptly the heat faded, his vision cleared.

He sank back against the tree, mortally exhausted.

And slept.

A dream found him: sky, clouds swirling around him like pieces of some alien landscape, as he had seen them from a plane once—or better, as he had seen them far more recently in the shape of a falcon. No longer remote, they were things to be touched, felt, toyed with, dived through.

But he was not alone. There were others there, darting down from either side to flirt with him: a pair of peregrines. And that told him something:

Falcons were his totem, because they—like him—could see things others could not. And he knew enough of the mystical to know that many events had a mystical interpretation.

This was therefore a Dream of Power.

He was also flying, though he had no body, and part of
him was afraid because he had been a falcon once before
and had perhaps enjoyed it too much (in spite of his fear)—
so much that he had nearly lost himself that time, too—
though he had not told even Dave about that.

Do not be concerned, a voice in his mind interrupted.
*It is only your soul that travels, and a soul can take what-
ever form it pleases and never lose itself.*

Follow, another thought insisted. *Follow, see.*

And Calvin did follow, vaguely aware by the slant of
the sun that they were flying north and west. For a long
time they flew, until a hump of gray granite rose from the
horizon, one he recognized as Stone Mountain. The birds
began first to circle it, then to fly in patterns which they
repeated over and over, leaving contrails of feathers in the
air. At first those designs were indistinct, but as the falcons continued to repeat them, Calvin was able to recognize some of them: the cross-in-circle that was a symbol
of Power both for his own folk and for the Sidhe, and
then—and part of him laughed at this—the circle bisected
by a diagonal that was the international NO sign, and then
the circle surrounded by three triangles that meant RADI-
ATION HAZARD. Others there were too, but less obvious.
And abruptly he realized the falcons were gone, had worn
away their very selves to become feathery sigils in the sky.
He stared at them stupidly, trying to find some elements
of unity. And then it came to him: they were all round
symbols, all symbols of Power. But they also all carried
a warning.

A warning of what?

A chill shook Calvin, and he shuddered. And when he
did, a branch poked his bare side. He awoke at that, stared
at the sky across the creek. There was a trace of duskiness
there, and the breeze sliding up from the river held a hint
of evening cool.

There were also two things moving in the sky: a pair of
peregrine falcons.

And he had dreamed of falcons, and earlier that afternoon he had seen a falcon fly off with a snake . . .

Darkness fell upon him, of a sudden, as if a cloud had

slipped over the sun, but still his gaze chased the birds. They were gliding west now, but very, very slowly. Calvin followed, slipped into the forest that bordered the creek, felt that world engulf him, knew it found resistance in such simple things as the smell of the soap he had cleaned up with.

"Sorry," he whispered. "Can't help it, I'll be more careful in the future."

And the trees seemed to whisper back, seemed to urge him on.

Calvin simply drifted then, and was not surprised when a moment later he found himself approaching the stump of a lightning-blasted cypress, which was very strong medicine indeed. He scrambled up a buttresslike root that was taller than he was—and found himself atop a sort of natural altar within a ring of forest: decaying wood a carpet beneath his feet, the darkening sky a vault above his head. He could feel the air playing about his naked body.

And there came to him, distantly but distinctly, a familiar, disturbing cry.

A glance above showed him *four* falcons—the single most magical number—all flying in a circle just at the edge of the ring of trees. Round and round they swooped and swirled; faster and faster. One had something in its talons, but he couldn't tell what it was.

And then, all at once, all four arrowed inward, seemed to collide, but then winged apart again.

But at that instant when Calvin was certain they were going to impact each other, one let something fall.

It landed at his feet, but he did not flinch, did not look down. Rather, he continued to stare after the falcons as they flew in single file northwest.

Only when they had vanished beyond the froth of treetops did Calvin dare venture a glance at what his totems had abandoned there.

His hair prickled as he knelt before it, stretched a hand out at the baseball-sized blob of white and red, and rolled it over so that he could identify it.

A face grinned back at him: tiny sharp teeth drawn back

in death's rictis, beady red eyes still glittering with a hint of life.

It was the head of a 'possum. An albino 'possum. And with that realization chills shook him all over again. For the name Uki had given Dave Sullivan in Galunlati was *Sikwa Unega:* White 'Possum.

This, Calvin reckoned, was an omen he could not ignore. Four falcons, a white 'possum's head, and the birds had flown northwest with great urgency.

So what did it mean?

But he already knew, for those birds had tried to tell him before. This was a warning. Something was happening in the northwest, or was going to happen, something that involved snakes—or some similar threat from the Underworld; involved Stone Mountain, involved danger; and now, evidently, involved his buddy Dave.

"Never leave business unfinished," Calvin's grandfather had told him, "especially not when it involves magic."

As if in confirmation, four falcon feathers drifted down from the sky. Calvin did not hesitate to claim them. Maybe Sandy had been right. Maybe this *was* a Vision Quest—in which case he'd better start observing the prohibitions.

Suddenly Calvin Fargo McIntosh was *very* uneasy.

Chapter V: Conjurations
(east of Whidden, Georgia— sunset)

So much for getting his head straight, Calvin mused an hour later as he busied himself cutting palmetto fronds for a certain part of the ritual he was planning. Evidently the Powers-That-Be had no intention of leaving him alone— or at least that's what the visions of the past few hours seemed to indicate. And here he had, perhaps foolishly, assumed he was through having adventures for a while. Books were like that: the hero triumphed, the villain was vanquished, and then you looked for someone else's trials to entertain you.

But, as he was beginning to discover, the crises of real life were not so easily assuaged: rather, they snuck up on you and attacked unaware, often from forgotten or unexpected quarters, and did not then line themselves up in order of priority and present themselves for optimum convenience. And *lately* they'd been mixing and mingling and jostling with each other in such a mad quest for ascendency that even Calvin, who was normally pretty laid back, sometimes found himself at a loss as to how to proceed. It was too bad, he reckoned, that he could not check ahead now. At times like these it would be really nice to read the last page first and find out how everything turned out. But he was beginning to wonder if there even *was* a last page to his particular story. Perhaps not, at the rate weird things were accumulating.

Or perhaps he really *had* been simply dreaming, in which case he was behaving like an utter fool. But his heart did not believe that for an instant.

Not a day had passed, after all, since he had been involved in a desperate quest to help Dave rescue their Faery friend Fionchadd from a heretofore unknown realm of the Sidhe where he was being held hostage—a captivity that had precipitated war among the tribes of that World, which had slopped over into this World as such massive storms that Dave had found himself with no choice but to try to stop it once he had learned of the effect it was having both in his World and in Galunlati, where it was actually moving the sun. Calvin had been involved from the time he had helped Dave's buddy Alec use the prophetic ulunsuti crystal he had acquired on their first visit to Galunlati to ascertain the source of the aberrant weather. It had shown them the war in Faerie—but worse, it had revealed a possible future in which their friend Gary Hudson's fiancée was struck dead at the hour of her wedding by a bolt from those same sorcerous storms. That had led Dave and his comrades to orchestrate an end to the war—which eventually had succeeded, but not without cost to all of them.

Calvin's problem had been simply one of having to use powers he was not fully in control of yet, spells and rituals Uki had taught him, or which he had picked up from him, but which he had been advised again and again were only to be used with caution. He *had* used them, too, and successfully as far as he knew—but now he was beginning to wonder if perhaps he had not been a little too full of himself, a little too vain about his own fledgling shamanhood. But it was also damned scary when the fate of reality as you knew it depended on how you used a few talismans and a smattering of obscure information. And now, Calvin very much feared, he was going to have to use them again—although he hadn't a clue what for.

But such speculations were not doing an iota of good.

There was nothing he could find out for sure until midnight—which was the next of the four optimum times of day for working magic. His only recourse, then, was to funnel his nervous energy into preparations.

A Vision Quest, Sandy had called this time in the wilderness, yet she had not truly known of what she spoke, except that it referred to a ritualistic seeking after truth which was often so intense it amounted to a rite of passage. It was not even a phrase his tribe used, but had its source much farther west; yet the Ani-Yunwiya had a form of that ceremony as well, used to sanctify all important activities.

Calvin knew the form of that rite, though he had experienced the full ritual only twice, and each time had been subtly different. The first was when he had reached puberty and his grandfather had made him fast and sweat and breathe fumes and listen to chants until he had had a vision of his spirit guide—the falcons that had subsequently come to warn him. That had not been a strictly Cherokee ritual either, but his grandfather had undergone one like it on a sojourn to Oklahoma, and incorporated it into his own body of lore—mostly herbal medicine, though he also utilized some of the old spells and chants and charms.

The second time had included Dave and Alec—and Fionchadd—and had been contrived by the human wizard/seer Oisin. They had opened a gate between the Worlds then, and the four of them had journeyed to Galunlati. It had been an opening of another kind of gate for Calvin, too; for the World had never been quite the same after.

What would tomorrow hold? he wondered. What did the visions mean? If he could only make it to midnight without going bonkers, that much, at least, might be revealed.

Thwack! And with that last swipe with his knife he decided he had procured enough palmetto. He paused where he was, staring at the pile. It occurred to him (not for the first time, such had been his indecision over the past few hours) that he probably ought to zip into town and give Dave a call and let him know something might be up. His buddy had surely had time enough to get home by now, and while he was at it, he could try again to get hold of Sandy.

But common sense got the best of him instead. There were a certain number of things he *had* to do, and all were more easily accomplished by daylight. Beyond that, it would be preferable to tell his friends something than nothing, and if he waited until tomorrow to report, all of them would be rested and thus more receptive, and Calvin would be better informed.

And since the sun was flirting hard with the horizon, he'd best get moving.

Sighing, Calvin gathered up his fronds and lugged them the twenty or so yards back to his camp. He had already set up a framework of sweet gum sapling there: a low dome around his fire pit, lashed together at the top with bits of grape vine. In the remaining light, he covered it as best he could with the palmetto, leaving a smoke hole at the top, and a door opening facing the creek. He was *trying* to construct an *asi*, a Cherokee sweat lodge, but wasn't at all certain how well he had succeeded.

Roughly an hour was spent completing this project, and by the time he had finished, it was full dark and the forest had begun to resound with the cries of crickets and night birds. Indeed, Calvin had never heard the former so loud. They were like white noise, almost drowned out all other sounds, and he found himself more than once unconsciously looking for some kind of volume control.

Or could they themselves be a sign? Ritual properly demanded drumming, but perhaps the insect cries were some sort of surrogate, conjured by whatever power (he dared hope it was Uki) had sent the earlier visions.

He stood, feeling an unexpected stiffness in his back and legs that surprised him. He maintained a fairly physical lifestyle and certainly was not averse to a little bit of hard labor, but this perplexed him. Maybe he was pushing himself too hard, maybe he really did need to just take it easy.

And maybe if he took the easy way out, he would queer whatever quest he was about to embark on before it was begun. After all, overcoming one's natural instincts and aversions was part of the process. Once on a Vision Quest, you *had* to do exactly what you thought was right in your center-soul. You could not act frivolously, and you absolutely could not lie. Any one of those would insult the Powers he would be invoking. And such Powers, Calvin now knew, were not to be trifled with.

Sighing, he began a series of stretching exercises, let his body slide at its own speed back to form. His stomach growled, and he grimaced, wishing he dared eat something, but fasting was another part of the ritual. Ideally, he should have begun that long ago (not that he'd had a really filling meal lately, excepting the one back at Whidden's Steak-and-Seafood). Seven days' abstinence was sometimes prescribed, though he'd always made do with less. But for now he'd do as best he could—with one exception. No one could last long without water—or some liquid refreshment—and certainly not in the sticky heat of a south Georgia summer. He was therefore allowed a beverage. Something called black drink was specified—a bitter brew made from a species of holly. But, though various hollies grew wild in these very woods, he had no time to chase down the appropriate variety—and no knowledge of how the concoction should be prepared. Uki did not use it much and had never shown Calvin the art of its making, but since the active ingredient, according to what Calvin had read, was caffeine, strong coffee had been deemed a suitable alternative in the past—and of that, fortunately, he had God's plenty.

Another sigh, and he busied himself rekindling the fire, using bits of Spanish moss as tinder. As soon as it was blazing along, he filled the peanut can and set it to boiling atop it, then took a flaming twig and used it to ignite a second, smaller fire within the asi.

That done, he checked the sky—he had no watch, but fortunately it was clear—and, deeming that there were still a couple of hours until midnight, set himself to alternately meditating and beating off mosquitoes until the water was done bubbling and he was able to take his first dose of bogus-black drink. A double helping of dark crystals made sure it was bitter enough.

And made sure that Calvin, who had not had a proper night's sleep in longer than he could easily remember, would probably not get one that night either.

Four cans later it was approaching midnight, and Calvin was so wired he could practically hear himself shaking. His stomach was also giving him grief—not surprising, given that it was awash with acidic liquid mixed with grilled catfish. Purgation—likewise part of the ritual—was doubtless not far off, but he knew it was not proper to artificially induce it, which he could have done with little prompting. He was sitting on the ground now, as he had been since he'd finished the first batch of black drink, gazing across the tiny fire and at the water. He had been trying to center his thoughts, to determine a battle plan, but that had proved a near impossibility.

The best he'd been able to manage was that the smart thing was to try to contact Uki, though he did not know precisely when he had decided that. He did not even know if such a thing were possible, for always before Uki had summoned him, had opened the gates between the Worlds himself; or else Calvin had simply burned an uktena scale and gone to Galunlati that way. Trouble was, teleportation scales had to be specially prepared, and the one he still possessed had not been so empowered. They could make you shapeshift in their native form, but to use them to gate between the Worlds took special effort—which Calvin could not duplicate with the resources at hand. Not that he *expected* his make-do ritual to actually pierce the World Walls, but he thought that his spirit might possibly somehow be able to slip through.

And then he could delay no longer. Moving with the near-silence born of long years of pride in that art, Calvin followed the creek to a point a dozen yards south of his camp, where the bank dipped low enough for him to wade into the water. That was important: water was powerful and you had to approach it reverently, otherwise it could turn on you. Calvin wished he still had his medicine bag—

some of the things in there would be of use now, notably the colored clays he needed to mark himself; but perhaps he would be forgiven that omission this time. First thing in the morning, though, *first* thing, he would start looking. No more would he find himself unprepared.

A glance at the sky told him it was as close to midnight as estimation could account for—and so he began. A moment only he hesitated on the shore, and then he stripped very quickly (he was only wearing jeans and a T-shirt to start with, and them mostly to keep the wretched mosquitoes at bay) and marched very slowly into the water. He did not spare a thought for what might lurk beneath that inky surface, though he had checked on the whereabouts of the grandpa snapper with the last of the light—and found it gone, which was some relief. But he was really too wired to focus on such things; his thoughts were bouncing everywhere, and—he realized to his dismay—the coffee-and-catfish stewing in his gut had finally come to loggerheads. For as soon as the water reached his belly, his stomach began to spasm, and he found himself vomiting copiously into the creek.

Which was *not* the style in which this sort of thing was supposed to be accomplished. He had no prayer of apology to offer the water, either, as he lowered himself the rest of the way into it, letting the dark liquid sweep away the last of the drool that unheroically decorated his chin.

That done, he proceeded to feel his way along the muddy bottom until he was as close to the middle as guesswork would allow—a point where he could *just* touch bottom and keep his head above water. And there he stayed for one hundred and twelve breaths—twenty-eight breathed as he faced each direction. He felt a little stupid doing it this way, but could think of no other rituals—the one he had undergone at puberty he could not remember, and the one Oisin had spoken when first he had gone to Galunlati, and which Calvin had subsequently memorized, was not appropriate. *It* was for men going to the ceremonial ball play, which was sometimes surrogate for war, not for half-crazy kids on a Vision Quest. The hundred-and-twelve-breaths bit was one of his own devising: four the number of power of his people, and seven that of his adopted folk. That seemed right, and Calvin knew enough about magic to know that what seemed right—and was attempted with absolute sincerity—often *was* right.

. . . *twenty-six, twenty-seven, twenty-eight*—those addressed to the north, and Calvin began making his way out again. Nothing seemed different, except that he felt cooler, and of course emptier. Maybe a little light-headed, in fact, which was undoubtedly desirable.

The rest of the ordeal was simple: once on the bank, he gathered his clothes and returned to camp. He did not re-don them, but quickly removed the palmetto-frond door of the asi and scooted inside. Heat hit him like a wave—the dull light of the bit of fire far out of proportion to the warmth the hut retained. Calvin wasted no time, though, in building up the fire as hot as he dared—which was not far; the hut was maybe four feet at the tallest, and he had to be very careful of both sparks and smoke. Almost immediately he began to sweat profusely and his stomach to knot tighter, and he closed his eyes and concentrated on his breathing. A few herbs rested on the stones near the fire—certain ones he had found in passing and decided might be of benefit and as the stones beneath them heated, he became aware of their fragrance blending with the smoke that was almost making him gag all over again.

But it was working, was slowly drawing him out of himself, which was what one needed to do. A bit of water dashed on the edge of the fire when it threatened the roof filled the hut with steam, and made it a little easier to breathe, and it was at that point that Calvin took the bundle of cattail reeds he had gathered and began to flagellate his thighs. He could not do it well, there was no room in the cramped space for him to work over his entire body, which was what the ritual really required, but it served its prime function, which was to further sunder his soul from his body. His eyes were closed—had been since he'd raised the steam—and he kept them that way, but now he focused on the red landscape inside his lids, watching the circles there appear and dance and recede. He tried to follow, to imagine them going beyond the World Walls, and began

slowly trying to recall Uki's face. Like his own, somewhat, or at least with the common characteristics of the
Ani-Yunwiya, which Calvin had seen often enough, though
somewhat muted in his father's line by the white blood
that had sneaked in a few generations back. Wide cheekbones and arched nose (Calvin's differed there); almond-
eyes and long head, square chin, the skin white as chalk,
the eyes an unlikely blue, though the hair was black. Calvin tried to picture the demigod in his most characteristic
pose: standing at the edge of the cliff above *Hyuntikwa-
layi:* Where-It-Made-a-Noise-as-of-Thunder, which in his
own World was called Tallulah Gorge. He would have his
arms lifted until they were level with his shoulders and
would be chanting, summoning the rain, or the sunshine.

But nothing happened. Calvin would construct the image, hold it a moment, and then, as he began to compose
an invocation, something—a spark fallen upon his leg,
maybe, or a snap from the fire, or a surfeit of smoke that
made him cough—would distract him, and it would dissolve and he would have to start all over.

Finally he gave up in disgust. This method had failed;
there remained only one viable alternative—one of which
he was far more dubious, but which might therefore ulti-
mately be more productive.

Sighing, he rose to a crouch and eased out of the *asi*,
leaving the fire to die of its own accord, since any other
way would be an insult to that most capricious of servants.
The first impression he had was of coolness—largely an
illusion this far south in June, but he did not dare let himself be distracted, for he was still more than a little dis-
tanced from himself and that was good. Otherwise, that
work, too, would be to do all over.

What he was about to attempt would be a thing he had
done only once before in this World, and that was to raise
a fog. Then—it had only been a day and a half ago—he
had not been careful, had raised a mist far and wide in
order to summon the Little Deer so that he would not have
to poach on a friend's land when he needed blood for the
ritual he had used to help Dave rescue Fionchadd. That
had created problems, though, for he had almost been un-

able to see, so thick had that mist become. This time he would raise a very little fog, one whose limits he could control, and in that nether-place between the Worlds, he would try to send his spirit to reach Uki. That was something else he had done only a few times, and never without supervision. He didn't know if it would work now, he only knew he had to try.

Sighing the softest of sighs, Calvin reached into his backpack and drew out the potent-looking Rakestraw hunting knife. With the back of the blade he incised a six-foot Power Wheel in the sand, and when that was complete, laid himself in the middle of it, with his head to the north, his feet to the south, his hands to east and west. He could feel the sand grating against his still-damp body, bonding to his sopping hair, but that did not matter now, for it was the earth he called on, his figurative mother, for he was born of earth as much as water. The chant he used was a silent one: lips shaped the sounds but did not set them into the air; rather he willed them down into the soil, awakened it, told it to send forth its enemy water, to blend it with its ethereal brother, air. It was the magic of the *between* things again: fog which was often born of earth, but was a mix of air and water, and which could likewise suffer at least a small amount of fire. A powerful thing indeed: strong enough, sometimes, to dissolve the Walls Between The Worlds.

He could feel it rising around him, feel the ground exhale as it gave up the moisture it had hoarded for the next day's dew. And now he could see the ghostly white tendrils floating up around him, merging with the moonlight, twining around the trailing beards of Spanish moss. It grew thicker, whiter, and before long, Calvin could not tell where fog and moonlight and moss began or ended.

He closed his eyes, focused on his breathing, felt his eyes roll back into his head as he entered light trance. His body became a distant thing, a weight upon his spirit, and he willed himself to rise, to leave it behind.

And did, floated farther, wanted badly to merge with the night wind and ride the skies, and see the Georgia landscape spread below him. But he resisted, concentrated on only one thing. *Hyuntikwala Usunhi*, he called in his people's ancient tongue: *Uki—Darkthunder! It is I, Edahi, that the men of this land call Calvin, who seeks you. I have a quest before me and would have your aid, your counsel. Hyuntikwala Usunhi, hear me, hear my prayer!*

He repeated the impromptu invocation twice more, became gradually aware of being drawn in a certain direction—but could go no farther. Once a presence tickled his spirit, but before he could reach out to embrace it, to know it for what it was, it vanished—or was cut off, he could not tell for certain which.

Four more times Calvin tried to contact his mentor. Four more times he failed, and by the time he had reached the last repetition, the wind was beginning to disperse his fog. Fearing he might become lost in the Lands Between, he returned to his body, and as the last of the mist drifted away into the woods, he rose once more to his feet. Not a grain of sand stuck to his body. And he was completely dry.

Okay, he told himself, *you've tried to contact Uki, and failed. That only means you have limits; it doesn't mean you'll fail at whatever it is that's before you. You know no more than you did, but neither do you know any less. Tomorrow you will go into town and call Sandy and David. Tomorrow you will . . .*

But before he had finished planning tomorrow, he was sleeping.

PART II

STRONG SUSPICIONS

Chapter VI: Sneakin'

(east of Whidden, Georgia—
Wednesday, June 18—
just after lunch)

"You're a *good* girl, ain't you?" Robert Richards drawled at Allison Scott from behind the slightly tawdry gleam of her mama's Sunday china and silverware—the stuff Daddy hadn't wanted Mama to keep on account of it had been in his family before him and Mama were married. The stuff Mama had insisted on retaining after the divorce. Allison remembered that, too: the fights, the hollering, and Daddy stomping out and not coming back again. New Daddy hadn't cared much, 'cause he hadn't lasted long enough to get upset about things like china: a hunting accident had claimed him not a year ago. Allison wondered if red-headed Robert Richards would become Third Daddy someday. He'd lasted longer than any of the others, anyway; why, he was a regular fixture at Sunday dinner now, and had got to be just about as bad to drop by for lunch during the week, like he was doing right now, though he wasn't wearing his policeman's uniform like he usually did 'cause he was off until tomorrow morning. But if he thought he was gonna get on Allison's good side by telling her how good she was, he was mistaken.

Of course, she *was* good, she knew that without being told. Or at least she was when it counted, like when Mama told her to eat everything on her plate and she could have an extra dessert—that was what Robert had been referring to. She wasn't *always* good, though; she knew that, too. But she was careful not to get caught at it—at least not by Mama. That was easy enough to do, too, when Mama was mooning and cooing over her latest beau. Then it was simply a matter of staying out of the way and doing what she was told (which often enough *was* "Stay out of the way like a good girl," or, "Allison, honey, could you stay in your room for a while?" or, "Allison, baby, me and Robert're goin' to a movie, so you mind your brother like a good girl, okay?").

And she'd nod *yes* and then go right on and do what she wanted to, because she knew that Brother Don couldn't do anything to her no matter what she did, on account of the fact that she knew Brother Don had plenty of secrets of his own—like those magazines he'd hidden under his bed until he'd moved 'em to his and Mike's treehouse (or that's where she *thought* they were; that was one place even she didn't dare violate). Or what he did while he was looking at those same magazines in the bathroom, or some of the things she'd heard him and Mike mention about looking in a certain young lady's window down the road, which just happened to be about the time there were rumors of Peeping Toms (she thought that was the term) in the neighborhood.

Yeah, Don Larry Scott might be a lean and hungry fourteen, but he sure wasn't lord of the manor. At least not when nine-year-old Allison Jane didn't want him to be.

He was staring at her now, too: or glaring, rather: aiming a mixture of scorn and envy at his younger sister that was only slightly less virulent than he fixed on Robert, whom he cautiously admired, but did not want to encourage in the art of Allison flattery, even when it made Mama happy.

That was the key these days: make Mama happy.

And that's what Allison was good at.

Mama chose that moment to lay a hand on Robert's before gazing wistfully at her only daughter. "She's been mighty sweet these days," Mama said. "Mighty sweet indeed."

Don rolled his eyes and started to say something but puffed his cheeks instead, which Allison thought made him look even more like a chipmunk than he usually did. Margo—that was her best friend, Amy's, older sister—said he was cute, but Allison didn't think so. Least he wasn't as cute as she was: no curly blond hair (his was dark brown and sort of spiky-burry), no bright blue eyes (his were greenish-gray). The only thing he had over her, she figured, was long black eyelashes. Or that's what she'd heard Margo say one time: "That boy's got the prettiest eyes I ever seen. I wish I had eyelashes like that." To which someone had replied that yeah, it was a pity poor little Allison was so blond, 'cause it made her eyelashes go invisible. Mama had told her she could wear mascara when she was eleven. Allison couldn't wait.

"Can I be excused?" Don asked as soon as decorum allowed.

"Sure," Mama said absently. "But just remember it's your turn to do dishes."

"*Maaaaa!*"

"Now don't argue, Don Larry, you know I can't trust Allison with my good china. It's supposed to go to her when she gets married. Suppose she dropped a piece? It'd break her heart."

"Sure would," Allison affirmed triumphantly, and Don Larry knew he was stuck. He was usually stuck now, 'cause anytime it was her turn and Mama wasn't around, she'd just threaten to mention a thing or two, and good old Don'd take over. She'd have to start being a little cleverer, though; 'cause Don had lately taken to arranging to be elsewhere when dish-washing time rolled around, and Allison knew she couldn't delay too long. Having two sneaky kids in one family was a problem. But at least, of the two, she was the best.

"I'm goin' over to Mike's to game in a little while,"

Don told Mama. "And we're goin' campin' later, don't forget."

"Then you'd better hurry up with them dishes," Mama told him back, with a shake of her hair (which gesture Allison had taken to imitating lately, which made Don so mad he could spit when she did it to him).

"Can *I* be excused?" Allison asked primly. "I don't think I want any dessert right now."

"Yeah, run on," Robert chuckled, dismissing her with a wave of a freckled hand.

And that's just what Allison Scott did. She ran right to her room and changed out of the white-and-pink sundress Mama had made her wear to lunch 'cause there was special company, and into her red shorts and the blue-and-yellow Simpsons T-shirt and her little white Reeboks. And as soon as she heard the door to the den close at one end of the hall and the dishes start rattling and clinking at the other, she was making a beeline for the front door.

She paused with her hand on the knob and stood on tiptoes to peer through the peephole.

She was about to do something bad—something *really* bad. She was going to go play in the woods. But not the oak woods behind her house; that was her brother's domain, and besides, that way eventually turned into swamp, and that kind of scared her. No, she was going to play in the nice pine woods right beyond the railroad tracks. She had a playhouse there: a collection of boxes within a grid-work of carefully laid out pebbles. Trouble was, she couldn't get there very often, and didn't dare stay there very long when she did, because Don didn't know about it yet, and if he ever found out, she'd lose one of her prime advantages over him.

But there was still the thrill of the forbidden, though Mama had not, in fact, lately said she couldn't go there, just not to go outside the reach of her voice. That that admonition conveniently superseded the much more ancient one not to cross the road, and Lord knows not to play on the tracks beyond, was not lost on her. If she got caught, she'd just plead ignorance of the law (that was a phrase she'd learned from Robert, who was morning shift commander in the Whidden Police Department).

One final glance toward the back of the house, one final check to see that the coast was clear, and Allison slipped outside. She had already started to run across to the nearest of the fifteen loblolly pines that dotted the wide expanse of newly mown yard (another thing teenage brothers were good for), when something brought her up short.

She stopped in her tracks and stared, brow wrinkling in perplexity. The yard ended a short way farther on, where it ran up against the dusty yellow-white length of the upstart logging road that meandered past the new ranch house Daddy had built Mama when she was five. Beyond it was a fringe of weeds, and beyond them the slight elevation that carried the Georgia Pacific on down to Brunswick. She knew its habits quite well: once in the morning going west through Whidden with a burden of ragged tree trunks, and then east again in the afternoon, laden with rolls of newsprint and other paper products. Even on Sunday.

Beyond the tracks were the woods that were Allison's destination, but what had stopped her cold was that, while the coast had most certainly been clear earlier, it definitely wasn't now.

For as Allison slipped around to the road side of her pine tree, she saw somebody come hobbling down the tracks from the west. An old woman, it looked like, probably *real* old, though Allison couldn't see enough of her face to tell. But the way the poor old thing was walking— sort of hitching along like she had a limp, or maybe like her feet were too heavy; and the way she was all bent over with almost a hump on her back seemed to indicate that was the case. And the clothes more or less clinched it, for the woman wore a grayish-tan shawl flipped over her head like a hood and trailing over her arms and back, largely obscuring the long, shapeless dress beneath it. Allison found this curious not only for itself, but because it didn't jibe with the oppressive south Georgia June heat. But she just couldn't imagine that poor old woman wearing shorts and a T-shirt like her mama did when she didn't have company. The old woman looked dirty, too; and Allison was sure she could see bits of leaves and twigs sticking out of the ragged fabric.

Maybe she shouldn't go play in the forest after all; maybe the old woman would be there. Maybe the old woman was a witch who would eat her up.

Except that was silly, and if Don Larry knew she even considered things like that, he'd make fun of her for days. and that settled it. Soon as the coast was clear, she'd run right on over.

As soon as the coast *was* clear, 'cause it was taking the old biddy a *long* time to make her way down the tracks. Allison watched her, as if hypnotized, and realized she'd nearly dozed off just following the methodical step-and-hitch that was the rhythm of the crone's progress. It was almost like every step made the ground vibrate—which made Allison's eyes tingle in turn, kinda like they did when she got sleepy, but it was the middle of the day and she wanted to play, and didn't like that at all.

The woman didn't seem to have noticed her, though; didn't seem to notice *anything* as she moved with slow precision from Allison's right line of sight to her left. Eventually she passed from view behind a screen of oleander, and Allison breathed a sigh of relief and concluded her dash for the road. She'd be okay, she knew: the old woman was gone, and if she crossed the tracks quickly and silently, as she knew she could, she'd be at her playhouse in no time. It was kind of to the west, anyway. And the old woman had been heading east.

In fact, when Allison dashed across the tracks and entered the woods, she was nowhere in sight.

Chapter VII: Off the Beaten Path

(east of Whidden, Georgia— early afternoon)

Calvin was practically beside himself with irritation when he awoke. The sun was shining square on his face (which is probably what had roused him to start with), and a gritty-eyed squint in its direction through the froth of live-oak leaves indicated that it was clearly afternoon— which meant he had slept rather more than twelve hours. Time he had certainly not planned to let slip by.

"Damn," he grumbled under his breath, as he rummaged through his meager gear in search of breakfast, then remembered the Vision Quest and checked himself abruptly, wondering if he should continue his fast. Good sense won out, though: he had *sought* his vision and failed, and while some sort of threat was evidently still laying for him, and he still ought to be on his best behavior as far as things like lying went, it was not necessarily wise to confront . . . whatever it was . . . half sick from starvation. Besides, the fasting was to help sunder soul and body, not weaken that body when the actual trial began. With that bit of rationalization giving him a degree of comfort, he broke out a stick of beef jerky and began gnawing it reflectively. He did not, however, make coffee.

By the time he had got himself cleaned up and his camp in order, his course of action was clear. He would go into town (he needed to anyway, since if there *was* trouble brewing it would be a good idea to know what goods and services were available), and once there, he'd ring up Dave and Sandy and alert them both to his situation. He hadn't a clue *what* he'd tell Dave, of course, only that he should beware, but he had a pretty good idea what his conversation with Sandy would be about, which was basically everything that had happened to him in the past three days. It occurred to him, though, that she might already know most of the story, since while he wasn't reachable by phone, Dave was, and she might very well have wrung a detailed briefing out of him when Calvin proved unavailable. But still, it would be awfully good to talk to her, and he *had* promised her a call and not delivered—though that was not, strictly speaking, his fault.

He was just making final preparations for his departure—checking the fires for embers, and secreting his bow inside the trunk of a nearby hollow tree—when his eyes fell on the copy of the *Savannah Morning News* he had bought yesterday and never got around to perusing. The article that had drawn his interest then jumped out at him once more: JACKSON COUNTY WOMAN FOUND DEAD UNDER MYSTERIOUS CIRCUMSTANCES. Now, as then, it intrigued him, not merely because he had recently *been* in Jackson County (and of course, there was also the slightly sensational use of *mysterious*), but also because Jackson County was a long way from Savannah, and thus small happenings there were not likely to make the front page unless it was a slow day for news—or unless it was not, in fact, a small happening.

An impatient grunt, because he really did need to get his ass in gear, and Calvin flopped against his tree and scanned the article.

His hair stood on end as he read it. Not only had one Evelyn Mercer been found dead outside her trailer, but that selfsame trailer was apparently right off Lebanon

Road, only a mile or two from where Calvin and his friends had camped on their way from Sandy's to Stone Mountain the Sunday night just past. As for the ''mysterious circumstances,'' they remained frustratingly obscure. All Calvin could piece together from the article's oblique language was that the woman had risen early to fix breakfast for her husband, stepped outside to feed the chickens, and simply not come back in. Her husband had found her in the yard hours later, with the chickens pecking at her body. There were a few veiled references to mutilation (''The body, dressed in a housecoat over a T-shirt, appeared to have been tampered with in an unconventional manner, resulting in unconfirmed reports of possible removal of some viscera. When questioned, the local coroner had no comment,'' was the way the paper put it), but nothing really concrete. The rest of the article was a brief bio of the late Ms. Mercer and the usual rejoinder about further information being withheld pending investigation. There was no actual mention of murder, though that was certainly implied, and was what the dead woman's husband was quoted in print as suspecting. Bizarre stuff, all right.

Calvin suppressed another chill as he refolded the paper and stashed it inside the rapidly collapsing asi. Still, he supposed, sensationalism, no matter how un-sensational, had never yet failed to unload a few piles of pulp. Maybe when he got to town he'd pick up another and see if there was a follow-up.

It took Calvin perhaps thirty minutes to make his way through the woods to the road that led into Whidden, but he miscalculated his trajectory slightly, so that when he slipped out of the brush and slogged across an unexpectedly marshy bit of right-of-way and onto the shoulder of the only major highway around, he didn't recognize the place at all. The so-far-unseen metropolis had to be fairly close, though; he could just make out a pair of steeples and what looked like a clock tower looming above the treetops to the right, no more than a mile or so away. Fortunately the terrain looked a little dryer across the highway, so he crossed it at a lope and headed north beside one of the ubiquitous pine plantations, with the sun mercifully hidden behind a puff of clouds that might be vanguard of an afternoon thunderstorm.

He was not thinking very hard about anything at all—or thinking so hard about so many things at once that it amounted to the same thing—when he became aware of the crunch of tires behind him. That was strange, too, because he was facing traffic. Whoever it was would have had to whip across four lanes to come upon him from the rear.

Trying not to appear alarmed, though he was—with some reason, given his looks and circumstances—Calvin risked a glance over his shoulder and saw more or less what he expected: one of the bronze Chevy Caprices that belonged to the local constabulary—probably a County Mounty this far out. Whether there even *was* a city police force, he hadn't a clue.

A whirr/whistle/buzz of siren, and the car ground to a halt, whereupon a public address speaker broadcast a rattly "This is the Willacoochee County Sheriff's Department. Please remain where you are and turn around slowly."

Calvin obediently stopped in place and eased around to face whatever music might be playing, having no desire to do anything to upset these people, who might, after all, have perfectly good and reasonable intentions. Nor was he surprised when both the Chevy's front doors popped open and a pair of mirror-shaded officers climbed out, each of whom outmassed Calvin by at least forty pounds of—in the driver's case particularly—solid muscle. Indeed, though both gray-haired and balding, the guy looked *remarkably* fit—much more so than his much younger sidekick, who sported a bit of a paunch and a vestigial auxiliary chin. Unfortunately the driver also had a hard, thin mouth Calvin did not much like—as if he were used to getting his own way most of the time and didn't hesitate to let it be known when he didn't.

His partner, by contrast, seemed far less certain of himself, a quality he evidently tried to mask with a snappy precision of movement that was almost prissy. Calvin had to bite his lip to suppress a smirk when he saw the guy's inky sideburns, which had to weigh at least a pound apiece. Even Willacoochee County, it appeared, harbored the occasional Elvis wanna-be. Maybe this redneck rube moonlighted at the local honky-tonk or something. Calvin wished suddenly he still had his harmonica; music might help charm this possibly savage beast. Perhaps because he was nervous and wanted something to do with his hands, he reached unconsciously for the pocket where he usually kept his Hohner, then realized to his horror that he still had the hunting knife clipped to his belt—which he probably shouldn't be carrying. No doubt the officers had noticed it by now, but he froze anyway, lest his intentions be misconstrued.

The driver's brow furrowed ever so slightly, as if he had caught Calvin's gesture and was filing it away under "additional charges." "Mind if we have a few *words* with you, mister?" he drawled as he came to within about a yard of Calvin. Calvin had to raise his head to look him in the face. Mirrored RayBans shielded the man's eyes, though, and beyond the unpromising mouth Calvin couldn't get any feel for him at all. No hostility—but no friendliness either. Basically business. The nametag on his light tan shirt read W. LEXINGTON. His badge indicated that he was the local sheriff.

"Sure," Calvin replied as casually as he could.

"What we was *wonderin'*," Sheriff Lexington informed him, "was what you 'uz *doin'* 'long here. Hitchhikin's 'gainst the *law* in these parts, 'case you didn't know."

"I wasn't hitchin'; I was just hikin' into town," Calvin replied carefully, trying not to appear either nervous or confrontational—and keeping his hand well away from the knife hilt.

"You're not from around here, are you?" the other officer barked with more aggression than Calvin thought necessary. He paused, his forehead likewise wrinkled, and then: "Hey, didn't we see you down at the Magic Market yesterday?"

''Probably.'' Calvin hoped very hard he wasn't coming across as a smartass, but was beginning to suspect that any response would be subject to that interpretation.

''You didn't look too glad to *see* us, son,'' the sheriff noted pointedly. ''Any *reason* for that?''

Oh Lord, Calvin thought, *here it comes.* He'd have to level with them because he didn't dare lie when on a Vision Quest, but he doubted they'd like the answer.

''Well,'' he began, ''uh . . . well, when you . . . look like . . .''

He broke off, not liking the direction he was heading in. ''Well, I guess you've noticed that I'm an Indian, or mostly one.'' he blurted finally. ''And I've been around enough to know that not everybody warms to us, especially in small towns.'' (And *that,* he realized as soon as he had said it, had been a mistake. Last thing he needed was to sound patronizing.)

There was no obvious response from the officers, though Calvin wished desperately that he could see their eyes. Or that they couldn't see his, guiltless though they were.

''What's your name, son?'' This from the sheriff.

''Calvin McIntosh, sir.''

''You got any ID?''

Calvin shook his head. ''Lost it.''

''*Lost* it? How'd you *lose* it?''

''Mind tellin' us *where?*'' the other—ADAMS, his name-tag read—added.

''I'm not sure,'' Calvin replied truthfully. ''Last time I remember havin' it was in the Stone Mountain a couple of days ago.''

The officers exchanged startled glances, and Calvin could tell from their subtle tensing that his words had struck some chord with them.

''When's your birthday?'' Adams snapped. ''And what's you Social Security number?''

Calvin told him, whereupon Adams spun smartly and trotted back to the car. He picked up the mike inside and began speaking into it, but Calvin couldn't catch what he said.

"Nice knife," the sheriff noted casually.

"Thanks."

"Handmade?"

"Yeah. Guy up at Commerce makes 'em."

"*Commerce?*" The man's brow wrinkled again. "Ain't that in Jackson County?"

"I'm . . . I'm not sure. Could be, I guess."

"Just wonderin'."

And then an uncomfortable silence, while the deputy continued his business on the radio.

"Look," Calvin sighed finally, with more exasperation than he intended, "what is it, exactly, that you want from me?"

"Don't get smart!" the sheriff warned, but before he could continue, his partner was back, easing around to the forest side, as though to block Calvin's movements in that direction. He clutched a piece of paper, which he passed to his superior, who frowned at it for a moment, then looked back at Calvin.

"The name Maurice McIntosh mean anything to you?"

"He's my father," Calvin replied automatically, and his whole body stiffened as a host of unpleasant possibilities came flooding over him, chiefmost being that Dear Old Dad had called the law on him for busting down the fence around his beagle lot, never mind that there'd been extenuating circumstances—and that Calvin had not been driving. He *had* left some gear back in the clearing there, though; and—his heart skipped a beat—probably his wallet was among it.

Sheriff Lexington advanced another step. " 'Bout this Stone Mountain business you 'uz talkin' 'bout—you don't happen to know *which* day you uz there, do you?"

Calvin frowned thoughtfully, puffing his cheeks and wishing fervently he could lie. "Let's see . . . I got here yesterday—that's when you guys saw me—so it must have been . . . yeah, it was Monday mornin'."

"*Monday* mornin'? You *sure* about that?"

"Positive," Calvin affirmed, not flinching.

"And how'd you get here?"

"Some friends brought me. I can give you their names if you like."

"No need—yet."

"When did you see 'im last?" Adams inserted, earning a warning glare from his superior.

"Christmas—briefly. Sometime in the fall. I don't remember before that. I don't live there anymore."

"He throw you out?"

Calvin shook his head. "I left. I was in high school. Dropped out to go and try to get my head straight."

"And did you?"

"I don't know. See, Dad was half Cherokee, but he didn't want anything to do with that, but *Mom's* dad was Cherokee too—one of their last great medicine men, in fact—and he more or less took me under his wing when Mom died. I'm a lot more my grandfather's son than my father's. I—"

The sheriff silenced him with a scowl. "An' you ain't seen your daddy since Christmas?"

" 'Fraid not. Like I said, I was by his house Monday, but he wasn't home. That may be where I lost my billfold."

"And you're *certain* it was Monday?"

"Absolutely."

"Can anybody prove this? Any witnesses?"

"Like I said: some friends up north. Maybe the clerk at the Golden Pantry in Winder."

"What about *since* then?" Adams broke in. "What about *yesterday?*"

"I was here, mostly—campin' out in the woods."

"Anybody see you?"

"You mean besides you guys? Well, there was the waitress at a restaurant. Cashier at the Magic Market. Couple of kids there."

"Any idea what time?"

Calvin shrugged. "Early afternoon? Two-thirty, maybe?"

"What about last night?"

"I was here."

"But nobody saw you?"

"Right."

"And this mornin'?"

"In the woods."

"And nobody saw you then, either?"

Calvin shook his head, wondering what they were getting at, and becoming more uneasy by the second.

And then the clincher: "You mentioned somethin' 'bout bein' in Winder, and that knife comin' from Commerce. You spend a lotta time in Jackson County, Mr. McIntosh?"

"Not really."

"Been there lately?"

"I spent Sunday night there."

"Where?"

"Friend's place, south of Jefferson."

"This place got a name?"

"Yes."

"Watch it!"

"Lebanon Road."

"Anybody see you *then?*"

"Like I said, just some friends."

The sheriff's scowl deepened. Once again he consulted the piece of paper Adams had handed him. "Well, then, Mr. Calvin McIntosh, I'm afraid we're gonna have to arrest you."

"Arrest me? But why? I haven't *done* anything!"

"It's suspicion of murder, son. They found a woman dead up near Jefferson Monday mornin', and some sign you'd been nearby. *And"*—he held the pause for effect—"they found your *daddy* dead this mornin', but he'd already been dead at least twelve hours. There 'uz evidence you'd been there too. I tell you *what,* son: I sure do hope you've got a good . . ."

"Dead!" Calvin whispered dully, not listening to the rest of the accusation, for the implications of the word had struck him like a physical blow.

Dead!

His father was *dead!* He was an orphan! He was alone in a strange place, and his father was dead, and that Ev-

elyn Mercer woman was too . . . and these yahoos
thought he'd done it!

But that was ridiculous! Oh, true, he and his dad didn't
get along, had fought like cats and dogs when Calvin was
in his teens, but that didn't mean Calvin wanted him
dead. At worst, he just wanted to be left to do his own
thing.

"No!" Calvin mouthed numbly, and without really
thinking about it began backing away.

"Just come along quietly, son. We"—and Calvin
caught the gleam of handcuffs in Adams's hand.

He started reflexively, and when he did his hand accidentally brushed the knife hilt.

"Watch him!" the sheriff yelled. "He's got a knife!"

Adams lunged forward and grabbed Calvin around a
bicep, but once more Calvin acted on pure reflex and
wrenched free. What was wrong with these people?
Couldn't they see he wasn't a killer? Wasn't it obvious
he wasn't a patricide? And he had things to do, friends
to warn, a quest to undertake . . .

But then Adams tackled him again, and this time the
sheriff joined him, and together they dragged him down.
Calvin struck out reflexively, blindly, still only half aware
of what he was doing.

A fist slammed into Calvin's cheek hard enough to jar
his teeth. "Ain't no sense fightin'," Adams grunted as
Calvin felt arms trying to pin his knife hand from behind,
which he only barely managed to evade by twisting violently. "You're resistin' arrest, boy!" the sheriff added.
"*And* assaultin' an officer. We'll have to *shoot* you if you
don't calm down!"

But Calvin barely heard. His mind was drowning in
adrenaline, the same adrenaline that was making his body
wriggle and twist as he struggled to win free of a pair of
lawmen thirty percent bigger than he was, each of whom
was snatching and poking him for all he was worth. He
saw a gleam of dark metal appear in a hand, but that only
made him struggle harder. And all the while his rational
part was receding further and further, unwilling to deal

with the news. *Dead! Dead! Dead!* Out of the clear blue his father was dead—and they thought he'd done it!

Pain exploded in his face again, as one of Adams's blows landed square on the jaw; but then, somehow, he wrenched free, was on his feet and running. He did not look back, merely charged straight for the woods, only half aware of what he did, for his mind was flirting dangerously close to overload.

"Stop or we'll shoot!" a voice bellowed behind, and he could hear the steady thump of heavy feet across the grassy shoulder. He was faster, but not so fast or so far ahead that the sound of a .38 being fired didn't explode in his ears loud as a cannon. Something whizzed past his neck, and he thought for a moment he'd gone deaf, but by then he'd reached the edge of the forest and darted inside.

Gotta get away, gotta get away.

Bang!—And another bullet zipped past, and he zigged around a tree.

Two more, then, and, after the briefest of pauses, a fifth.

"Yiiiii!" he screamed as he felt fire lance across the outside of his right thigh, which meant—he thought—that they were still only shooting to wound.

But he had to escape now, 'cause if he didn't they'd never believe he didn't do it. And there wouldn't be anybody to warn Dave, or fill in Sandy, or . . .

His life, he realized dully, was probably ruined.

But he was gaining on them, was making decent progress through the pines, with the men pounding along behind. Except that he wasn't going the way he wanted, because there was just enough fallen timber to force him back toward the highway—and if he got there again, they'd have a clear shot.

But there was suddenly no choice, because Calvin came barrelling through a stand of oleander and found himself back on the shoulder. He hesitated only an instant— glanced left to see a car approaching, followed in quick succession by several others. And gambled. A quick sprint across the pavement just ahead of the startled woman in the Chrysler, and he made the other side, then flung himself to the ground beyond the shoulder and continued rolling into the sliver of marsh that separated the woods from the road. Four more cars passed, and each bought him time, for the officers had evidently lost sight of him, or at least were no longer pressing their pursuit.

A final check, a quick, furtive scoot through the cattails, and Calvin was once more in the forest—this time on the east side of the highway—and heading straight to his camp, which was seriously stupid.

But he was scared. His heart was thumping hard and he was sweating like a pig. Without thinking about it, he slapped his hand on his chest to still the thudding—and felt it close over the uktena scale.

The scale!

Calvin broke stride. There was one sure way to escape—if he only had the time. A quick glance back showed the deputies still in the woods on the other side, having apparently lost his trail in the brush there. He had a couple of hundred yards on them, but he doubted that would help much when they found his trail again. Grimacing, Calvin turned and ran as fast as he could toward the densest brush he could find.

And there, in the lee of a windfall, he stripped, stuffed his clothes under the rotting trunk, and grabbed the scale, thinking of only one thing: escape. But in what form? Falcon, or 'possum, or—

His subconscious made the choice for him.

Pain wracked him, flung him forward, tore his body apart, and reassembled it. And when Calvin rose again he was a deer: a handsome whitetail buck with a set of half-grown, velveted antlers and a bullet burn along one tawny thigh.

And in that guise, he ran once more toward the river, while the part that was Calvin simply went into hiding.

Chapter VIII:
The Doll-Maker

(east of Whidden, Georgia—
mid-afternoon)

Allison was getting bored and just a little bit anxious. She'd been playing a long time—far longer than she ought to have been, she supposed, since the sun seemed to have slipped more than a couple of widths across the circle of treetops that ringed the clearing where she had made her playhouse. Maybe she'd give her day's work a final survey and be done with it. She stood, backed off a little, and gazed with immense satisfaction at the additions. She'd moved one whole set of walls farther out, so that the spaces they delineated were closer to the dimensions of a real house. And she'd found bigger and better stones to mark those walls— and used a double row on the outside so she could tell which they were from the porches. Maybe when her birthday rolled around in another two weeks she could get some better boxes to use for furniture too. Maybe even one of those Cabbage Patch dolls she'd been wanting. And then she'd . . .

She paused in mid-thought, for something had caught her attention. A thread of melody, she reckoned, but not precisely like anything she'd ever heard. No, this was subtle and—and *foreign* sounding, but not at all unpleasant. It was low-pitched and full of vowels and esses, and before she knew what was happening, the melody had sort of wound its way through her brain and pretty soon she could not stop listening.

There was something a little troubling about it too, though she couldn't focus on exactly what. Just a vague unease that made her brow furrow and the pale hairs on her arm prickle ever so slightly.

Without really being aware of it, Allison turned away from her playhouse and started off through the pine woods—not back home, though, but deeper into the forest—toward the source of that singing.

She could hear it clearly now. It was a woman's voice (which ought to worry her, but every time she tried to think why, the thought sort of slipped away from her). Yet, though she seemed to be getting closer by the step, Allison still could not make out the words.

On and on she went, with the song sneaking into her ears, and she gradually left the pines behind and was making her way through the live oaks and willows and maples and the occasional wild magnolia of the older woods. All those trees had thick green leaves that shut out the sun and plunged her into a kind of gloom that was neat in a way 'cause it made her feel closed in and comfy. There was a lot of undergrowth as well: oleanders and sweet gum and wild black cherry, but it didn't grow where she was 'cause she'd evidently happened onto one of those deer trails like Don had shown her one time when his buddy Mike was off with his folks on vacation and he had to make do with her for company. She wished he was that nice all the time; maybe then she might do her own dishes.

The trail was getting softer, too; in fact, the moss and leaves were getting downright soupy, and she wished she hadn't worn her good sneakers, 'cause if she got mud on 'em Mama would know she'd been off where she shouldn't and get mad.

Mama! The thought chimed into her mind like a bell rung at midnight, and all of sudden she realized that she had no idea where she was except that she was a long way from home, and there really was no good reason for somebody to be singing out here. She felt a chill, but though her thoughts were rational once again, her feet kept right on following that song.

All at once the trail bent around a fallen treetrunk, and she found herself unexpectedly in sunlight so bright it made her eyes water. The singing was *really* loud now, and she could make out the words, though she didn't understand them.

> Uwelanatsiku. Su sa sai.
> Uwelanatsiku. Su sa sai.

That was it, just those nonsense phrases repeated over and over. She wondered what they meant, and then found herself trying to recall what it was she'd been thinking a minute ago. It had been important—she thought—but what was it?

Did it really matter, though? Did *anything* matter when she could listen to such singing?

She followed it now, and quickly found herself back in dark woods again, but this time they didn't go far, and when she saw the sun again, she was standing by the banks of a stream. It was Muddy Branch, she thought, from the width and the color of the water. She'd been swimming there a time or two, but that was before Don had told her about 'gators and snappin' turtles and what they could do to a little girl's feet. She preferred the public pool down in Whidden now. Let Don and Mike have the creek—maybe one of those snappers'll take a nip out of them. Maybe one would even take a bite out of that thing Don liked to play with in the bathroom. Wouldn't *that* fix him!

> Uwelanatsiku. Su sa sai.

The song shocked her out of her reverie, and another few yards down the bank she found its source.

There was a good-sized clearing by this part of the branch, and most of it was covered with sand, as if it had once been a sandbar that had got too big for its britches— the sudden kink in the creek to her left seemed to indicate this. But curiously, the clearing was not surrounded by trees and bushes like it ought to be this close to water. It was sort of shielded in by stones—a whole bunch of big gray and tan rocks just poking up out of the paler sand like the teeth of a monster.

Except that there was no monster here, just a poor old woman. Allison frowned when she saw the dingy, shrunken form hunched over a mound of pebbles to her right. It was her that was singing, she knew that; but there was something troubling about that old woman, if only she could think what. Maybe Allison had seen her in town. Old ladies were always going up to her in town and telling her how pretty she was. Maybe it was one of them.

Uwelanatsiku. Su sa sai.

And with that, the singing stopped and did not resume again. Allison felt something twitch in her mind, and started to turn and run, but by then the old woman had glanced up and Allison found herself staring straight into her eyes. They were black, absolutely black, like two lumps of coal embedded in skin that looked dry and hard, almost like sun-baked sand. Those eyes had no pupils she could see, but they glittered, and she found she could not look away from them.

The woman broke contact instead, and pointed first to the ground, then to something in her lap, and Allison saw that what she'd taken for piles of rounded river rocks were in fact dolls—rather attractive dolls, especially given that they seemed to be made out of nothing but pebbles. There was another in the woman's lap, half completed; Allison could see the feet, legs, and lower torso. Boy, it sure was neat how she found rocks just the right shape to make the various parts. Like rocks with little ridges in 'em for toes (the closest doll had feet like that), or slightly elongated pebbles in varying sizes to make the toes of another one. And . . . why, that one even had pieces of sea shell for nails.

And their faces! Allison squatted down to see, amazed at how the woman had used the natural lumps and hollows to make faces, and had added lines of dark sand for eyebrows and swatches of redder sand for lips (she wondered how she got it to stay on, too—*she'd* never had any luck sticking things to rocks). There was something strange about those faces, though: they didn't look like the kind of people Allison was used to. In fact, now she really examined one, it looked a whole lot like an Indian.

"You may play with my children," a sort of creaky-rumbly voice said—one that sounded like it had to fight its way up a long way to reach the air. Not at all like the singing, though it had the same deep, gravelly undertones.

Allison jumped, having discovered that she'd gone right up to the old woman, squatted before her, and started staring at her dolls without bothering to speak to her, and without being told it was all right to do so.

"They're made out of rocks, ain't they?" Allison inquired carefully. Then, as curiosity caught up with her: "Did *you* make 'em?"

"Bone and muscle, pebble and rock," the woman replied, and Allison blinked as she said that. An eyebrow lifted in perplexity, for she was pretty sure the woman's mouth hadn't matched the words she'd heard. But just as she began to consider that, her thoughts brushed the tune that was still hiding among them, and the notion drifted right on away.

A soft click, and Allison's gaze shifted to the work-in-progress in the woman's lap. She had on a filthy-looking rag shawl, which served her as a sort of work surface across her knees. But what Allison found curious was the way she was putting the dolls together. As best she could tell, the woman simply picked up a pebble about the right size from the pile at her feet, whispered something to it, and then stuck it where she wanted it to go and it just stayed there. And if the shape hadn't been quite right to start with, why, all of a sudden it was. But there was something else queer about the way the woman worked, too; and Allison realized that she was doing everything with her right hand. The left she kept hidden, sort of thrust up under a fold of the shawl. Maybe there was something wrong with it she didn't want folks to see.

"You *do* like my children?" the woman prompted, and

Allison remembered she hadn't responded to her earlier invitation to play with the stone poppets.

"Can I have one?" Allison asked suddenly.

"You may have them *all!*" the woman chuckled.

"Really?"

"All."

"No kiddin'?"

"All. I ask only one thing in return."

Allison was suddenly wary. "What?"

The black eyes found hers again, and Allison felt herself growing dizzy, though it really wasn't such a bad feeling.

"Let me comb your hair," the woman whispered, stretching out a gnarled hand, and rising just enough that the doll she'd been working on shifted and clicked in her lap.

Allison's fingers sought automatically for the blond curls that were so obviously superior to the lank gray wisps she could see peeping out from beneath the woman's shawl.

"Pretty hair," the woman murmured. "Maybe I should call you that: Pretty Hair."

"Thank you," Allison said, because it was polite. And true, and certainly true if you were comparing it to the crone's dusty-looking locks.

The woman patted a smooth place on the stone to her right. "Come, sit, lay your head in my lap."

Allison hesitated, but just as fear came sneaking back, so did the song, and without really wanting to, she slipped around to the old woman's side and sat down there, so close she could hear the rasp of the shawl's coarse fibers against each other.

"You heard my song, didn't you, my little one?" And Allison felt an arm slide around her shoulders and draw her down into the woman's lap. She flinched a little, because the crone was so old and wrinkled and bound to smell bad, but the only odors she caught were of hot stone and a sort of musty smell like dusty rags. Not her favorites, but they weren't really unpleasant.

What *was* unpleasant was the feel of the old woman's skin against her bare arm. Though thin and wrinkled, it felt—there was no other word for it—*hard*. But not hard the way leather can be made hard: no, this was more like how sand can be firm and yet yielding.

Uwelanatsiku. Su sa sai!
Uwelanatsiku. Su sa sai!

The song was crooningly soft now, almost a lullaby, and Allison found herself relaxing. Before she knew it, her eyes drifted closed. She felt the woman's hand on her head, gently probing, then slowly dragging something stiff and pointy through her hair, sorting through the snags and tangles the woods had given her, tugging now and then to remove a twig or leaf. And all the while the song kept on, sent her drifting further and further down toward sleep.

At some point the woman shifted, and Allison started awake, but then the song returned, and Allison was only vaguely aware that there were two hands at play amid her curls. No, wait, one was slipping down across her shoulders until it rested on her side. She could feel it there, like a bag full of warm sand. A movement, and she realized the woman had slid her shirt up and was resting the hand on the bare skin just below Allison's ribs. Her flesh was hotter: *too* warm—like rocks that have lain in the sun all day.

Allison stirred, but just as she did, she felt something poke her right beneath her bottom rib. She gasped, but by then the pain was gone.

Uwelanatsiku. Su sa sai!

And Allison's eyes slid closed. She dreamed of sliding down sand dunes. And then she dreamed of nothing.

Chapter IX: Runaways

(east of Whidden, Georgia—
late afternoon)

The first thing that Calvin noticed when he began to return to himself was *pain:* a pervasive soreness that bounced all across his body when he tried to zero in on it, that moved as he moved, sending long, dull tugs of agony along his muscles.

Gradually, however, his senses began to clear and he became sufficiently aware to focus on the more persistent spots. The worst was along his thigh—a kind of thin-edged burning; another was along his jaw, which was duller but still sensitive to the touch of his tongue. There were a couple of others along his ribs and around his right arm—those felt more or less like bruises. He opened his eyes then—and almost cried out, for the world had gone strange and blurry and he couldn't see colors right, could not perceive distance the way he thought he should.

No! he cried. And got another shock, for the word had come out as a sort of snort. That hurt his jaw, and he slapped his tongue across it automatically—and found that he had licked the tip of his nose! And that nose was altogether wrong, was long and brown and . . .

Christ! I'm still a deer!

And with that realization, Calvin began to reassess his situation, though he had to fight hard to remember how he had come here to this sheltered place by the riverbank. He could recall the fear easily enough, and running for what seemed like hours through the woods, running until he could run no more. But he didn't remember choosing this particular spot or collapsing, or why he should be so sore. And he could only with difficulty conjure back the lawmen and their dreadful words: *"They found your daddy dead this mornin' . . . and there was evidence you'd been there too."* Every time he started to think about *that*, his memory promptly clouded up and a new set of instincts made him want to leap to his feet and flee, and eat the thick foliage around him, and never be human again.

He had to get a grip on himself, had to let his rational side regain command.

A movement startled him; triggered cervine reflexes before the human could override. Something was stalking him, watching him. Maybe if he were still it wouldn't notice. (That was the deer again, a part of him noted.) He froze, but cast his gaze about, seeing only the gnarled trunk of an oak, the riverbank, the shrubs that grew close around—and, crouching almost as still as he was beside a decaying cypress stump, what appeared to be a boy about eleven or twelve. He was short and thin, fair and tow-headed, and sported the remnants of a hi-tech haircut. He was also rather dirty, and looked to be rather trendily dressed, to judge by the number of zippers and pockets and tags and loops and studs that adorned the jeans and vest he wore with his B-52s T-shirt. Finally, he sported a dangling earring, but Calvin couldn't make out what form it took.

The boy was watching him, peering intently with wide, dark-lashed eyes, and it came to Calvin then that he was probably behaving damned peculiarly for a deer.

The boy shifted subtly, extended a hand in one slow, smooth gesture as he hunched forward a half step. Probably trying very hard not to alarm this poor hurt animal he had discovered. Slowly, slowly, and Calvin could feel

his heart rate increasing, as one set of instincts fought
another.

Slowly . . . slowly, and then a dragonfly lit on the boy's
hand and he yipped and flinched and utterly lost his cool.

And with that abrupt motion, the wariness that ever
haunted the deer-mind asserted itself, and Calvin rose to
his feet, staggered for a moment, then commenced running, the deer taking more and more control as it coor-
dinated four legs instead of two.

But . . . but . . . he *hurt,* was dizzy . . . A twig poked
his injured jaw and he bleated in pain, and then the diz-
ziness claimed him and he slumped to the ground, barely
conscious.

The boy was there in a moment, his thin face crammed
full of the rounded eyes and lips of astonishment, his body
a-fidget with headlong energy that he suddenly checked as
he began to creep closer and closer to his quarry. "Don't
worry, deer," he pleaded desperately. "I'm not gonna hurt
you; I'm gonna help you if I can. Oh, don't worry. I'm
not a hunter, I *like* deer, but you're gonna have to relax
and trust me if I'm gonna help you."

Calvin jerked his head around but did not rise. The pain
returned with the movement—and brought sickening
flashes of darkness which neither consciousness desired
and which incited real fear in both parts of his awareness.

"Shit," the boy yelped. "Oh shit!" And with that he
turned and crashed away through the bushes.

Calvin tried to rise, to follow, but his body wouldn't let
him, it was too full of pain. He thrashed, trying to get to
his feet, but could not. As he moved, though, something
gouged his throat, which brought more pain. If only he
could escape it, if only he could win free for just a moment.

And then he *did* feel pain, as spasm after spasm wracked
his body.

And then, without warning, it was over, and he lay
gasping and panting on the ground.

It was a moment before Calvin dared open his eyes, but
when he did, it was to glimpse bare, smooth skin. "I'm

back," he croaked in his own voice, and fainted once more.

This time he woke to a blessed coolness across his forehead, trickling down his cheeks and into his eyes, sliding down the angle of his jaw and onto his neck and chest. Somebody was holding him, he realized dimly, cradling his head against bony shins. And he didn't hurt nearly so much now, though he was still getting occasional twinges from his jaw and hip.

Water found its way into his mouth and he choked on it before he could swallow. That made him open his eyes, which showed him a splatter of blue sky above a lacework of branches—and, closer in, filling half his field of vision, the wild blond hair and dark brows of the boy he had seen before.

Another spasm, and he sat up, though he could feel the boy's hand on his shoulders trying to ease him down again.

"You okay, mister?" The boy's voice was softer now, and it took Calvin a moment to figure out that he was hearing it with human ears, not the deer's more finely tuned senses. He couldn't place the accent beyond generic South.

Another round of coughs, and Calvin finally gasped, "I'm fine. I . . ." And then the peculiarity of his situation dawned on him. The boy had gone off looking for help for a deer, had come back to find a naked man in roughly the same location. If he was a sharp-eyed lad, he'd probably noted the uktena scale on its thong around both sets of throats. (And it was a wonder he still had it; a miracle it had neither been torn off during his headlong flight nor garroted him when he'd transformed.) Suddenly Calvin would have given a lot to know what was going on in that boy's head right now.

A final series of coughs cleared his lungs, and Calvin scooted around in place to face his benefactor. "Thanks," he whispered hoarsely. "Thanks a bunch."

The boy regarded him levelly, and with more than a trace of suspicion. "You're just lucky," he replied, with the tone of someone trying to act cool and not quite certain he was succeeding. "I . . . I was lookin' for a sick deer and found you instead."

"That why you've got water?"

The boy nodded sheepishly when Calvin indicated a plastic juice jug still half full by his side. There was a wadded pile of blue fabric nearby too, which looked disturbingly like the jeans he'd abandoned earlier.

"You're countin' on a lot if you think a deer'll let you near enough to give it water."

"It was hurt, and I was gonna clean its wounds."

"Hurt?"

"Had a bad scrape along its thigh, looked like it couldn't walk easy."

The boy's eyes shifted lower, and Calvin dared a glimpse at his bare thigh—and was both relieved and shocked to note that there was no wound there, only a thin, pale line almost invisible amid the long shadows that dappled him.

"Maybe not," Calvin countered quickly, "but it'd be a powerful stupid deer—or a powerful trustin' one—that'd let you get that close."

"I wasn't gonna *hurt* it!" the boy protested. "I think it kinda knew that. It sure let me get close, though."

"Maybe."

"*Real* close," the boy emphasized.

"Uh, yeah," Calvin muttered noncommittally. "But, uh, look, you said something about wantin' to bandage that deer, and . . . well, I can't help but notice you've got some clothes with you . . . and I imagine *you've* noticed that I don't have a whole lot on, so . . . well, do you think I could maybe give 'em a try?"

"Yeah, sure." More grunt than answer.

"Thanks," Calvin sighed, rising. Most of his previous soreness was gone—except a twinge in his jaw. That was curious, too; he'd have to think about that when he had time. Still moving a little stiffly, he wandered over to the pile of clothing, which indeed proved to be his jeans. He made a point of checking the waist size, though, in case the kid was even sharper than Calvin feared.

"These yours? They look a little big." (Was that a lie? He hoped not.)

The boy shook his head. "Found 'em."

"*Found* 'em? You just found a pile of clothes in the woods?"

"I just found a naked *guy* in the woods too. That's a little *more* unusual, I'd say."

"Touché!" Calvin laughed, as he began tugging on the britches, hoping by his light tone to draw the conversation away from the obvious question.

"Look like they *fit* you, too," the boy noted wryly.

"Lucky for me."

"Cops was hangin' around," the boy added.

"They see you? You might get in trouble."

"I'm careful and quick," the boy replied. Then, so suddenly it caught Calvin by surprise, "They after you?"

"Yes."

"What for?"

"For killing my father."

The boy tensed, and Calvin was afraid he was going to bolt, but he stood his ground.

"You do it?"

"No."

The boy relaxed a tad, though Calvin thought he still looked wary. In fact, he had the appearance of someone who was used to being wary.

"Those *your* clothes?"

"Yes."

"Why'd you take 'em off?"

"To throw the cops off my trail."

"Yeah, but—" And then the boy grimaced. "Never mind. I won't ask nothin' else. If the cops find me I don't want to have to lie to 'em."

"Any reason they *should* be lookin' for you?"

"Might be."

"I was straight with you, man; you owe me a secret or two. At the very least, you owe me your name."

"You ain't told me yours!"

Calvin took a deep breath, and debated the wisdom of replying, then: "It's Calvin. Calvin Fargo McIntosh."

"Fargo? That's a funny middle name."

"It's a version of my Cherokee name."

"Which is . . . ?"

"I'd rather not say."

"You'd tell me that you're wanted for murder, but not your *name?*"

Calvin grimaced in turn. "It's a matter of principle. Names have Power, and if you give somebody your true name, you're givin' him power over you. You have to really trust somebody a lot to do that. You get me now?"

"Yeah," the boy replied. "It's like magic, I guess."

"Right," Calvin affirmed. "More or less."

Silence, while the boy pondered this.

Calvin broke it. "Two questions, then, and I promise I won't ask any more. You act like a boy with secrets, and I've got a few of my own, so I won't ask anything personal."

"Go ahead—but I'm not sayin' I'll answer."

"Okay. Well, first, I'd *really* like a name, just a first name, so I won't have to call you *boy*, or *hey you*, or whatever all the time."

"Brock."

"Brock?"

"It's an old name for badgers, and badgers like to dig and hide and fight."

"That your real name?"

"No."

"Is that what you like to do, then? Dig holes and hide and fight?"

"When I have to."

"Okay, fine," Calvin said. "One more, now: what're you doin' sneakin' 'round in the woods? You don't look local and you don't sound local, either."

"Neither do you!"

"I'm not, but answer my question."

"I'm . . . I'm a runaway, I guess. Me and my sister ran off from Jacksonville. My stepdad beat me and . . . and did things to her, and we just couldn't stand it. We're goin' to Savannah and try to get on a ship. Robyn's got a friend over in England."

"Think they'll take you?"

"Her friend will!"

"On the ship, stooge!"

"We'll stow away."

"Yeah," Calvin chuckled after a moment's consideration, "I'll bet you would."

"You gotta place to crash?" the boy asked suddenly.

"If the cops haven't found it."

"They're workin' the other side of the highway, I think.
I watched 'em for a while. 'Course, if it's over there, you're
in trouble."

"It's not. I—"

Calvin's stomach growled loudly.

Brock started, then giggled and checked his watch.
"Christ, it's almost five—and I've gotta get goin'—
Robyn'll kill me." He paused, then, "You can have dinner with us if you want to. That way you can meet my
sister. She'd probably like you."

"Would I like her, though?" Calvin teased, flexing his
muscles experimentally as the boy rose.

"Probably. Most guys do."

With that, Brock turned and started down the ghost of
a trail. And Calvin found, to his surprise, that he was
following.

He shouldn't do that; he had enough problems of his
own without getting tangled up in the affairs of a couple
of runaways. But there were so *many* of them all of a
sudden that he had no real notion of where to begin, and
the cops were after him, and his . . . his father was dead—
which seemed so remote from him he almost thought he
had dreamed it. A part of him suggested he was blanking,
running on automatic until he could get time to think it
through. Also, if this kid and his sister helped him and
the cops found out about it, it could get *them* in trouble,
not to mention landing them right back where they came
from—where they obviously had no desire to be.

He sympathized, he'd run away a time or two himself,
and while he didn't approve of it in principle and knew
far too much about its dangers, he also suspected that the
kids probably had good reasons for what they did, it what
Brock had hinted at was true. At the very least he ought
to meet the sister, get a feel for their situation. There came

the Vision Quest again: you had to do the right thing as
your heart perceived it. And right now his heart told him
to go with Brock-the-Badger No-name.

It took a fair while to get Brock's camp—long enough
for Calvin to figure out that he'd evidently run far south
during his madness—but a good ways before they reached
it, Calvin had a strong suspicion of where it was, for the
simple reason that he'd tromped that territory himself the
day before while searching for the place Don Scott had
told him about. Shoot, he'd even rested there. Hopefully
he'd left no trace of his passing—that was one of the things
he was trying to achieve as a matter of principle, but it
was real hard to disguise everything.

He'd guessed correctly, too, for when he followed Brock
past a stand of oaks and through a thick fringe of palmettos, he found himself gazing at the short grass, ferns, and
mosses of an almost circular depression a little lower than
the surrounding land—a sinkhole, he was nearly certain;
possibly dangerous, if not for the recent rains that had
surely raised the water table under it. Though the promised sister was not present, there were plenty of signs of
habitation: a small fire in the center of the ring; two backpacks in mighty disarray; a pair of expensive sleeping bags;
assorted bits of clothing and food wrappers; the rest of his
clothes, including, thank God, his sneakers—and a couple
of sooty-shiny masses among the coals that Calvin suspected were potatoes baking. Smaller lumps might have
been onions or apples.

"Cheap and filling," Brock volunteered, noting the way
Calvin was sniffing for odors. "Some of it free, some of
it borrowed from home 'fore we left, and—"

"Some stolen," Calvin finished.

"No meat, though."

Calvin raised an eyebrow and hoped he didn't look too
disappointed.

Brock caught the expression and puffed his cheeks in
consternation. "Oh, we're not vegetarians or any shit like
that, I mean I *love* meat. It's just . . . well . . ."

"You don't have money to buy it, the skill to catch it,

or any way too keep it if you did. Yeah, I know, I've been there.''

"I caught a fish, though," Brock informed him, squatting to turn the potatoes with a stick. "But that was yesterday."

"I could probably hunt something up if you like—if I had my bow. It's back at my camp.''

"Don't bother, this'll do for n—''

"Brock, you little asshole! What the hell do you think you're doing?'' The woman's voice was low, but with a sharp, nervous edge to it. Calvin whirled in place. He had not heard anyone approaching, which alarmed him, because picking up on that sort of thing was usually second nature to him.

Brock's sister, who was now pushing through the undergrowth at the northern rim of the pit, could have stepped out of a Joan Jett video—except that he doubted Joan Jett ever let herself be photographed in mud halfway up to her thighs, even if it was slathered over black leather. Calvin caught his breath in appreciation.

"It's cool, sis," Brock called. "He's okay—like, one of us, I guess. I invited him to dinner.''

"Isn't enough for the two of us, much less an extra,'' the girl growled, slumping down grumpily and starting to tug at one of her boots—obviously expensive black items, as far as Calvin could tell under the muck. But not so uptown they didn't look able to deal with a long day's hike. Maybe the kind of thing a biker queen would wear. "Damn!" the girl continued, as she found herself thwarted. "Friggin' things are waterlogged—probably ruined.''

"Need some h—'' Calvin began, but Brock had already scooted around to tug on his sister's ankle while she yanked the other way.

"*No, I* don't need any help! Unless you can zap us outta this goddamned swamp!'' the girl shot back acidly.

"Sorry," Calvin mumbled, beginning to wish he hadn't accepted Brock's invitation.

Except then he'd have missed meeting this fox, and that would have been a shame. Not that he would *do* anything to risk his relationship with Sandy, he hastened to add. And certainly not while on a Vision Quest, 'cause anything unethical he did while on that would just come back to haunt him. But he could still look, couldn't he? And he sure liked what he saw.

No more than seventeen at the outside, Brock's sister was slim and dark, most unlike her brother, though they shared the same pointed features and Calvin doubted her hair had been that black when she was born. It was cut fairly short and bound to her head with a black and white bandanna, but he supposed that when properly arranged it had a sort of fountain effect. Her face was full of dark eyes and full lips and strong cheekbones, all showing to good effect without the conceit of makeup. As for clothes, besides the boots and the leather pants, there was a wide leather belt complete with studs, some kind of pack arrangement on it (sort of Banana Republic-meets-Essdee Evergreen), and a sleeveless black tank top that covered breasts that were small by the standards of the world at large, but plenty enough for Calvin's tastes. She wasn't wearing any earrings, but Calvin could see multiple holes in both lobes. That was good, 'cause it meant she had sense enough to avoid frivolities that would jingle in the woods or get snagged on branches. Unlike her brother's rather too intricate garb.

"*Shit!*" Brock spat softly, as a particularly sharp tug freed the remaining boot, sending him sprawling and earning him an Olympic-level glare from his sibling.

"Dammit, Brock, I told you not to cuss!"

Calvin couldn't help chuckling, which prompted a guffaw from Brock, who narrowly dodged the boot his sister chucked at him.

"Uh, I'm Calvin," Calvin managed awkwardly, trying to regain some sense of decorum.

"Robyn," the girl replied flatly. "With a 'y'. That's all I'm sayin'."

"It's all I need," Calvin told her civilly. "I, uh . . . well, I kinda gather it wouldn't be too cool to ask questions, so I won't. I'd appreciate the same—not that there's anything you guys need to worry about—beyond the cops.''

Robyn froze in the process of trying to scrape her pants clean. *"Cops?"*

'' 'Fraid so,'' Calvin admitted. "County Mounties, anyway.''

"Lookin' for you?''

"I imagine.''

"Gonna find you?''

"Not if I can help it.''

"Any reason we should worry?''

"Not unless they find you guys too. That happens, the less you know, the better. Besides—from what Brock here tells me, they'll have plenty to ask you about without draggin' me into the deal.''

Robyn glared daggers at her brother, who simply shrugged.

"I trust him, sis. I don't know why, 'cause I *know* he's got a *lot* of secrets, but I trust him.''

"I don't,'' Robyn replied. "Not yet.''

"Well,'' Calvin said, squatting down to inspect the baking veggies, "I'm mostly Cherokee, if you haven't figured it out yet; and one of the things we say is that if you've shared food and fire with a person, he's under an obligation to you not to harm you.''

"Yeah, and Eskimo men are supposed to offer you their wives, too,'' Robyn shot back. But there was a trace of softening in her voice.

"I'm your *brother!*'' Brock grunted in exasperation.

"You're a damned nuisance, is what you are,'' Robyn told him. "And if I was you—both of you—I'd stay right where you are, and keep on looking exactly where you're looking, 'cause I've gotta get outta these friggin' britches.''

Calvin and Brock exchanged an appropriate combination of winks, eye-rolls, and grins—but dutifully did as instructed, though Calvin did risk a glance across the clearing (which was *away* from the scrape of fabric and buzz of zippers) and noted for the first time what looked suspiciously like a holster amid the piles of gear. Empty, but he had an idea where the occupant was.

"These ready?" Robyn asked, joining them by the fire a moment later, then reaching behind her to excavate a fork from her pack, with which she prodded the nearest foil-wrapped tidbit.

"Oughta be," Brock told her. "They've been cookin' since three!"

"Watch it!" Robyn shot back, but Calvin noted that she was finally taking time to give him a once-over, and apparently liking what she saw.

"Wanta stay the night?"

"Huh?" *That* had come so unexpectedly it shocked Calvin speechless.

"Not afraid, are you?"

Calvin finally found his voice. "Of course not. But it's probably not the smartest thing I could do. Besides—well, there's some things I've gotta do some hard thinkin' about, and I just can't do that with folks around."

"She likes you," Brock confided under his breath, as Robyn captured a potato and began unrolling it with delicate tugs and stabs of lacquered (but functionally short) nails.

"Coulda fooled me," Calvin muttered back, as he claimed his own spud.

"So . . . you stayin'?" From Brock this time, and Calvin imagined the kid was desperately glad to have another male around. Robyn, for all her looks, had an attitude that could doubtless wear thin pretty quickly.

"I really shouldn't," Calvin reasserted. "I—"

But before he could finish, he heard the muffled thump of powerful wings flapping, followed almost immediately by the swish of air across his face as something flew right above his head. He glanced that way, and saw—to little surprise this time—that a single peregrine was perched on a limb not fifteen feet from the fire. It had something in its claws too, but just as Calvin noticed that, whatever it was won free and flew away. No, Calvin amended, had been released. The falcon had deliberately freed its prey.

But before he could investigate further, the peregrine like-wise spread its wings and wafted away through the woods.

"Cool," Brock shouted. "Hey, did you see that, sis?"

Robyn looked puzzled. "What?"

"That bird!" Brock continued excitedly. "A falcon, I think. Wasn't it, Calvin?"

"Yeah," Calvin acknowledged softly. "It was."

"What kinda bird was that it had, though?" Brock went on. "Man, that was *weird*, I swear it *let* it go."

"It . . . did," Calvin replied slowly. "And that *is* strange."

"But what kinda bird was it?"

"A robin," Calvin whispered. "Maybe I *will* stay the night." It was not a nonsequitur, though Brock stared at him askance when he said it. No, it was a response to yet another omen.

Chapter X: Frettin' and Worryin'
(east of Whidden, Georgia— supperish)

"I don't know *how* long she's been gone," Liza-Bet Scott was sobbing into the phone when Don came tumbling in the door, engaged in a tickle battle with Michael Chadwick. Don silenced his best friend with a glare and an elbow punch in the ribs, then gently deposited the bags of junkfood they'd snatched off Mike's dad onto the counter, his attention fully focused on his mother. Beside him, Michael nodded and simply slunk back out of the way between a counter and the refrigerator, as if he too could sense the tension that permeated Liza-Bet's every word and gesture.

"No, she knows better'n that," Liza-Bet went on and Don could tell from the way her gaze suddenly hooked his way and locked with his that something really bad was going on. Probably something to do with Allison, to judge by the way Mom's face was: all wild-eyed and scary, and with a few dark smudges on her cheeks and around her eyes to show she'd been crying. She was picking at her clothes too: the sweatshirt and gym shorts she'd put on when Robert had left to give his 'coon hounds a final run before he went on call again in the morning. And *that* was a real bad sign, 'cause it usually meant that the bottle'd come prancing out from below the sink real soon. Then . . . who knew what could happen.

More noise on the line that Don could not make out, then from Mom: "No, that's what I said: five hours!" She turned then, looked his way: "You haven't seen your sister, have you? She say anything 'bout goin' off?"

Don shook his head, a score of emotions at war within him, from concern for his mother, through irritation at his sister (whom he divined to have gotten lost sometime while they were taking their own sweet time returning from Mike's), to that horrible sick thunk of dread that something awful *had* happened and that he was at fault. And finally to guilt, which he didn't even need to feel yet. "Last I saw of her she was headin' for her room."

"She didn't say nothin' 'bout goin' out to play?"

"No," Don replied, trading apprehensive shrugs with Michael. "But she's started sneakin' off a lot lately," he added, in part through genuine concern, and in part because it might make him look better if Allison did turn up. Another exchange of glances with Mike, who was starting to look *really* troubled and was probably wondering—as Don was—if this would put paid to their camping trip. "Want us to go hunt for her?"

Mom's brow wrinkled and she started to reply, then held up a finger to put him on hold while the voice on the other end of the line—Don bet it was the ever-conscientious Robert checking by the department just in case—rattled on again. Her frown deepened, but then she nodded a little resentfully. "Yeah, I'll hang on till you get here. But hurry, Rob, I just can't stand this waitin', I—Just a minute."

For there had been a noise in the front of the house. "What was that?" But Don had not even had time to figure out what *that* was when footsteps pattered across the living room floor and Allison popped into view at the other end of the hall—dirty and bedraggled, to be sure, but as far as Don could tell, relatively intact. She had something with her, too: a bunch of pebbles wrapped in a scrap of rag.

"Mom!" Don cried, pointing.

And with that Allison thudded into the kitchen and screeched to a halt in the exact center of the floor, her muddy sneakers making twin red streaks on the pale linoleum. Don's nose wrinkled automatically. He'd been right, she wasn't only filthy, she was smelly as well.

A startled "Oh!" escaped from Mom, and then her eyes grew very large indeed, and tears of relief flooded into them, even as Don felt a vast relief of his own course through him like a hot drink on a cold day as he realized that his camping trip was not going to be shot to hell after all.

The phone crackled inquisitively.

Mom stared at it as if dumbfounded for a moment, then resumed her conversation. "No, Rob, just forget it. She's come back."

More crackles.

"No, she looks fine. Tell you what, I'll call you again when I know something."

Noise.

"Yeah, I love you too."

And with that, Liza-Bet hung up the receiver and knelt before her daughter. A long moment passed as they stared solemnly at each other, but then Liza-Bet threw her arms around her wayward offspring and hugged her tight. "Oh baby, baby, where've you *been?* Don't you know I've been worried sick about you? Why, I just called Robert. I . . ."

She blubbered on, heaping endearments atop exhortations not to do that again, *ever,* and mixing the whole thing with paens of relief.

For his part, Don simply rolled his eyes at Michael, who rolled his back and emerged from his patented impression of a piece of wallpaper to snag a bag of goodies and start toward the hall. "Just a minute," Don called him back, uncertain if he should just go on with business, which was what he *wanted* to do, or show some concern for his evil sister, which he supposed was what he *ought* to be at, or at least making lip-service to. Trouble was, it was hard to be worried about somebody being lost when you didn't know they *were* lost until they'd been found again. As for hanging around to find out the what and where, he supposed he'd hear all about that soon enough. Finally, he laid a hand on Mom's shoulder. "You need me, holler, okay?"

She nodded, and Don felt vastly relieved. He snagged his own bag of snacks and started down the hall, already tugging off his sweat-soaked T-shirt.

"Got any Cokes?" Mike called from ahead of him.

Don spun around and returned to the kitchen. Mom was still kneeling by her daughter, her back to him. But from the door Don could see Allison quite plainly.

And then she saw him too; and for no reason he could think of, a chill raced over his body. There was something about Allison's expression, something to do with a complete lack of the fear or guilt or contrition he knew should be there. Maybe it was shock, but then he got a closer look at her eyes and realized that sometime since lunch they had grown harder and much more calculating. Though awash with what Don suddenly had an uncanny feeling were crocodile tears, they stared at him hard and unfeeling, and Don had the eerie sensation he was being evaluated—rather like a piece of meat in the grocery store.

"You bringin' them Cokes?"

Don broke eye contact with his sister and shook his head, then trotted over to the fridge and snagged a pair of colas. But as he dashed back to his room, he could feel Allison's eyes on him every step of the way. He was suddenly glad he'd be sleeping in the woods that night.

Chapter XI: Moonstruck
(east of Whidden, Georgia—dusk)

Calvin took a final lick of apple-flavored fingers and then nothing remained of the supper he'd shared with Brock and Robyn except full tummies and the satisfaction they brought. Brock was already burying the aluminum foil veggie wrappers; Calvin had made him.

Robyn poked up the fire a little—mostly for light and comfort, Lord only knew they didn't need the heat—then settled back atop the sleeping bag she had stretched at full length on the ground. "Maybe I *ought* to tell you about it, just so you'll know," she conceded finally.

"You don't *have* to," Calvin replied. "I mean, I'm curious, and all; but I'm not sure it'd be best . . ."

Robyn took a deep breath but wouldn't meet his eyes. "No, I *want* to—haven't told a soul except my friends, and most of them don't really understand—either that, or they want me to go too far."

"They wanted her to *kill* the old fag," Brock confided from where he was shaking out his own bedroll. Calvin quickly found himself in the middle, lying on the grass-padded ground.

Robyn snorted contemptuously. "That's the *one* thing he wasn't."

"Wanta bet?" Brock shot back. "I seen him watchin' me plenty of times that same hungry-kinda way he looked at you. And he was all the time tryin' to come in the bathroom when I was in there, and . . ."

"Sounds like a real asshole," Calvin interrupted, feeling his first real pang of regret at his failings with his own father. They'd had differences, sure, but it was over ethics and philosophy, not actual abuse. Most of the whippings Calvin had got he'd deserved. And his dad had damned sure never laid a hand on him any other way!

"He *was* an asshole," Robyn continued, her voice a little shaky, but Calvin marveled at how much she'd changed in the few hours he'd been in her company. Though still trying to play the tough broad, she was starting to soften, to let her hair down some. And that was dangerous, because Calvin knew he'd have a tendency to follow suit but didn't dare.

"I'm listenin'," Calvin prompted, when Robyn seemed at a loss as to where to begin. "I can keep a secret," he added hopefully.

Robyn sighed and folded her arms above her head, not looking at him. "Oh, jeeze," she began. "It's such a long story. But I guess what really kicked it off was when our real dad died. We were living in Miami then. It was a really nice neighborhood—we had a pool and all—but it was kinda close to one of the Cuban ghettos. I guess I was about twelve or thirteen, Brock was probably—"

"Seven," Brock supplied, then lapsed back into silence.

"Right. Well anyway, Mom was your basic housewife, and Dad worked for the city. But one day Mom went out shopping, and . . ." She paused, sniffed, then went on, ". . . well, basically, this Cuban kid raped her. She didn't say anything to us about it, but then one night we heard her crying, and I asked Dad about it the next day, and he asked Mom what was up, and she told him, and he went looking for the kid, 'cause Mom knew who he was—the son of the woman who cleaned for us sometimes. And Dad found the kid and was gonna beat him up—maybe even kill him—except that . . ."

She hesitated again, and Calvin knew she was having a hard time. He wondered suddenly what it must have been like to have a father you loved.

"The kid's brother came in on 'em and shot Dad in the back," Brock finished.

"Jeeze!" Calvin whispered.

"Yeah," Robyn echoed, her voice stronger now. "Well, the outcome of *that* was that we moved to Jacksonville, where Mom was from, and then Mom met this guy there . . . and married him. Things were fine for a while, and the guy was actually pretty decent to me and Brock, but then . . . well, I think what began it all was that Mom never told him about what had happened, and she never really liked to have sex after she was raped, so that eventually they just quit doing it. But our stepdad was a lot younger than she was and didn't understand, and when he finally found out, it messed him up good, 'cause he wasn't gettin' any on the one hand, and 'cause Mom had kept stuff from him on the other, and 'cause he couldn't stand the idea of what he called 'damaged goods' on the third.'

"*That* was when it really hit the fan," Brock inserted.

"Yeah," Robyn sighed in agreement, "I reckon he just got mean. And since he couldn't stand the idea of sex with Mom anymore, he got to messin' around, only that made him feel guilty, so he started drinkin', and *that* made him mess around more—you can see where this is headin', can't you?"

" 'Fraid so." Calvin nodded. "I bet one day he got drunk. . ."

"And raped *me*," Robyn whispered, her voice once more aquiver.

"*Shit!*"

"Oh, Brock tried to stop him," she went on, "never mind that he was only about eleven, but the guy knocked him around and hurt him, and made us swear not to tell. But Brock *had* to tell Mom, 'cause the guy had nearly broken his arm, and then the shit really hit the fan, and after that it was hollerin' and fightin' all the time, and Mom takin' us off and our stepdad comin' back to get us, and court, and lawyers, and social workers, and all."

"And all the while he was still . . . well, you know," Brock put in.

"*Both* of you?"

Brock shrugged uncomfortably. "Like I said, he never did anything but look at me funny—unless you count beatin' the crap out of me 'bout once a week. Man, I couldn't do *anything* right."

"I know the feelin'," Calvin confided. "But you still haven't told me how you actually ran away, like how long you've been on the road and all."

Robyn took up the tale again. "We planned it a long time, but didn't act until last week. I was kinda lucky in a way, 'cause by the time things had really gotten messy, I'd got old enough to be on my own, though I hated to leave my little bro, so I just stayed gone a lot: slept over at my girlfriends' houses and stuff. Even ran off once before, but came back after three days 'cause I got worried about Brock."

"Who had meanwhile learned how to dig and hide and fight," Calvin guessed.

"Yeah." Robyn chuckled in spite of herself. "Kids kinda tended to get down on us 'cause of our folks. I don't know which of us spent more time takin' up for the other."

"You did," Brock volunteered instantly.

"But anyway," Robyn continued, "last week we just couldn't take it anymore, and when Brock's final grades came in and weren't the straight As our stepdad wanted, he just flipped, and that's when we decided to head out. We stole his credit cards and charged up a bunch of camping gear and stuff, and stashed it with some friends, and then just walked out last Sunday and said we were goin' to a movie, and never came back. Had a friend was gonna take us to Savannah, but it was rainin' like a son-of-a-bitch by then—and we had to stop along the road 'cause we flat couldn't see, and then when we tried to start the car again, it wouldn't go, so he had no choice but to call home for help, and *we* had no choice but to hit the road."

"So you've been hikin' . . . ?"

"Since Monday night. Found this place yesterday. Gotta

move on tomorrow. We're afraid to hitch,'' she added. ''Cops are probably on the watch by now.''

''So what happens after you get to Savannah?''

''We hop ship for Europe and get as far away from our stepdad as we can.''

''What about your mom?''

''We'll write her when we get the chance, but not till we're safely out of reach.''

''Wish we could have brought her with us,'' Brock mumbled sleepily.

''Yeah,'' Robyn affirmed wistfully. ''She was a really neat lady.''

''*Was*,'' Brock yawned back.

Robyn was looking at Calvin expectantly.

Calvin slapped at one of the mosquitoes that had begun to plague him. ''My life's not been real great either,'' he admitted.

''We're waiting,'' Robyn replied pointedly.

Calvin shrugged uncomfortably. ''There's not much to tell—not that's interesting. Mom and Dad were both Cherokee, but Dad was only half, and city-bred in the bargain, and she was born on the reservation up in North Carolina.''

''I've been there,'' Brock piped up.

''Hush!'' This from Robyn.

''Yeah, well, Mom died when I was born, but right from the start her folks and Dad disagreed on how to raise me. Dad said I'd only be unhappy if I tried to be an Indian in a white man's world, and Mom's folks said I had a right to my heritage, and should be exposed to both sides, and make my own choice. Her dad was their main advocate, I guess. He was a kind of—you'd call him a medicine man— and I started spendin' summers up there when I got old enough, and he started teachin' me things, and so I just naturally got interested in that side of the family. Eventually Grandfather tried to adopt me, 'cause the descent goes through the female line in Cherokee. That was when the *real* trouble with my dad began. I was tryin' to find out everything I could about my people, and Dad was tryin' every way he knew to stop me. He kinda had a point, I guess, 'cause I really do have to live in the white man's world, and just then—I was maybe fifteen—I wasn't doin' real well there. My grades started slippin', though fortunately I stayed away from drugs and booze; I've seen too much of what they can do. Anyway, Dad finally laid down an ultimatum and told me I could do whatever I wanted to do Cherokee, as long as I *also* did what he wanted me to do, which was to make good grades, and play sports— white men's sports—and go huntin' with him, though even that was the white man's way: with dogs and stuff. And he wanted me to date only white girls, by which I mean *very* white girls, like live in Chamblee and Sandy Springs and all. Finally I just couldn't stand it any longer, and then Grandfather died, and I went to the funeral, and I decided then I was gonna follow my heart.''

"Which was?''

"To soak up as much of the real world—of my people's world—as I could. See, white people don't really think of themselves as a part *of* nature; they think of themselves as apart *from* nature—and apart from history too, I guess, to judge by what some of the preachers say. Basically, what this meant was that I dropped out of high school and bummed around a bit, spent a while up at the reservation, and then last summer started hikin' the Appalachian Trail, and then . . . that's when things really changed.''

"How?''

"Met a girl, for one thing,'' Calvin replied, oblivious to the glimmer of disappointment that clouded Robyn's features until it was too late. "Uh, actually, she's twenty-five,'' he added awkwardly. "Her name's Sandy, and she teaches physics in a high school near Sylva, N.C., and has a real neat cabin on a mountaintop near there.''

He paused to poke the fire again, noting how the ruddy light made Robyn's too-pale skin seem to come alive.

"Like I said,'' Calvin went on, "that was last summer, and a couple of months after I met Sandy I went on down to Georgia and ran into some really sharp folks—first folks I'd met who were really into the things I'm into.''

"Like magic?'' Brock suggested a little too eagerly.

"Yeah," Calvin grunted, wishing the kid wasn't so quick. "Like magic."

"I play D&D some," Brock volunteered eagerly. "I've got a tenth-level cleric who—"

"Not *now,* Brock," Robyn told him, but with more sadness than hostility.

"No, not now," Calvin echoed. "Maybe sometime, though. I promise."

"So how'd *you* wind up here?" Robyn asked finally. "I mean, if you don't mind telling."

"I *can't* say," Calvin replied wistfully, " 'cause I don't want to lie, and if I told you the truth, you wouldn't believe me."

"Try us."

Calvin shook his head. "Not yet. Suffice to say I was takin' care of some stuff with my buddies, and we finished it up, and I asked them to let me off here, 'cause I found out a bunch of things while we were doin' . . . what we did, that really kinda weirded me out, so I wanted to just hang out in the woods for a while and get my head straight."

"And then *we* came long and messed it up," Robyn finished.

Calvin shook his head. "Not you, the cops. Them—and the death of my father."

"They think Calvin killed him," Brock supplied.

Calvin rolled his eyes in dismay. That was the last thing he needed.

Robyn's eyes narrowed, but she kept her cool. "Did you?"

"No."

"When did you find out?"

"This afternoon."

Her voice softened, though it retained a note of apprehension. "Wanta . . . talk about it?"

"No."

"Sure?"

A pause, then: "No to that, too."

"Life's a bitch."

"And then you die," Brock concluded.

"No," Calvin countered, *"life's* great, it's people not bein' straight that screws you up—that, and people who won't wake up and smell the roses, who wanta make the world into their image of it 'stead of what it really is."

"Like your dad did?"

"Yeah."

They talked for several more hours—or Robyn and Calvin did; shortly after it became full dark Brock rolled up in his sleeping bag and, in spite of his best efforts to the contrary, was soon snoring softly. Most of what they discussed *was* fathers, and though Calvin was reluctant to elaborate at first and recounted his encounter with the sheriff in the sketchiest possible terms, he discovered that Robyn was almost as easy to talk to as Sandy. Eventually she began to open up as well, and after a while Calvin realized they'd both sort of regressed to their childhoods, were exchanging tales of small family doings before crises had hit. Robyn spoke of going to Disneyworld with her folks, and how her dad had enjoyed the rides as much as she had, and had insisted on going on all the E-tickets twice, never mind her mom's protests.

And then Calvin told about his dad sneaking off from work to watch Calvin play in Little League, and how he'd comforted him when they'd called him names. It was catharsis, Calvin decided, for both of them. Maybe that was what the omen had meant: that by staying here he could get the sort of outpouring of grief mixed with relief that would otherwise be slow in coming. By the time it was over, both of them were misty-eyed and Robyn's nose was running. She wiped it daintily. "So much for being a tough broad, I guess."

"We're all soft in the center," Calvin told her gently. "Either that, or we *have* no center."

"Yeah," Robyn yawned. "And tomorrow'll come whatever."

"Yeah," Calvin echoed. "Guess it's time we turned in."

"Guess so."

The fire had burned to embers by then, and neither of them had any desire to poke it up. Robyn unzipped her sleeping

bag and slid inside, fumbled for a moment, then dragged out
her jeans, which she rolled into an untidy cylinder and handed
to Calvin with the single word "Pillow."

"Thanks," Calvin murmured. He slid it under his head,
then stretched out on the ground where he was, arms
folded across his bare chest, staring at the sky. Brock was
a small lump beside him, his back snuggled against Calvin's side, his legs drawn up like a tiny child.

Silence for a while—except for the sounds of the night.

And then Calvin felt a soft touch on the hand he'd
cupped around his left elbow. A glance down showed him
Robyn's fingers; a shift of his gaze further left revealed
her reclining on her elbow looking at him. Their eyes met,
and she lifted the flap of the bag a fraction. "There's room
for two."

"I can't," Calvin whispered, but she did not withdraw
the hand from his.

But the hand was gone when Calvin awoke sometime
later—near midnight, to judge by the position of the moon
and the stars. The sky was clear, though the wind still
held a hint of rain, and Calvin could just make out the
Cygnus corner of the Summer Triangle. For a while he
simply lay where he was, wedged between Brock and Robyn, almost as if they were family. It was strange, too, for
he'd been sleeping soundly, dreaming something about
swimming in Galunlati, and then abruptly he was awake.
But what had roused him?

Beside him, Brock stirred and whimpered and frowned
in his sleep.

Somewhere to the west a dog barked—far off, but clear.
Calvin started full awake at that, and could have kicked
himself. He'd been an utter fool. Of *course* a dog had
barked—he *was* a fugitive, after all. No way they'd just let
him run off in the woods and not look for him. But white
men were lazy, were sorry trackers, so they'd naturally
use dogs to do their dirty work, and in a little county like
this, they'd probably have to bring 'em in from outside.
Only . . . didn't they usually use bloodhounds for stuff
like that? And weren't they usually silent? Calvin strained

his hearing and caught another set of distant, excited yips. Those certainly didn't *sound* like bloodhounds. Beagles, then, like the ones his dad used to chase rabbits? Except that it was night, which made that unlikely, though not impossible—and they didn't sound quite right to be beagles. More likely it was somebody out 'coon hunting. Only it wasn't season, unless somebody was just out running their hounds to hear them sing; he'd known plenty of people who did that.

He sat up to try to catch the bays and bells more clearly, and made out the deeper, more resonant tones of a treeing walker. 'Coon hunters for sure, he decided; keeping their hounds in tune.

But maybe he ought to investigate, anyway. No telling what'd happen if a bunch of hunters stumbled on him and the runaways. For an instant he thought to rouse his companions and have them abandon their sinkhole hideaway, but something told him *no*, that the cries were too far away to pose much threat.

And then something else caught his attention. He could not tell for certain if it was an actual sound or merely a vibration in the ground, it was so low-pitched. Like rocks sliding together, maybe; like the earth muttering to itself as it cooled. But then he noticed something far more troubling: the crickets and the birds—the chuck-will's-widows—had all fallen silent, as had the frogs in the swamps nearby. So had the dogs. Even the mosquitoes had ceased to buzz.

That did it; something was up. He had no choice but to investigate.

Sighing, he slid out from between the siblings, using the smooth, silent movements in which he took so much pride, and indeed he made no sound at all as he crept across the depression and snagged his sneakers—dread of what he might step on in the dark overriding his fear of noise. He made no move to put his shirt on, though, and the moonlight laid blue shadows across his body.

Moonlight was his friend, as was the night.

Still soundless, Calvin pushed through the bushes that fringed the camp and entered he forest.

It enfolded him like a brother, and he had a sudden urge to halt dead in his tracks and simply stand among the starlit trees while he slowly cleared his mind until there was nothing left but self, until he had no body and could simply drift away on the rising wind.

Almost without thinking, he found himself gripping the scale, and wondered, suddenly, if he could use it to achieve exactly that—abandon shape entirely, and become pure, mindless consciousness. But after a moment good sense got the better of him and he moved on, tiptoeing barefoot until he was out of range of the camp, then leaning against a maple to slip on his shoes. He was one with the night now, and from then on he knew he would make no sound.

He strained to catch the cries of the dogs again, but could not. The thrumming continued, though, like something drumming in the earth—no, it was more as if something bowed the ground, drew on its very structure to play a long, slow fiddle tune. There were almost words, too, a sort of sighing on the wind, but Calvin could not make them out. They had a direction, however—north-north west—and he followed them, slipping among the trees, letting the moonlight catch and blend their shadows with his own, sliding across his hair and down his shoulders, teasing him alive with light and wind.

He ran, then, as softly and nearly as swift as the deer he had recently been. On and on he trotted while the thrumming got fainter and fainter and finally faded away entirely. For a moment he halted, at a loss as to which way to continue, then shrugged and continued on, more or less the way he had been heading. He had slowed to a jog, though, ears ever alert for a resumption of the thrumming—until, quite suddenly, he found himself on the edge of a stream—very likely a tributary of good old Iodine Creek. At least the width looked about right, and there was the same sort of bank.

What *wasn't* right were the stones. Coastal south Georgia was flat, Calvin knew; had been underwater until fairly recently, thus the predominantly sandy soil. To hit rock worthy of the name you had to dig deep, and even then it was likely to be limestone.

Not handsome sandstone monoliths like those that reared up from the sandbar before him, gold-glimmering in the moonlight—impressive, yet somehow sinister as well, for each was taller than he was, and most were wider than his arms could span.

No way stones like these could be natural.

Indians, then? He tried to recall all he knew about aboriginal Indian stonework. He didn't think the native Yuchi had worked stone, and was pretty sure they wouldn't have lugged boulders like these around without a very good reason. Maybe it was the folks who had built Rock Eagle away to the north, or the ones who'd piled the pseudo-forts on Fort Mountain.

Or perhaps it was none of these things—for Calvin could not put from his mind what he had sensed as he followed the thrumming: that something was playing with the forces of the earth itself. Maybe *that* was it; maybe something had *raised* these stones, dragged them up from the center of the world—or perhaps simply fused them together out of the abundant sand. The color was the same, in fact.

But who or what?

Was this what the omens had pointed to? If so, what did it portend? Did it mean anything at *all*?

Or was he simply being paranoid again?

The trouble with magic was that once you knew it worked, you never quite trusted anything you saw afterward, especially if it was in any way out of the ordinary. But Calvin had also seen enough of hard-core mundane reality to know that plenty of remarkable things had perfectly natural explanations.

So, he supposed, the first thing to do was check out the stones. With that in mind, he slipped around the first one—and got a shock so strong that a low cry escaped him before he could suppress it.

The rocks constituted an irregular half-ring where they butted up against the stream. But to Calvin's left was a series of lower shelves, and on the bottommost lay the body of a small blond girl. She was naked, Calvin saw as he drew nearer, lying on her back as if in repose. Maybe about nine or ten—certainly younger than Brock, who claimed thirteen and looked eleven. Her face was pretty, her soft, smooth skin rendered smoother yet by the moon-light that caressed it and hid the pallor Calvin knew was there without bothering to check—perhaps because his senses were already so attuned to the night he could have heard the sound of her breathing had there been any. But the tiny chest did not rise and fall; the lips did not stir; the eyes did not twitch beneath their translucent lids.

The child was dead—but she had died in peace, that much he could tell by her expression. Yet it had not been natural causes, that much was equally clear. Calvin bent closer, scarcely daring to breathe lest he shatter the illu-sion—though his heart knew that was the thing he wished *would* happen, for no child as lovely as this should be dead. Closer, and he stood directly over her, trying very hard to fight the tears he felt welling up in his eyes, to banish the memories of his father the image before him suddenly evoked.

Logic advised that he get the hell out of there—an In-dian boy caught looking at a naked dead white child in the middle of the night was a situation custom-made for trou-ble. But there was something about *this* night, this *place;* something about its almost mystical stillness that made him linger a moment longer.

Soundlessly, Calvin knelt beside the child, and when he did, he noticed what she held in her nearer hand. It was a doll—a sort of articulated manikin—completely made of artfully jointed pebbles. In fact, when Calvin turned so the moonlight was full upon it, he could see that—though every form was made of unshaped rock—they were joined to each other in some way he could not make out so that they could move and twist like a natural body. There was something a little *too* strange about that, too. It smacked— there was no other word for it—of magic.

But magic or no, Calvin had to get word to the author-ities, never mind what they might do to him. There were a thousand reasons to do so, most having to do with simple ethics, with doing "the right thing," and trusting to the courts to acquit him of any improper allegations. And since he was on a Vision Quest, doing the Right Thing was very important. Trouble was, they were looking for him back in town, very likely had a murder warrant out on him, and if they had any sense really would have bloodhounds on his trail before long.

And now he, the fox, had to chase down the hounds! Because if there was one thing he could not do, it was to leave this poor child here for others to find Lord-knew-when.

He thought briefly of waking Brock and Robyn and dispatching them to phone in an anonymous tip, but quickly brushed that notion aside. They were in almost as much trouble as he was; no way he'd ask them to further risk themselves in his behalf.

But if something had killed this little girl, most especially if it was something supernatural, no way was he gonna leave the runaways unprotected. That, at least, he could do something about.

"A-woooo-ooooo-oooooo!"

Calvin almost jumped out of his skin, and whirled around just in time to see a large black-and-tan 'coon hound lope into the clearing. It paused when it saw him, staring soulfully at him with confused brown eyes that questioned his presence there.

"Easy, boy," Calvin whispered, and began backing away, edging toward the encircling woods opposite the way the hound had entered. Evidently the monoliths had deadened sound somewhat, for now he was almost clear of them, he could make out the cacophony of the hunt at full cry—and growing closer by the instant. He hesitated, torn between the very reasonable desire to get the hell away from there, and curiosity. For the hound had lost all interest in him, was nosing around the little girl's body, yet keeping a certain distance, as if it mistrusted what it smelled. If it stayed there, Calvin now had every good reason to believe, the hunt would proceed no further.

As if in answer, the hound set back its head and bayed. The tone and cadence were different than earlier, though, and Calvin suspected the dog's owner would know what it implied.

Well, he supposed, if push came to shove, he could

always change skin again. And with that in mind, Calvin slid back into the cover of the forest—but not so far he could not see or hear what went on inside the ominous stone circle.

He did not have long to wait, because the hound's belling was quickly joined by others, and an instant later, the sandbar was awash with canine bodies—tails wagging, pendulous ears flopping every which way. Most were black-and-tans, but there were a few redbones and blueticks as well, and—sure enough—a single treeing walker.

An instant later, two men followed. One was tall and slim and red-headed, maybe in his middle thirties; the other shorter, blockier, and younger, yet somehow the more elegant of the two. Both wore jeans, flannel shirts, and purposeful-looking boots, and both had impressive battery packs slung around their waists, which connected to equally heavy-duty flashlights.

If he'd had any doubts before, the men's appearance dispelled them. They were 'coon hunters without a doubt—probably out for a practice run to keep their hounds in tune.

"Jesus Christ!" the shorter man cried abruptly, as his beam raked across the little girl's corpse. Then, "Fuck, Rob! That's a goddamn *body!*"

"Jesus *H.* Christ!" the taller man echoed, pushing past his companion to stare down at the form on the stone. Then, "Oh, shit, Larry! Why, this is . . . this is my woman's girl: this is poor little Allison Scott!"

The shorter man frowned and waded through hounds so he could peer over his companion's shoulder. "You're shittin' me!"

The taller man stood, towering above the other, his face almost blank with shock. "But . . . but that just can't *be*, Larry!" he whispered, sounding suddenly much younger than he had a moment ago. "I . . . well, I was over at th' station right 'fore we came out here, and Liza-Bet called in and reported her missin'—took the call myself. But then Allison turned up right in the middle of everything, so they closed the case before it was even really opened. Liza-Bet figgered she'd just got lost in the woods."

"Yeah," Larry breathed. "I 'member you tellin' me 'bout that. You *sure* that's her?" he added.

The red-head nodded. "I saw her today at lunch over at Liza-Bet's. Told her how good she was. I . . ."

Larry laid an arm around his shoulders and drew him back. "That's okay, Rob. You don't have to talk 'bout it now. I reckon you know what we've gotta do."

"Yeah," Rob replied heavily. "Guess I'd better give the sheriff a call."

"I'll do 'er if you want me to," Larry told him. "I'll stay here and wait, if you want. You can stick the dogs in the pickup and then I suspect you'll be wantin' to hightail it to Liza-Bet's. Figger she'd rather hear it from you as anybody."

"I 'spect so," Rob acknowledged heavily, in somewhat better control of himself than heretofore. He reached for the walkie-talkie that hung at his waist, unhooded it, and stared at it stupidly but did not turn it on.

Meanwhile Larry was sweeping the sand with the beam of his flashlight, moving it back and forth with great precision and following the large, bright circle with equal intensity. Most of what it showed was dogs milling around and getting fidgety (though they hadn't approached the body, which he thought curious), but then . . .

"*Aha!*" he cried, and knelt down right by Allison's corpse. "Tracks," he continued, looking up at Rob. "Middle-sized male in tennis shoes, unless I miss my guess. You know anybody like that?"

"Yeah," Rob sighed, rising once more and switching on the walkie-talkie, " 'Cordin' to what I heard Wilson goin' on about back in town, I've got *one* idea already; so I guess I'd better get the wheels to turnin'."

"Guess you had," Larry agreed. And with that Robert Richards sent the bad news out of the forest and into Whidden.

Chapter XII:
"Uwelanatsiku. Su sa sai!"

(northeast of Whidden, Georgia— Thursday, June 19—near 1 A.M.)

There was one thing he could always count on when he went camping, Don Scott reflected with a yawn: sooner or later he was going to have to get up at least once in the night to pee. It happened *every* time, and usually at the most *inconvenient* times, like when he was crammed between two buddies, or was the one closest to the wall, or when he was in the top bunk, or when it was raining, or— sometimes—just when he was in a particularly enticing dream. That had been what he'd been aroused from this time, and aroused was a pretty good word, too; 'cause he'd been dreaming about Janie Morris, who was a year ahead of him in school, but who'd winked at him in town yesterday morning. Lord, it gave him a hard-on just thinking about it, and that wasn't what he needed to be thinking about at all when his bladder was crying out for relief.

Oh well, he decided philosophically, glancing down at Michael snoring away beside him; ole Mike's log-sawing would have woken him up sooner or later anyway. Or the skeeters, he added to himself, as he paused in the process of sliding his legs out of the bag to slap a couple he could feel sampling his arms and neck.

Or, he realized suddenly, very possibly the humming in the ground. It was a wonder Mike couldn't feel it, 'cause *he* sure as heck could. Curious, too: it was like an endless train running at a great distance, like far-off thunder in the earth. Or like drumming. It crept up through his body, thrummed into his bones.

And inevitably reached his over-stressed bladder.

"Shit," he muttered under his breath and slid the rest of the way out of the bag, not caring now if he woke Mike up or not, and thinking rather strongly that if the—whatever it was—was still going on when he got back from his pit stop, he'd wake the SOB up and see what *he* thought about it.

The bag fabric hiss-buzzed against itself as he rose beneath the scanty shelter of the lean-to he and Mike had lashed together the previous summer. Another yawn, another glance at Mike, and Don padded skivvies-clad into the warm night.

He hesitated at the foot of his bag to check out the river: a glittering ribbon of black below the bank to the right. A pair of laurel oaks backed the lean-to, and to the left and ahead were miles of woods: hardwood here, but a little farther out—beyond the single strand of barbed wire he'd aloofly ignored—they gave over to one of Union Camp's endless loblolly pine plantations.

But it was night, and it was the woods, and him and Mike were out in it, and it was great. He could feel the warm wind against his bare chest and shoulders as he trotted along searching for a place where the bank sort of overhung the creek and he could whiz into the water unimpeded. The sand was soft underfoot, too—soft as flour. But for some reason that troubled him—maybe because he could still feel that weird-ass thrumming, and he didn't think you should be able to feel that kinda thing through something as soft and unstable as sand.

It took him a little longer than he expected to find the place he wanted—maybe fifty yards up from the camp. A tree crooked over the river there, its trunk curving out and then up again. He balanced there precariously, one foot on land and one on the knobby bark, flopped Rambo Jr. out, and let fly, hearing the distant tinkling splash—and the startled croak of a suddenly baptized bullfrog.

Finally relieved, Don returned to more stable footing and headed back to camp. He was almost within sight of it when he heard something—some*one* singing. Simultaneously he caught a glimpse of something white winking ghostlike through the already disquieting streamers of Spanish moss. He froze in place, as every haint tale he'd ever heard (and he'd heard plenty, 'cause they were a sort of specialty of his) came sneaking back to him, so that all in a single sharp breath the night woods were transformed into something sinister.

The singing was getting steadily louder, too; and pretty soon Don could hear words, though they didn't make any sense:

Uwelanatsiku. Su sa sai!

Just that same nonsense phrase over and over. But the voice gave him the willies worse than ever 'cause it sounded a whole lot like Allison's voice, and *she'd* given him the willies once that day already. Her eyes had been the worst, 'cause they hadn't looked like Allison's eyes at all. Or rather, they'd looked like Allison's eyes rendered into cold, dead stone. And the way she'd stared at him . . . jeeze! Like she'd wanted to eat him or something.

If Mike hadn't been there, if they hadn't already done a million things to prepare for their trip, if Mike had been even halfway likely to have listened to him when he said something was wrong with Allison and maybe he ought to stick around home for a while, he *would* have stayed home, just to keep an eye out. But this trip meant a lot to Mike, and they hadn't been out all night in a while, and . . . well, it really had seemed silly when he thought about it. "Something's wrong with my sister? Yeah, sure!"

It did not sound at all silly now.

Don could not have said what kept him rooted to that

spot. Maybe it was fear, maybe it was curiosity. Maybe it was some other hand guiding him (he felt that way sometimes—like somebody was watchin' out for him, making him lucky and all.) Whatever its source, he stayed where he was, while the singing got louder and closer. Don noted absently that the thrumming had stopped, but that didn't make much difference now, not when his sister was out roaming through the night like a crazy woman.

Uwelanatsiku. Su sa sai!

For when the half-seen figure finally pushed through a particularly thick beard of moss and came full into the clearing, Don had no doubt whatever that it was Allison.

He also had no doubt that there was something wrong with her. Common sense—and a good chunk of emotion—said what he ought to do was run out to her and hug her and ask her what in the world she was doing out there a mile from home in just her nightie. But when your sister stared at you like she had earlier, and then showed up singing strange songs, it might be wise to watch her for a minute first.

Thus torn, Don swallowed and squatted down in place, hoping against hope that the tree he was crouched behind would be sufficient cover.

He could hear the song clearly now, and this time there was no doubt: it was Allison singing, and it was not English. But even as he strained his ears, the song slowly shifted, and then it *was* English, and the words sure enough kept Don frozen in his tracks:

> *Liver I eat! Su sa sai!*
> *Liver I eat! Su sa sai!*
> *Liver I eat! Su sa sai!*

And with that last strange word echoing around the clearing, the small blond figure removed its left hand from where it had been hidden in a fold of nightgown and flourished it on high.

And Don saw that which came within an ace of making

him scream his lungs out. For his sister—no, it couldn't be; better say that *thing*—had an index finger that was at least twelve inches long, on which glittered a nail that looked far too much like the chipped and flaked head of a stone spear.

And she was walking right toward Mike, who slept all unaware.

"No!" Don tried to scream, but only then discovered that he could not move. No, he *could* move, but so slowly it was like pulling his way through hardening concrete. He could breathe, could feel his heart pumping extra as it tried to supply the blood desperate muscles needed. But something was interrupting.

It was, Don realized dully, that damned song. For as he watched Allison calmly walking toward his buddy, she kept singing, and every time she came to that set of non-words, *Su sa sai!* the air gave a little buzz, and the ground gave a little thrum, and together they just sort of slipped up into his nerves and held him cold.

He could only watch, then; watch in horror as Allison skipped to within a foot of Michael Chadwick's head, knelt beside him, dragged the flap of the sleeping bag aside— and with obvious relish, plunged that awful finger into his naked right side.

And Don could do nothing but watch: could not flinch, could not gag, could not scream. He could not even cry much, though he felt his eyes burning. That was *Michael* over there, lying on his back with his left arm resting on his flat, tan belly, and the other curled languorously above his head, as if he were *offering* his side to that monster. His face, though, was the worst, for it did not change, kept that smile of peace that Don loved—and would have died to keep Mike from knowing he loved; that smile Mike wore only when he was sleeping, that Don saw only when he awoke beside Mike in the night and watched him and wished he really was his brother.

Why didn't Mike move?

Why didn't he do something? But Don knew, with a pang of resignation: because he could *not* move. If Don, who was awake, had fallen under that spell, Mike stood no chance at all.

But Allison *was* moving, and Don wished he didn't have to watch that, wished he could close his eyes tight (for he could no longer move even that much), because he *certainly* did not want to see the smile of relish that crossed his sister's face as she wiggled that finger around inside his friend's body for a while, and then, very slowly, dragged out a hunk of something dark and shiny, something that she let dangle from her fingers before lowering it into her mouth, whereupon she sucked it down with a sickening slurpy noise and swallowed.

Three times Don had to watch that grisly rite repeated, and all the while he fought the paralysis, and all the while it held, though he could feel it slip a little from time to time, but not enough to help.

Finally Allison was sated. She stood, turned—and then stared right at the place where Don was standing, just looked right at him with those eyes as cold as stone.

"*You* I will hunt," she mumbled slowly, as if she were not familiar with English. "I have pumped your liver full of fear, and it will taste even better than this simple fare—but not now. Farewell, Don Scott—and live in fear, for when I will, I will find you."

And with that she turned and strolled back into the woods.

Don did not move—*could* not move. He had just heard his death pronounced and he knew it. He only became aware that the numbness was gone when he abruptly lunged forward onto the ground, as muscle fibers finally found themselves able to twitch again and did so all at once.

He screamed. It was true: Allison wasn't Allison but some kind of monster, and she'd done something awful to his best friend.

"Mike!" he yelled, and scrambled forward to embrace his buddy, but the instant Don touched him he knew he was too late.

Michael Chadwick's skin was already cooling, his body far too limp. And he was a light enough sleeper that having his head yanked up and his cheeks slapped around by an hysterical, sobbing friend would have awakened him fast enough—and probably earned Don a wrestling match in the bargain.

But he did none of these things.

He was dead.

Which meant that Allison might be too, 'cause *something* had sure happened to her. But Allison had been at home when Don had left her, sleeping off her ordeal (so he supposed) in her room.

Which meant . . .

"Mom!" Don cried, and leapt to his feet. He had already run a half-dozen yards down the trail that led home when he discovered that he was still in his drawers, and that he probably shouldn't leave Mike unprotected like that. Impatience nearly consumed him as he made desperately short work of zipping his friend all the way into his sleeping bag, and of getting dressed more or less on the fly.

In less than a minute he was stumbling through the dark forest, a shape of silver and midnight blue where moonlight and shadow grappled endlessly for him.

Run run run. That was all he could think. *Gotta help Mom, gotta help Mom, gotta save Mom. Oh God, don't let me be too late.*

Branches dragged at him, fallen limbs tripped him, Spanish moss captured him in itchy silver-gray nets. He fell, scraped himself against trees, got dirt in his already-streaming eyes.

But he made it home in what surely would have been record time.

Which was *just* in time to see a Sheriff's Department car drive away with what looked like his mother hunched over in the passenger seat.

"Mom!" he screamed once more, ineffectually, and then simply stood there at the edge of the no-longer-friendly forest, stood with his hands clenched and his heart pounding and his eyes streaming like a baby's.

"Mom! Oh God, no!"

And with that he sprinted toward the house. If he

couldn't catch her one way, then, by God, he'd call somebody and warn her.

Warn her about what? Not to come back? That Allison was not Allison? That something had sung Michael Chadwick to death and eaten his liver?

Or maybe that hadn't even *been* his mother. Maybe whatever it was had gotten home ahead of him (and he should have passed it in the forest, he realized in retrospect).

He was on the patio by then, dashing up the back steps, fumbling for his key.

Inside—and what would he do?

Call, yeah, that was it. Just call, find out what was going on, warn his mom. Warn Mike's dad. Call . . . who first?

But then he saw the sheet of notebook paper on the kitchen table.

He picked it up shakily, stared at it through blurring eyes as he wiped his nose on a filthy hand. The writing was wobbly, the paper damp in a place or two as if tears had fallen upon it, but it was his mother's script all right.

Don,
Something's awful's happened to Allison, and I've gone with Robert to try to find out what. I don't know when I'll be back, but if you find this, give the sheriff's office a call and they'll tell you. I can't.

Love,
Mom

P.S. I wanted to come get you, but Robert said it was urgent and that there wasn't anything you could do anyway, so we'd just as well leave you happy.

Sorry,
Mom

Don crumpled the sheet in his hand and trotted across the kitchen to reach for the phone. His fingers had just brushed the plastic when he saw something out the adjoining window that made his blood freeze all over again.

For as he gazed out into the moonlit backyard—across

the newly mown grass, the patio, the neat octagonal concrete flagstones that led back to the wading pool and the
flower garden—he saw what he first took to be the world's
largest molehill slowly forming not five feet from the edge
of the patio.

The thrumming was back too, and rising in intensity.
He wondered whether or not it had been present when he'd
been running through the woods, 'cause it seemed to be
in some way connected with . . . whatever-it-was.

He was still gripping the phone and staring foolishly
when the molehill ceased to grow, and before he knew
what had happened, Don Scott saw the surrogate Allison—now stark naked—push up out of the soil there.

"No *way!*" he cried to the empty kitchen, and before
he took a second breath was out the front door.

He hesitated then, not having the vaguest notion of
where to go or what to do. But he was so far gone into
shock now he scarcely cared. Run, that was what he should
do: get the heck out of there. But he should not do that
until he knew what was going on.

Steeling himself, though his whole body was trembling
and his mouth was dry as dust, he eased his way left and
off the tiny porch, then turned left again so he could survey the side yard. Nothing was there, but as his gaze darted
over the pair of uniformly dark windows, the farther one
suddenly blinked alight. It was the den.

And he just *had* to have one more look, just had to see
what it was that could rise up through solid earth and take
Allison's form.

Moving as silently as he ever had in his life, Don slipped
around until he was under the window. Then—and it was
maybe the most nerve-wracking thing he had ever done
because he expected at any moment to be surprised from
behind or to finally get his eyes up to level and come face-
to-face with whatever-it-was staring out at him—very
slowly he stretched far up on his tiptoes and lifted his head
above the sill.

Fortunately there were curtains, thin though they were.
And fortunately he was gazing from dark into light, not
the other way around.

Yet he still felt chills race over him when he saw "Allison," newly clad in jeans and T-shirt, pause for a moment by the light switch, then pad toward the sofa and curl up expectantly on the far end. She was gazing curiously at the television his mother had evidently forgotten to turn off in her haste to depart—but the eyes were cold as stone.

Don slumped back down against the bricks, his heart still pumping like Dixie, and his lungs like flaming bellows. He was drenched with sweat, yet he was cold. He was scared shitless, yet he was calm.

And he had nowhere to go. The house was out, *it* was in there. And when his madly darting eyes finally came to rest on his mom's year-old Mercury Cougar, the flash of hope that ensued quickly evaporated as he realized that she always kept one set of keys with her, and the other set—and that was his luck—in the end table right beside the couch where his sister's alter-self was lying in wait for his mother's return.

That left one alternative:

Mike's house was more than a mile away overland—and at that, still the closest neighbor. He'd go there. And maybe he could save a little time by cutting through the woods.

With that in mind, Don Scott once more started running.

Chapter XIII: The Lurkers in the Shadows

(east of Whidden, Georgia— just past 1 A.M.)

"Okay, kid,"Calvin whispered to himself, "time to start gettin' your act together."

He did not know how long he had lingered in the fringe of oaks beyond the strange stone monoliths, but it seemed an eternity. His goose was cooked for certain now, 'cause circumstantial evidence had suddenly written "serial killer" all over him. Never mind that he was innocent, even had an alibi. *That* kind of thing didn't matter in little podunk towns like Whidden, Georgia. No *way* a local jury would believe a pair of weird-looking runaways, even if he could get Robyn and Brock to testify in his behalf—presuming, of course, that they didn't simply split at the first sign of trouble. After all, the woods would be full of cops in no time, and Calvin didn't know how wide they'd range in search of evidence. Brock looked to be a fairly light sleeper, too—wired kids like him usually were—so there was a good chance he'd already gotten wind of whatever was going on and urged his sister to boogie right on out of the county.

Which would leave Calvin back at ground zero. Shoot, they wouldn't put him *in* jail, they'd put him *under* it—and that would be *before* the trial.

A couple of things bothered him, though. Like why the cops thought *he* had killed his father. He'd been dead at least half a day when they found him, they'd said. But they'd only discovered the body that morning, which would have put his death no later than Tuesday evening—and Calvin had been *here* then; had been having dreams and seeing visions out the wazoo, in fact. So when . . . ?

Well, he and his friends had been by his father's place just before sunrise Monday *morning*, but they hadn't seen any sign of anything unusual then. His father's truck had been gone, true, but that only meant he'd left for work. The dogs had been locked up properly as well, and seemed to have been fed, so presumably his father was still alive then, which meant his murder had to have happened after . . .

. . . after he and Dave and Alec and Liz had used a little clearing in the nearby woods to open a gate into another World so that he and Dave could go through to rescue Fionchadd. That had been when the shit *really* hit the fan. Oh, they had sprung the Faery boy, all right, and made it back intact; but in doing so they had attracted the attention of a horde of Faery warriors, who had followed him and Dave all the way into this World. Dave had rammed his car through the fence around Calvin's dad's dog lot then, that being the only way they could escape, since Faeries feared iron and steel. But the warriors had nevertheless pursued them in eagle form until he and Dave had found themselves with no choice but to burn uktena scales and zap off to Galunlati with Finny, while Alec and Liz continued in Dave's car toward the coast, which had been their original destination because Alec's ulunsuti had shown a Faery fleet massing nearby. As for his father's place . . . who knew what had gone on there after Calvin's crew had departed—or what the Faeries might have done to his father if he'd stumbled onto 'em accidentally.

But why did the cops think *he* had done it? Except . . . "Shit!" he grunted to nobody. "Yeah, of course."

No way anyone could have missed the shambles Dave had made of the dog lot. It would have been pretty obvious that there'd been a car involved—and any even moderately thorough investigation would also have turned up the gear they'd abandoned in the nearby clearing—including, he'd have bet anything, his missing wallet. Worse, they'd have discovered much of the paraphernalia that allowed them to gate between Worlds, all of which their hasty departure had forced them to leave behind.

And the cops would have been sure to draw *really* wrong conclusions from that stuff. *I'm not only a serial killer,* Calvin thought grimly, *I'm a patricidal Satanist as well.* Only . . . there were holes throughout the case. Like why were the local authorities looking at him suspiciously on *Tuesday,* when they hadn't found Dad's body until the following day? And since they had obviously *seen* him on Tuesday, which was the most logical time for the murder to have been committed, why did they still suspect him? Did they think he'd somehow shopped at a Magic Market one afternoon, then hiked across two hundred miles of state, offed his dad, and zapped back in time to be arrested for it twenty-four hours later? Didn't make a lot of sense to *him,* that was for sure. Or maybe that had merely been local paranoia.

A much more troubling thought struck him then: if the cops were smart—had matched paint samples and tread widths, say—they could have figured out what kind of car had flattened the fence, and might even have connected it to the red Mustang the State Patrol had found abandoned near Crawfordville late Monday night, which a few phone calls could link to him rather nicely. Unfortunately those calls would have led to Dave first, and might—his heart flipflopped at the thought—implicate *him* in this mess as well. Probably had already, in fact, since Calvin's attempt to get in touch with him that afternoon had gone so preposterously awry.

Not that there weren't a few points on his side, too; 'cause, depending on when the authorities finally decided the murder had been committed, there were several people who could testify to his presence elsewhere. Oh, true, as far as anyone beyond his partners-in-crime on the quest knew, he'd last been *seen* in or around Stone Mountain on Monday morning. (His last actual contact with anyone else prior to that had been with the clerk at a convenience store in Winder.) After that he'd been in various Otherworlds until sometime the following night (it was a little hard to tell exactly, because time ran differently in Galunlati) when he'd linked up with Uncle Dale again near Crawfordville and headed south with him to Cumberland Island, where they'd joined up with David once more. That had been Tuesday morning, and there were plenty of people around who could prove it—like the ferryman down at Cumberland, like the waitress at the seafood place, like the cashier at the Magic Market. Like the cops themselves.

So maybe there was hope after all.

The tough part, then, was going to be accounting for his whereabouts Tuesday evening.

And there were still two other questions: who or what had killed that little girl, and were his two erstwhile companions still okay?

And one thing was for sure, he'd not find any answers by hiding behind trees feeling sorry for himself and practically begging to get caught.

By the time he made it back to camp, Calvin had an idea and had already collected most of what he needed. It shouldn't take long either, and that was a blessing, because he had pretty much decided that as soon as he could, he really did need to go back and check on the goings-on at the stone circle.

As quietly as he could, he slipped down into the sinkhole and snagged Brock's empty backpack, wishing he had time to zip back to base and retrieve his own. A pause to check on the runaways and to retrieve his shirt and socks, and he was merging once more with the night.

When he was maybe ten yards out, he set his plan in motion. A stick from a cypress tree—one of the plants of vigilance—made do for a wand, and with it he began scratching a circle in the leaves and moss and undergrowth completely around the camp—far enough out, he hoped,

that he would make no noise beyond the low chanting he
had begun under his breath: a spell Uki had taught him
the last time he'd spent any time in Galunlati.

Yuhahi, yuhahi, yuhahi, yuhahi, yuhahi,
Yuhahi, yuhahi, yuhahi, yuhahi, yuhahi—Yu!

Sge! Ha-nagwa hinahunski tayi. Ha-tasti-gwu gun-
skaihu. Tsutatalii-gwatina haluni. Kunigwatina dulaska
galunlati-gwu witukti. Wigunyasehisi . . .

It was not precisely a charm of protection. Uki had told
him that it had originally been used to "frighten storms."
But it had the *effect* of turning things aside from a certain
path, and with a wording change here and there Calvin
thought it would suffice to detour snoops from the camp
at least long enough for him to get a better idea how the
land lay back at the scene of the crime.

Fortunately, the chanting made the scribing go faster,
so it was not long at all before he had completed the first
part of his work. It wasn't a perfect circle, for he had to
zig around a tree or two, but it seemed adequate. The next
stage was simpler: four lines leading inward from the cardinal directions, making what Uki called a Power Wheel,
except that the center was incomplete. Finally, Calvin set
sticks at the four points of the compass and marked them
with scraps of cloth torn from his clothing: blue from his
jeans for the north, white from his socks for the south,
bandanna red for the east, and T-shirt black for the west.

A repetition of the chant at each quadrant, a final one
for good measure, and Calvin stepped into the Wheel,
feeling, to his relief, a gentle tingle of Power there.

Only one thing left to do now, and that was a thing he
dreaded.

Following the by-now-monotonous procedure, Calvin
removed his clothes. But instead of simply abandoning
them as he'd often had to do before, he bundled them into
Brock's backpack and arranged the straps into a very wide
loops around his neck—loops hopefully wide enough that
they would not choke him when the *change* came.

The rest was almost too simple, and the ease with which the transformation was accomplished took Calvin by surprise. Eyes closed, one hand on the scale, and think what it was like to be a deer, then the pain, and the shifting and the pulling, and the distortion of vision, the dulling of some senses, the sharpening of others, and the falling onto all fours.

The pack was too tight, though, and he almost gagged before he managed to shake it into a looser configuration.

As prepared as he'd ever be, Calvin trotted away.

And Brock, who had heard him and followed him, and had seen everything, sat alone in the night for a very long time, his mind awash with wonder.

Even in deer shape, it took Calvin longer than he'd hoped to make his way back to the clearing, though mostly that was due to problems with the form he had chosen. He'd tried to transform gradually, so as to keep his own thoughts in control. But what he hadn't counted on was that there would be other whitetails about that this body would scent and want to investigate, which made the animal consciousness want to assert itself even more strongly. There were a *lot* of deer in Georgia, too: about one for every five people, he thought. But he hadn't counted on ever inhabiting a body that wanted to get to know them on a one-to-one basis—and certainly not one that could tell a buck from a doe from a fawn by smell alone.

He was having trouble with his antlers, too. Apparently the *change* more or less translated you into your equivalent age and the appropriate physical aspect for the season which meant that Calvin's head was crowned with the half-grown rack of a very healthy two-year-old stag—still growing, still in velvet, but already starting to itch.

And another, though very different, concern was that the weird thrumming in the ground kept starting up and then stopping again, and *that* he did not understand at all. It smacked of magic, but what kind? For that matter, what sort of magic could there *be* in Willacoochee County? Most places had some kind if you looked deep enough for it, he'd discovered. But how would it manifest around here? He didn't know squat about Yuchi mythology, except that it was apparently fairly close to Creek, and therefore Cherokee. As for the Spanish, who'd come and gone from the coastal isles before the English arrived and stayed—who knew what kind of weirdness *those* poor little monks had practiced when the loneliness and the swamp fevers got to them.

Maybe the thrumming was connected to the little girl's death.

But how?

He was still pondering that question when keen white-tail hearing caught the first distant sound of voices talking excitedly. Almost certainly the sheriff he'd encountered yesterday, he decided as he crept closer. And probably the guy who'd gone off at a run, whom he suspected of being some kind of law-enforcement type as well. There was also the 'coon hunter who'd remained behind, and another man, whose voice was smoother and a little more cultured, along with another whiny-voiced man, and what sounded an awful lot like a woman giving vent to frequent bouts of high-pitched hysterics.

Gotta watch it now, as he crept closer, taking what advantage he could of the frequent shadows and wishing he could get rid of the blasted backpack, since it made movement awkward and noisy. Noise was the key thing, too, because Calvin had hunted enough deer to know that you heard a lot more of them than you saw. Shoot, he'd once watched a whole herd of them wander to within thirty feet of him and spread out across practically his whole field of vision. But so effective was their camouflage that even when he knew they were there he had a hard time distinguishing them from the surrounding forest. It had been sound that had tipped him off to their presence then; he had to be careful that *he* did not make the same mistake himself.

A few steps closer, and he could finally see somewhat, smell better, and hear well enough to make out even whispers.

What he saw was the rock-girt clearing—only the five people clustered beside the farthest boulder didn't seem at all impressed by the fact that there shouldn't be stones like those in south Georgia. Understandable, given the circumstances.

He'd been right about their identities, too: there was Sheriff Lexington, plus Larry the hunter and Rob the policeman, all of whom he had seen before. But there was also an unsavory-looking skinny guy he didn't recognize, also in Sheriff's Department togs—and a thin, attractive, thirtyish woman, who seemed to be sticking close to that Rob fellow, even though the sheriff was asking her a lot of questions. They kept calling her Liza-Bet, and from the way she was carrying on, Calvin guessed she was the dead child's mother.

The sixth person—who was nowhere *near* a monolith— was a heavyset man of indeterminate age, but old enough to dress with no attention to style and to be bald. He had just set down a video camera with which he had evidently been preserving the whole grisly tableau for posterity, and was now kneeling beside the body and muttering to himself at a furious rate, mostly things like, "Yeah," and "Okay," and "Hmmm," and then quite suddenly and much louder, "Now *that's* odd."

"What is?" the sheriff wondered. "You got somethin', Bill?"

"Maybe."

"Well don't keep us in suspense, boy; spill it."

The man looked up but did not rise. "You're *sure* you found this body just like this?" he was evidently addressing the hunter.

The man nodded vigorously. "Just like that. Just exactly like that."

"And you didn't notice anything strange about the body?"

"Nothin' beyond what you see. Rob'll vouch for me there."

The red-haired man escaped Liza-Bet and wandered over to peer over the bald man's shoulder. "What'cha found?"

"Well," Bill said slowly. "Now don't quote me as gospel here, and I won't know for sure till I can get her back to the morgue, but I've been examinin' this body as best I can and . . . well, this is gonna sound mighty strange, but . . . uh, well, the fact is that I . . . I can't find no liver."

"What the hell?"

"No, come here, sheriff, and feel for yourself if you don't believe me."

"I'll take your word for it; 's what we pay you to be coroner for."

"Okay, then . . . well, see, it's like this: your liver sorta sets down below your ribs on the right-hand side. It's pretty big, and on a moderately skinny person like this poor little child is, anybody that knows what he's doin' can feel it." He paused, as if for effect. "Thing is, when I do that to her, all I can feel is . . . nothin', just a hollow place. It's like something's *removed* her liver, sheriff; taken it clean away without makin' hardly a mark on her body."

"You're shittin' me!"

"Not on your life, sir. There ain't no liver, and the only sign I can find of how it might have vanished is this little slit of a thing over on her side. Can't see it too good in this light's the problem."

"Oh Lord," the sheriff moaned. "Not only've we got us a goddamned serial killer here, but we've got one that mutilates his victims."

"There was Satanic paraphernalia they found up where that Indian boy's daddy died, 'member?" the skinny guy whined.

"So I've heard," Robert inserted. "And there may be another victim as well, if what they said about that woman up in Jefferson's true . . ."

But Calvin did not pay heed to the rest. Something the coroner had said had set his mind to working feverishly, as if a key piece to a puzzle had just been found, which only required turning the right way in order to fit.

No longer caring if he was seen or not, Calvin turned and bolted, noting with a bit of amusement the shouts and exclamations that followed, the loudest and clearest of which was the sheriff's: "Aw, shucks, Bill, it wasn't nothin' but a goddamned deer."

Goddamned deer indeed!

That goddamned deer was running lickety-split away from there as fast as it could, with its brain awash with ideas that were right on the verge of coming together but wouldn't. It was the deer instincts reacting to strong emotions with a desire for flight, Calvin's human aspect knew. But by doing so, it was also muddling the finer points of his reason.

Which meant he had to change back if he was going to accomplish anything at all. *That*, in turn, meant he had to get a good ways off.

Before long though, Calvin had found an appropriate place: a dogwood thicket fringed with palmettos.

Except that to return to his own shape he had to prime the scale with blood while thinking about how it felt to be a man. And maneuvering a scale around so that it could poke you enough to draw blood wasn't easy when you were a quadruped and had hooves. Last time had been an accident: a lucky adjunct of his half-delirious thrashings. This time he *had* to do it—but how?

Sliding his neck up and down against a tree with the scale between, hoping to impale himself on one of the scale's three points, didn't work—mostly because of the pack that was hanging awkwardly around his neck. Attempting the same thing on the ground didn't succeed either, for the same reason plus the fact that the scale tended to dig into the soft soil. Finally, in desperation, Calvin bit his tongue hard enough for the blood to trickle down his jaw and reach the talisman. Hopefully that would be enough to at least get the transformation started. Truly he hoped that, and was gratified when he felt the beginning of the *change*.

It hurt like hell, though; far more than it should, and for a long moment Calvin thought he was going to get hung up between forms. Evidently whatever reaction went on between the blood and the scale was dispersed throughout the body by the bloodstream, and if the magic couldn't *get* to the bloodstream, well . . . Blood spat upon the scale was evidently enough to get it going, but not to finish it. Already Calvin could feel the *change* slowing, and he made one final gamble. Although it had not worked before, he was far more desperate now, so once again he concentrated on altering only one part of himself: his hand. If he could return *that* to human, he could grab the scale and complete the transformation.

Fighting back the agony that wracked him as his very cells

tried to respond to conflicting orders, he wished with all his might for a human right hand. Nothing happened for a moment, but then he felt the hoof shift, draw up, his fingers fly apart, and the instant he could he grabbed for the scale and felt blessed relief as the edges sliced into his flesh.

The pain of transformation was quickly over, and then relief flooded through him as his human shape returned. He crouched beneath the limbs, shivering more from fear than cold, but did not dress lest he'd have to shift again in a hurry. Instead, he kept his hand clamped firmly around the scale and tried to lay out the facts in some kind of logical order. It had been real interesting, he mused. Seemed like everytime he *changed,* he learned something. Trouble was, it also looked like he had to be in desperate straits for anything much to happen. Maybe that was part of it, though; maybe the process needed adrenaline to trigger it, or at least to speed it along. And what about this wound business? He'd bit his tongue enough to bleed, and though it was still sore, it certainly didn't hurt as much as it should. As for his other injuries—the bruises, the bullet scrape, and the pounded jaw from that afternoon—not a trace of them remained. He supposed it was possible that when you *changed* back to your right shape, your cells were simply remembering what you were supposed to be like—and in effect, rebuilt a perfect you.

But that was not dealing with the matter at hand—though he now had a partial answer to that too: one he had known as soon as the transformation was complete; one word from the myths of his people, one *name* that had haunted his darkest dreams since childhood.

Utlunta!

Literally it meant ''she has it sharp,'' but to him it conjured a far darker and more specific image: *Spearfinger!*

It all fit. Calvin thought back over what he knew of the myth, which he'd both heard as a child and encountered again recently in Mooney's *Myths of the Cherokee.*

As far as he could remember, Spearfinger had no real origin, she simply *was.* Typically she'd appear as an old squaw wandering alone in the woods. She was usually singing some strange little song which translated as "Liver I eat!"

That was a reference to one of her several bad habits, because if she came up on you alone, she was likely to stab you with a long spearlike finger and then chow down on your liver. Sometimes it didn't even kill you, sometimes you went home as if nothing had happened, but began to wither and pine, and eventually you died, and sometimes folks found out then that the deceased had no liver, because Spearfinger had taken it.

She was also a shapechanger, and that made her doubly dangerous, because she could kill a person and then take their form and impersonate them when they went home and so be in a prime position to wipe out the rest of the family. Well, she might *be* a skinchanger, but so, by God, was he.

There was another peculiarity about Spearfinger too, though most folks forgot about it on account of her evocative name and bad eating habits. And that was that she was sometimes called *Nunyunuwi,* which more or less meant "dressed in stone." Actually, though, it was a reference to the fact that Spearfinger supposedly had skin like stone and had mastery over it—which would neatly explain how there happened to be sandstone boulders on the edge of a south Georgia swamp, not to mention how articulated dolls could be made out of pebbles.

"That's a pretty wild conclusion to jump to, though," Calvin confided aloud to the half-grown raccoon that had wandered into his sanctum and was now eyeing him with beady little eyes.

The most perplexing question was what such a being was doing in this World at all when by rights she should have been terrorizing Galunlati. She'd even followed Dave for a while, the first time they'd gone there. Dave had told Calvin all about it—how Yanu, the bear who was his guide at the time, had casually mentioned that Spearfinger had come close the previous night.

Dave!

Another part of the puzzle clicked into place.

Spearfinger had pursued Dave at least once, and Dave had obviously eluded her. That meant that there was a reasonable possibility that she might have become angry—or maybe curious to match wits with a different kind of quarry than she was used to. And then that prey had slipped through her fingers and returned to another World . . .

But if this whole shaky theory was correct, how in hell had she got into *this* World—and conveniently found her way to the exact spot where one of Dave's friends was camping?

And then Calvin knew.

He could see it all so clearly: a scrap of dirt road in a private woods in Jackson County, a towering oak tree, the moonlight shining down on a certain red Mustang parked nearby, Dave and Alec and Liz laid out in sleeping bags . . .

It was the night before the ritual they had used to open the gate to the Otherworld that held Fionchadd captive. But in order to facilitate that ritual, they needed the blood of a large animal.

Calvin, rather too eager to try his hand at some of the charms Uki had been teaching him, had decided to circumvent the numerous POSTED signs that dotted the wood by summoning Awi-Usdi, the Little Deer, to aid him. And in order to facilitate Awi-Usdi's passage from Galunlati, Calvin had raised his first-ever fog, for it blurred the distinctions between the Worlds, and Awi-Usdi had obligingly come.

And apparently the premier evil of Galunlati as well.

Calvin could have kicked himself. How could he have been so stupid? No reason at *all* that Awi-Usdi had to be the *only* thing to answer the call; probably anything with Power in Galunlati would have heard him if the Little Deer had; and certainly a being as powerful as Spearfinger, who had doubtlessly seen—and heard—him already. Given that, there was no reason why, having heard him, she couldn't have decided to investigate—especially when she had a score to settle with upstart prey that had escaped her before. And if Spearfinger had entered the human World when Calvin had raised that fog, she would certainly have sensed Dave nearby.

But why hadn't she attacked him then? For that matter, why not attack them all and leave no witnesses?

All the pieces were laid out now, but a few still hadn't found their proper places.

Like his dad's death.

Except . . . If Spearfinger *was* after Dave, she obviously hadn't got hold of him as of Tuesday noon, because Calvin had been with him almost constantly until then. In fact, she would probably have had a hard time keeping track of him at all during the past few days, what with him zipping out of the World at least twice, with only about fifteen minutes between, and that at the coast, hundreds of miles from where she'd first entered the World—assuming she'd come through in Jackson County. That could have caused her *real* trouble, especially if she was trying to follow Dave's actual route, since his trail would have led her first to Stone Mountain—where she'd then have lost him completely, because Dave hadn't been in this World for nearly a day after that. Maybe she'd hung around there for a while, though, *trying* to locate him, during which interval she'd found occasion to snack on Calvin's unfortunate old man. Yeah, that made sense, 'cause when Dave returned from Galunlati at the coast Monday night Calvin doubted he'd have been there long enough for Spearfinger to sense him—especially if she didn't know where she should be looking. And after that Dave had been moving so quickly (usually in a car, which could have confused her as well, if it didn't mask his trail entirely) there was no way anyone not used to dealing with technology could have kept up with him by conventional tracking methods. The longest time Dave had been in one place was at the seafood restaurant, so if Spearfinger *had* finally sensed him, there was a good possibility it would have been then, and she'd have headed that way next.

But if Dave had returned Tuesday *morning* and Calvin's dad had died Tuesday *evening*, why had Spearfinger waited so long to leave Stone Mountain?

Maybe he was wrong. Maybe Spearfinger *couldn't* detect Dave this far away—until the magic Calvin had fooled with Tuesday night in his vain attempt at contacting Uki had given her a lead.

Yet if that was true, how had she got here so *fast?*

"Too many questions," Calvin told the 'coon, shaking his head. "But," he added with a grin, "if it really *is* Spearfinger committing these murders while she's goin' after my friend, *I* know how to defeat her!"

He did, too. For the same mythology book that had given him the lowdown on Spearfinger had also spelled out the manner of her demise.

What had the myth said? Something about a group of hunters that had trapped Utlunta in a pit and shot her full of arrows that wouldn't pierce her stony skin—until finally Tsikilili the Chickadee had told them to aim for the palm of her left hand . . . because she kept her heart there?

Calvin didn't know about the heart, but the rest made as much sense as any other conclusions, and more than anything the law would likely have considered.

That she had already been killed once yet evidently lived again did not concern him; he had pretty much come to accept the fact that beings from Galunlati never stayed dead very long.

The next step, then, was to retrieve his bow, check on Robyn and Brock, and prepare to seek his quarry.

PART III

FEAR AND
TREMBLING

Chapter XIV: Chance Encounter

(east of Whidden, Georgia—twoish)

So much to do and so little time to do it in, Calvin reflected, as he jogged through the woods toward Brock and Robyn's camp. He had decided to remain in man-shape, though he knew he ran serious risk in retaining that form. Still, he thought he was far enough from the murder scene to venture it; and besides, he was becoming leery of constantly changing skin. That kind of thing had to be a shock to the system, and he didn't know how long he could keep it up. For that matter, *was* there a limit? Did it get easier all the time (as it sometimes appeared to be doing, though it still hurt like hell), or did your body eventually wear out and simply stop cooperating? And what about your mind? Did sharing two consciousnesses cause any sort of lasting mental harm?

And what of the scale bouncing up and down against his chest? It was the source of the *change*, but could *it* wear out? Was the magic it contained also finite—especially here in this World, cut off from the source of its Power?

He fervently hoped not.

Spearfinger was in this very county, and he was almost certain she was looking for Dave. Now more than ever Calvin needed to call his friend and tell him to be on guard. The *smart* thing, though, would be to try to contact Uki first, on the odd chance Calvin could breach the Barriers Between this time; that way he could give Dave maximum information. Yet to attempt *any* of those things right now would not only leave his new friends unprotected, but risk his own capture as well—which would leave him unable to aid anyone at all.

He slowed for a moment, flopped sweating against a tree, and tried to think clearly. Did he *really* have to go after Spearfinger tonight? But if he didn't, she'd be free to work more mischief, and he couldn't stand the thought of another life being lost because of him. There were two on his conscience already, and very likely at least one more. Robyn and Brock would not join that company—not if he had anything to do with it.

Unless—a sudden chill shook him—they already had. Was his warding strong enough? When he had set it he had not considered that it might have to hold against one of the great evil powers of Galunlati.

No, he *had* to stop Spearfinger as quickly as possible. Every second wasted was a second in which she could kill. This, he realized dully, was what the omens had all been pointing to.

He started off again, though he did not feel at all rested, and bent his trail to the left, hoping to come on the camp from the north side. The forest was not so thick there, and he made good time, loping along like a wolf, with the wind whistling gently past his ears, and every footfall striking light upon the earth. The thrumming had stopped, he noted absently, but just as he began to wonder why, he heard something crashing noisily through the woods. The footfalls sounded vaguely human, and Calvin was instantly on guard, for fear someone was already on his trail—or worse, Spearfinger herself. But when a particularly sharp crack was followed by sudden silence and then an angry "Son-of-a-bitch!" he knew otherwise.

"Brock?" he called softly before he could stop himself. "Hey, Brock! That you?"

No answer, and Calvin had no choice but to investigate. Moving as quietly as he could, he eased toward the cursing, making sure it wasn't a trick or a trap before he revealed himself.

He need not have been concerned, for the slender form that lay panting breathlessly among the ferns was definitely male, clearly not Brock, and almost certainly in very bad condition, to judge by the way he was shaking and trembling. He was older than Brock, or at least bigger, and his hair was dark whereas the runaway's was fair, though it was so snarled with leaves and twigs and streamers of Spanish moss that Calvin almost couldn't see it. His clothes—blue jeans, a white T-shirt, and oversized, big-tongued British Knights—were a mess too; torn and filthy, and with more than a little blood patterning the fabric.

"Jesus," Calvin muttered, scrambling across the fronds to crouch beside the boy, whose gasps and pants were mingling with intermittent sobs. "Hey, kid, you all right?"

"No!" the boy moaned. "They're dead, they're all dead!"

"Dead!" The word cut through Calvin's heart like a knife. *"Who's dead?"*

"All of 'em!"

"Come on then, let's get you straightened up, and you can tell me about it."

The boy did not stir, just went on sobbing, but Calvin slipped an arm under him and helped him turn over and sit up. "You're not hurt or anyth—" he began, then, "Christ! You're the kid at the Magic Market!"

"Don," the boy managed between sobs. "Hey, *you're* the guy with the cool-ass bow!"

"Calvin," he supplied. "I—" But his sentence was cut short when Don suddenly wrapped his arms around him and started crying uncontrollably. It was as if Calvin's presence had released some long-pent-up tension that now flowed out so fast it was backing up and making the boy shake. All Calvin could do was hold him and pick the leaves out of his hair. "You're okay, I've got you now," he whispered. "It's gonna be all right."

At last the boy's grip eased, and he shrugged out of Calvin's embrace. A quick wipe of his nose on the tail of his T-shirt, and he blinked up at Calvin, his expression a mixture of fear, rage, and adolescent embarrassment.

"Okay, now," Calvin murmured softly, "who's dead?"

"Mike is . . . my best friend, and I think my sister is, and I'm afraid my mom's gonna be if I don't get help fast!" He started to his feet but Calvin caught him by the waistband and dragged him back down. "Not so fast, Don. What makes you think your buddy's dead?"

" 'Cause I *saw* him! We were campin', and I got up to take a leak, and my sister came up through the woods, only it wasn't my sister, and she was singin' some kinda weird song that made me freeze, and she just walked up to Michael and . . . and *killed* him!"

"Okay, okay," Calvin said in his most reassuring tones. "I believe you, don't doubt it. But I have to ask you, was there anything strange about your sister? Anything out of the ordinary?"

"Everything was strange."

"Yeah, I know, but anything in particular? Did she look different, or anything?"

"It was her finger . . . she had a . . . a real long finger, like a spear or a sticker-thing, or something. She stuck it in Mike while he was sleepin' and . . . and started eatin' his *guts!"*

"And you're sure it was your sister?"

"Of course I'm sure!"

"What does she look like?"

Don told him, but it only confirmed what Calvin already knew.

"Okay, Don," Calvin said carefully, "just relax and try to think clearly, 'cause I really am gonna try to help you, but there's some things I'm gonna have to tell you that may be hard to believe, so just hang in there and trust me, okay? You've had a bad shock, but I think I know some of what's caused it, and if you'll help me, maybe we can stop this from happenin' to anybody else. You with me so far?"

"Sure," Don sniffed dubiously. "But I really gotta go warn Mom!"

"She'll be all right, I think," Calvin said carefully, not certain if he should say more. "I've got a pretty good idea where she is."

"She went to town with her boyfriend—he's a policeman."

Calvin shook his head. "Not to town, to a place near here where there's been another murder."

"*Another . . .*"

"Now hear what I'm sayin', Don. Bad things happen sometimes, and when they do you just have to accept 'em. You've just gone through probably the worst thing that's ever gonna happen to you, and you've already made it past the hardest part, so it's really all downhill from here. I got some news nearly that bad just this afternoon. But I'm gonna have to tell you one more bad thing. You know what you said before? Well, you were right about—"

"It's Allison, ain't it?" the boy interrupted. "She really is dead, ain't she?"

Calvin regarded him levelly. "Yeah, I think she is."

"Figgered as much."

"Yeah. But look, guy, I need to know everything that happened, every detail you can remember about your friend's death. I know it's gonna hurt, and I know you're in a hurry to catch up with your mom, but if you can tell me everything, maybe I can do something to fight it."

"Well," Don began, "it was like I told you: me and Mike was goin' campin', but Allison had disappeared, only we didn't know, and . . ."

He went on then, recounting as much as he knew about Allison's disappearance and subsequent strange return, about the camping trip, about Michael Chadwick's murder, and what he'd done thereafter. It took Calvin a while to sort all the facts into some kind of logical order, because the boy kept glossing over things, or getting sidetracked, or trying to hurry, but eventually Calvin had a pretty clear idea of the chain of events, plus a fair notion of where Don's house was and the layout of the surrounding terrain. That was information he'd need when he went Spearfinger hunting.

"Okay, Don," Calvin whispered when the boy had finished. "Now think hard: that song you said your sister was singin'—think you could remember the words?"

Don shook his head at first, but then looked thoughtful. "Didn't make sense, but . . . I *think* the first word was something like *Owie-lan-at-siki,* or somethin' like that."

"*Uwelanatsiku,* maybe?"

"Yeah, that's it."

"Were there any *other* words? Think hard!"

Don's brow furrowed. "Just some kinda nonsense syllables, something with esses. I can't remember what."

"Maybe it doesn't matter," Calvin muttered, mostly to himself. Then louder, "I think that clinches it, Don-o: the finger fits, the shapechangin' fits, the mastery over stone fits—and the song fits. You know what *it* means, don't you?"

"It means 'Liver I eat,' don't it? She sung it once in English right there at the end."

Calvin gave his shoulders a brotherly squeeze. "Thanks a bunch, guy. You've told me a lot of useful stuff, like that business about travelin' through the ground and all. And I—"

"You believed that?"

"Sure I do. Folks as freaked out as you are don't lie, even when it sounds crazy. Besides, I've . . . seen some things myself."

"And you think you know what this thing is?"

"Yeah," Calvin replied. "And I'll tell you what I can, but some of it's gonna be hard to believe, and I'll have to let you in on a couple of secrets for it to make sense. Deal?"

"Deal." And was that maybe the ghost of a smile?

"Okay, well, first of all, you know I'm Cherokee, right? Well, do you know anything about Cherokee mythology?"

"Just a little. Some stuff I learned in Boy Scouts."

"Ever hear of Spearfinger?"

Don shook his head. " 'Fraid not. But . . . hey, you're not sayin' my sister's turned into some kinda monster out of Cherokee legends, or something, are you?"

"Not . . . exactly. I . . . I'm afraid it's a lot more likely that Spearfinger killed your sister and took her form."

Calvin proceeded to tell the boy all he could recall about the legend of Utlunta, then continued with a quick rehash of his finding of Allison's body, ending with a radically edited account of the conversations he had overheard at the murder scene, including the coroner's speculations about the missing liver. He did not, however, mention that *he* was implicated—or his earlier encounter with the sheriff, or his father's death. Kid had enough on his mind without having to deal with Calvin's problems.

"There's a couple more things I gotta tell you, though." Calvin concluded.

"Shoot."

"Ever hear of the uktena?"

"Ain't that some kinda snake monster, or something?"

"Yeah, but there aren't any around anymore, at least not in this World—but there are in Galunlati."

"What's Galunlati?"

"The Cherokee spirit world."

"You mean like heaven?"

"More like a magical version of this World. No technology or anything."

"You talk like you've been there."

"I have."

"You're *shittin'* me!"

"No," Calvin assured him solemnly. "Listen: you yourself have seen something tonight that you'll have to admit isn't part of this World. And it happens that it fits a Cherokee myth almost perfectly, okay?"

"Yeah, sure."

"Right, then doesn't it stand to reason that if one supernatural creature exists, more might?"

"Maybe," Don conceded dubiously. "What're you gettin' at?"

Calvin took a deep breath, wondering if he wanted to finish what he was about to begin. Finally he reached into his neckband and dragged out the uktena scale on its thong. It glittered in the moonlight, strangely bright. "Know what this is?"

The boy squinted at it. "Arrowhead?"

"Nope."

"Shark's tooth?"

"Wrong again."

"Hey, man, just get on with it, okay?"

"Okay, okay, hold your horses. I'm just trying to break this to you gently."

"Break *what* to me?"

"This is the scale of an uktena, Don. And it . . . helps me to work magic."

Don stared at Calvin askance. "No shit?"

"Swear on my life."

"What *kinda* magic?"

"I'd . . . rather not elaborate just now. Let's just say I think I may be able to use it to destroy Spearfinger."

He paused then, wondering how to proceed, since he obviously did not need a sidekick right now. Don had indicated that he wanted to warn his mother, which was certainly not a bad idea. And they probably needed to get word to the dead boy's parents as well. But Calvin didn't want to send Don off alone to find either, nor did he feel he had time to accompany him on those errands himself. He also doubted he could trust what the boy might say in his present condition. Finally, Calvin puffed his cheeks and said, "Don, I know you want to get hold of your mom and your friend's folks, but . . . I *think* you're better off stickin' with me for the time bein'. I've got some friends near here I can leave you with, and—"

"*Leave* me with?"

"Yeah," Calvin acknowledged with a sigh. "I can't delay any longer. Spearfinger might be killin' again already . . . but I'm startin' to get some ideas about what she's up to."

"But you don't wanta say, right?"

"You got it! Now come on, guy, let's boogie. You *are* okay to run, aren't you?"

"You got it," Don echoed, rising. But Calvin knew his conviction was largely an illusion.

Both of the runaways were sleeping—or going through the

motions, anyway—when Calvin escorted Don into their camp. But Brock awakened a little too quickly, as if he'd been lying there with one eye open already. A couple of the palmettos looked disturbed too, and Calvin suspected that the warding had been breached at least once from within. *Something* had certainly been at it—he could tell by the way it had tingled beneath his feet when he had crossed it.

"Where've *you* been?" Brock demanded, trying to sound groggy, but Calvin thought his yawns were a tad *too* wide. The runaway's eyes narrowed when they fell on Don. "Hey, who's your friend?"

"What's up?" That was from Robyn, legitimately confused. "Jesus God, Calvin, who's *that?*"

"His name's Don. He's . . . had some real bad news tonight, and may still be in trouble. I—"

Robyn raised an eyebrow, instantly suspicious. "What *kinda* trouble?"

Calvin squatted beside her and dragged Don down with him. "I'll tell you what I can," he began, "but that won't be much, so you've gotta trust me. We've all got secrets here, and there may be more before the night's over—or everybody may know everything. The point is, right now I've got something I need to do somewhere else and fast—and I need somebody to take care of Don. He's just seen one of his friends . . . die, and it's kinda freaked him out, so I thought—"

"Oh Christ," Robyn moaned. "Why didn't he just go to the cops?"

"I *can* talk," Don grumbled indignantly.

"I know you can," Calvin told him. "But you're gonna have to be real careful about what you say for a while, okay? At least until you get your head on a little straighter. Just remember what you told me and what I told you, and then think how that'd sound to somebody who wasn't there."

Don nodded meekly. "Yeah, sure."

"Besides," Calvin told the runaways, "do you really *want* him talkin' to the cops just now? As wired as he is, it'd be *real* easy for him to let something slip about you guys."

Brock was staring suspiciously at both of them. "Something really weird's goin' on, ain't it?"

Calvin puffed his lips in exasperation, wishing the boy was not so observant. "You could say that."

"*How* weird?" Robyn asked pointedly.

"Weird enough."

"And you're involved in it?"

"Yeah."

"And you won't tell us what it is?"

"It'd take more believin' than you've got in you," Calvin sighed, "and more time to convince you than I can spare. For now, I just need you guys to keep an eye on Don here until I get back. Feed him if you can find something; help him clean up a little. He may start goin' into shock, and if he does, just keep him warm, and—"

"I've *had* first aid," Robyn noted with a touch of sarcasm.

"Good. Let's hope you don't have to use it. But as I was sayin': there's something goin' on that—" He paused, then: "Oh hell, I wish I could just lay it all out straight, but I can't. Suffice to say that Don's sister's *also* been killed, and under peculiar circumstances, and that I found the body, but that somebody else found it before I could report it, so that the cops think I may have done it."

"You mean like they think you killed your dad?"

"Uh . . . yeah, actually."

Brock's comment elicited a startled scowl from Don, and Calvin wished he had leveled with him about that earlier. Last thing he needed was to destroy Don's shaky confidence now.

"Shit!" Brock exclaimed, before Robyn cuffed him.

"The point I was tryin' to make," Calvin went on, "is that there're cops in the woods less than a mile northwest of here: sheriff's men, mostly, and they don't much like me. They're pretty much staying' put, though, and they've gotta get a body back to town, but they may be snoopin' around some too, so you'd be smartest to just lie low. I've . . . I've done something to make this place harder to find, but it may not work. So just be as quiet as you can, and remember: no lights, no fire, and no more talkin' than you can help."

"Right," Brock agreed.

"Robyn? I need a promise. I'm sorry, but I really do."

"I don't promise what I don't know."

"You'll have to this time. Tell you what, I swear I'll tell you everything as soon as it's over."

"What if it's *never* over?"

"Then we're all in deep shit. Now, promise. And let's see those hands. I don't want any crossed fingers."

Robyn sighed sourly, but displayed both palms. "I swear."

Calvin put an arm around Don's shoulders and gave him a quick, reassuring squeeze. "You gonna be okay, kid?"

"Yeah, sure."

"Positive? If there's somewhere else you wanta go, I'll take you there as soon as I can, but like I told you, time's real critical right now."

"Sure," Don sniffed miserably. "But it's gonna be real hard waitin'."

'I know," Calvin told him, squeezing him again. "But twelve hours from now the whole thing may be over."

"No," Don shot back bitterly. "Mike'll still be dead. So will my sister."

Calvin could find nothing to say to that.

"Need some help?" Brock asked suddenly.

"Yeah," Calvin replied. "But I think this is kinda over your head. I . . . I *know* I ought to level with you guys," he added to the group as a whole. "But I really don't want to say any more now, 'cause I simply don't have time to explain. Except . . . well, there's more to me than meets the eye . . . I guess. A little."

"Figured as much." Robyn nodded. "I sure can pick 'em."

"*I* picked 'im," Brock pointed out.

Already nearly at the edge of the sinkhole, Calvin turned, and stared at Robyn. " 'Fore I go I need a favor."

Robyn raised an eyebrow. "Yeah?"

"I really could use some lipstick—if you've got any."

The eyebrow went higher, but she was already reaching for her purse. "What color?"

"Many as you've got, and the wilder the better."

Robyn thrust a handful of plastic and metal tubes in his direction. "I'm not even gonna ask."

"Just as well." Calving grinned as he accepted them and stuffed them in his pack. "Thanks a bunch . . . see you when I can."

A short while later, Calvin returned to his own camp for the first time in what seemed like days, but was in fact slightly less than half of one. Everything was still where he'd left it: the backpack with its meager store of clothing and supplies, the ruins of the asi—and most importantly now, Dave's Galunlati-made bow. He slipped his hand up into the hollow tree truck where he had left it, felt the reassuring smoothness as he drew it out and examined it in the moonlight. Even in the dimness, it was still a thing of beauty, and he could still make out the many kinds of wood that composed it. Funny, though, how rarely he'd actually used either it or the near twin that had been lost in Faerie, that actually belonged to him. Still, he could think of no better use for it than defeating Spearfinger, though he doubted even Uki had foreseen that when the shaman had bestowed it upon Dave in reward for helping slay the uktena.

A glance at the sky showed the night moving well toward morning, which meant he didn't dare waste much more time before setting out toward Don's house.

But before he could do that, there were still a couple fo things Calvin had to accomplish.

Chapter XV: Plotting

(shortly after 2 A.M.)

Robyn was more than a little pissed at Calvin when she saw him scramble up the low embankment that ringed the camp and disappear among the palmettos at the top.

What did he *mean* sneaking off in the middle of the night like that? Going Christ-knew-where, and then coming back with this . . . *stranger* in tow like he had some God-given right to tell the whole world where she and Brock were and what they were doing? And then cutting out mysteriously all over again? He'd seemed like such a nice guy, too; though she had to admit that she'd been dubious when Brock had first dragged him into camp. She was *still* dubious about a lot, most of it having to do with the fact that she knew—and Calvin had admitted—that he had a lot of secrets. Trouble was, secrets were that for a reason, and often enough that reason was dangerous.

That was the last thing she needed now, when she and Brock were only a few days from making the final break. No, she amended, the *last* thing she needed was someone to take care of in the middle of the night.

Why, then, did it bother her to be pissed at Calvin? Why did he have to *be* such a nice guy: so friendly, so relaxed, so open—as far as that went. Nice looking, too; and she loved the way he wore his body so unselfconsciously, how he moved soft and quick and sure, almost like Malcolm McDowell had done in *Cat People,* only it worked even better on Calvin because he did it completely unaware. He also liked Brock, and Brock liked him, and that was good. She'd even toyed with the idea of asking him to accompany them on their run to England; had, in fact, almost worked up nerve enough to spring the question when he'd innocently let drop that he had a girlfriend. *That* was just her luck too: the good ones were always taken; and Calvin was too tied up in his own ethics to allow her even a nibble when no one was looking. There was only one thing that troubled her . . .

"What'cha starin' at, sis?" Brock's voice broke in on her reverie, and Robyn realized she'd been gazing at the gap in the shrubbery Calvin had departed through for a good minute after the bushes had closed behind him. She could feel herself blushing (which she hated, but at least it wouldn't show in the half-light) and let her eyes drift first to the moon, which was still visible through the leaves above them, and then down toward their latest visitor, who was squatting on the ground staring at the topsoil.

"Nothin'," Robyn informed her brother, with more irritation than was deserved. "How's *he* doin?"

"You tell *me,*" Brock shot back, then scooted around so that Robyn could take a look at their charge. "You're sweet on ole Calvin, ain't you?" he added, as she rearranged herself so that a maximum amount of light fell on Don.

"He's a nice guy and nice lookin'," Robyn replied tersely, then laid a hand against Don's forehead. "You don't have a fever or anything," she observed. "How do you feel?"

"Like I been shot at and missed and shit at and hit," Don told her. She chuckled in spite of the tired old line. Apparently the kid was trying to make the best of a bad situation with humor. Or maybe not, for right after that, he seemed to withdraw into himself again, as he'd been doing off and on ever since he'd first arrived. That was bad. She considered chasing down the flashlight to better check him out, but decided it'd do as much harm as good, as well as possibly attracting undesired attention.

"Of *course* he don't have a fever," Brock drawled sarcastically from where he was rummaging in Robyn's backpack—Calvin having gone off with his. "He's had the crap scared out of him, not been bit by germs! 'Sides," he continued, "shock makes you cold, not hot, and that's what Cal told us to look out for."

"*Do you mind?*" Robyn snapped at him. "If you wanta do some good, how 'bout handin' me what you've got in your hand?"

Brock bared his teeth, but passed his sister the Hershey bar he'd excavated. "I was gonna give it to 'im anyway."

Robyn snatched the chocolate and delivered it to Don, who slowly began to unwrap it. "Mind tellin' us what's goin' on?" she asked, scooting around behind him and starting to work the worst of the detritus out of his hair. Don did not resist.

"Yeah, spill it," Brock urged. "Where'd you run into Calvin, anyway?"

"He told me not to tell."

"He *would* have," Robyn snorted. "I wish to God he didn't have so goddamned many secrets."

"I know one," Brock volunteered smugly.

"What?" Don asked without much interest.

"He's a *were-deer!*"

"A *what?*" Robyn could not help herself.

"No shit?" Don echoed.

Robyn wondered if that was incredulity in his voice (which it certainly should have been), or acknowledgment of pre-existent information. "Come *on*, Brock, get real," she finally managed.

"No, it's true," Brock insisted. "I ain't had a chance to tell you, since he's been around all the time, and I didn't wanna talk about it while he was here, and *then* we was all asleep—but there was something kinda weird about the way I found him." And with that he recounted the tale of the hurt deer he'd happened on. Mostly this was for Don's benefit, since Robyn had been there when he'd come running in all perplexed and excited, first about the clothes he'd found abandoned while on a supply run, then about the wounded stag he was going to bandage. Eventually he got to the part where he'd gone back and found a stark-naked Calvin instead, and how Calvin kept evading Brock's questions about the deer and why he was minus his duds.

"And you didn't suspect a thing?" Robyn asked suspiciously when he had finished. "You were gone a *long* time before you came in with those clothes . . ."

Brock stared at the ground. "Yeah, well . . . maybe I was kinda not tellin' everything."

"Maybe it's time you did!"

Brock sighed wearily. "Well, it's like I said—only more so. I went up and stole those apples you wanted from that fruit stand south of town—that was right after lunch, Don. But then on my way back I saw this police car pull over and start talkin' to this guy. Well, I kinda hid and watched, 'cause I was afraid they might think the guy had something to do with us, except that I also thought I might be able to find out if they *knew* about us—and the next thing *I* knew the guy was runnin', with the cops *shootin'* at him. And right after that he zapped across the highway almost on top of me, only he didn't see me. And 'fore I knew what was happenin', he was takin' his clothes off, only I couldn't see much 'cause there was bushes in the way—but the next thing I know this *deer* runs out, and there ain't no sign of the guy. So I kinda zipped over there and picked up his clothes. Figured—I dunno—figured the cops'd find 'em otherwise, and that way I was givin' the guy a fair shake."

"And you were curious as hell," Robyn concluded. "I know you."

"Yeah," Brock admitted. "But you'd have done the same thing, if you saw what I did."

"*I'd* have run like blazes."

"Right after 'im," Brock added with a giggle. "It was weird, sis—*too* weird to resist. Only I suddenly found myself with these clothes and nothin' to do with 'em, but I couldn't find the guy again and I was afraid the cops'd see me, so I couldn't hang around and check for tracks. So anyway, I brought 'em back here, and figured I'd look for the guy again later.''

"And *lied* to me," Robyn noted.

"I'm not *finished*," Brock snapped. "I still haven't got to the proof!''

Robyn could feel Don start at that, and nearly reprimanded her brother's rudeness, then decided she didn't really feel up to a row—especially since Brock evidently knew things she didn't. To keep herself from fidgeting, though, she shifted her machinations from Don's hair (it was essentially clear of debris now) to his shoulders and began to massage the wiry muscles there. It helped her relax and probably would do the kid some good too. He tensed briefly—until he figured out what she was about— then settled into a sort of resigned slouch.

"What kinda proof?" Don challenged.

"Saw him do it."

"You *saw* him?"

"Yes," Brock affirmed, gazing smugly at his sister. "You was asleep, but I felt ole Calvin move, and saw him get up and sneak off. I started to follow, but decided he'd just gone to take a leak or something, so I didn't. But he was gone a *long* time, and when he came back, he was actin' real sneaky, and got my backpack and took off again. I followed him that time 'cause I *knew* he was up to something. And sure enough, he did this ritual-kinda thing, and then got naked and grabbed that whatchamacallit he wears around his neck . . . and turned into a deer!"

"Give me a break!" Robyn snorted, and squeezed Don's shoulders so hard that he yipped. "Sorry," she added off handedly, and started working her way down the boy's spine.

"No, it's true, sis," Brock insisted. "I know it sounds absolutely crazy, but it's the honest-to-God truth. I wish there was some way to prove it to you, but 'less you actually see him do it, there's not."

"Brock, get real."

"I swear on my life, Robyn. If I'm lyin', it's 'cause something's playin' games with my head, or somebody's slipped me a mushroom, or somethin'.'' He stared at her hopefully, totally guileless.

Robyn stopped her massage and returned Brock's stare. It was preposterous, of course, but there was something about the tone of her brother's voice—that shakiness it acquired when he was really passionate about something, maybe—that made her want to believe him, or at the very least give him the benefit of the doubt until she could get independent corroboration.

Finally she broke eye contact, shrugged, and nodded. "Okay," she said, *"if* he can do that, *how* does he do it?"

Brock shrugged in turn. "I'm not sure, unless—"

"It's the scale," Don supplied quietly. "That's what that thing around his neck is. He told me it was magic—or that it let him *do* magic. Said it came from a monster from another world called an uktena."

"Oh, Christ," Robyn began, but Brock interrupted.

"When'd he tell you *that?"* he asked eagerly, then, "Oh—guess there's only one time he could have."

"Yeah," Don replied, looking down, "and I shouldn't even have mentioned it, 'cause it was supposed to be a secret."

"You didn't promise, though, did you?"

"I don't remember . . . I was kinda out of it at the time."

"The only thing anybody *promised,"* Brock reminded them, "was to stay here until he gets back. And *that* was only Robyn, technically."

Robyn looked at Don expectantly. "Well, now that you've *started,"* she sighed, "you might as well spill the whole thing."

"But Calvin didn't want me to—" Don began, then, "Oh crap, why not? I reckon he was afraid you wouldn't believe me, but Brock's seen something just as weird, so I don't guess there's any harm . . ."

And with that he repeated the tale he had earlier recounted to Calvin, as well as most of what Calvin had confided to him.

It was even more difficult for Robyn to accept than

Brock's preposterous story had been—she was too much a child of the cynical eighties to be otherwise. But there was something about the absolute sincerity with which the boy spoke, the tears in his eyes, the catches in his breath, that made his account ring true. *Something* had freaked him, that was obvious. And here, now, with the frogs singing, and the Spanish moss floating on the breeze, and the smell of swamp water in the air, it was somehow easier to believe that the world might hold more than she expected.

And then there was the thrumming in the earth. She'd noticed it off and on the past day or so, but always assumed it had something to do with passing pulp-trains, or being near the swamp, or in a sinkhole, or something. But Don's explanation made as much sense as anything else did—more, really, if you allowed for such a radical worldview. But if the thrumming *was* magic, and Calvin really *was* a shapechanger, and people really *had* been murdered . . .

"Oh my God!" Robyn cried suddenly, digging her nails into Don's shoulders so sharply he gasped. "Oh my God! I just had a *really* gross idea!"

"What?" This from Brock.

"I . . . well, you said Calvin could shapeshift, right? Or at least change into a deer. Now, I'm not exactly saying I *believe* that—wouldn't at all if I didn't know you like I do, and even then it's a reach. But what happens if—just for the sake of argument, say—he could turn into *other* things too? Suppose . . ." She gulped. "Suppose he could turn into another *person!* Suppose he's just *pretending* to be a good guy, and all."

"No way!" Brock protested instantly, but his eyes were troubled. "Calvin was here when Don's friend bought it!"

"No he *wasn't,*" Robyn whispered. "He was gone at least an hour. You weren't the only one who couldn't sleep."

Don looked as if someone had knocked the air right out of him. "And that'd be plenty of time for him to have killed Mike, and then run into me in the woods on his way back here," he finished slowly. " 'Specially if he could change into a deer . . . Jesus! Maybe it really *could* be him."

"Yeah, think about it," Robyn continued quickly, dark imaginings suddenly usurping her intuition. "Calvin was in bad shape when Brock found him, but you said your sister was missing a long time, and didn't show up acting strange until right around suppertime. That was almost certainly *after* Brock met him, which means whatever happened to your sister had to have happened earlier still—while Brock couldn't find Calvin, probably—which means Calvin could have been recovering from doing something to her when Brock first discovered him."

"No!" Brock insisted. "You're wrong—he was runnin' away from the cops then! Dammit, I *saw* him. Calvin's my *friend*, for Chrissakes!"

"But he's sneaky," Robyn countered. "You'll have to admit that."

"So're we."

"Yeah, but *we're* not suspected of killin' our father. Oh, sure, me and Cal talked about that some, and he *seems* to be pretty sincere. But then why won't he give us the straight scoop about that?"

" 'Cause it's tied up with magic again?" Brock ventured. "And I bet whatever happened to Don's sister is too. Shoot, I bet they think he did that as well!"

"Don? How 'bout you? What do *you* think?"

"I don't *know*," Don replied so quietly they almost couldn't hear him. "I mean I'd *like* to believe Calvin—he's been *real* nice to me—but you're right: some stuff just don't quite fit, like that crap 'bout killin' his dad. I really do wish he'd told me. 'Cause *not* tellin' makes me feel like he's hidin'—"

"You don't believe *that*, do you?" Brock interrupted. "Gimme a break, man! Shit—the guy *helped* you! If he'd wanted to kill you, he coulda done it right then and there, 'stead of draggin' you all the way back here!"

"Or he could be goin' to bring some other were-things so they can eat us *all*," Robyn snapped back—though a part of her wondered why she was suddenly arguing a position she didn't want to believe herself.

"Bullshit!"

"You ever hear of a friendly werewolf?"

"He ain't a werewolf."

"Same thing."

"Don?"

"Who knows?" he grunted doubtfully. "*I* don't."

Silence, but for the sounds of the night.

"Well," Brock announced finally. "I'm gonna see what's *really* up. And if I'm not back by dawn you guys better just head for high timber, 'cause I'll have been dead wrong about Calvin."

"Damn," Robyn muttered under her breath.

"Yeah," Don echoed. "Shit's really hittin'."

Chapter XVI: Being Prepared

(Calvin's camp, east of Whidden, Georgia—late)

Back at his camp, Calvin was staring with trepidation at the waters of Iodine Creek. Not wishing to subject the same bit of territory to ritual two days in a row for fear of exhausting its intrinsic Power, he had trotted a few yards downstream of the scrap of shore he had used the previous evening. A carpet of moss replaced most of the sand there, and the stream looked dark and cool and inviting. But now that he was faced with actually wading in, the notion disturbed him—which didn't make a lot of sense, given that he'd bathed in this same creek only yesterday, never mind last night's pre-Vision-Quest Going-to-Water. Tonight's repetition of that rite carried much more serious consequences, though, and he did not want to have his concentration disturbed by scaled or furry visitors.

That had never been a consideration before; the critters in his ancestral hunting grounds to the north seemed instinctively to know what he was about and ignore him. But the coast was Yuchi turf, and not all of the creatures there owed allegiance to Galunlati. Or even if they did, they might be denizens of the Underworld—and that meant they could be in league with Spearfinger. For, Calvin realized suddenly, the only things around here that could really hurt him were reptiles: snakes—both moccasins and coral snakes; 'gators, of course, which could move silently and fast; and snapping turtles, which could bite clean through your bones without trying real hard. Shoot, he'd already *seen* one of those!

And every one of those things could be in that water!

But he had to complete the ritual or he'd be starting out with everything wrong, and maybe confronting such fears as these was part of it.

Steeling himself, Calvin backed up to where he was standing entirely on soft moss (not rock or sand, which were presumably the Stoneskin's minions), and once there he began to strip. He did this slowly and methodically, staring at the water, willing himself to calm, thinking the solemn thoughts appropriate to the occasion. He was a warrior—maybe the last of his kind—preparing to embark on a venture that could very well cost him his life. But if he did not try, others would die, and that was an incontrovertible fact. Thus he gazed steadily at the glittering creek while he undid buttons and zippers and knots, folded each article neatly as he removed it, then set it aside. Even the uktena scale, though it was the last to go, and he placed *it* in front of him so that it was centered in a patch of moonlight he had chosen for just that reason. He squatted then, retrieved the four small objects he had removed from his pocket when he had first come there, and folded them into his fist before standing again.

Turning to face the north, he took one of the objects— it was a tube of Robyn's lipstick with a definite bluish cast—and with it, he marked his chest and his arms, his thighs and his cheeks with lightning bolts, and while he drew, he chanted:

Sge! Ha-nagwa asti unega aksauntanu usinuli anetsa unatsanuntselahi aktati adunniga.

Utlunta utadata, Utlunta tsunadaita. Nunnahi anitelahehu igeski nigesunna. Duksi-gwu dedunatsgulawategu. Dasun unilatsisatu. Sakani unatisatu.

It was the prayer he had learned from Oisin the first time he had gone to Galunlati, the one that was normally invoked before the ceremonial Ball Play, since war was now unknown in that land. Though he had not understood the words then, Uki had later explained them to him. Basically, the chant ridiculed the other participants—this section asked the Terrapin to hold onto them so that they lost all strength. When he had finished, Calvin set the blue lipstick on the ground, substituted a red one, and faced the east, then marked himself again, the scarlet lines paralleling the blue; and again he chanted, this time invoking the First and Second Heavens, and with them the Red Bat and the Peewee and the Common Turtle:

Nunnahi dataduninawati ayu-nu digwatseliga anetsa unatsanuntselahi. Tlamehu Gigagei sagwa danutsgulaniga. Igunyi galunla gesun iyun kanunlagi uwahahistagi. Taline galunla gesun iyun kanunlagi uwahahistagi. Henilu danutsgulaniga. Tlama unnita anigwalugi guntlatisgesti, asegwu nigesunna.
Dutale anetsa unatsanuntselahi saligugi-gwu dedunatsgu-lawistitegu. Elawini dasun unilatsisatu.

South, now, and the color was white this time, and the chant was in invocation to the Third and Fourth Heavens, to the Red Tlaniwa and the Blue Flycatcher.

Tsaine digalunlatiyun Saniwa Gigagei sagwa danutsgulaniga, asegagi nigesunna. Kanunlagi wahahistagi nugine digalunlatiyun. Gulisguli Sakani sagwa danutsgulaniga, asegagi nigesunna. Kanunlagi uwahahistagi hiskine digalunlatiyun Tsutsu Sakani sagwa danutsgulaniga, asegagi nigesunna.
Dutale anetsa utsanuntselahi Tinegwa Sakani sagwa danutsgulaniga, igeski nigesunna. Dasununilatsisatu. Kanunlagi uwahahistagi sutaline digalunlatiyun. Anigastaya sagwa danutsgulaniga, asegagi nigesunna. Kanunlagi uwahahistagi kul-kwagine digalunlatiyun. Watatuga Sakani sagwa danutsgulaniga, asegagi nigesunna.

Finally Calvin took black lipstick and turned his eyes to the west, *Usunhiyi:* the Land of the Dead, the place he feared he might soon experience firsthand, and then he began the last chant.

Dutale anetsa unatsanuntselahi. Yana dedunatsgu lawsistaniga, igeski nigesunna. Dasun dunilatsisatu. Kanunlagi detagaskalauntanun, igunwulstanuhigwud-ina tsuyelisti gesuni. Aktati adunniga . . .

He went on for some time before concluding the invocations to the Bear and the Blue Dragonfly and the Chimney Swift, and to all twelve Heavens. Eventually, though, he rose and once more faced the east (which was toward the river) and without flinching, without moving his eyes up or down, left or right, marched straight into the water.

It was cooler than he'd expected, though *anything* would have seemed cool after the heavy, blood-warm heat of the day. Further he waded, feeling the water rising up his body, the mud squishing up between his toes. When the water lapped around his chin, he stopped and began, very softly, to repeat the chants, addressing each verse to the appropriate direction.

There was logic in his actions, though it was that peculiar sort that governed the Ani-Yunwiya worldview. Water was the strongest thing there was, for it could wear down mountains, drown fire, shut out air. By giving himself to water, he was confronting that thing; by offering his Power to it, as he was doing by allowing it to lick away at the signs he had painted on his body, he was making a bond with it and hoping it would give him back Power at his need. A white man would have seen echoes of birth or rebirth in that ritual, of death and resurrection. That was fine; they fit too.

There were still untouched symbols on his cheeks, though, and Calvin could not complete his bond with the water until all the signs had been tasted. He took four deep breaths, each facing a cardinal direction, with the last one addressed to the east, which was where new life was born—and with that air still filling his lungs, he ducked his head underwater and held his breath.

It was like death must be, he thought distantly, as he felt the water close over his head, lifting his hair, filling his ears, making little raids on his nose and mouth and eyeballs. Very slowly Calvin began counting: seconds, officially, but each was a symbolic year he hoped to live. He made it to twenty—his own age—without any trouble, kept on going to forty, fifty—seventy. At eighty his lungs began to hurt; at ninety he could hear the blood starting to pound in his ears. He was counting more slowly too, and almost did not make it to the last five numbers . . . *ninety-six, ninety-seven, ninety-eight, ninety-nine, one hundred.*

And with the breaths of a hundred years begging for release from his lungs, Calvin broke surface and exhaled.

He emerged from the creek then, sleek and shiny as the newborn child he figuratively was; felt the caress of wind against him: the second strongest elemental. A glance down made him smile. The water had done its work—and more, for it had washed away every single mark he had made upon his body, which normally it could not have done. Moving silently (for he would not speak now unless unless he had to), Calvin gathered up his clothes and his talismans of Power, and walked back to his camp.

And then he began to vest himself for war.

It was in the Lands of Men that he would fight this battle, and so he would wear the outward dress of that World. But beneath he would be a warrior of the Ani-Yunwiya. The lipsticks returned, and with them he once more painted lightning on his chest and on his cheeks. Deer he drew on his legs, for he would need to run swiftly; a falcon he sketched on his forehead, for it would be good to be sharp-eyed. A snake decorated his left forearm, the one that would aim the arrow, for he would have to strike fast and sure; even as the bear on his right was for the strength he would need to shoot true. And as an afterthought, he drew a snow-white 'possum above his heart, in honor of the one for whom he did this thing.

Clothes followed: the clean ones he'd never had a chance

to wear: fresh underwear and socks, blue Levi's, and a black T-shirt bearing a white wolf's mask. He'd have preferred a falcon, but in a hurry, you took what you could get. Finally, he bound back his hair with a red bandanna, into which he stuck the falcon feathers he'd kept since he'd found them in the woods after the third vision.

And then it was time for his weapons.

He retrieved them with care, stowed them with pride: the Rakestraw hunting knife in his belt, the bow, and the deerskin quiver that carried the white-fletched arrows of Galunlati.

A deft movement of arm, calf, and thigh strung the bow, and he was ready.

And so, in the early-morning hours of Thursday, June 19, Calvin Fargo McIntosh, called Edahi, strode north along Iodine Creek in Willacoochee County, Georgia, to do battle with Utlunta Spearfinger, called Nunyunuwi: the Stoneskin.

Chapter XVII:
Confrontation
(east of Whidden, Georgia—late)

Calvin was possessed. It had come upon him abruptly, but was not the dark and evil thing people usually implied when they used that expression. No, *this* was a sort of feyness that was maybe born of a combination of fatigue (he hadn't had a lot of sleep in the past several days), shock, wonder, and anticipation. Perhaps the ritual he had just concluded had something to do with it as well, or possibly it was simply that he was finally acting, not wondering what to do. Whatever it was, it filled him with a surge of energy that was all at odds with his predicament, and he suddenly found himself almost looking forward to his encounter with Spearfinger.

So it was that he ran nearly all the way to Don's house without tiring. In fact, it was as if each breath drew Power into his lungs along with oxygen; as if each footfall upon the spongy ground took only the pain from his muscles and not his strength, as if it *gave* strength back, and added some of its own. He was one with the night; and the shadows that flicked and slid across his body seemed to caress him, not set obstacles in his way. The tree trunks that littered his path, he hurdled; the branches that thrust before him he brushed aside—but even they seemed to stroke him, to massage his muscles loose, not to claw, or scratch, or poke at his eyes. The woods, it seemed, were clearly on his side.

He hoped he was not dreaming, hoped his high would last long enough to see him through what he had begun.

A blue/white glimmer through the trees ahead marked Liza-Bet Scott's security light, and a quarter minute's trot that way brought him across the tracks and the road and onto the fringe of the Scott clan's yard.

He halted in the shadow of a pine, assumed stealth mode as he made a slow, detailed survey of the house. Nothing was obviously amiss—it looked a typical south-Georgia brick ranch, no different from those in the suburbs of Savannah or Brunswick—or Atlanta, for that matter: set back off the road within an acre or so of yard dotted with the ubiquitous pines whose needles made a soft mat beneath his feet, while their spicy odor mingled with the ever-present pulp-mill sulfur in the air.

The only things that set the house apart from its more urban analogs were that there were no others nearby, and the fact that the road it fronted on was not asphalt but sandy dirt.

This far out there was no sign of Spearfinger, though the den lights were on, as Don had told him they might be. Calvin kept his eyes fixed firmly on the bright rectangle as he dodged from tree to tree until he was roughly thirty feet from the nearest of the azaleas that ringed the red brick walls.

He paused there, with his shoulder pressed against a stickily oozing pine, glanced right and left, straining his eyes for any sign of surveillance—and decided the intelligent thing to do would be to head straight for the window, on the theory that if Spearfinger was still where Don had left her, Calvin would be able to see her before she saw him. *If* she had normal eyes.

Two deep breaths and he ran for it, and an instant later paused directly beneath the sill. Unfortunately the house, like most of its kind, had windows tucked close up under the eaves, so that Calvin had to stretch to peek inside. Very cautiously he did, seeing the white ceiling, the ivory walls with their matching paintings of shrimp boats above the long brown sofa.

Which was empty.

The television was still on, crackling static, but Spearfinger was almost certainly not in the room—at least not in human form.

Did he dare break in to seek her, then—or should he continue prowling around out here? He much preferred the latter: houses didn't give you much room to stalk, and his plan depended on him taking Spearfinger unaware.

With this in mind, he skirted left, slipping from window to window with shadowlike silence, raising his head carefully from below, or sometimes from the side—to see nothing but drapes, a glimpse of a boy's cluttered bedroom, a swatch of shower curtain, a bit of kitchen.

But no Spearfinger.

He was beginning to lose his nerve now, for while the house was finite, the environs were not. There was a heap of yard, and a mess of woods around it, and the whole bloody state of Georgia beyond. A troubling thought struck him then: what if Spearfinger had abandoned her wait for Don's mother and departed, seeking other, more accessible prey? Or was there some method to her feeding? And hadn't she told Don that she planned to hunt him? That seemed to indicate that she intended to hang around. Maybe it took a lot of strength to travel between the Worlds, and she had to rebuild for a while before she could move on. Maybe she'd even given up on finding Dave. Or perhaps she was still trying to figure out where he had gone. What would *he* do, Calvin wondered, were he in Spearfinger's situation?

Well, if *he* had zapped into another World in search of someone, *locating* that party would naturally be his first priority. Everything else—food, clothing, shelter—would take a backseat. But what if the quarry kept moving around on you more quickly than you could keep up: in Stone Mountain one day, then gone entirely, then suddenly on Cumberland Island, then in Willacoochee County, and then back in Enotah County three hundred miles to the north? That would drive you crazy in no time, so maybe you'd stay in one place and plot and wait. But you'd still get hungry, and you wouldn't want to draw too much attention to yourself, so you'd find yourself a family living far out, one with several members, and one by one you'd kill them off, but you'd keep their shapes handy in case you needed to fend off folks asking questions . . .

Yeah, all that was possible, Calvin decided, but it still didn't give him any clear notion what to do.

A resumption of the thrumming in the earth made the decision for him. And this time it felt—sounded, whatever it did—really close. In fact, Calvin thought he could determine an actual direction: northeast, toward the darkest part of the woods. He had not taken four strides across the short backyard grass when he literally stumbled on something that gave him pause: a low ridge in the earth, almost exactly like an immense mole tunnel. One end terminated with the expected mound and hole, the other led toward the woods—and the source of the thrumming.

"Uki, go with me," Calvin whispered, and followed the ridge into the forest.

The thrumming kept up, stronger and stronger, and Calvin increased his vigilance, fearing that, since he knew he faced a shapeshifter, *anything* he passed might be his foe. Trees suddenly became sinister where before they had seemed almost sentiently benign; stumps could no longer be taken for granted as merely rotting wood. He found himself wondering if the Stoneskin was bound by the same rules of skinchanging he was, then recollected with a scowl that he hardly knew all the nuances either.

But at least he had a trail, and that was something, never mind that it was leading him deeper into the woods; it was also—thank God—leading away from his friends.

And then he heard it: a ghost of the song that had haunted his childhood. "Spearfinger will get you," his grandmother had whispered. "She will sing you the song: *'Livers I eat, su sa sai!'* And when you hear that four times, she will have you!"

And Calvin was hearing those words now. Already he

could feel the melody insinuating its way into his head, making his thoughts grow dim, his body and reflexes leaden.

And how many times had he heard it already?

It didn't matter; he dared not hear it again, and with that, he dropped to the ground and scrabbled among the mosses on the forest floor until he scraped up enough to cram into his ears as makeshift plugs. He could still hear the song, but not clearly, not as a whole.

But the fact that he had heard it at all meant that he was getting pretty close.

Almost *too* close, and had Calvin not been alert, he might have stumbled upon his quarry before he was ready.

As it was, he noticed a subtle increase in the amount of light on the way ahead and slowed, slid into shadows, resumed a furtive darting from tree to tree.

And finally peered between the twin trunks of a pine tree and gazed upon Utlunta Spearfinger, the Stoneskin.

She had found herself another clearing in the woods—no more than twenty or so feet around. And once more she had raised up stone monoliths to surround it—the closest, in fact, was scarcely five yards away.

But Calvin's first actual sight of his adversary almost disappointed him. She looked no more than an old Indian squaw, clad in rags and tatters of coarse fabric and leather; like something from one of Curtis's nineteenth-century photos—or Dame Judith Anderson's feisty old squaw from *A Man Called Horse*. Stooped and bent she was—no taller than Calvin's chin, if that—and with long gray braids hanging to the ground. Her face he could not make out, for it was veiled by the shawl she wore wrapped around her head and by her crouching stance. But he could see her hands quite clearly—including the great long awl-finger that had begat her appellation. Worse, though, was what she was doing with those hands.

There was no stone in south Georgia; at least not in great slabs like these. But Spearfinger had either *wrought* stone from sand or had called it from the bowels of the earth and made it rise at her bidding. And now she was embarked on a far more ambitious project, for there in the middle of her circle she was sculpting a life-sized man. It was almost finished, in fact, though every now and then she would reach to the ground and mumble (this disrupted the rhythm of the song a little), and fold her hand around something which she would then affix to the work-in-progress. Calvin was intrigued in spite of himself, and now he examined it more closely, he could see that the manikin was made of lumps of pressed-together stone, augmented here and there with colored pebbles.

The troubling thing was that the statue looked familiar. It was male—that was pretty obvious, since she was making it nude and it was facing toward him. Its build was slender, but there was enough fullness of muscle on arm and chest and leg to hint at a gymnast's poise and strength. She was still working on the face, but Calvin knew he had seen it before: angular chin, level brows, full lips, a nose that was neither stubby nor yet quite straight.

David!

There was no doubt about it, Spearfinger was making a simulacrum of his buddy Dave!

And that gave Calvin whatever proof he needed that his best friend was the Stoneshaper's quarry.

It was time to fulfill his mission.

A deep, slow breath; another; and then Calvin slid his hand back over his shoulder, snagged an arrow, and drew it soundlessly from the deerskin quiver. Another fluid motion and he had nocked it, and with another he took aim.

But he could not see her hand clearly from where he was and finally admitted that he really did need another vantage point. He had good night vision for a human—and the moonlight was plenty bright. But he had to hit dead on the first time or he might not get another chance.

Which meant he needed to get closer. He edged to the left a little, but one of the stones blocked the best angle, so he slipped a half dozen steps to the right.

And brought his foot down on solid rock.

The air suddenly filled with a high-pitched shriek like the sound of fresh-broken stones sliding together.

Calvin sprang back reflexively—but found he had fallen flat on his back instead, and then he saw why.

Without skipping a beat, Spearfinger had changed her

song, and the rocks had obeyed, had wrapped themselves around his feet and held him fast. He fumbled with the bow, but before he could get his shot realigned, other stony pseudopods had prisoned his arms, forcing him to sprawl spreadeagled on the ground with all his limbs trapped and the stone beginning to twitch beneath his back. Spearfinger was looking at him too, gazing straight between the monoliths and right into his face. He could see her beady little eyes, the cruelly hooked nose: every archetypal witch in the world rolled into one.

She raised that awful finger, then, and stared at it as if she were seeing it for the first time. Her eyes glittered balefully, and there was a look of triumph on her face. With a brief, admonishing pat, she left her sculpting and began slowly hitching her way across the intervening few yards between herself and Calvin. She did not bother to walk around the rocks that stood between; rather, she simply altered her droning song, and they slid aside of their own accord, so that in an instant her dirty bare feet were inches from the stone that held Calvin's, and she was glaring down at him gleefully.

He got a good look at her then, and this close he could see that her skin had a rough texture to it, like coarse beach sand that had dried hard. Her face was full of moles and warts and excrescences—or were those simply pebbles?—and her eyes looked like nothing so much as lumps of polished coal. She smelled, too: but not the sour stench of a dirty old woman, though there *was* a hint of musty cloth, and of long-mildewed leather. More it was the odor of fresh mud and sun-baked stone—almost a pleasant smell, if not for what it portended.

For a seeming eternity they stayed that way, with Calvin feeling his legs and arms gripped tight, and her peering down at him with a crooked, almost bemused grin. A puzzled tilt of her head, a frown, and she bent over—and stabbed the awl-finger straight into his face.

Calvin winced, but at the last minute she flicked that dreadful digit expertly aside and with appalling finesse scooped the moss out of his ears, so that the night was suddenly awash with sounds. When she straightened again, Calvin could actually hear her joints cracking and popping.

"You are Yellow-Hair's friend," she spat. Her voice was harsh and flat, like rocks tumbling, and seemed to come more from her belly than her lungs. "You are the one who showed him the way to Galunlati; do not think I do not know that! I have seen you there—more than once I have seen you lurking—spying—*speaking* to that soft-one Uki as if he were a god; listening to the foolish knowledge he would impart to you—as if it were true wisdom! But I tell you, Edahi, Uki knows nothing of wisdom. I was in Galunlati before he came, I will be there after he passes, for Galunlati and I are one bone and blood, and I will not allow anything to endanger it!"

"You're crazy!" Calvin gasped. "I know what you are! You have no right part in the way of things!"

"You lie—though that is nothing new to one who comes from the Lying World. But there is a thing you would know, Edahi, and that I will tell you, and that is the reason I have come here."

"So tell me then and kill me, and get it over with—since you mean to deny me a *proper* death."

"Your *death* will be as is," she snarled back. "But unlike your friend, whose liver I will only in part pluck from his living body and slowly devour before I return him to his folks all unknowing, so that he will die oh so very slowly—unlike him, *you* will die knowing the full tally of what you have done, and with full knowledge of the guilt that is yours."

"Why bother?" Calvin gritted bitterly.

"Because you are of the blood of the Ani-Yunwiya and have always tried to live true to that. I respect that, and therefore I will not let you die in ignorance."

"I'll still be dead."

The finger flashed down again, and Calvin was certain he was going to find an eyeball skewered, but it did not happen. "You will be alive without a tongue if you do not be silent! Do you think livers are *all* I eat?"

Calvin bit back a retort, though his glare spoke eloquently.

"*Revenge* is what I seek, Edahi! Listen, while I tell a tale."

And Calvin had no choice *but* to listen.

"In *hilahiya,* in the Ancient Times," Spearfinger began with the traditional formula, "Galunlati lay close to the Lying World—so close that most men could not tell where one began and the other ended. We of Galunlati were free to come and go, as were the men of the Lying World. Sometimes they hunted our folk, but we did not begrudge them that so long as they thanked their kills for their lives and covered their blood. Sometimes we hunted their folk, too— by we, I mean myself, the Raven Mockers, the Underground Panthers, the Water Cannibals. They feared us, as men do, but we too had our place beneath the sky. And then came the white men, like your yellow-haired friend. They brought lies, they brought deceit, they brought disease. 'Give us this piece of land,' they would say, 'and we will ask no more.' And so the Ani-Yunwiya would give them the land—since it was everyone's, how could they begrudge it? 'But that land is not *enough,*' the white men would say again; 'give us more.' And then, 'Give us more yet,' and finally, 'Give us *all!*' And all the time the Ani-Yunwiya kept their word, and all the while the white men lied. Worse still, the Ani-Yunwiya tried to be like the white man: they wore his clothes, they spoke his language, they lived in houses like his and tilled the land as he tilled it. They even took his names in preference to their own, *Calvin Fargo McIntosh!*

"And they turned away from Galunlati. Magic could not be, the white priests told them, and so the Ani-Yunwiya ceased to believe. 'Sorcery is wrong, witches all must die!' This they came to believe.

"Finally it became too much. This World had been tainted beyond healing by the white men, but Galunlati most of them could not see. Yet still their lies reached there, and so it was decided by the Chiefs of Galunlati that the Land Above must be removed from the Lying World. And so it was made to be."

"But what does this have to do with me?" Calvin protested. "What's it got to do with Dave? He may be white, but he respects the land. He thinks more like one of us than many of our own tribe."

"Your own tribe! You and I are *not* of one blood, do not forget that!''

Calvin simply glared.

Speafinger nodded with a touch of amusement. "Your friend knows of Galunlati, he has taken others there, his words seduce even Uki, even Yanu the Bear and Tsistu, the Rabbit-Chief. How long will it be before he returns, and with him others? How long before the lies begin again?"

"He'd never do that!"

"How do you *know?* Knowledge is Power, Edahi, and David Sullivan knows a great many things."

"But he'd never use it, I promise you."

"No, he will not," Spearfinger agreed gleefully. "For within a hand of days I shall feast upon his liver."

"No you won't! If I can't stop you, someone else will. Dave's got more powerful friends than you know!"

"Who are forbidden to enter this World! Do you think Uki is the only one with an ulunsuti? Do you think he is the only one who can watch between the Worlds?"

Calvin gaped incredulously. "It was you! You've been blocking the Barriers Between! No wonder I couldn't get in touch with Uki!"

"Silence!" Spearfinger hissed. "I will leave you here for a while, Edahi, to think on things, and to fear. It will make your liver oh-so-toothsome!"

"Is that what you did to that little girl, too?" Calvin spat. "Did you make her cry, make her beg, fill *her* with fear before you killed her?"

"It would have spoiled *her,*" Spearfinger chuckled. "It is a warrior's flesh that fear seasons best."

She hunched around until she was at Calvin's right side, then squatted and ran a hand along the arrow he still gripped ineffectually. Then with great delicacy, she slipped the finger into the waistband of his jeans.

He closed his eyes at that, gulped, fearing to be emasculated before he died.

But Spearfinger was a true expert at her craft: she simply hooked the stony nail a fraction and yanked upward, ripping Calvin's wolf-mask T-shirt open to his neckband,

and laying his belly bare. A further series of deft flips and yanks, and she had exposed his entire right side.

Calvin gritted his teeth and waited, but the expected pain did not come. Instead, there came a gentle prickling along his ribs, and he realized that Spearfinger was simply drawing the nail of the terrible finger gently along his flesh, so precisely, so carefully, that it sent chills and shivers stampeding across Calvin's body. He could feel goose bumps forming, and tried to twist away, but still Spearfinger continued stroking him. It was torture, that's what it was: she was toying with him, playing his body like an instrument, making it feel tickle and itch and pain and even a pleasure that was almost sexual, all at once.

And then she stopped, rose, and stared back down at him. "The next time I examine your liver, it will be as bare as the flesh I have just caressed above it," she cackled. "I must go now, and finish my poppet so that I can send it to find your friend."

"No!" Calvin groaned, and wished instantly that he had remained silent.

"Yes, Edahi," Spearfinger croaked offhandedly, "you are correct: I do not know where he is. But wherever Yellow-Hair goes, there will be earth and stone close beneath him, and wherever they are, I can follow. My man of stone can follow too, and much more quickly, for while I can swim in stone, he *is* stone."

"One question," Calvin cried desperately. "You've said you want me to die in knowledge, not in ignorance: why livers? And why pick on Don and his folks? You say you don't want attention paid to Galunlati, yet by killing an entire family, you're raisin' suspicions that make that even more likely to happen."

"No, I make them suspect *you!*" Spearfinger cackled back. "I am more wise about this World than you imagine. And when they find you with your liver gnawed and your knife in your hand where you have carved it out and feasted on it, they will think you have gone mad with remorse. There will be no more questions." She paused then. "As to why livers? Why is it that some beasts live on fruit and others flesh, and cannot exist either on the other? But I grow hungry once more—perhaps it is time I sampled the boy.''

"Bitch!" Calvin shouted helplessly.

But Spearfinger was through paying him any need. She turned and shuffled back to the clearing, where she resumed to work on her statue. All the while Calvin lay prisoned, bound by stone around both legs and arms.

How long he lay in helpless fury, he didn't know, for Spearfinger had started up that damned song again, and with it came a resumption of the thrumming. Calvin knew what it was now; he had no choice *but* to see: it was the Stoneskin keeping rhythm with her feet upon the earth while she worked her craft. Every pat resonated through the ground like an immense, ancient drum.

And then, abruptly, the song and the thrumming stopped. Spearfinger stepped back from her handiwork and admired it critically. She muttered a word that Calvin did not catch, and then to his utter amazement, simply melted into the ground in front of the statue, whereupon the thrumming started up again with renewed vigor, but in a subtly different form—like sound heard under water, not in air. For its part, the manikin turned an exact stone-and-pebble copy of David Sullivan's face toward him, grinned wickedly, then spun about and started walking north. But, Calvin realized, it was also slowly sinking into the earth, which produced a softer thrumming of its own. Unbidden, the lines from the Book of Job came to him: "Going to and fro in the earth, and walking up and down in it." He also remembered who it was that had said them.

Chapter XVIII:
Sweating Bullets

Calvin lay flat on his back on the dully thrumming slab of ensorcelled stone—still struggling against his rocky shackles, though there seemed nothing he could do to free himself. He was therefore also trying—with little success, because the damned vibrations made him muddle-headed— to remember his death song.

He had started it long ago in the comfort of his grand- father's cozy cabin up near Qualla, still remembered that gloomy December day he had begun:

"You should always be ready," the old man had told his twelve-year-old grandson, puffing on one of his hand- rolled cigarettes. "You are a man now. Already you take life from the world in the creatures you hunt, but now you can give life as well, and that is a wondrous thing. But do not become so proud that you forget Life's twin: the Black Man of the West, Lord of Tsusginai, the Ghost Country in Usunhiyi. Him you will meet when you least expect it, and when you do, you should know the words to say: your name, the tale of your life, the things you have accomplished, and the people you have affected. Know them all, commit them to memory, for the Black

Man may not give you time to sing them all with your tongue, maybe not even the first word. But by thinking on it, you *have* sung it. Beware, though, for the Black Man will not be fooled.''

More than a little frightened by this, Calvin had commenced immediately, scrawling clumsy iambic pentameter couplets into his junior-high notebooks and committing them to memory over the next several days. It had grown over the years, spread and branched like a tree: separate songs for each unique occasion, and not always with the same rhyme or meter, for as he became more musically sophisticated, there came ballads, laments, lyrics—even rock and country and jazz—and lately he'd been adding to it something he called the ''Werepossum Blues,'' which detailed the adventures of Dave Sullivan and Calvin's increasingly important role within them.

But that came late in the opera, and looked like it might be the concluding aria.

Just now, he was having trouble remembering how the damned thing *started*.

That frigging, persistent *thrumming* kept getting in the way—coupled with Spearfinger's song, which he could no longer hear with his ears, but which it still seeped up through the ground to dull his brain. It was really hypnotic, too, and for an instant before he realized he was doing it, Calvin had begun affixing words to match the beat:

. . . *deep shit . . . deep shit . . . deep shit . . .*

He tried to resist, tried to think clearly, but could not.

. . . *Uwe . . . lana . . . tsiku . . . su sa . . . sai . . .*
. . . *deep shit . . . deep shit . . . deep shit . . . deep shit . . . deep shit . . .*

And then the rhythm shifted slightly. Calvin puzzled over that a moment, even as the stone's grip finally ceased growing tighter. The beat had become more halting, which meant—if Calvin was correct in his half-formed theory that the drumming was either Spearfinger drawing on the Power of the earth or sending her Power through it in the rhythm of her steps—that the ogress had resumed an even more halting pace. More interestingly, though, the beat had become distinctly bluesy, so that before he was quite aware of it, Calvin found he was softly humming the "Werepossum Blues."

"Oh Lord, my name is Calvin, an' Indian blood run
    through my veins.
Yeah, my name is Calvin Fargo, an' Cherokee blood
    be pulsin' in my veins.
I've had some wild adventures; seen an awful lot o'
    wond'rous things . . ."

He had just commenced the second verse when some-thing clicked inside his head.
Werepossum!
Lord, he'd been a fool. The solution was no farther away than the uktena scale. With that he could shift to a smaller form and escape—presuming the stone shackles didn't change with him to accommodate. They seemed to have pretty well solidified now, appeared to be holding him rather passively, not with the active grip they had maintained when the song began.

The thrumming had ended, too; had just sort of tapered off without his noticing it. Maybe that meant—troubling thought—that Spearfinger had reached her destination. Or perhaps she'd simply passed out of range. Certainly his head was clearer now.

So he could escape after all—*if* he could somehow ac-tivate the blessed scale. Where was it, anyway? It should have been on its rawhide thong around his throat, but then Spearfinger would have noticed it when she'd laid his torso bare—but no, when he strained his head up to check (yanking at his hair, for the rock had ensnared a good part of it), he felt the scale poke him in the left armpit.

Trouble was, there was no way to *activate* it. He tried twisting his arm and body and shoulder around within the narrow bounds of his confinement, but that only rubbed his skin raw. He could not reach his knife, nor twitch the arrow he still held enough to bring blood from its point, at least not where it could reach the scale.

That left the technique he had used before: biting him-.self until he bled. It had worked, after a fashion, though he hated the thought of doing it again because, like everything else involved in shapeshifting, it seemed to require a lot of pain. One thing, though, it would not be his tongue this time. No way!

Steeling himself, he closed his eyes and curled his lower lip over between his incisors, then concentrated, striving to fix on his teeth, not the damp flesh between them, as he bit down. His lip resisted like an alien, living thing; writhing and twisting as the pain increased, and once it hurt so much that he gasped and it slipped him entirely.

He started over.

Harder and harder, and he had to force himself to continue. He felt like a fox he had once found. It had come limping into his grandfather's yard on three legs, dirty and emaciated and still bleeding from the stump of its right forepaw. Grandfather had cared for it, but it had died soon after. It was more than a week later that Calvin, on one of his rambles, had found a trap containing the gnawed-off foot of that same fox.

And now he was gnawing his lip for much the same reason. Succeeding too, finally, for he could taste blood. He strained his head forward as much as he could, tilted it, half-blew, half-spat between his teeth. Could feel something warm trickling down his chin and onto his throat—and stopping there.

Seeking to augment the flow, he bit harder—and was rewarded with a slight increase, but still not enough.

He wiggled his torso and jerked his head, trying to urge the recalcitrant blood to flow into the hollow of his arm. If he could just get the transformation started, he thought he could manage.

But it wasn't working! He wasn't situated in a way that allowed him to feed the talisman enough blood.

Calvin ground down even harder, and pain beyond belief shot through his lip. He felt it trying to free itself, but that only added to the agony that engulfed it from inside and outside alike.

Another, stronger gush of blood, and Calvin spat again, then choked and gagged as too much ran down the wrong way.

Another bite, sliding his teeth back and forth now, gnawing away—

And cutting through! He could feel a section of his lip flop down against his chin, almost bereft of feeling. The very concept made him retch, forcing him up against his bindings as blood fountained across his chest, slid down his throat—and, thank God, ran in a steady stream down his chin, across his neck, and into the hollow of his left arm where the scale lay. He waited until a sticky warmth accumulated there, and began to concentrate:

'Possum, 'possum, 'possum . . .

'Possum was what he would become, because it was small enough and he had been a 'possum, and thought he could handle a smaller form if it were one he had worn before. He had to fight, though, had to resist the nausea that threatened to overcome him, the agony of his wounded lip, the distancing from his *self* that signaled the *change* about to begin. What was 'possum? Small, furry, furtive; pointy nose, beady eyes, long naked tail, and paws like tiny hands.

The *change* hit him all at once, not gradually like before, and he had to make a conscious effort to maintain control as alien instincts once more invaded his mind and took up lodging there. But the rock was loosening as his body shrank away from it. In seconds he could slide his left hand free, and when he did, he clasped it around the scale and let the points sink in.

That speeded things and smoothed them out. He took a deep breath and let the *change* proceed, keeping his mind firmly locked on self-awareness as he felt his joints shift, the twitch at the base of his spine that was his tail making its presence known, the strange pulls and tensions, the sudden loosening of clothes as his body altered and they did not.

And then, abruptly, he was free. He had to struggle to escape the piles of empty fabric where most of his body had been, but then he really was loose. Already the pain of transformation had faded, already the agony in his lip was dulled.

Quick now, before the 'possum got other ideas: he fumbled around his throat until he found the scale again. Clamped his paws around it, and thought, very hard, *human*.

That was accomplished very quickly indeed, in one long upward rush that made Calvin dizzy as his head shot into the air and he found himself crouching at the edge of a wide flat boulder. As quickly as he could, he slipped the scale necklace over his head and gathered up his clothes and weapons. Fortunately none were damaged, and the rock did not resist, though he did have to yank vigorously to free one of his sneakers.

Maybe a minute later he was dressed again, and only then did he dare check on his lip. It didn't hurt as badly as it had initially, that much was clear. But he had done it some pretty solid damage, and in spite of two *changes* it was still occasionally sending little stabs of bright agony shooting into his chin when he tried to move it. His stomach churned and flip-flopped as he raised a finger to his mouth experimentally—and met, thank God, the thin rough ridge that meant it was already scabbing over.

Satisfied that he was as well as he could be, given the circumstances, Calvin checked his bow once more, turned, and jogged off toward Don Scott's house.

Chapter XIX:
Catching Up

It was strange, Calvin mused grimly as he trotted through the moonlit woods, how radically things could change in fifteen minutes.

This forest, for example. The first time he had emerged from it beside Don's house, it had seemed friendly, almost as if it were making a conscious effort to assist him. Perhaps it *had* been, too; maybe so few people paid it any real heed anymore that it had been grateful when Calvin's rituals had given it the obeisance to which it was anciently due.

But if the woods had aided him then, they overlaid stone and sand, and those were Spearfinger's allies. And since she now knew he was onto her, perhaps she had pulled rank on him, as it were, and the forest had withdrawn its support and replaced it with hostility.

For surely there could not be so many buried roots snaking along the earth at just the right height to trip him. And *surely* there could not be so many sharp twigs and broken branches to stab at him as cruelly as that awful finger had. Nor could the terrain itself otherwise have grown so uneven that his feet twisted and slipped at every

192

turn. Already he'd stumbled twice on a series of wash-board ruts he could have sworn had not been present earlier, and he had to maintain constant vigilance against the skull-sized stones that seemed to have erupted beside Spearfinger's mole-mound path like toadstools after a rain. These he gave a particularly wide berth, for *they* might do anything from snap at his passing toes to communicate word of his approach to the Stoneskin.

In spite of his growing sense of urgency, Calvin took a quick break, leaning against the trunk of a convenient sweet gum—maybe the only thing the worthless weeds were good for. A tendril of Spanish moss tickled his ear and he batted it away, and simply stood for a moment, chest heaving, the air disturbingly full of the heavy hiss of his breathing.

He was dog-tired, he realized, and with good reason: it was getting close to dawn now, and he'd been on the go almost constantly for the past several hours—didn't even want to *think* about the miles he'd covered in various skins and guises. Fortunately he was in good condition—excellent condition, in fact; and shapeshifting seemed to have some sort of rejuvenating effect—but even the best of athletes eventually began to wear down, and Calvin thought he was about to. Lord knew his legs were getting stiff, his feet sore, and his lungs hurt like hell. He bent over, bounced a couple of times to try to loosen his spine a bit, did a quick series of waist twists, then laid down the bow and gave his thighs and calves a thirty-second massage.

But he was still not ready to move on. Fatigue and trepidation had replaced energy and elation all in the space of a quarter hour.

Okay, guy, he told himself firmly. *It's only another half mile or so to the house, and you know you can do that. And once there, just a little while sure enough to put an arrow through a witch's hand—presuming that's where the old biddy is. Then you can rest. An hour from now you could be curled up asleep beside Robyn.*

All of which was probably bullshit, considering that he had no idea where Spearfinger actually was—and that the cops really *would* be after him when dawn rolled around. Probably there were APBs out on him already.

But that didn't exempt him from his responsibility.

Calvin took five more deep breaths to calm himself, inhaling through the nose and exhaling through the mouth, like you were supposed to do when you got nerved out. They helped, but it was still not enough when he started off again.

Nor was it enough to keep his pulse from racing when he once more emerged from the woods at the edge of Don Scott's backyard.

He paused there, surveying carefully. It looked the same as before. The mole-mound he had been following was certainly still present and looked, if anything, to be maybe a little rougher around the exit end, though that was the only difference.

Except . . . there were no lights on.

So what did that imply? Had Spearfinger got wise and turned them off? Had she—appalling thought—actually put on Allison's shape and gone to bed? Was a Cherokee ogress sleeping soundly between the K-Mart sheets of a south Georgia ranch house?

Calvin had a sudden chill and swept his gaze across the yard again. Or perhaps she was still out *here*. Maybe she was watching him now—from a bush, from a tree, from a clump of grass. Maybe she *was* a bush or a tree or a clump of grass.

Maybe he should try to beat her at her own game.

Except that to kill her he needed to be able to use the bow.

Still panting slightly, Calvin began a second cautious circuit of the environs. This time, though, he swung left from where he had emerged from the forest and made his way to the logging road on that side, staying within the tree cover as much as possible, even though it meant exposing himself to the hostile woods.

No luck that way: every window was dark.

The other direction now, to much the same effect, and Calvin's eyes were actually starting to smart from trying to focus on tiny details obscured by the night.

A quick pause for another series of calming breaths, and

he made his way across the backyard, flitting from shadow to shadow with as much stealth as he could muster, disturbingly aware of how his muscles seemed much more reluctant to respond than heretofore.

Eventually, though, only fifteen feet separated him from the house, and he made the dash from utility shed to back corner on one held breath, to flop panting against the wall beside the kitchen door. Moonlight shone on a window directly above his head, and, unlike the others, it was cracked open perhaps six inches at the bottom, though there was still a screen. He hesitated with his head inches below the opening and listened, alert for any sounds that might hint at Spearfinger's presence. Nothing out of the ordinary: only the hum of a refrigerator, the deeper growl of an air-conditioner, the ticking of the grandfather clock in the other room that seemed to synchronize itself with his heartbeat and remind him at once of "The Masque of the Red Death" and "The Tell-Tale Heart."

Or maybe "Masque of the *Stone* Death" and "The Tell-Tale *Liver,*" he decided wearily, and continued his survey.

His plan was different this time, however. Before, he'd hoped to catch Spearfinger inside and simply shoot her through a window. But since none of them were open, it now looked as if he was going to have to break in and stalk her from room to room—assuming she was even here. He didn't dare risk *not* checking, either, since if she *was* present he wouldn't get a better chance to do the deed.

Still, he was a little uneasy; it would be just his luck to take the time and trouble to pick a lock and walk in to find himself face-to-face with his adversary. Thus it was with considerable trepidation that he checked the windows once more with about as much success as previously. He could see nothing clearly through them, and every one except the kitchen was closed and latched—and even that, when he managed to get the screen off, was jimmied, for he could push it no higher than it already was.

Which meant he was reduced to picking the door locks. Okay, front or back?

The front door was one of those thick, solid oak jobs behind a solid-looking screen and had been securely fastened when he'd tested it on his previous circuit. The back-door screen was much flimsier, though, and in fact had a hole in it right beside the handle that seemed to indicate that someone had pushed through before and unlatched the screen from inside—probably someone in the household, to judge by the fact that the wire ends looked to be a bit rusty. Calvin thought it unlikely it would have gone un-repaired for long otherwise.

Propping the bow against the doorframe, Calvin took a deep breath and worked his hand through the slit and found the hook. As gently as he could with thumb and forefinger, he lifted it free and slid his hand out again, swearing softly when the broken wires gouged him as he went against their curvature. He wiped the blood on his jeans—as far away from the scale as he could, just in case.

Another deep breath, and he eased the screen open.

This door was one of those cheap hollow affairs, once yellow, but with the paint peeling off some kind of veneer. There was only one lock, and fortunately no deadbolt—a little odd for a woman living alone. But then, this *was* the country, and he'd bet there was a stash of guns around somewhere—a kid like Don would almost certainly have at least a couple.

An idea struck him: the legends said Spearfinger had been slain with an arrow through the hand where her heart had been relocated. But the folks who had originated that story had not known of firearms, so was there any real reason a gun *wouldn't* do just as well? He was a pretty decent shot with a pistol, okay with a shotgun, and hell-on-wheels with a .22 rifle. Maybe if he made it inside he'd do a fast search for one and get after-the-fact clearance from Don.

If he didn't encounter Spearfinger first.

If he didn't rouse her trying to pick this goddamned lock.

If.

Fortunately Calvin was good at picking locks. Lord knew he'd had enough practice, since his dad had lost the key to the front door when Calvin was twelve and had never bothered to replace it. That had been the same kind of lock as this, too: one that responded very well to your basic paper clip—which was one of the very few pieces of equipment Calvin had with him.

A quick search of his pockets confirmed it, and Calvin dragged out a nice stiff one and unbent it. He had just started to insert it into the keyhole when he noticed something that gave him a sudden chill. There was a smear of clay next to the doorknob, and beneath it the dirty handprint of a small-to-middling child. Calvin could see them both quite clearly in the glow of the back-porch light, but what gave him pause was that the mark showed no sign of fingerprints—and that the index finger seemed unnaturally long, though perhaps not the foot or so he had so recently observed. Well, that answered one thing: it settled Calvin's curiosity about how accurate Spearfinger's copies were: close, but no cigar.

He got a solution to another mystery almost as quickly, too, for with the screen open, his eye was drawn to a dark object lying atop the doorjamb. He picked it up curiously and noted, to his surprise, that it was a key. Not just any key, though: one made of stone. But even as he touched it, it crumbled into sand and slipped away between his fingers.

He wished *he* were as facile with magic; maybe he'd have better solutions to his problems than trying to break into other people's houses. *Maybe.* Taking a deep breath, he returned to his work. The first tumbler fell almost immediately, the second followed quickly.

He had just poked and prodded his way to the third when he heard a twig snap behind him, but before he could even glance over his shoulder, a voice barked, "Boy, if I was you, I wouldn't move even a *muscle!* I got a gun on you, and this time I ain't gonna miss."

Calvin's heart almost leapt from his body. It was the sheriff, and he'd caught Calvin red-handed—literally, since his fingers were still trickling blood from the wire gouges.

He couldn't run, either; two men were behind him and approaching at a steady trot, to judge by the increasingly loud clump of their footfalls. Calvin took token relief from their number because it sharply decreased the likelihood that either one was Spearfinger in disguise.

"Jus' ease them hands right on up that door above your head," the sheriff continued, "and just you spread them legs as wide apart as you can."

Calvin obeyed, though he had to fight back disappointment so tangible it almost made him nauseous. He'd been so close to resolving this mess—either by confronting his quarry or by finding a weapon that might be better than anything he had against her—and now it was all for naught. Now he was going to jail and Spearfinger would be free to ravage the land.

But there won't be anything you can do about it, a part of him insisted. *If you can't get at her, how can she be your responsibility?*

That was true. It was also a world-class cop-out.

Boots thumped onto the patio then, and an instant later, Calvin felt heavy hands clamp around his sides, then give him a thorough frisking: up his torso, down his thighs and calves, and then up again, even including his crotch.

The sheriff knew his stuff too, for he quickly found the knife at Calvin's belt, which he appropriated, along with the bow and quiver. So thorough was he, in fact, that when he spun Calvin around to face them and cuffed his hands together, the sheriff even slipped the uktena scale over his head and stuffed it into a pocket. This possible procedural violation elicited a disquieting, green-toothed grin from his younger companion—the unsavory-looking whiny-voiced guy Calvin had seen before—but his superior simply grinned back and said something about not wanting any sharp objects around, nor any mumbo-jumbo.

The next few moments—when Calvin was being hustled across the yard—were muddled with confusion. The sheriff told him he was under arrest for suspicion of murder; Whiner mumbled through his rights, and then he was thrust into the backseat of one of the bronze Caprices that he'd foolishly failed to notice parked just beyond the trees at the western edge of the yard—the one quadrant he hadn't closely investigated.

Calvin fell into the seat hard enough to jar his teeth, but

though both officers climbed back in, neither made any move to crank the car.

And so Calvin had no choice but to slump against the cushions and feel utterly helpless and furiously pissed at himself for being so careless and not thinking ahead to this eventuality.

The officers up front weren't going to any trouble to conceal information from him, either, though they'd said they'd put off any interrogation until they got to town, where they could, as they put it, "goddamn *see*." From snatches of their conversation, Calvin was pretty much able to piece together what had happened.

Liza-Bet Scott had gone with her policeman beau to identify the body of her daughter—that much Calvin already knew. But evidently she'd gotten so hysterical they'd taken her on to town to await confirmation of cause-of-death and release of the body to the mortician. Apparently the coroner was insisting on performing an autopsy, though; which concept had sent Liza-Bet off all over again. Eventually, she'd calmed down enough to answer questions, and several of those had involved a certain Indian boy her son had been seen talking to down at the Magic Market. *That* much she'd remembered: how Don had gone on and on about this neat Indian he'd met, but she hadn't paid him much mind—he was always doing things like that. Finally, though, she'd recalled that Don had asked the Indian to go camping with him and his buddy—that'd gotten through to even her.

And that, coupled with the fact that it was getting near dawn and Don would be coming home from that trip soon and would need to know what was going on, had been enough to make the guys put the house under surveillance. The current delay was for the reappearance of a second deputy, who was evidently scouring the woods for Don and his friend. Once he showed up, it was off to the slammer for Calvin.

He *hoped*. This far out in the sticks, and considering ethnic heritage, Calvin suspected that trial by jury was frequently more formality than fact.

"Here he comes," the sheriff rumbled from the front

seat, peering through the windows, though how he could see anything through the coating of white dust was anybody's guess.

" 'Bout time, too," his companion allowed, aiming a disgusted glance at the nonfunctional LED clock in the dash.

"Jesus tit!" the sheriff exclaimed, rolling down his window to stare outside. "He's got *another* goddamned body!"

"You're shittin' me!"

"You look."

Calvin did, along with the two officers, and saw, just as he'd feared, that a second deputy—Adams again, as it happened—had emerged from the woods on this side of Don's house, and that he held a body in his arms. He did not need to see it to know that it was the corpse of Michael Chadwick.

And he doubted anybody had bothered to check for footprints this time. Which was too bad, because they'd have found the tracks of someone who was supposed to be dead, and that might have saved Calvin's ass.

"Critters was snoopin' around," Adams told his boss when he got within range of the car. "Didn't have no choice *but* to move him." He patted the radio at his hip proudly. "I already called for an ambulance."

"Dead?" More a statement than a question.

"Yeah, and he ain't got no goddamned liver, neither."

"Shit," the sheriff grunted, fixing Calvin with a glare that said he wished he could skin him alive with a hot knife right there.

Deep shit, Calvin thought, as the car rumbled to life.

As if in reply, a single drop of rain splattered the windshield.

Chapter XX: Spyin' on the Spied-upon

(Brock and Robyn's camp— the wee hours)

"No!"

Brock's shout of dismay cut through the night, but no one paused to listen. The big Chevy continued on its way without slowing, leaving only a vast cloud of white dust to mark its passage—a cloud that was quickly beaten into submission by the random patter of a sudden halfhearted shower. In less than a minute only the damp remained— that, and the erratic thrumming that had been getting on Brock's nerves off and on for the past day now.

Hunched miserably in the shadow of the pine where he had taken shelter, Brock folded his arms on his scrawny chest in disgust, oblivious to the occasional drops that continued to pepper his head and shoulders. A sort of blowing/whistling sigh escaped his lips as he shifted his weight from foot to foot, helpless with indecision.

Where to from here? he wondered.

Well, the *cops* had Calvin, and since he'd started out after Calvin—for no clearer reason than to prove to Robyn that he was correct about his friend's integrity—it stood to reason that he should continue trailing the Indian, especially since it looked like his new friend was *really* in for it now and would probably need all the help he could get.

Trouble was, they were almost certainly taking Calvin back to town, and to jail—and Brock didn't have a clue where the jail was or what the procedure for seeing prisoners was, much less for getting one free again.

But he had to try, never mind that he'd risk exposing himself and his sister in the bargain.

He really had no choice. Strange things were happening, and that was a fact: Calvin could change his shape by fooling with that scale-hickey around his neck, and Brock had seen him doing some ritual-kinda stuff twice—once right outside their camp—and had sensed an unpleasant tingling in his feet both times he'd sneaked out of the sinkhole. But Cal had also been accused of murder that he swore he did not commit. And far more troubling yet was the wild tale Don had told about Spearfinger. Brock wasn't quite sure he *believed* it yet; but it fit the available facts, and *something* had sure as hell scared the bejesus out of Don, as well as making Calvin act like the devil himself was after him.

The thrumming in the ground strengthened abruptly, as if in response to the threatening storm. Brock shuddered, since he now knew what was causing those disturbing tremors. He wondered, indeed, about the wisdom of being out alone in the forest with that . . . *thing* . . . roaming around as well. But it was too late now. To admit he was frightened would be to admit defeat. It would also leave a mystery unresolved, and that he could not allow—not considering the amount of effort he'd put into spying out the truth already.

Sighing, Brock turned back into the forest, hunching his shoulders against the scattered but heavy drops, and as he jogged along he considered how remarkable it was that he had even made it here at all.

He hadn't had much trouble keeping up with Calvin after he'd split camp, and had tailed him long enough to witness the end of that weird-ass bathing ritual. But when the Indian had started off again, he'd run like the very wind, and Brock's shorter legs had not been able to follow suit. That he'd found himself at Don's house at all was more or less an accident. He'd only heard the guy mention a general direction and something about railroad tracks and the river, so he'd simply struck off north until he found tracks and followed them, to arrive just in time to see a pair of Sheriff's Department cars cruise up with their lights off right as Calvin came skulking around the opposite corner of the house.

He wished desperately that he'd been able to get close enough to really tell what was going on. As it was he'd seen the flash of the yard light on handcuffs and a pistol; and the sheriff confiscating Calvin's bow and knife and even the scale from around his throat. Brock's heart sank when he remembered that, because whatever Calvin had to accomplish almost certainly involved magic, and the one magical thing Brock knew absolutely he possessed was the scale.

And, Brock forced himself to admit, that was pretty damned scary, because once the novelty of Calvin's shape-shifting had worn off, he'd set himself to some serious thinking about how the proof of one kind of magic more or less left it open for 'em all—like Don's Spearfinger story. Suddenly he regretted not going to church, regretted making play-acting stabs at occult rituals he'd gotten out of nut-cult magic books—and regretted most deeply being in the woods when something magic was definitely afoot, something that was hostile, and which only Calvin had any chance of ever elucidating for him—or (troubling thought) saving him from.

And *that* clinched it. Rain or no rain, it would be town, but he really did need to let the sibling unit know what was going on.

Not that she could stop him from whatever he decided to do.

Not ever.

Not even when the ground was drumming.

Twenty nerve-wracking minutes later, a somewhat damper Brock pushed aside the prickly fronds of palmetto

and hopped down into camp. The rain had followed him
a way, but evidently had not reached here—which he feared
was the end of his fortune.

Robyn was on her feet in an instant, leaping up from
where she'd been leaning against her pack with one arm
around Don, who raised an eyelid apprehensively at
Brock's approach. Brock suddenly wished he'd never told
them about Calvin being a were-deer, much less anything
else, because that had paved the way for Don to open up
a *really* smelly kettle of fish which Brock felt obliged to
poke around in—while Robyn did her damnedest to keep
him away. It wasn't *their* problem, after all.

Yeah, sure.

He hoped, from Robyn's scowl, that he didn't have a
fight on his hands.

He hoped in vain.

"Where the *hell* have you been?" she raged at him, her
voice so loud in the darkness that Brock flinched and made
frantic shushing signs.

"After Calvin, of course." Brock thought that should
have been obvious.

"I know *that*," Robyn snapped. "So where's he *gone?*"

Brock flopped down in front of her and helped himself
to another candy bar from the seemingly endless stash,
not bothering to towel off. "He went to his camp and did
some kinda ritual. And then he went to Don's house, only
I lost him for a while, so I didn't get there until the cops
was hustlin' him away."

"The cops! *Shit!*" Robyn rolled her eyes. "Dammit, I
knew that'd happen. Well, that finishes it; we're outta here
come sunrise." She whirled around and began stuffing
gear into bags, oblivious to Don's wild-eyed confusion and
Brock's outright disgust. He made no move to assist the
packing, though, so that a moment later Robyn turned
again and glared at him.

"He's in trouble," Brock said simply. "*Lots* of trouble."

"So are we—and if we're not extra careful, old Calvin'll
send the fuzz right back here!"

"No reason to."

"No reason, hell! If it's the kinda crap he was talkin' about—murder and all—he'll need *somebody* to account for his presence, and we can't, only he might think we can, and then we'd really be up the creek.''

"So you're just gonna let a friend down just like that?''

"I'm not really sure he *is* a friend," she grumbled sullenly, "at least not anymore. He sure as hell hasn't leveled with us!''

Brock glared at her. "He told us he had secrets and we told him we had some. That's levelin' in *my* book!''

"But not mine!''

"You mean you *really* think that he killed Don's sister and then stole her shape and killed his best friend?''

"He *might* have. Lots of folks act nice and then turn out to be assholes.''

"*Tell* me about it," Brock replied, cocking an eyebrow meaningfully. "But if that's the case, why would he do all that stuff to hurt people, and still help us? Why would he threaten to kill Don and then look after him like a brother when he runs into him in the woods a little later? Why *didn't* he kill him then, 'cause he sure could have if he wanted to and nobody woulda known any different! And don't give me any of that b.s. about bringin' in others, either; you *know* you don't believe that!''

"She said something about fear seasonin' my liver," Don began, but his voice trailed off as he caught sight of Robyn's face.

Robyn ignored him and regarded her brother seriously. "Damn, you're good,'' she chuckled. "You oughta be a lawyer when you grow up. Anyway, I'll grant you that Calvin's a nice guy—at least on the surface—and I'll also accept that he helped us out. But we still didn't ask him to do any of those things, he just *did*—and he's got us in a heap of trouble because of it.''

"No, he's *protected* us from trouble as best he could,'' Brock countered desperately. "He *understands* what we're into and all, he wants us to stay out of it. Problem is, he's not sure it'll stay away from us, so he has to look after us.''

"How's he gonna do that from jail?'' And then Robyn

noticed her brother's sudden grin, and appeared to realize she'd suddenly argued against her own case. "Brock, we *can't* go there, they'll ask questions, they'll want names and addresses, IDs. They may have already heard the missing-persons reports on us, 'cause you know damned sure Dad'll file 'em even if Mom won't. Somebody's bound to recognize us."

"So you're willin' to leave a friend in deep shit and go on off to England to save your ass?"

"Don't *talk* like that! Besides, it's like I said. Calvin knows what we're up against. He won't expect us to hang around."

"Yeah, but could you forgive yourself? *I won't!*"

"I won't either," Don echoed quietly. "I don't know, but . . . I reckon maybe Brock's right. Yeah, there's some stuff that points to Calvin possibly being involved in some murders. But he doesn't *feel* like a murderer. I mean I met him yesterday—before you guys did, I reckon—and he didn't act nervous or anything. Sure, he was kinda in a hurry-like, and sorta preoccupied and all, but . . . well . . . ain't *nobody* that good an actor!"

Robyn frowned. "*You* don't get a vote. Come sunrise we're gonna go watch your house, and soon as anybody official shows up, off you march. They're gonna be searchin' for you in a few hours, anyway."

"Uh-uh," Don shot back hotly. "No *way* I'm goin' back there! Not with that monster maybe hangin' 'round! Only people I trust right now are folks that've had somebody with 'em every minute since this thing started!"

"That's *nobody*," Robyn pointed out with a touch of sarcasm.

"Yeah, but I could *tell* something was wrong with my sister by the way she was lookin' at me. I don't see that in either of you, and I don't think y'all could hide it."

"What about Calvin's eyes?" Brock inserted. "Wouldn't that hold for him too? Wouldn't *they* be proof he's okay?"

"Wasn't thinkin' 'bout it then," Don admitted. "Was dark, anyway."

"Okay," Robyn sighed. "But what are you gonna do

about your friend's folks? They've gotta find out some-time.''

"Probably already have," Brock noted, "considerin' that the cops have found his body.''

"He's only got a dad, anyway," Don informed them. "And if they did call him, I'm *sure* he's gone by now.''

"Okay, okay," Robyn announced resignedly. "Maybe we *ought* to at least check out what's goin' on in town and make sure there's nothing we can do.''

"Good job," Brock cried, slapping his sister on the back. "I knew you'd see sense.''

"I *see* disaster," she snapped back. "But maybe it's like you said, maybe I couldn't forgive myself.''

"Okay, so let's boogie.''

"Not so fast," she replied. "I still think we need to move camp. That way if Calvin does spill the goods on us, the cops won't find us as quick.''

Brock frowned, but finally nodded. "And *then* we go to town.''

"All of us?" Don wondered. "They're gonna be lookin' for me too—and Mom's gonna be worried. I'd kinda like to touch base . . .''

Brock's frown deepened. "Good point. And since they know your friend's dead now, they're *bound* to want to ask you questions.''

"*Hard* questions," Robyn appended. "And if all this magic stuff's true, you're gonna have to be *real* careful how you answer 'em, or you'll wind up in the funny farm.''

"Yeah," Brock continued, with a glare. "So maybe you'd better lie low until we get back.''

"I'm *goin'* with you," Don said flatly.

"Yeah, maybe he's right," Robyn conceded, eyeing Don narrowly. "You in good enough shape to truck through the woods for a while?''

"I'm tough," Don replied.

And then the ground began to thrum ever so subtly. And that brought an end to discussion.

Chapter XXI: Put to the Question

(Whidden, Georgia— just before dawn)

. . . a bare light bulb, plain white walls, and three faces leering out of the shadows, angry and piggish . . .

"You do it?"

"No."

"You have anything to do with it?"

"Indirectly, but not by design."

"What's that s'posed to mean?

"I can't tell you."

"Why not?"

"It's a . . . religious thing, like confession . . . I took a vow."

"Is that like the Fifth?"

"Stronger."

A exasperated sigh. "You know who done it?"

"Maybe."

"Who?"

"I can't tell you."

"*How* d'you know, then? You witness it?"

"No."

"How, then?"

"By the signs."

"You mean them livers?"

"Yes."

"An' you won't tell?"

"*Can't* tell."

"How come?"

"You wouldn't believe me."

A long pause. "Boys, I'm goin' for a cup of coffee. Might check on the fuse box while I'm at it. Wouldn't want that video camera to go off at the wrong time, would we? Might be gone 'bout twenty minutes. You boys look like you could use a little exercise."

PART IV

EARTH AND WATER

Chapter XXII: Comin' To

(Whidden, Georgia—Thursday, June 19—morning)

It was something wet trickling into Calvin's eyes that awoke him, and he thought for a moment it was more blood, because that was certainly what had been running into them when the sheriff's thugs had finally left him alone the night before—or this morning, or whenever it had been. Morning, probably, because he thought he remembered the sky being pale when Deputies Adams and Moncrief (as Whiner's nametag proclaimed his real name to be) had dragged him out of the County Mounty car and across the parking lot and into an unlighted and azalea-shrouded side door of Whidden's Gothic courthouse, whence they'd pushed and shoved him down about a million hard-edged stairs and then down a long, humid corridor full of pipes and boilers and mechanical hums, through a steel door marked STAFF ONLY, and thence along a dank, brick-walled tunnel and through another STAFF ONLY door to a surprisingly homey interrogation room where they booked him and printed him and were assertively polite for about five minutes (taping all the time)—or exactly until Calvin had begun to relax just a smidgen. *Whereupon* the sheriff had vanished, and it had been back to the brick tunnel again, this time into a cramped and dirty room that opened off it where . . . *things* had happened, and then, finally (when the sheriff returned from his "coffee break"), to this cramped detention cell that was—Calvin had decided before he passed out—truly under the jail.

And there wasn't a sharp corner or projecting object along either route that he hadn't somehow "stumbled" into, or "fallen" upon—with maybe just a little bit of encouragement. Just like they'd "helped" him stay awake with assorted attention-getters in the form of fists—and once with a cup of remarkably hot coffee "accidentally" spilled into his crotch.

It was still wet too, but clammy cold now, and as Calvin slowly dragged himself to greater wakefulness on the narrow cot, some part of his consciousness informed him that if blood were running into his eyes it would be warm, whereas this liquid obviously was not.

He blinked then, or tried to, for his left lid was crusted shut, and the right only slightly better from having been lately soaked in whatever it was. The blink let in a stab of light, though, that made his head hurt—or hurt worse; it was already pounding, and come to that, everything else was too. A grunt, a groan, a yawn (not a good idea—his jaw wasn't just optimum either, never mind what he'd earlier done to his lip, which was yet another, though fortunately much dimmer ache), and Calvin swung himself upright enough to manage a stiff-shouldered slump.

A gust of damp, chill air from somewhere above and behind made him shiver, but it also helped him focus enough to see that it came from a missing pane in the barred window hard up under the ceiling—the same one that was letting in occasional spits of rain, which (coupled with an impressive leak directly over his head) were evidently what had awakened him.

Knuckles to his eyes then (when had he scraped them like that?), about a ton of dried ick dragged out of the left one, and he was finally able to take stock of his surroundings.

In spite of the barred window and the grillwork that replaced the door, he doubted that the stone-walled eight-

by-eight-foot room had either started out as a cell or been
intended for long-term occupancy. But then, he imagined
a little county like Willacoochee didn't have a lot of need
for spacious criminal quarters, and when you had a real
desperado like he supposedly was that you wanted to keep
in solitary (especially if he'd gotten a little too roughed
up—Calvin doubted all the local cops were as brutal as
his interrogators had been), you just stuck them where you
could.

Like here, which he suspected was some kind of con-
verted storage cubby—safe enough with the stout bars, the
concrete walls, and the high (easily twelve-foot) ceiling.

Furniture? Only the cot bolted to the wall and a chamber pot in the corner.

Calvin eyed it warily, wondering whether it was wiser
to toss his cookies into it (as his pirouetting stomach was
beginning to suggest) or to use it for its more traditional
function first.

He was still debating when the sound of a door opening
drew his attention to the narrow bit of corridor he could
see beyond the bars. Two men were talking, one angrily,
one definitely on the defensive, their voices accompanied
first by the slap of feet against bare concrete, then by a
sudden pause.

"You better watch it, Moncrief," the angry voice
snapped. "I don't care *what* he's wanted for, all *you*
guys've got him for's attempted breakin'-and-enterin' and
criminal trespass—and that ain't enough to justify beatin'
the hell outta nobody. Wilson's *way* outta line on that. He
may *think* he runs the county, but this jail's mine as well
as his."

Calvin perked up immediately. This was the first time anyone in authority had shown the slightest sign of being reasonable. He wondered who it was—local police, maybe? But
before he could speculate further, a chillingly familiar voice
whined, "Shit, chief, ain't you ever heard of circumstantial
evidence? Boy's wanted on s'picion of murder up at Stone
Mountain, and they found his tracks everywhere 'round that
little gal, and—"

"Suspicion of murder *ain't* murder. They found Larry

Mather's 'coon hound's tracks too, and it there, but that don't mean *she* done it.''

"You *believe* that Injun's story?"

"Wasn't there when you interrogated him, since Wilson didn't bother to contact me. But I've seen the tape, *what there is of it,* and he don't *sound* like no criminal to me.''

"Don't sound like much of nothin' 'cept a crazy man," Moncrief snorted. " 'I can't tell you' ain't no answer— and that's what he said 'bout half the time.''

"He also said he found the body and was on his way to report it when he heard you were lookin' for him. Wouldn't that kinda put the wind up you, especially if you knew you were already wanted?''

"So you *are* on his side, then!"

"I'm on the side of the law, Abner—and don't forget it. But there's somethin' weird 'bout this case that don't make sense.''

"Like what?"

"Like them missin' livers."

"Nothin' to that; boy's a goddamned Satanist—you seen that tattoo on his ass. We got *that* on tape real good.''

"That's not one of their symbols, though; I took that seminar up in Atlanta and they showed us a bunch and it's not one.''

"What *is* it, then?"

"Hell if *I* know. But I don't think that boy cut out them livers. 'Cordin' to Bill, they was kinda scooped out from inside through a little bitty hole 'bout as big as your finger. I don't think there's any way that boy coulda done that.''

"Maybe he had an accomplice."

"Maybe."

"Shit!"

"We'll know more when they get them tests back. Find out what was in them dirt traces they found in the wounds.''

"*Shit.*"

"You buckin' for suspension, Moncrief? I may not be your boss, but the Ordinary listens to me much as he does to Wilson and likes me better. There's *plenty* of folks can be deputies. Some of 'em even got brains.''

"Yes, sir." The voice was tinged with hostility—the same hostility the owner had vented against Calvin in person last night. Not a sterling example of *Homo sapiens*, that was for sure.

The steps started again. "Good, then you go see that boy gets cleaned up and put in a proper cell. Get the doc to sew him up if you have to."

Calvin was feigning sleep when the steps paused outside the barred doorway. "You there," a voice barked.

Calvin grunted and wondered suddenly if dissimulation counted as lying.

"You there!"

Calvin flinched at that and pretended to come full awake, though he tried to look groggy and didn't have to fake moving stiffly. He blinked at the man leering at him from outside the bars—and wished he didn't recognize him. As he had assumed, it was one of his tormentors from the night before—the one who'd been with the sheriff when they'd apprehended him. Tall and thin and youngish, he sported a mustache that looked too dark for his fair hair. High-school sneak gone pro, or Calvin couldn't call 'em.

"Police chief says I'm t' get you cleaned up an' move you," the man spat resentfully.

Calvin did not reply but rose obediently, keeping his arms where the deputy could see them. Another gust of breeze assailed his chest (the T-shirt was in even more tatters than he recalled) and he shivered and hoped the gesture would not be misinterpreted.

For his part, the deputy glared at him, rattled keys and locks, and finally got the cell door open. Calvin coughed nervously—and unintentionally—and abruptly found himself staring straight at the muzzle of a Smith and Wesson .38. "Sorry," Calvin murmured quickly, but the apology was met with a deepening of the glare into a full-fledged snarl of contempt as the man motioned him out. He kept the revolver trained on Calvin while he shut the door one-handed.

A short walk down the corridor, and Calvin was ushered into a locker room that appeared to have been cobbled together inside the shell of a much larger restroom. There, with the man looking on with rather more interest than Calvin felt was strictly procedural, he tended to nature's functions, undressed, and stepped into the shower, noting gratefully that his war paint had not survived two transformations. As the cold water beat him to full alertness, Calvin tried not to think about hostile eyes flitting over his bare body, tried instead to arrive at an accurate assessment of his situation.

He *had* to escape—that much was a given. Spearfinger was loose in the woods; he had friends there; and there wasn't a soul around to protect them. Now that he was starting to think clearly again, a part of him took grim comfort from wondering what would happen when bodies kept turning up minus their livers while he was safely stashed away in the hoosegow. Would his captors see sense then, and let him go? Or would another such occurrence merely convince them he was an accomplice to some vast and degenerate mutilation cult? Or might they simply brush the whole grisly affair under the rug, proclaim him guilty, and details be damned? The sheriff and his cronies evidently thought he was their man; the police chief wasn't so certain; and he didn't have a clue which way the coroner was leaning.

More to the point, though, he was worried about Brock and Robyn—and poor Don. The first two might make it okay, if they were smart and boogied on out, but he really had his doubts about Don. Surely the two runaways would take care of him, see him safely to the authorities. If he was lucky, Don'd even help Calvin out of his scrape—*if* they believed him. Calvin's only hope was that he'd somehow be able to get somebody to check out the boy's campsite again and see if any of Allison's prints had survived the morning's rain. If there *were* some and there was some way they could be dated. If . . .

Lord, this was a complicated mess! And a whole lot of its resolution depended on getting people who were used to looking at the world in a certain way to consider it otherwise. But how *did* you prove supernatural intervention? If Calvin'd had his scale, he could have demonstrated quickly enough, but he hadn't seen it since they'd taken it last night, officially, at least, as evidence.

Another thing that might be useful too, was if they could get a geologist in to investigate those stone formations that were so patently unnatural in south Georgia. *Or* maybe get a forensic specialist to examine the wounds on the bodies (he had some hope there). *Or* find someone to analyze that weird doll they'd surely discovered by now. Yeah, now that he thought about it, there were a *lot* of details that could be looked into, but the fact was that people were turning up dead, Calvin was obligingly in the neighborhood and sufficiently unorthodox, and the law was just jumpy enough for the facts to get lost in convenient suppositions.

He wondered what he should do about a lawyer. Maybe Sandy'd have one. He supposed that'd be his one phone call.

But another thought struck him. What about *Dave?* Calvin'd hoped to solve this whole thing without involving his friend, but now . . . what?

"That's enough, boy," the deputy barked. "Get dried off and let's get movin'. Sheriff's gonna want to talk to you later."

Calvin shut off the water and reached for the scratchy, threadbare towel the deputy tossed him. He felt much better now, though his body was a mass of scrapes and bruises and he suddenly found himself vainly wishing he could shapeshift a couple more times and dispose of them the same way his lip was healing.

Once dry, Calvin dressed quickly in the clothes they'd provided for him: cheap jeans, T-shirt, and sneakers. At least it wasn't prison blues—yet.

That done, he was escorted back into the corridor, where the deputy held him at gunpoint while he delivered Calvin's clothes to a hard-faced woman who promptly ducked into a door marked STORAGE/EVIDENCE, whence she soon returned empty-handed.

"Put it with that arrowhead-hickey and that bow and quiver and knife—that all right?"

"Fine," the deputy grunted, and prodded Calvin onward.

Another steel door—this one with some kind of fancy electronic locks attached at both top and bottom—let onto a staircase kinking upward in short flights with frequent landings. But just as he set toe to the first tread, voices sounded somewhere above, quickly rising in anger.

"I don't care *what* procedure is!" a woman was protesting violently. "I wanta see the son-of-a-bitch that killed my baby!"

"Now, Liza-Bet," a familiar male voice replied softly, "you know you're not s'posed to do that."

"Bullshit!"

"Liza-Bet . . ."

"You let me in to see him!"

Some inarticulate mumbling followed, and somebody said it wouldn't do no harm, especially since they were just bringing him up now anyway, and then a door slammed and there were footsteps which quickly grew louder. Calvin and his escort had reached the first-floor landing by then, and through an archway, Calvin glimpsed a hallway and a series of doors open to what were probably offices lit with daylight—the nearest of which was abruptly filled by the guy who'd first discovered the body (Rob, he thought, now in policeman's blues)—and Liza-Bet Scott, whom Calvin had last seen bemoaning the death of her daughter.

Both parties halted awkwardly and abruptly, and for perhaps ten seconds the woman stared at Calvin.

She would have been quite striking, he thought absently, if she hadn't obviously been up all night—he could tell that by the way her eyes were red, and the circles of smeared makeup around them which she'd evidently tried unsuccessfully to remedy. She was shaking and held a cigarette in her hand.

"Where's Don?" she spat abruptly. "Just tell me that one thing: what have you done with Don?"

Robert eased behind her, clasped his arms on her shoulders, and drew her back. "Now, Liza-Bet," he murmured, "you know you're not supposed to talk to 'im.

We're probably violatin' procedure right now! Might wind up with a mistrial, or somethin'."

Calvin said nothing but he regarded the woman calmly, meeting her eyes straight on without flinching. "I haven't done anything to him," he stated quietly. "I've—

"He needs a lawyer," her escort interrupted quickly, urging her away. "They've got one on the way, but he's gotta come from Jesup, and it's gonna take a while."

"I want to call *my* lawyer," Calvin insisted.

Robert raised a warning eyebrow. "All in good time."

"I'm entitled to a call . . .''

"I know," the policeman replied softly, "but—"

"You're a goddamned murderer," Liza-Bet snarled and whirled around, then stamped back down the hall toward a second, closed door.

Robert regarded Calvin apologetically. "Something strange is goin' on, Mr. McIntosh, and I wish to hell you'd help 'em, 'stead of bein' so damned obscure."

"Part of it they wouldn't believe," Calvin told him simply, sensing that this man was not overtly hostile, though he had more reason than most to be. "And the rest I'd need other folks to corroborate."

"We could get 'em," Robert offered.

"It'd be too much of a risk for them," Calvin replied. "They've got problems of their own."

And then his tormentor poked him none-too-gently in the back, and they were off again, up more stairs to a simple barred door (unlocked, Calvin noticed to his surprise, though there was another electronic bolt) which opened upon a short corridor lined with cells five to a side.

Another set of bars slammed in Calvin's face, and he was once more alone. At least this cell—the second on the eastern side—was better than his earlier one: fresh cream walls (though they were pockmarked with paper wads and gum), newish furniture, decent bedding, better light. And there was a sink, a toilet, and a built-in desk, as well as the cot he flopped down on. A few minutes later there was breakfast, served by the same hard-looking woman who had stashed his clothes. Calvin eyed the coffee and doughnuts a little dubiously, wondering if his stomach was up to them, but finally decided to risk it and found the coffee to be surprisingly good—probably from the same Dunkin' Donuts he had spotted on his ride into town.

He asked Old Hardface if he could make a call, but was rewarded with a terse *"I* can't give you permission, I'm just the dispatcher.''

So Calvin had no choice but to sit and wait and wonder—and increasingly, as the minutes dawdled by, to worry about his friends.

Were they still alive, or was he already fretting in vain? Don still hadn't turned up here, but he didn't know what that portended, whether escape, holdup, or death.

Death: *that* brought back memories of Allison. He almost couldn't stand the thought of that pretty little girl lying dead, got an awful sick feeling in his stomach every time that image paraded across his inner eye. But at least he'd never known her when she was alive. Brock, though, and Robyn, and Don—and Dave—them he *did* know: had talked to them, laughed with them, touched them, and felt them aflame with the supple energy of life. The notion that they too might now be lying cold and stiff and empty almost made him gag. That it would be his fault *was* more than he could tolerate. Against his will, he felt his eyes misting.

For God's sake, get a grip *on yourself, McIntosh!* he told himself firmly. *Self-pity won't do* anybody *any good.*

With that, he began once more to consider his options. If he was extremely lucky, the legal system would grind along and get him in contact with a lawyer. (Had they said something about one coming from Jesup? He hardly remembered.) Hopefully, there'd be bail. (Could Sandy afford to post bond for a murderer?) But he had no idea how long that would take, and he imagined Spearfinger would have accomplished her goal long before then.

That left him back at escape, and *that* seemed extremely unlikely—unless he could get thirty seconds alone with his uktena scale.

But *it* was sequestered as evidence, so Hardface had intimated. *Lord,* he hoped they didn't fool with it too much. He could just imagine some lab tech somewhere trying to do analysis on it and cutting himself while he was wishing he was one of the humpin' bunnies in the next cage—and then slam, bam . . . The idea struck Calvin as ludicrous enough to prompt a chuckle, but then noises reached him from the floor below, only a little muffled by distance: doors slamming, shouting, and footsteps running on tile, while a woman (maybe Old Hardface the Food-bringer?) shrieked hysterically, "The little son-of-a-bitch bit me! The little son-of-a-bitch bit the goddamned shit out of me!"

Calvin wondered who the little son-of-a-bitch was and whether the woman had had her shots. More to the point, he wondered whether the "little son-of-a-bitch" had had his.

Chapter XXIII: Frayed Nerves

(Whidden, Georgia— mid-morning)

"Catch him!"

"Where'd he go?"

"Damn! Shit! Fuck! He *bit* me, goddamn it!"

"There he is!"

"Shit!"

Calvin couldn't help perking up at the explosions of shouts and profanity that were wafting their way up from the downstairs offices to his cell. He couldn't tell for certain what was going on, but more doors were slamming and (apparently) being locked; things were falling over (or being pushed)—and at least one of them had to have been a file cabinet, to judge by the volume of the metallic crash and the wails of an unfamiliar female voice shrieking, "I just finished alphabetizin' them records!"

There was also a veritable cacophony of footfalls, one fairly rhythmic and light-sounding, the others (usually accompanied by heavy, uncomfortable grunts) those of larger bodies bouncing off things and each other. Calvin heard glass shatter; the lights flickered and went out—and then, abruptly, there was silence. Curiosity having gotten the best of him, he padded to the cell door and peered outside.

"Where'd he go?" a man yelled from somewhere directly beneath Calvin's feet. Calvin had no trouble understanding him, though his words were muffled by a thump and the rattling of a lock a fair bit closer.

"Shit if I know, I thought *you* had 'im."

"Where'd he come from, anyway?"

"Hell-if-*I*-know!"

"Hell, you *better* know!"

"I—"

"Shit! He's locked the goddamned door!"

An alarm began to shriek and bells to clang, all accompanied by the nasty buzz of something electrical shorting out. The sharp, bitter odor of ozone filled the air even on the second floor, and Calvin found himself gazing out into a gloomy corridor bathed only in the dim light of the thunderous sky diffusing through cell windows. Even the red-eye of the electronic security system on the barred stairwell door was out, and Calvin could tell by the crack of light dimly visible at one side that it hadn't been closed properly in the first place, which meant it had probably *never* worked correctly—which in turn implied that the locals rarely dealt with really dangerous prisoners. That *might* give him an advantage.

And below, chaos exploded once more:

"What the *fuck?*"

"Little son-of-a-bitch must've pulled the fire alarm."

"Fire alarm, *hell!* Must've pulled the *circuit* breaker!"

"My computer!" the woman wailed again.

"Marvin, you get that goddamned door open an' I'll check downstairs. Abner, you get a flashlight and investigate up top. Shit . . . son-of-a-bitch! We gotta get some friggin' *light* in here!"

"I ain't *got* no friggin' flashlight!"

Calvin couldn't resist a grin. Someone had evidently set his captors into a top-notch tizzy.

That was when he saw the stairwell door slowly open and a hunched-over shadow appear there.

For a moment Calvin's heart stuck in his throat, for the

outline was humpbacked and shrunken, exactly like Spear-finger. He suddenly realized, too, that the walls of his prison were stone and there was probably no reason in the world that the hag couldn't make her way there through the earth, rise up through them, and come at him that way. But then the shadow moved again, and he heard its steps, and they sounded too light, too sure, to be his adversary's.

And then a boy's voice whispered hoarsely from the wall beside his door. "Calvin? Hey, Cal, man it's me, Brock!"

"Brock! Jesus, guy, what're *you* doin' here?"

"Tryin' to rescue you," the boy replied breathlessly, glancing over his shoulder. "I've locked 'em out downstairs, but I've only got about a minute 'fore they do in the door."

And with that the shadow moved to the other side of the bars and Calvin got a good look at the boy.

He was wearing the oiliest, scuzziest jeans and T-shirt Calvin had ever seen, had smeared every visible bit of skin with either dirt or ashes—and had somehow become a brunette in the bargain, probably by the application of spray-dye, to judge by the trace of chemical odor that lingered around his dull-looking hair.

"Like my disguise?" Brock asked eagerly, grinning like a fool. "I was afraid they'd recognize me, so I had to kinda switch things around."

"You better get the hell outta here!"

"No, man, I've gotta get *you* out. The"—he swallowed nervously—"the ground's poundin' again!"

"Shit!"

"Yeah. It's part of it, ain't it? The ground poundin'? Part of the magic."

"Yeah."

A pause, then: "I know about you. I—"

A lock clicked, a door creaked, and footsteps sounded in the hall, slow and fumbly. Calvin and Brock held their breath, but the steps receded down the stairs—evidently in quest of the fuse box.

"What'd you *do*, anyway?" Calvin wondered.

A low chuckle. "Knocked the water cooler over into

the computer terminal. It wasn't grounded or nothin'. Then zipped into the hall, locked the door behind me, and pulled a bunch of switches. And *then* I locked—''

"*All* that?''

"Don told me how. I—''

More steps, and a light flared fitfully at the foot of the stairs. Abner had apparently located a flashlight.

"Quick! How can I help?''

"Find the scale,'' Calvin whispered urgently. "It's in the basement somewhere: room marked STORAGE. There's some kinda secret tunnel between here and the court-house—that's where they interrogated me. Now get the hell *outta* here!''

"Figured as much.'' Brock nodded. "I—''

The flashlight beam lanced up toward the second-floor landing. Brock flung himself in one smooth leap to the sliver of wall beside the stairwell door, just as a head poked cautiously into the corridor. The boy flattened against the stone, melting into shadow.

Calvin wrenched off a shoe and flung it skittering down the hall in the opposite direction from the stairs.

The figure—sure enough, it was Abner—dashed into the corridor, revolver poised in one hand while his flash-light prodded the far shadows with the other—and thereby missed Brock, probably because Abner was not expecting his quarry to be so close.

Until it was too late.

As soon as Abner's back had cleared the doorway, Brock dived for the opening, careening into the startled deputy with enough force to set him staggering. The man swore, half-danced a series of steps farther into the hall, then whirled, sending flashlight beams everywhere. Calvin caught the glint of a .38 and hoped Brock wasn't so fool-hardy as to go up against something like that.

But the boy was gone, though a final explosion of shouts from downstairs gave proof that he was not forgotten:

"There he is *again!*''

"Catch him!''

"Damn, I *missed!*''

And then the lights came on, only to flicker off once more and stay that way.

"*You're* still here, anyway," the deputy growled, when he saw Calvin staring calmly through the cell door. "Get back over there and set down!"

Calvin complied obediently, but he could tell that the man was giving the whole corridor a thorough once-over. In less than a minute he was back, holding Calvin's decoy shoe at arm's length as though he expected it to bite him. He dropped it onto the floor outside the cell and kicked it through the bars to him.

"You know anything 'bout this?"

Calvin picked up the sneaker and scrutinized it with exaggerated care before slipping it back on. "It's my shoe," he stated flatly. "Or technically, the shoe you gave me to wear."

"Don't get smart, boy!" the deputy snapped. "You mind tellin' me what it's doin' at the end of the hall?"

"I threw it at something."

"At what?"

"The floor and the wall."

"I'm warnin' you boy! Mr. *Po*lice Chief ain't 'round here now."

"I'm tellin' you the exact truth."

"You know that boy that 'uz up here?"

"Yes."

"Who is he?"

"A friend of mine."

"What's his name?"

"I don't know." Which was the truth: Calvin had never learned Brock's legal name, but he hoped this grilling ended quickly, because he was afraid that sooner or later this dim bulb would ask him something he couldn't answer with an evasion and still be truthful.

"What'd he want?"

"To see me."

"He some kind of accomplice?"

"Not by my choice."

"Shit! You a *liar,* boy!"

"No," Calvin countered calmly. "I absolutely am not."

"You got a plan?"

"No." Which was also true, technically. He had desires, but no clear idea how to execute them. That did not constitute a plan in his book.

"What'd you tell him?'

"I can't remember, exactly."

The man's eyes narrowed suspiciously. "What about *other* than exactly?"

"It wouldn't be smart for me to say."

"I'll tell you what'd be *smart,*" Abner snarled, pushing his face up close to the bars. "It'd be *smart* for you to watch your mouth. It'd be *real* easy to mistake you for a rat in this light. And we *shoot* rats 'round here."

"You'd have a problem, then."

"Why's that?"

" 'Cause then who'd you blame when folks kept turning up dead without their livers?"

"Abner, you okay?" a voice shouted up from the floor below.

"Yeah, I reckon," Abner called back.

"Then get your skinny ass down here and help us pick up this goddamn file cabinet!" A pause, and then nearly as loudly, to the folks in the sheriff's office, "No, that's okay, sheriff; reckon the little son-of-a-bitch got clean away."

"Right!" Abner called back, then aimed a searing glare at Calvin. "I'll be seein' *you* again right soon, never fear."

The rustle of something slithering through the bank of kudzu ten yards to her right made Robyn start. She swallowed nervously and peered out from where she'd been avoiding the current sprinkle in one of the range of bricked-in archways that comprised the lowest level on the back side of the old Whidden Hotel, but found her view blocked by a stack of two-by-four scaffolding. (The building was presently undergoing a lull in restoration and the supporting clutter of construction materials and equipment in its long-neglected hinder regions made it an ideal base for clandestine activities—when it was not obstructing Robyn's line of sight.) Leaning against a granite pillar across from her, Don merely added apprehension to his already grim and unhappy expression. "What?" he began. "I—"

Robyn had just raised a finger to shush him to silence when a final scrabbling ended in a frustrated grunt and indecipherable mutter that was probably profane. She gave herself a mental kick in the butt for being so jumpy. It was only her brother, failing at stealth at last. For his part, Don simply exhaled slowly and looked relieved.

"Your turn, sis." Brock grinned from under the coat of grime he'd had so much fun applying twenty minutes before. It was rain-streaked now, and he looked even scruffier than when Calvin had seen him.

"Took you long enough," Robyn snorted. "What'd you find out?"

Brock eased in beside them and casually commenced removing the clothing he had liberated from an unmonitored dumpster near the point where the railroad track crossed the town line. He seemed enormously pleased with himself.

"What about *Calvin?*" Robyn persisted. "You *did* find him, didn't you?"

"It's 'bout what Don told us to expect," Brock panted, tugging on fresh jeans. "They've got him in a cell on the second floor. He looks okay, but he's *real* worried, you can tell. The rest is just like we figured: he ain't escaped 'cause he don't have his scale. That's what we've gotta get."

"What *I've* gotta get," Robyn corrected sourly.

"It was your choice that I check things out," Brock told her, looking up for an instant before applying himself to the grime on his face and arms with considerable assist from the drizzle.

"Fortunately," he continued, "Don was right about their security bein' really sloppy. All I had to do was wander in and look homeless and lost, and then ask 'em where my mother was, and keep my eyes open while I got the lay of the land. But then they started askin' me stuff I couldn't answer real good, and then I tried to split, but one grabbed me, and I bit her."

"What *kinda* stuff?"

"Oh, just my name and all."

"What'd you tell 'em?"

"That I didn't remember. I was tryin' to play poor little shell-shocked runaway. Made a big deal outta suddenly actin' scared, like, and tryin' to get away. 'Accidentally' knocked a bunch of stuff over, and then tipped the water cooler over on a computer and shorted the lights out. After that it was a cinch to zip into the hall, lock the doors, and trash the fuse box and fire alarm."

"Oh, so *that's* what all those bells and whistles were about? We could hear 'em even down here."

Brock grinned so wide Robyn thought the top of his head would fall off. "Yeah. Neat, huh?"

"Yeah," Don echoed. "So they were exactly where I told you, right?"

"Dead on—good thing your mom's fellow gave you that tour that time."

"Yeah," Don chuckled in spite of himself. "Told me every way there was to break into that jail. Bet he never thought I'd use it against him, though!"

"So where *is* the scale?" Robyn inquired pointedly.

"Downstairs somewhere: room marked STORAGE."

"Well, *that's* just great! How'll I get down *there?*"

Brock frowned abruptly. "Well," he began, "that may be kinda complicated. I guess I better draw you a picture."

"Get at it then, before I lose my nerve."

Brock stuck his tongue out at his sister and picked up a piece of rusty rebar with which he began sketching in a sheltered pile of sand. Before Brock's mission Don had already drawn a gridwork like a tic-tac-toe board, but now Brock was filling some of the squares with smaller ones. "Okay," he began, indicating the top-middle section: "We're here behind this old hotel, graveyard's to the left, depot to the right." He paused to inscribe a prickly-looking line above the map. "These are the railroad tracks we followed in, and right beyond them's the river."

"I'm *not* stupid," Robyn noted sarcastically. "Besides, Don already told us that much."

''Just gettin' you oriented,'' Brock went on patiently, pointing to the rectangle inside the central square. ''Courthouse's in the middle—that's the funny-lookin' buildin' with the tower. Jail's to the right—the east, I guess. Entrance to the west, toward the courthouse. Calvin's on the second floor—that's up one flight of stairs—but the stairs go down at least one level below the street, too, which would jibe with what Calvin said 'bout there bein' a tunnel between the jail and the courthouse.''

''A *tunnel!*'' Don slapped his forehead in frustration. ''Shoot, yeah! I *forgot* about that, or you coulda probably used *it* to get at Calvin.''

Brock regarded him incredulously. ''You *know* about it?''

Don shrugged. ''Everybody's *heard* of it, but not many folks know for sure, 'cause I don't think it's really supposed to be there—or to be used. I think it was part of the Underground Railroad, or something, 'cept that they supposedly closed it up when they redid the courthouse back in the fifties 'cause it wasn't on a public level. Rob showed me a door that was s'posed to go to it that time he gave me that tour and all; but he said he didn't have a key or nothin'. I don't think he was supposed to talk about it anyway; leastwise he looked kinda funny when he mentioned it to me, like he'd slipped up or somethin', and he made me promise not to tell.''

''So much for promises,'' Brock inserted, winking at his sister.

''Yeah, but that still doesn't tell *me* how to get to the basement—since you've pretty well blown the direct approach!''

''Yes it does!'' Don countered, more perkily than heretofore. '' 'Cause if there *is* a tunnel from the jail to the courthouse, that's where it comes out! That's where the door Rob showed me is.''

Brock's face was a-beam. ''All *right!*'' he crowed.

Robyn regarded them dubiously. ''So all I've gotta do is get myself out from behind this derelict hotel without being noticed, then get into either the jail or the courthouse without attracting attention, then find a scale in a

three-story building, and *then* get it to somebody on the
second floor of a jail . . .''

"Piece of cake.''

"Bullshit!''

"*Sis!*''

Robyn glared at him. "I'll do it,'' she snapped, "just
to show you I can!''

"Go to,'' Brock challenged gleefully.

"Just as soon as it stops raining,'' Robyn told him. She
rummaged in her backpack until she pulled out a bar of
soap, which she handed to her brother. "Now why don't
you see if you can get your golden locks back like they
oughta be again.''

"Yeah,'' Brock chuckled. "They'll be lookin' for a
dirty little black-haired kid, and they'll get a squeaky-clean
blond one instead.''

As if it were a spotlight highlighting his impending
transformation, the sun chose that moment to finally slide
from behind the heavy clouds—though it was still driz-
zling steadily, and looked even more threatening to the
north and east.

Brock glanced at it hopefully. "Good omen?''

A shrug from Robyn. "Calvin'd probably say so.''

"So what're you waitin' on?'' Don asked edgily, and
Robyn could sense him drawing into himself again. That
was bad too, for as long as he was busy—helping them
shift camp, or hiking here, or planning Calvin's escape—
he was okay. But she wondered what would happen when
he finally had time alone.

"Sis?'' Brock prompted.

Robyn sighed. "Nothin', I reckon,'' she replied, "I
guess I'm off to the wars. Brock . . . soon as you get your
hair clean you probably oughta sneak up top and keep an
eye out from the shadows, just in case anything happens.
And, Don . . .'' She paused, staring at the boy thoughtfully, not wishing to leave him alone, nor yet to place him
in a situation where he might be noticed—though they'd
all agreed that he *would* go to the cops if their wild plan
hadn't borne fruit by dark. "Don,'' she repeated, "I guess
you oughta hang out down here until we get back. But if

we're *not* back in, say, an hour . . . you probably oughta just go ahead and turn yourself in and tell what you know, 'cause they'll have us by then anyway.''

Don nodded absently and sat down, his back firmly lodged against his security pillar.

"Sorry," Robyn apologized, "but it's the best I can do in a pinch.''

"Like I said, I'm tough," Don mumbled dully, and fell silent.

Robyn sighed once more, and—after a bit of additional discussion during which she clarified Brock's observations and Don's directions as well as she could—made her way nonchalantly up the opposite bank from the one Brock had used, then darted across the side street and entered the graveyard from the hotel side. The main gate was to her left; the courthouse diagonally beyond it. Robyn took a deep breath and started toward them.

"Uh . . . excuse me," Robyn whispered five minutes later, "but I . . . uh . . . could you, like, point me to a *restroom?*"

The gray-haired man behind the tag-office window looked up at her wearily and motioned to his right. "Down the hall, it's marked.''

Robyn nodded and cast a glance back toward the glass doors through which she had entered the west end of the courthouse. *A storeroom in the basement of the jail, huh?* And one she had to get to via a secret tunnel. Shoot! Might as well have been a needle in a haystack. Still, if Brock had the balls to make a shambles of the jail, she supposed she could do no less to the courthouse.

"Down the hall," the man repeated, and Robyn realized she'd been standing there gawking—which might attract suspicion, the last thing in the world she needed.

"Thanks," she mumbled, and trotted off. She made a show of going into the ladies' room, remained there perhaps a minute, then reemerged, trying to look irritated and uncomfortable, which did not in fact take much effort. An instant later she was back before the tag window.

"Yes?"

"Uh, I'm sorry, but . . . well, I've got a . . . a *female* problem, and the *machine's*, like, *empty.* Is there maybe another . . ."

"Upstairs."

"Thanks."

Good, her plan was working, Robyn thought, as she made her way toward the staircase to the right of the door. Nobody'd think anything about somebody roaming around the building looking confused now—or if they did, she had a witness to her rationale. With possible opening lines still jumbling through her head, she strolled casually into the stairwell, then made a very loud and obvious show of going upstairs but only paused at the first landing and slipped quietly down again, not exiting this time on the main floor. A quick check showed at least two underground levels—the topmost with more offices and such, their windowsills level with the lawn—but the stairs continued down another flight to terminate in a gray steel door that read SUB-BASEMENT: MAINTENANCE STAFF ONLY.

She hesitated there, fingering the flashlight in her purse and wondering if this level was more or less analogous to the basement of the jail; and—more to the point—if what Robert had told Don about the connecting tunnel was even true.

Well, there was no way she'd find out without looking. Taking a deep breath, Robyn twisted the doorknob. It did not move, but fortunately had one of those simple sort of locks that acquiesced easily under the assault of a determined credit card, in which art she'd had considerable practice at various summer camps. An instant later, Robyn found herself peering around the doorjamb into a long, dim chamber filled with boilers and pipes and humming machinery. Blessedly, the space was not brightly lighted, and a lot of what *was* present was blocked and dimmed by the plethora of machinery, so she felt relatively secure scouting along the perimeter. Assuming Don's hasty instructions *were* accurate, there ought to be some sort of opening on the other side leading to the tunnel that ran to the basement of the jail. She only had to navigate the length of the room to find out.

And twice more luck was with her, for there was no one minding the place, and the door she wanted was in plain sight of the other side, again simply noted as STAFF ONLY, and again secured with an easily carded lock.

Another deep breath, a furtive peek through the door, and Robyn was squinting into a long brick-walled corridor whose damp mustiness and general air of decay hinted that it was both old and infrequently used. There were no lights on, nor did there seem to be much provision for any, and Robyn almost couldn't believe her luck in finding it also empty. She was almost starting to believe her plan—"I was only lookin' for the bathroom, officer, and I got lost"—might succeed. It was a *long* corridor, though, maybe a hundred yards or so, and it sloped gradually upward, so that her feeble flashlight beam went to diffusion without ever reaching the opposite wall. And she wondered what purpose it had served—probably no legal ones, but whether it had been built for clandestine Klan activities, Prohibition foolishness, or even, as Don had intimated, the Underground Railroad, she had no idea.

Nor did it matter. What was important was getting through it and into the basement of the jail as quickly and quietly as she could. Her footsteps would be loud on the bare floor, so she slipped off her shoes and padded softly along the damp stones toward the other end of the tunnel, where another, newer door glimmered. She paused there to catch her breath and steel herself, and had the presence of mind to press her ear to it before trying the grimy handle. As best she could tell, there were no sounds at all from nearby, but a fair number of raised and/or irate voices filtering down through the ceiling indicated some sort of ongoing chaos one floor up.

And to her surprise, the door opened at her touch— evidently it had had some sort of electronic lock that had lost its grip when Brock's ruse had overloaded the wiring. Another corridor greeted her, this one much newer and cleaner, and to her everlasting relief, the second door she passed was marked STORAGE/EVIDENCE. Its lock yielded to a deft touch with a credit card as well and Robyn ducked inside. A rank of metal shelves faced her, most piled with uniforms or bits of gear, but one labeled, unmistakably, EVIDENCE.

A hasty inventory of the baskets—there were only ten, of which nine were empty—and she found Calvin's clothes. Right on top were his knife and the uktena scale, still on its thong. An instant later, the scale was in her pocket. She considered collecting the knife along with it, and actually picked it up before deciding it might be a little *too* obvious if she were apprehended. Reluctantly she put it back.

Now came the hard part. She'd hoped, by taking the back way in—the way most folks weren't supposed to know about—to come upon the jail from its unprotected underbelly. Now she had to get the scale to the prisoner and hope she wasn't caught. A quick survey of the hallway outside showed it still empty, and a dimly-lit rectangle at the end indicated the entrance to a flight of stairs. She paused to put her shoes back on, then squared her shoulders and marched purposefully toward the stairs. There was enough noise going on above that her footfalls were lost in the shouts and scrapes, and so it was that she made the second landing—halfway home—without being noticed. The power still wasn't on, and apparently they were conducting business either with lanterns or by the scanty daylight filtering in through the jail's narrow windows. But as she started up the next flight she found herself face-to-foot with a harried-looking policeman. He froze for an instant, stared rather stupidly at the top of her head, then recovered. "What're *you* doin' in here?" But it was more surprise than demand.

Robyn tried to look flustered and shocked. "Oh jeeze, man," she began, "like, this isn't the way to the *rest-room*, is it? Like, they told me over *there*" (and here she waved in some vague direction) "that it was, like, down the stairs and to the right, and I started goin' and got lost and then the light went out and there was all these, like, pipes and *things*, and . . ." She stopped in mid-sentence and tried to look unhappy and scared and imploring. "I've *really* gotta go, man!"

The cop, already frazzled, looked taken aback, and

pointed back the way he had come. "Through there, door to your left. But be careful, we've had a power outage, and—"

"Yeah, *tell* me about it, man," Robyn interrupted. "Like, I was tryin' to find a place to . . . you know?"

"Yeah," replied the cop, obviously baffled. "I know." And with that, he edged past her and continued his descent.

"Thanks," Robyn called after him, executing a little twist, as if she couldn't hold it any longer, but once more proceeded up the stairs. She let her feet slap hard the first part of the climb, then tiptoed quietly past the chaos of the offices and up to the second story.

A barred door greeted her there. She peered through it and saw a corridor lined with cells, exactly like Brock had described.

Let's see, she thought. *Calvin's in the second one to the left*. But how to get his attention? There was no hope for it; she'd have to call and hope no one else heard.

"Calvin," she hissed. "Ca—"

She did not need to risk further summons because the Indian appeared at the entrance to the second set of bars almost as if he had teleported there. He raised his finger to his lips and made hushing motions, then sketched a question mark in the air. She nodded and brandished the scale. He stuck his arm through the bars and mimed her throwing it. She hesitated, uncertain of her skill, but finally took a deep breath and flung it skittering along the floor.

Almost she missed, but Calvin strained his reach to the limit and managed to snag the thong with a fingertip. Robyn held her breath until he had reeled it in. She nodded; he mouthed *thanks*. And she turned and headed back down the stairs.

The man was still there, fooling with the fuse box with a flashlight. She came up behind him, making no secret of her presence now. "Like, *where'd* you say that restroom was?" she whined. "I *really* gotta go."

"*Next* landing, turn *left*," the man repeated, exasperated and preoccupied.

"Oh, *left,*" Robyn echoed dumbly, and started up the stairs again. This time she entered a darkened hallway, the left side of which was evidently (to judge by the signs) the domain of the Whidden Police, while the right was home of the Willacoochee Sheriff's Department. The only open door was to the right, and she went that way—and blundered into the chaos that still reigned in Sheriff Wilson Lexington's main office. A hard-looking woman noticed her immediately, and Robyn noted with an ill-suppressed smirk that she had a bandaged hand. Robyn made the preemptive strike, though. "Guy downstairs said, there was a restroom up here?"

"Where'd *you* come from?" Hardface muttered suspiciously.

"Got lost, and then the power went off and I got loster and wound up in, like, a *bunch* of tunnels and all."

The woman did not look convinced. "It's right over here," she barked. "But you've been in unauthorized areas. I'll have to search you goin' in and comin' out."

"Far out," Robyn said without conviction.

"I'll *teach* you far out if you ain't careful," the woman informed her.

Robyn had no choice but to allow herself to be escorted into the restroom, no option but to allow herself and her purse to be thoroughly examined (fortunately she'd left her real ID and credit cards with Brock; the ID in the billfold was one of several fakes she' procured just in case), and no alternative but to allow the procedure to be repeated again when she had performed her stated function.

As she marched back out into the morning light of Whidden, Georgia, she hoped Calvin appreciated what she was doing for him. She hoped he appreciated it a hell of a lot.

Chapter XXIV: Breaking Point

(behind the old Whidden Hotel— mid-morning)

Don was beginning to wonder if he was as tough as he had thought he was when he'd assured Robyn and Brock that he'd be okay if they left him alone long enough to conclude their quest for the scale. He'd said it before, too: when they'd first set out to shift camp prior to coming to town. But it was one thing to make that kind of assertion in the middle of the night when you were tired and sleepy and shell-shocked, because then the whole thing seemed unreal—like the journey to Calvin's camp had seemed unreal: a trek with two silent, moody ghosts among tree-shaped shadows. But now, in the clear light of day with the leavings of the brief morning shower still dripping fitfully off the crumbling cornices above him and the odd sprinkle still making circular interference patterns in the muddy pools behind the derelict hotel, he was beginning to have misgivings.

Somewhere in the brief time since his keepers had departed he had dozed off, scrunched into the blind arcade with his back to a pillar of rough-hewn stone. He had not dreamed, that he knew of, but when he had awakened, it had all come rushing back to him with such force that it almost overwhelmed him.

Last night was *not* a dream. None of it was. The sun was up—battling it out with bouts of shower and winning. The air was clear and tasted fresh and well-scrubbed, and for once was free of the underscent of sulfur.

And his best friend and baby sister were dead.

That was an absolute. But every time he forced himself to think about it, his mind sort of slipped sideways from accepting it. *Fact:* he *would* never see either of them again. *Fact:* he would never fight with Allison over the dishes; had had his last tickle-battle with Michael. *Fact:* there'd be no more arguments over the TV set on Sunday night with his sis; no more exchanges of confidences with his almost-bro. *Fact:* no more sister's first date to ridicule (but secretly look forward to); no more forestry school with Michael. No, he had to face it now, look it straight in the eyes and not flinch: *all* those *ifs* and *maybes* and *mights* were gone. Absent. Finished. *Over.* And he was alive, but so empty he might as well have been dead, because he felt as if someone had reached into his chest in the night and scooped out two enormous holes that could never be filled.

No more . . .

No more *nothing*.

For a long time Don stared out at the railroad tracks and the river beyond, all lit by the sun of what was turning into a remarkably pretty morning—and tried to think of nothing. He didn't know whether he was hot or cold, wet or dry. He cared not a whit if the wetness on his cheeks was rain or tears. He simply wanted with all his heart not to *be*.

At some point he closed his eyes and actually tried to accomplish that: to merge his body back into the stone pillar, to will his legs to melt into the ground, to send his spirit floating off into space. That way he would not have to confront the hard fact that eventually Brock and Robyn would return, having succeeded or failed, and that sooner or later he would have to leave this island of security and find out what was going on with his mom (she'd need him, he supposed, now that her favorite was gone), and that not very long after *that* he'd have to go to a pair of funerals. Somewhere in there, too, he'd be asked some questions that he knew absolutely he would not be able to answer and be believed.

Maybe they'd just decide he belonged on the funny farm and lock him up, and maybe that wouldn't be such a bad idea. Maybe that would be very close to not being, and would save him from ever having to make decisions again.

Maybe—

It was then that Don noticed that the ground was very softly, very gently, beginning to thrum once more, as if someone, miles distant, was pounding on a drum whose skin was the whole wide world.

For a moment he sat very still and listened, but then, so suddenly he could not have anticipated it until it actually happened, the vibrations that were slowly filtering their way through his bones somehow merged with the fear-born chills they had awakened, so that, quite abruptly, he leapt to his feet—and yelled.

The pain was an edge of reality in his throat, a paean of life in his ears. But it was not enough.

He *had* to get back home, *had* to check on Mom, *had* to have more comfort than Brock and Robyn and Calvin could provide . . .

Without consciously willing it, he found himself trotting toward the railroad tracks that had brought him into town.

An instant later he had crossed the river on the trestle and was confronting the woods, oblivious to Brock's frantic cries far behind.

The thrumming grew louder, and with it came a suggestion of melody . . .

Chapter XXV: Changing Times

(the jail—Whidden, Georgia— mid-morning)

Calvin had about decided he believed in luck after all. What *else* could explain the fact that Brock had actually managed to contact him, and even more remarkably, that Robyn had beyond all expectation succeeded in retrieving the uktena scale?

Trouble was, luck had two sides: good and bad; and no sooner had he managed to snare the talisman and secrete it in his pocket than he heard irate voices, and footsteps were once more clumping up the hall toward the stairs—which meant that he didn't dare *change* right then—not and risk losing the scale all over again, never mind the questions his peculiar concern for it might prompt his captors to ask. Indeed, too much of *that* could very well exchange one sort of captivity for another. No more jail (if they believed his explanation, or if he actually *changed* in front of them); but years, perhaps, of being poked and prodded by frustrated scientists would certainly be just as bad.

Which meant he had to hide the damned thing, and do it fast.

Someone was on the stairs now—which gave him about ten seconds. He scanned the bare room frantically.

Not on his person, that was for certain; they'd be sure to check there first, and ditto the bed. The corners? Still too obvious, and likewise the window.

No, wait: the window was open beyond its grillwork (it *was* summer, after all), and he didn't need the thong and wire loops, so he could dispose of them that way. And fortunately the cell, though clean, was not in perfect repair, so that occasionally globs of gum or cement or plaster dotted the walls, at least one of the former of which was relatively fresh and ready to hand. Moving as quickly as he ever had in his life, Calvin untangled the scale from the silver wires that bound it, smeared it with gum, and smacked it into the corner of the doorway directly above a hinge, then dashed back to the cot, leapt atop it, and tossed the thong and binding through the high window above—just as he heard the hall door being unlocked. (They'd rightly gotten paranoid about that, now that it was too late to do them any good).

He had barely gotten himself composed in the chair when Deputy Moncrief sauntered into view beyond the bars. He glared at Calvin, trying to look threatening, while Calvin simply tried to appear alert and expectant and guileless, and tried *not* to let his gaze drift toward the scale. One good thing, at least; if they were searching for something, they wouldn't know what it was, so he might have the upper hand there.

"You ain't had any more *visitors* lately, have you?" the man inquired in a tone that indicated he already knew the answer.

"No," Calvin replied, choosing to interpret *visitor* in the narrowest possible definition, and ditto for *lately*.

The deputy regarded him dubiously. "You *sure* 'bout that?"

"No."

An eyebrow shot up.

"You wanta explain that?"

"No."

The other eyebrow joined its fellow, and the man's lip

stuck out so far he looked like a Ubangi woman. "Well," he drawled, glancing sideways, as if fearing observation, "I reckon I don't have no *choice* but to check you out myself, then, 'cause we sure did have an unexpected visitor just now—that makes two, if I can count. So," he added, as he fumbled out keys with one hand and his revolver with the other, and somehow managed to get the door open between them, "why don't you just start by gettin' outta them clothes—just in case you might be, you know, *hidin'* something?"

Calvin rolled his eyes but complied, starting with his shoes and scooting each article toward the guard with a foot as he removed it. The man would pick them up, knead them carefully with one hand, and toss them to the floor behind him, but his eyes never left Calvin, and the revolver never wavered. Finally, for the second time in about an hour, Calvin was as bare as the day he was born, and stood staring at the man quizzically, hoping thereby to keep him as off base as he could.

"Raise 'em and spread 'em," the man barked. Calvin did, and suffered the less obvious regions of his body to be inspected with the cold barrel of the .38.

"Open your mouth!"

Once again, Calvin acquiesced, thinking maybe this guy was sharper than he'd first thought—and *knowing* he was a lot more sadistic.

"Well, I reckon you *are* empty," the man muttered finally, as if disappointed. "Now why don't you just get yourself over there in the corner while I check out the rest of this shit?"

Calvin could only watch helplessly while the guard stripped the cot of its single sheet and blanket, upended the mattress, examined all the seams, then shone his flashlight along every edge of the room, including the corners of the doorway. He almost caught himself holding his breath then, which would probably have been a dead giveaway, but the man's eyes passed right on over the glob.

Finally satisfied, though still suspicious-looking, the deputy turned and glared at Calvin. "I *ain't* convinced," he spat. "But I reckon we'll just keep a real close eye on you for a while. Won't be here long anyway, so I've heard; seems they're transferrin' you up to Atlanta.''

"Can I get dressed now?" Calvin asked, not having to fake a chill, for the front that had brought the rain was still heaving the odd gust of wind through the window.

"Not till I get outta here," the deputy grunted.

And that was not quickly enough for Calvin.

As soon as the door clanged behind the man's khakied back, Calvin picked up his skivvies and slipped them on, then reached for his jeans. So they were onto him, huh? Knew something was up? That meant he'd have to act fast, and never mind what Brock had told him about the ground trembling, or what he already knew about Spearfinger's intentions, which only added to the urgency.

But still, it was probably wise to hold off a little while, in the event his captors reappeared suddenly, hoping to catch him at whatever *it* it was they suspected him of.

So Calvin returned to the chair and began to count backward from three hundred, and prayed no one else would have business with him.

It was the longest five minutes of his life.

When he had finished, he rose nonchalantly, sauntered to the door, and peered out, letting his hand slide absently up the doorjamb to the wad of gum, like he was just sort of casually leaning up against the stonework there. Good, he had it, and there was no one in sight. Now if his luck would hold one more minute . . .

Not bothering to undress again, for the shape he had already chosen would be small enough to slip out of the clothes with ease, Calvin sat back down on the bed, took three deep breaths to calm himself and clear his mind, then folded his hand around the scale.

Cat, he thought, because he had to be small, and something domestic would attract the least attention. (The caveat about having to change into creatures one had eaten—presumably so you could absorb their genetic imprint—didn't apply because he'd at least tasted just about everything there was, including, on a dare when he was a kid, a bit of roadkill tabby.)

The only alternative had been some sort of bird—a par-

tridge, say. But he'd have had to become a *very* small one
to slip through the grillwork on the window (his customary
falcon, for instance, was too large). Of course, he could
also have *flown* through the building until he found an
open window or door, but something about that likewise
gave him pause. Too many ceiling fans for one thing, too
many moving objects that could break fragile bones—too
many unfamiliar reflexes to assimilate in too close a space.
He was also—he forced himself to admit—extremely leery
of becoming anything *that* small. Something cat-sized he
thought he could manage.

Cat . . . cat . . . cat . . .

Small and sleek and soft-moving; pointed ears and slit-
ted green eyes and exquisitely sharp teeth—and claws that
were even sharper. Calvin tried to imagine himself on all
fours with a fine furred plume sprouting from the base of
his spine and his body twisting and arching.

Cat . . . cat . . . cat . . .

Calvin squeezed harder, until blood ran from his fist,
but the pain of transformation did not come.

Cat . . . cat . . . cat . . .

More pain, and a tighter squeeze, and the roots of the
scale grated against bone.

But no *change.*

The scale wasn't working.

Finally Calvin gave up in disgust.

Fifteen minutes later Calvin was still staring skeptically
at his hand. The scale was secreted in his shoe now, but
he wondered why he'd bothered, since it obviously didn't
function anymore, even after he'd removed every trace of
gum from it, in case *that* was what had been preventing it
from effecting the *change.*

Which left him back where he had been half an hour
ago, except that then he'd had hope and now he had none.
He was stuck here, forced to sit helplessly while people
he cared about were in serious danger. All because he had
trusted too much to magic, and not enough to the law of
the land. The police chief seemed to be a reasonable guy
after all, and he suspected that Robert fellow might give

him a fair hearing as well. Maybe he should have had faith
enough in one or the other to tell them the truth and where
to find evidence to back up his assertions.

Of course, he reflected, he would have looked pretty
stupid explaining to them he was a skinchanger and then
offering to prove it if they'd only give him the scale—
whereupon he would have failed and looked either stupid
or crazy, and have provided even more grist for any one
of several unpleasant mills he could already hear grinding.

But that brought him back to the scale and to curiosity.
Why *had* it failed? Was there a limit to how much it could
do, or how many times it could be used for a certain purpose? Perhaps it was like a battery—and like any battery,
it had only a certain amount of magical fizz and then would
run no more. That it worked at all was something of a
surprise, in fact, given that it had its origin in Galunlati—
though now he thought of it, Uki had once made some
reference to the uktena magic being born partly of this
World.

But this World had magic, too; you just had to be receptive to it. After all, Calvin had been born in this World
and yet had changed skin. Sure, he'd had magical aid, but
it had been *his* flesh and blood, *his* iron/calcium/carbon
oxides that had undergone that metamorphosis, *his*
thoughts that had altered his bones, *his* genes that had
reconstructed him more perfectly than before. He *knew*
how to shapeshift, dammit. He just needed the proper
stimulus.

He searched his memory frantically. What had he been
doing differently those other times? Well, for one thing, he'd
been under duress each time, and—No, he *hadn't,* he'd been
perfectly relaxed that time by the river when he'd tried to
change only in part, so that wasn't it.

So how was that different from what he had just attempted? How was it unlike wishing to be a cat?

Well, he *had* been wishing, for one thing, and perhaps
that was important, because while he *thought* he had been
wishing to be a cat, he was beginning to discover that your
mind sometimes had its own hidden agenda, and if you
thought you were desiring one thing, you might in fact be

hoping for another (like simply to be out of a situation), which could probably screw you up real good if what you were attempting involved much concentration—as it did to become anything significantly smaller.

So where did that leave him? Either the scale really wasn't working; or it *was* working and he just wasn't going about it right.

But was there something else, something obvious he'd overlooked? Well, he'd never *been* a cat; that was one thing. But he'd never been a 'possum either, the first time he had *changed—or* a deer, *or* a falcon . . .

But he'd *hunted* those animals! In one form or another he'd pursued them all. And he'd never done that with a cat. Maybe *that* was it! He'd been thinking like a white man again, had forgotten what bound him to the land and the beasts that roamed it. He hunted them, and they gave him their blood willingly; and the scale took his blood in return. But the cat he had sampled had been a simple roadkill. No one had asked it for its life; no one had covered its blood . . .

It was a tenuous supposition at best, but time was short, and at least he had something to shoot for now.

So Calvin retrieved the scale and flopped back on his bed, then clenched his fist over the talisman and closed his eyes again. But this time he did not think *cat;* this time he prayed, very fervently, to become a 'possum.

'Possum . . . 'possum . . . 'possum . . .

He let the word sink into his consciousness, tried to turn off as much of his intellect as he could, tried to center on only two things: his desire to become that beast, and his memory of how it had been when once before he had been one.

Nothing happened at first, but Calvin did not panic. He simply slipped deeper into himself, tried not to think of himself as a man on a mission at all, but as a 'possum wanting to escape a confinement it certainly would not like. It was scary, because he still had to retain some hold on his humanness—it would do no good to go 'possum and not be able to remember his goal.

'Possum . . . 'possum . . . 'possum . . .

And then, very slowly, Calvin became aware of the *change*.

It did not hurt this time. Rather, it swept over him in a tide of warmth, almost like going to sleep and then re-awakening. He was distantly aware of the thrust of his tail returning, of his skin crawling and twitching, of the odd tensions and loosenings of the clothes as he shrank within them. Before he knew it, he was blinking out at the world through the eyes of a middle-sized and decidedly russet 'possum.

In no time at all he had wriggled through two sets of bars and was scampering down the stairs, the scale clutched firmly, if awkwardly, in one paw. A skittering instant later he had reached the archway at the bottom and was navigating the hall beyond. The second door to the right was open, and he found himself peering into the sheriff's office, gratified to see that it was still operating without benefit of electricity, a situation exacerbated by the intermittent clouds that at the moment seemed to have plunged the whole room into an almost-twilight gloom. No one noticed him at first: the loathsome Abner Moncrief was drinking coffee, a secretary was repeating a string of numbers into the phone, and Old Hardface was glaring at them both. Fortunately the outer door had been cracked open for ventilation, which solved a problem he had not anticipated. That was just as well, too, because he could already sense the 'possum getting nervous at the presence of so many people. Fight or flight: his body was awash with both instincts, and he could feel his fur bristling out around him and was finding it almost impossible to resist a desire to hiss.

Calvin was just psyching himself for one final mad scurry when Hardface's eyes fell on him. She started, then proceeded to scrunch her face up into a remarkable scowl—all this in the matter of a second—and then she leapt to her feet and hollered. Abner reached for his gun but went fumble-fingered, and Calvin fought down 'possum reflexes just long enough to make a break for it—exactly as the woman chucked a copy of the Atlanta Yellow Pages at him.

Calvin dodged and scrambled for the door—which was also straight toward the woman. She sort of simultaneously sidestepped, stamped, and kicked at him, and he could not resist the temptation to give her a fast nip on the ankle.

"Get it! Get it! Get it!" Abner was yelling.

But the *last* thing Calvin heard as he dashed into the mid-morning light of a white-columned veranda was a high-pitched voice screaming, *"Rabies!"*

Calvin ducked under one of the low azaleas that marked the entrance to the jail's walk on that side, wishing vainly that he didn't have to maintain constant vigil against 'possum instincts.

He had gotten no further than determining which way east was when a Whidden Police car drove up practically beside him—Liza-Bet's Robert was at the wheel—and as it sat idling, none other than Liza-Bet herself trotted out of the courthouse and climbed in. There was another policeman with her, and she was moving rather shakily. Calvin strained his ears, but caught only one line: ". . . says it's okay for us to take her on back home . . ."

Home, Calvin realized dully, was probably where Spearfinger was.

Which meant he had to hurry double—which he could not do in this form.

But he had to go somewhere else to shift back to human; no way he could do that here. A naked Indian boy appearing out of nowhere in the jailyard was not exactly a spectacle to be ignored.

Or, he realized suddenly, did he even have to *be* human to transform again? Could he shift directly to another shape? He'd never tried, but his luck was running pretty good, all things considered, so maybe it'd be worth the attempt.

He closed his eyes, fed the scale blood—and wished, very hard, to be an eagle.

To blatantly kill one was taboo, he knew from bitter experience, never mind such minor constraints as game laws. But certain men at certain times could hunt them for religious rites (if they did not get caught). His grandfather was one of these, but had been half blind by then, and so Calvin had accompanied him, and his had been the lucky shot that had provided the eagle-flesh he had later eaten in a secret ceremony.

Eagle . . . eagle . . . eagle . . . The words became a sort of chant, and Calvin tried to remember the feel of the air beneath his wings.

The *change* came swift and sudden and caught him sufficiently off guard that he almost got entangled in the bush before he could win free.

But before he was truly aware of it, his vision had unclouded and he was looking at the world through the eyes that saw far and clear.

A minute later he was soaring over the marshes and oak woods of the eastern end of the county.

Chapter XXVI: Back and Forth

(east of Whidden, Georgia— near noon)

Don Larry Scott was pretty certain he was going crazy. Somewhere in the last ten minutes his entire perception had shifted until the whole world seemed like a dream. There was the eerie light for one thing: sunbeams lancing through the tumbling clouds making the woods at one turn dim and murky and the next alive with sparkling jewels where raindrops hung from limbs and leaves and flowers and caught the sunlight. But there were scraps of fog too: drifting in and out among the beards of Spanish moss, mixing the sunlit clarity with patches of dimness and haze. And there was the cacophony of tree frogs tuning up to mate after the shower: the Jew's-harp shrieks of the common green species mingling with the quacks of the squirrel type and the staccato bursts of the pinewood variety that sounded like a gaggle of Boy Scouts trying to learn Morse code. And in counterpoint to their tenor chattering, the constant thrumming of the earth took up the bass. Every footfall seemed to feed it, every mad-run step sent that thrum into his bones, and every one seemed to come louder. Once it had stopped, but even that cessation had frightened Don, because it felt so ominous. That had been when the shadow had found him—roughly five minutes ago.

But he was still running, through light and fog, through rain-gleamed leaves and mist-shrouded bushes. Perhaps this was Heaven, a part of him thought, for it was a beautiful morning and sufficiently uncanny to be not of this world. Or maybe it was hell, and he was doomed to run forever from a threat that never arrived, while his legs just got tireder and more numb and the pain in his side twisted deeper and his lungs refused to continue taking in air. Already that body was becoming distant, already Don almost fancied himself a mindless wraith slipping forever through the sparkling woods.

And then the shadow touched him once more: a darkness across his path that he felt before he saw. Again, and again; and now it was staying with him, flanking him as his legs carried him into a good-sized patch of riverside meadow. A brace of quail rose to his left, but he ignored them as the shadow continued on: a cruciform on the ground, swelling ever larger as he ran.

It had overtaken him now, was perhaps twenty yards ahead, and this time he caught the sound of vast wings flapping; and then a raptor shriek.

An eagle was gliding down from the sky in a graceful fan of wings and outspread tail. It landed in the yellow grass barely a dozen yards in front of him, and turned on its ocher talons to regard him through eyes baleful and yellow and strange.

Don stumbled to a halt and stared at it. To his surprise, the eagle blinked: closed its eyes as if it were trying to remember something—and then its shape began to alter. The head rose up, the legs stretched tall, the wings fanned out, and the feathers slowly withdrew as the head and thighs and torso expanded beneath them. Skin peeked through on chest and belly—ruddy skin that grew smoother even as he watched it. It was as tall as he was now, and the beak had sunk back into the face while the eyes were shifting color and the head feathers getting finer by the second.

No, not feathers, hair!

And Don Scott was staring straight into the eyes of Calvin McIntosh.

"Don, my friend," Calvin panted, when he had spat something bright into his hand, "I have a problem."

Calvin could sense Don's indecision as the boy swallowed and shifted his gaze to the ground. He crossed the few paces between them at a silent lope, then knelt before the lad and laid his hands on his sweat-drenched shoulders, forcing Don to look him in the eye.

"Yeah, it's scary, ain't it? Guess you never met a skin-changer before, have you? But you've gotta trust me—gotta help me. I think I know how to put an end to all this trouble."

"It won't stop," the boy gasped, his voice strained and distant. "I can't get away from it." Abruptly he threw himself into Calvin's arms and was once more sobbing desperately against Calvin's shoulder. "I can't get away. They're dead, and it's after me, and I wish I was dead, but I don't *wanta* be dead, but I can't get away, can't get out . . . oh God, Calvin, what am I gonna *do?*"

Calvin could only hold him, feeling the boy's heart thudding against his own. "It's okay," he whispered. "I'm here to help you, but you've gotta get control of yourself, gotta think clearly for just a minute, okay?"

"Yeah," Don managed finally, pulling slowly away. "Guess I wasn't as tough as I thought I was," the boy continued, as he flopped back on his butt and wiped his face with the tail of his T-shirt.

Calvin squatted opposite him, trying to look calm, though his nerves were so alive with urgency he could feel a scream slowly building. But he could not hurry this, not and do what he planned.

"It's what I told you," Calvin explained quietly. "It's Cherokee magic goin' on. But there's a couple of things I didn't fill you in on before. One's that I did something really stupid a few days and ago and *let* Spearfinger into this World. And the other's that she's after a friend of mine up north, but is evidently hangin' around here until she figures out where he is. I'm onto her, though, and she knows it, but the only way to kill her's with a bow, or, just possibly, a gun. I had a bow—the one you saw—but the cops took it and I didn't have a chance to get it back, so that's what I need you for.''

''What?''

''Have you got a bow, Don? Or do you know anybody's got one I can get hold of? Or a gun? Either'll do.''

''No guns,'' Don sighed. ''My stepfather got killed by one in a huntin' accident and Mom got rid of all we had. But I *have* got a bow—got it for Christmas. Not a lot of poundage, though. Don't know if it'd do you any good.''

''Your dad didn't have one?''

Don shook his head. ''Mom sold 'em when he died. She didn't even want me to have the one I've got, but Grandpa gave it to me.''

''And it's in your house?''

''Yeah, in the closet in my bedroom.''

''You got a key? I'd hate to have to break in again. Got into a little trouble last time, in case you haven't heard.''

Don fumbled in his pocket and dragged out a jingly ring of keys, searched until he located a particularly jagged dull-gold one. ''Here.''

Calvin took it and worked it off the loop. ''Thanks.'' He rose and yanked the boy up with him. ''I've gotta go now. Gotta try to get to your house ahead of your mom. I—''

The boy's face clouded, and he started shaking again. ''Mom! How . . . how's she doin'?''

Calvin steadied him with a hand. ''I'll be straight with you, Don. She's about half hysterical—and she's worried to death about you.''

''Then I gotta go home *too.*'' He blinked suddenly, as if he had only just remembered that. ''That's where I was headin', I guess. Except . . . the drummin' in the ground scared me, made me so I couldn't think, and there was the song again, only I could just sorta halfway hear it, but it made it hard to think too, and—''

"I know," Calvin inserted softly. "And I think you're right to try to get there now. But I don't think you should go alone. Unfortunately I can't escort you; it's too big a risk to me if I'm caught and there isn't really time if Spearfinger's doing what I think she is. But—" He paused suddenly. "Where're Robyn and Brock? I thought you were with them in town?"

"I was, but the drummin' started, and all I wanted to do was run . . ."

Calvin scowled thoughtfully. "But they were behind you, right? Brock and Robyn were?"

"Yeah . . . I *think*."

"Then that means they can't be too far behind, even if you've been runnin'. I tell you what, then: I *really* have to get to your house before your mother, 'cause she'll surely wanta go to your room, which is where *I* need to go—which means I don't have time to chase Brock and Robyn down right now either. But I *will* try to keep an eye out for 'em, and if I see 'em, I'll send 'em on to get you. But that means *you're* gonna have to stay put. Think you can manage that? It may be real hard on your nerves."

"But . . . *she's* out here. She'll get me! I can feel her comin' through the ground."

"Yeah," Calvin acknowledged solemny. "That's a risk, and I won't lie to you about that. But . . . I guess there's *another* thing I should have told you and haven't . . ."

He hesitated then, uncertain as to how to proceed, for it was a thing he had only just realized himself. He hadn't been entirely honest, either with himself or with Don; and that could be disastrous when on a Vision Quest. In fact, now he thought about it, it was pretty obvious that he'd had a secret agenda all along. But having accepted that, he knew there was no ethical way he could withhold the truth any longer.

"Calvin?" Don was looking at him quizzically and maybe a little afraid.

Calvin took a deep breath. "Don, I . . . I've not been completely straight with you, but now I think I've gotta be. There's a part of me that wants you to go home, to be safe, but there's . . . there's *also* a part of me that wants you out here to be bait.''

He expected the boy to flinch at that—call him liar and coward and betrayer—but Don did not. He simply nodded slowly. ''I thought that might be the case.''

Calvin shrugged helplessly. ''It was the only thing I could think of . . .''

''Yeah.''

''And I thought you could handle it. It'd certainly make things a lot easier for me.''

''Right.''

''There's one other thing . . .''

''What?''

''She's *hunting* you, Don. She told you that she was gonna do that sometime—that's why I didn't want you ever to be alone—but also why I didn't want you to go to the authorities, 'cause I thought if you stayed in the woods you'd draw her out where I could get at her. But then *I* met her and she told me *when* . . .''

Don swallowed and only managed to stammer, ''N-n-now?''

Calvin nodded. ''Since last night. Fortunately for us all, you've been with other people most of that time, or in town.''

''But that's why you want me to stay out here?''

''Yeah,'' Calvin sighed, ''it is. But there're a couple of things you can do,'' he added before Don could protest. ''One is to stop up your ears so you can't hear her song, and the other's to keep moving, 'cause I don't think she can move real fast right now, especially above ground. And . . .'' He paused, staring at the nearby woods. ''There may be a third, too; but it might be kinda risky.''

''What's that?''

''Well, she travels through the earth, we've both seen that, and she can shapeshift. But if you're not *on* the earth, maybe it'd be harder for her to get at you. Maybe if you climbed a tree or stayed close to a tree, that'd buy you some time.''

''I'm a good climber.''

''Good job! But I've really gotta be goin'. I'll be back

soon, I promise. I wouldn't leave you alone now if I didn't have to. But I think you'll be okay.''

"Right,'' the boy managed, trying to look brave.

"Okay, then,'' Calvin concluded, "now get back into the woods. The earth's her ally, but I'm not sure the trees really are, and trees have roots that can slow her down. Maybe they'll even help you.''

But Don was still hesitating. Finally Calvin reached down, dug through the matted grass until he found soil. He stuck two fingers in it and scrawled a hasty falcon on the boy's forehead. "Maybe that'll help,'' he said. "That's all I can do for now.''

"Right.''

"No problem,'' Calvin told him. "Now let's see you boogie. I want you under those trees before I leave.''

"Right,'' the boy repeated, then turned, squared his shoulders, and jogged off toward the nearest stand of live oaks.

Calvin stuffed the scale in his mouth so that he could bite it and bring forth the blood needed for the transformation, then wedged the key firmly between his toes and closed his eyes. But as he wished for wings and felt them once more returning, he wished even more desperately he could give that boy wings as well.

Five minutes later—it was amazing how short distances were when you could ride the wind—Calvin caught sight of the low, gray-shingled roof of Don's house. From the air it was apparent just how isolated the Scotts' place was: the narrow yard scarcely visible amid the pines which grew thicker to west and north, where they bordered Union Camp's plantations. But at least they were somewhat ordered; the south was mostly the unruly oak woods he'd become so familiar with the past few days, and the east held more and denser forests that gradually gave way to a shifting webwork of streams and branches, marsh and bog and swamp.

There was the railroad track too, and the narrow ribbon of road, but the nearest rooftop was more than a mile away. The unfortunate Michael's house, he thought.

Yeah, the place was certainly isolated, but that didn't mean it was deserted.

There were cops everywhere. He spotted at least five cars outside: three bronze Caprices and two blue-and-white Crown Vics: Sheriff's Department and Whidden Police, respectively. And the yard was full of uniformed men. Most were simply milling around, but a couple of policemen were prodding at the ridge of earth in the backyard where Spearfinger had emerged. As Calvin looked on, another pair sauntered out of the house talking about mud samples, just as two more ran in from the direction of Don's camp, shouting excitedly about footprints.

So much for using the key, Calvin thought, as he spiraled lower. He prayed no one would notice him, because though he was no longer human, he was not exactly unobtrusive in eagle form. It put him in a real quandary, too, because the house was overrun with cops, but he *had* to get inside to get the bow; and to either retrieve it or carry it out, he almost had to resume his own form.

But first, he supposed, he had to *find* the bow.

He waited until a maximum number of cops were occupied—fortunately most of them seemed intent on looking at the ground—and simply folded his wings and dropped the hundred or so feet to the ridge line, fanning his wings at the last minute to come to rest near the stub of chimney.

A shout from the ground heralded his arrival, but there was no helping it, though he saw a policeman pointing excitedly, and tugging on the arm of the coroner, who obligingly raised his video camera and started taping.

Calvin ignored them, but sidled around so that the chimney was between him and the men. Quickly he closed his eyes, bit down on the scale, and wished the *change*— amazed at how facile he had suddenly become at that, presumably because he had passed some threshold or other. It was 'possum again, to get him down the chimney and into the flue.

But it couldn't get him past the damper at the bottom. It was open a little, because he could feel air wafting through, but far too narrow to admit more than his pointy nose. He'd have to become something even smaller.

Sighing, Calvin chomped the scale again, and ordered the transformation—once again into a shape he had not worn before. He must have been doing something right, though, because almost as soon as the image formed in his mind he felt the alterations begin. His arms and legs shrank, he felt his tail and back stretch endlessly and become more fluid, felt his nose grow blunter, noted that sounds had become distant and blurred but that he could feel them through his whole long body. He shivered impulsively, alarmed at the alien instincts that were edging around his consciousness, and when he did that, something buzzed and rattled in the close space with him, and it took him a moment to realize it was his own tail. It had worked: Calvin had become a rattlesnake.

In that form he slid his head between the damper and the fireplace and peered out into the Scotts' living room.

It was empty—thank the gods—but Calvin wasted no time in uncoiling his rather considerable length into the space between the grate and the firescreen. He paused there, debating. He did not like this body at all, distrusted the insistent way disturbing desires were poking and prodding their way between his thoughts. 'Possum was far, far better. And so he caused it to be, and in that guise wiggled between screen and stone and was soon scampering quickly along the empty hall toward what he hoped was Don's bedroom.

Fortunately the door was cracked, and he was able to scoot inside, where he gazed up at the perfect archetypal room for a fourteen-year-old boy. There was a set of bunk beds—he thought—but over, under, and around them was a truly amazing clutter: clothes, camping gear, an empty gun rack full of cheap swords; various trophies and plaques, both academic and athletic; an antique desk piled with paperback fantasy novels and gaming manuals; several armies of painted miniatures; model cars (mostly Ferraris and Mustangs); a discount-store stereo; a small TV; maps of the heavens; posters for Def Leppard, Z.Z. Top, *Batman,* and *Top Gun;* and—covering nearly one whole

wall—a near-life-size print of a black Lamborghini Coun-
tach.

But where was the bow?

He tried to recall, but the 'possum mind kept getting in
the way—apparently it was worse when you tried to remember than when you tried to think ahead. But then he
had it; it was in the closet.

Calvin now had no choice but to become human again.

He did, his head spinning a little as the floor fell away
beneath him until he was once more at his full five-foot
ten. The chill of air-conditioning brushed his bare skin
from a vent on the floor, and he shivered, glimpsed his
nakedness in the mirror hung behind the door, but he had
no time to be concerned about modesty. A pair of silent
steps (not easy, given the clutter on the floor) brought him
to the closet, which had no option but to be open. Bracing
himself with one hand, he peered inside, saw more clutter:
clothes, ammo boxes, a baseball bat, Lazer-Tag equipment . . .

And leaning against one corner, a perfectly serviceable
recurve bow—blessedly *not* one of those compound things.
He dragged it out as quietly as he could and examined it.
It looked to be in good shape, though there was a trace of
mildew on the wood, and the string was a trifle frayed. A
forty-pounder, it appeared—a bit light for him and probably marginal for the task, but perhaps it'd do. He strung
it quickly and tested it, then reached back inside in search
of arrows. He found three—broad-tipped hunting items—
but was disappointed, for they were rusty and badly
fletched.

Now, if he could only contrive a way to get out without
attracting notice . . . Shoot, maybe he should just take
the obvious route: walk bare-assed through the house, tip
his imaginary hat to the cops in the kitchen, and saunter
on out the door, trusting shock to carry him through until
he could get to the woods, go deer or some such, and
run like blazes—and hope the bow didn't snag on something while he was at it. Or was there some other, less
risky alternative? 'Gator he had once considered—he'd
eaten it a time or two. But though he'd certainly have

shock on his side, and he knew 'gators could move pretty fast, he wasn't so sure about the bow. And that left bear and panther, but he hadn't eaten panther, so that was out. Bear, though—now *that* was an idea. They even had a little manual dexterity; possibly enough to manage the bow if he was careful.

But at the exact moment he bit the scale and began to enact the *change*, he heard the door behind him creak open and a startled male voice exclaim, "Sorry," then add, when Calvin caught his eye and saw recognition flash, "Well, I'll be a son-of-a-bitch!"

It was Abner again, and he'd caught Calvin red-handed in Don Scott's bedroom. But this time Calvin had the initiative, and before he knew it, his reflexes had taken over and launched a solid right into the man's jaw. He toppled instantly, but Calvin caught him on his way down and eased him to the floor. A fast check showed the man was still breathing. Calvin shut the door again, and this time he locked it.

Suddenly he had an idea. Acting quickly, he tugged off the man's shirt, pants, and shoes. It took a minute and made more noise than he liked, but he managed, and a moment later was putting them on. Both shirt and pants were too long and a little too snug around the chest and thighs, and the shoes were far too big, but perhaps they'd do. A final pause to load and pocket the man's .38 and see if he was still okay—he was—and Calvin scooped up the bow and arrows and headed for the door.

He had barely touched the knob when an insistent knock sounded from the other side. "Hey, Abner, you okay?"

Calvin quickly spat the scale into his hand. "Yeah," he muttered, trying to shift his voice into Abner's nervous squeak.

"What you doin' in there anyway?"

"Checkin' out some stuff."

"Why you got the door locked?"

"*Is* it?"

"Sho' is."

"Hang on a sec."

Calvin made a show of fumbling with the knob but took

care that it didn't unlock. He mumbled an assortment of curses under his breath—convincingly, he hoped.

But maybe not.

"You okay? You don't *sound* right."

"Yeah, I'm fine, just havin' trouble with the goddamn lock."

"Hell, *shoot* the friggin' thing."

"No need."

"You *sure* you're okay?"

"Yeah."

Silence then: "I don't like this, Moncrief, I'm gonna go get the lockpick and come in. You better be outside here to meet me."

"No need." But by then the man was gone.

And Calvin was up shit creek.

He stared at the still-unconscious deputy, now sprawled across the cluttered rug in his T-shirt and BVDs.

They expected Abner, huh? Well, he'd *give* them Abner.

A deep breath, and Calvin squatted beside the unconscious deputy. There was a little blood trickling from inside his mouth, and Calvin rubbed his fingers in it, then inserted them inside the man's cheek and found more. Acting before he had time to contemplate what he was actually doing, he thrust the fingers into his mouth and licked them clean. The taste of blood was thin and coppery, and he had to fight his gorge—not so much *because* it was human blood, but because it was Abner Moncrief's blood.

Now came the crucial test: he would transform again, but *not* into a beast he had hunted. This time he would become . . . something that had hunted *him!*

He closed his eyes, gripped the scale, and thought how it would be to look like Abner: to be tall and thin; and to have that funny mole on his jaw and that cynical sadistic leer and that burry hair and over-wrought mustache.

He felt the *change,* but subtly, like a shift in air pressure, a gentle set of tensions and tugs and relaxations that felt no different than the way your body did after an intensive workout.

But when he glanced into the mirror—it was Abner Moncrief's face that blinked back at him.

He also heard footsteps hurrying down the hall.

Quickly, he dragged the unconscious deputy's body around until it was out of sight of the door and tossed a pile of clothes over it, then retrieved the bow and arrows. He opened the door just as the footsteps halted on the other side.

"Sorry, boys," he mumbled to the gaping expressions that greeted him. "Had trouble with the lock and got kinda flustered." He brandished the bow. "Boy back in jail said somethin' 'bout a bow." (Which he had, when they'd asked him how he'd planned on feeding himself while camping out.) "So I thought I'd check this 'un out." (Which didn't make a lot of sense, but maybe would do in a pinch.)

And with that he marched past their incredulous stares, proceeded down the hall, and pushed through the kitchen door. He was well into the yard when a shout told him they'd finally found Abner.

But by the time he heard pursuit, he was in the woods and had shed his clothes again, stuck the arrows in his mouth along with the scale he was already biting, snagged the bow and gun with his right and left foot, respectively, and was winging aloft as an eagle.

He could not fly well thus encumbered—the balance and aerodynamics were preposterously wrong—but somehow he managed. A minute later he was gliding low above the oaks, eyes probing the shadows in search of his quarry.

Chapter XXVII: Treed

(east of Whidden, Georgia—noon)

He would be back soon, Calvin had said, and Don Scott was hoping fervently that was so. But how soon was *soon*? he wondered. Calvin had been gone maybe twelve minutes, but they'd begun to hang like hours because almost as quickly as he'd left the thrumming had begun again, stronger than ever.

Don had followed Calvin's advice and scampered to the edge of the meadow where he had climbed into a massive live oak that had branches conveniently close to the ground. And he was still there, scanning the skies with feverish anticipation for the return of his friend, who was also an eagle.

But Calvin was nowhere in sight, and Don was about to go out of his mind with dread and anticipation.

The thrumming was the worst part, because even as he surveyed the skies again, he felt the strongest cadence yet—vigorous enough to actually set the tree to trembling, so that he had to grab onto the branch above him to brace himself. Simultaneously, he heard a rumble, like the one earthquake he'd experienced two years ago on a Boy Scout trip to California. Chills raced over him as he looked down, across the scrap of meadow, and saw what he had feared: a sort of humping wave-motion in the land, as if an immense mole made its way along beneath the grass.

"No!" Terror took hold of him again and threatened to send him fleeing, but instead he climbed higher, until he found a place in the fork of a limb, with two more just at armpit level to hang onto—the whole perhaps fifteen feet in the air. But suddenly that did not seem far at all, for the ridge had now advanced up to the edge of his tree's shadow. It stopped there, sort of bunched and puckered, and he had to bite his lip to keep from crying out when he saw what slowly rose from the ground: a hideous old woman gray as gravel and dirty as ancient mud. She looked like an Indian—sort of, or at least had that kind of face and long hair in braids. Her clothes he could not make much sense of except that they were shapeless and filthy and smelled at once of earth and sand and mud. The sunlight struck her for a moment and he was certain she actually steamed, that vapor rose from her flesh and that new cracks opened in her already seamed and fissured skin as he stared at her. He heard her groan, as if in great pain, but then she peered up at him with her eyes like black stones—those same eyes he had seen in Allison's face, the ones that had glittered gleefully when this . . . *thing* had calmly devoured the living liver of his best and only friend.

And then she smiled, though it was more like mud flats splitting open in speeded-up film, and he could see her teeth: black and hard like melon seeds.

"I seem to have found you," the woman croaked, and Don felt every hair on his body rise in spite of the moss he had crammed into his ears. For though it muffled the sound enough to keep him from falling completely under Spearfinger's spell, it did not entirely obscure her voice, and he could sense some subtle power floating even in those words. It was suddenly all he could do to remain where he was.

The Stoneskin raised a ragged eyebrow. "You do not *like* this shape? It does not *please* such a delicate child as you? Then perhaps *this* one will suit you better!"

She bent over, and Don could barely hear a muffled buzz of language, but when she straightened again it was

Allison's smooth pink flesh and golden hair that showed
through the coarse shapeless drapery. "Shall I come up
and play with you, *brother?* Or would you rather come
down to me?"

"I'll stay," Don managed, wondering if he was being
an utter fool for even daring to address this thing. She
wore Allison's body now, and Allison could certainly climb
a tree, so there was nothing in the world stopping her from
coming up here and taking her own sweet time to eat his
liver.

"You'll *stay*, will you?" And the voice was hard as
stone, but so shrill it pierced the moss. "Maybe you *will*
stay, but that will not protect you." With that, the woman
began to sing. Her voice went abruptly low, like stones
grating against each other, and as she sang, bit by bit his
sister's shape slowly slumped back into that much more
fitting hideousness. He knew the song too: it was the hyp-
notizing song, the one that froze you, that made you come
to her: *Uwelanatsiku. Su sa sai!* But at the first inkling of
it, Don clamped his hands over his ears as tight as he
could and though he felt the rhythm (for Spearfinger had
started patting her foot in time with her chant), he was
able to resist the call. It took all his effort, though, for the
least bit of relaxation let the melody through the moss,
and twice he found himself almost releasing his ears so he
could hear better.

So why didn't she come up? Allison could have, and
Spearfinger had worn Allison's shape. But then he recalled
something Calvin had told him, that she was a thing of the
earth, and that trees were not all her allies. Maybe she did
not dare leave the ground, or perhaps she got weaker if
she did. Maybe—

The tempo of the thrumming suddenly became much
more intense and quicker, and the song changed into a
series of syllables even more unintelligible than heretofore. She was staring at the ground, pacing around a part
of it, pointing at the center of the small circle she had
already trod out in the marsh grass directly beneath him.
Faster and faster she hitched along, always focusing on

that one spot, and with every footfall booming through the land so that the whole vast trunk of the tree vibrated.

And then the ground was hunching up as if something sought to enter the upper world from far beneath. Don head his breath as a hump appeared where Spearfinger pointed, soon to be joined by others to either side, and as he watched in horror, that hump rose higher and higher, and he realized he was seeing a finger of stone being conjured up from the underground depths straight below him. White those stones were, like the underlying limestone, and they gleamed balefully in the noontime air. A drop of sweat fell from his nose and stained one, but then was gone, absorbed—or *drunk*—by the ever-rising boulders.

Spearfinger had slowed her chanting now, but the centermost stone continued to rise like a newborn sarcen until its top was barely three feet from his branch and level with it, with another not far behind on his other side.

"Do you *like* them?" Spearfinger crooned. "Perhaps your death will not be so bad for you, Don Scott, because you will have at least seen what few in this Lying World have."

And with that, Spearfinger laid a hand on a lump projecting from the nearest boulder and started climbing. Don shuddered, even as he scrambled higher. For it seemed to him that the stone had grown out under Spearfinger's feet and was slowly boosting her upward. Against the very bones of the earth, what chance did he have but to keep on climbing? Finally unable to continue—for she had once more begun her dreadful tune and he needed both hands to shut it out—he hooked himself into a mass of branches as well as he could and clamped his fingers on his ears and saw Spearfinger's hands push through the first of the leaves.

Chapter XXVIII:
Taking Aim

A harsh cry above and to the right startled Calvin so much he almost dropped both bow and gun, and he *did* miss a beat of wings, so that his steady onward rush faltered and he dipped a yard or so. A quick upward glance showed him something reassuring, though, for he was now being flanked by a pair of falcons: his totems acting as escorts.

Which must mean that he was finally about to meet his foe on even ground.

Assuming he could even *find* Spearfinger . . .

He flapped lower, glimpsed his wide-winged shadow rippling across the trees as he scanned the land below before, letting the eagle instincts take over as much as he dared.

Mostly he saw treetops, and to the left—the east—the gleaming twist of creeks amid the bogland. And animals, of course: the eagle never missed those, though here in the bright light of day it was mostly squirrels at play in the upper branches—and birds. More than once he had to suppress an urge to dive and feast, for this shape was ravenous—as, Calvin realized, was he.

But where was Spearfinger? Surely she was near, for both he and Don had felt the earth trembling, which meant that she was moving about. The last tremor had felt close to the meadow, too: too close for Calvin to feel comfortable about, not with a friend waiting there. Surely the ogress must surface sometime, but was he going to have to land to actually find her? This shape was so good for reconnaissance: swift and keen-eyed, but it could not see everything, was not supernatural—and Spearfinger was. She was also—

Something caught his attention, sent warning flashes tingling through his body before his human reflexes could override. People—a boy and a girl, emerging from the dense cover of the forest beside a sliver of open ground left by the collapse of a pair of trees.

Brock! Robyn! he wanted to cry out as he folded his wings to dive, but could not because of the scale and arrows in his beak.

But his shadow touched them, and the boy, looked up, puzzled, then tugged on his sister's sleeve excitedly and pointed. Calvin could not hear what he said, but his expression spoke volumes: wonder and fear and apprehension all.

Calvin alighted on the closer of the fallen trunks and balanced there for an awkward moment while he disencumbered himself of the bow and gun. That accomplished, he hopped down behind his perch, closed his eyes, and began the *change*.

There was almost no pain this time, and it came so quickly that when he eased himself up again from behind the tree, Brock hadn't made it more than a couple of strides closer. Robyn was still hanging back, but Brock assessed the situation pretty clearly and hollered over his shoulder: "See, told you so! He was the eagle, sis—only he . . . he ain't got no clothes on!"

Calvin emptied his mouth of scale and arrows and crouched as coyly as he could behind the windfall. "They don't *change*," he explained sheepishly, as Brock trotted into easy speaking range.

In response, Brock skinned out of his T-shirt and handed

it to Calvin, who draped it around his hips, seated himself on the trunk, and breathed a little easier. "Thanks," Calvin told the boy, then, louder: "It's okay, Robyn—come on over, we've gotta talk."

Robyn joined them, sat lower than Calvin, and tried not to look at him directly.

"First of all, I owe you both more than I can say," Calvin began. "So . . . thanks for helpin' to spring me. I don't know what *you* know about what's goin' on, and all; and there's not time to tell you much, but . . . well, I guess you know I'm a skinchanger by now. And I imagine Don's told you that there's *another* shapechanger out here as well, an ogress from Cherokee myth that I accidentally let into this World—that's what I've got this bow for: it *should* kill her. Trouble is, she could be anywhere and she's after Don, so I can't stay. I—"

"What about *us?*" Robyn asked pointedly, and this time she *did* look at him. "We saved your ass and you're gonna *leave* us here, with something awful on the loose?"

"I don't have any choice," Calvin replied. "But there's two of you, which makes you less likely targets, plus you're further away than Don is from where the thumping in the ground's coming from. If this works, I'll be back, I promise."

"And if it doesn't?"

Calvin shrugged helplessly. "Climb a tree, I guess. That's all I can think of. Stop up your ears if you even start to hear any kind of singing. What I'd *really* advise you to do is to get as far away as you can."

"No way," Brock interjected. "We're stayin' with you. You might need us!"

"Brock!" Robyn hissed under her breath, then spared Calvin a confused and rather apologetic shrug. "Sorry, but . . . well, we've *gotta* get goin', Brock and me. I mean I really just can't take any more of this . . . first runnin' away, and then the cops, and then all this *weird* shit. And we've *gotta* get outta here real soon. I mean I'm sorry, and all: I like you a *lot,* Calvin, I really do, but . . . but I'm just too wired. It's just too much!" By the time she finished her eyes were wet and her shoulders were shaking.

"But, sis, he *needs* us!"

Calvin regarded her soberly. "It's okay, Robyn," he said gently. "I *know* you're in a bad place. You don't owe me anything, and if you did, you've already paid it by getting the scale to me. But there's a couple of things you ought to know. One is that Spearfinger may very well come after you and Brock if I fail, in which case you *will* need to be as far away as you can. The other thing is that this place may be crawlin' with cops real soon: after me and who knows what else. So what I'd advise you to do is to lie low for the next few hours—presuming I accomplish anything. After that—"

"*Great,*" Robyn interrupted. "If we stay we're fodder for monsters, and if we go we're fodder for the cops and it's back to Dear Old Dad. We'll be eaten alive either way!"

Brock was obviously distressed. "But *sis,* we've gotta help him!"

"*How?* If it's something supernatural like he said, what good are *we* gonna do?"

"What's *he* gonna do?"

"He's a shapechanger."

"Brock's right," Calvin agreed, looking uneasy, for the tempo of the thrumming had speeded up. "There's nothing either of you *can* do except stay away. The fewer folks around, the less likely you are to get hurt. Lord knows I've got enough deaths on my conscience now!"

"But . . ." And then a look of horrified realization crossed Robyn's already tear-stained face. "Oh jeeze, Calvin—I'm sorry. I . . . I never thought of that, but I . . . I guess they *are* your fault. It's just that . . . well, I've never *seen* 'em—all these dead folks—so it's, like, remote to me. God, your conscience must be *killin'* you!"

"I can't worry about that now," Calvin told her. "And I've *got* to go. I may have wasted too much time already. You guys can watch or not, but this may be kinda disconcerting."

And with that, he returned the scale and arrows to his mouth, closed his eyes, pinned the talisman between his beak and tongue so that it pierced the latter, and once more worked the *change*. When he opened them again, he saw Brock gazing at him steadily, and Robyn looking away, with tears flowing steadily down her cheeks. Calvin seized the bow and gun with his talons and rose into the sky. The last thing he heard was Brock shouting vehemently, "No, we've *gotta* help him," and Robyn's sobbing reply, "I don't know, I just don't know!"

And then the whistling of onrushing wind and the heavy thump of his wings drowned out their voices.

Now that Calvin had touched base with Robyn and Brock, he badly needed to check up on Don—if he was not too late—and then get on with the business at hand. He was heading for the meadow now, could already see it shining gold amid the surrounding browns and greens. A moment later he crested a low rise and found his gaze drawn to an uncommonly tall live oak at the edge of the open space. There was movement among its branches, too: more than could be accounted for by squirrels.

Don was in trouble, no doubt about it, for the ground had squeezed out what looked like white termite mounds directly beneath the tree, and Calvin was now close enough to hear snatches of Spearfinger's song. He slowed cautiously, torn between his sense of urgency and the knowledge that for his plan to succeed he had to move stealthily, to give Spearfinger no sign that he was nearby.

Which meant that he had to avoid touching the earth as much as possible, for it seemed to be able to tell her things. With that in mind, he started gliding lazily among the trees, until he found a suitable perch perhaps forty yards from his foe—one that was thick enough to support his human form, screened him in shadow, yet gave him a relatively unobstructed view.

He managed to get situated without dropping either weapon—the strength of his talons helped there, along with the width of the branch and its slightly depressed upper surface—but did not immediately *change*.

And always he kept his eyes focused on his foe.

That was difficult, too, for she was perched atop the

tallest mound of stone and was working her way into the lower boughs, and even with eagle eyes he could only glimpse her obscurely: as a dusty shape among the small glossy leaves. This close her song came to him fairly clearly, and he had to fight its soothing, paralyzing effect. Fortunately the eagle body was an asset, the feathers over his ears muffling the sound barely enough.

But what of Don? Calvin could see the boy clambering frantically ever higher in the tree, pausing frequently to clap his hands over his ears—probably when he could no longer resist the song. But already he was straining the limits. Any farther, and the limbs might not support his weight, while Spearfinger had the whole strength of the World to hold *her* firm.

The song ceased abruptly, and Calvin could just make out Spearfinger's voice, taunting: "You can go no higher, boy—but *I* can. I will catch you, and when I do I will eat your liver! Just think of it: a few breaths from now you will find yourself trapped, and then you will hear my song in your ears so close you cannot escape it, and you will not be able to move, and then I will touch you, oh so gently, I will slide my nails along your naked side and I will find the place where your liver lies, and then I will slowly stick in my finger and drag out a little and devour it as you watch. It will take me maybe half a day—and all that time you will live in agony and fear and every morsel will taste better than the one before because of that, so I will want to prolong my feast as long as possible. But eventually there will be no more liver, and *then* I will commence on the *rest* of you until nothing remains save your mind. *Then* I will let you die. Think of *that*, boy: a day from now you *will* be dead. You will face the Greatest Darkness."

"No!" Don screamed desperately, taking advantage of the lull in the song to scramble to a yet more perilous perch, which brought him into clearer view. "You lie, you lie, you lie! Calvin'll get you! And *you'll* be the one that's dead, you . . . you ugly old woman!"

Spearfinger did not reply, but she took up the song again, louder than before, and much more vehemently.

Calvin noted with sick dread that the mound beneath her was rising again. He also saw that Don Scott had frozen where he was, evidently victim of the song at last. Probably at that range he could not resist it plugged ears or no.

Calvin could delay no longer. A deep breath, eyes closed, the *change* willed, and he was a man once more, balancing precariously on a tree branch. He removed the arrows from his mouth, spat the scale into his hand, and carefully stepped off the bow and revolver. Steadying himself with one hand, he retrieved the bow, nocked an arrow, and took experimental aim.

No good. There were too many leaves on his tree blocking his way, and Spearfinger was almost completely enshrouded by a particularly dense mass of Spanish moss on the other oak. He had to get a clearer view.

Which meant he had to wait until she was higher—but the only way to be sure she would go farther up was to make her stop singing so that Don could move again. And what would make her do that?

A distraction? But what kind? It had to be obvious, had to be threatening, but could not betray him. Maybe he could—

"No!" A boy's shout cut the silence of the meadow. Calvin's heart skipped a beat, and an awful sick feeling crept into the pit of his stomach. He was too late, Spearfinger had started working her vengeance on Don. Calvin lowered the bow in disgust.

Except . . . that wasn't Don's voice! And it had not come from the live oak, but from the ground somewhere between there and Calvin's tree . . .

Brock! His gaze darted frantically away from Spearfinger, probing the dark foliage to his right—

—And saw a small, slim figure dart into the meadow, still yelling "No"—except now the shouts were segueing into song: REM's "Radio Free Europe," of all things, loudly and badly rendered in an uneasy tenor, and with half the lyrics replaced by *da-das*.

What on earth was Brock doing? Calvin wondered. Then he realized that the boy's melody was clashing with Spearfinger's song, muddying it, disjoining the troubling harmonies of the spell.

"*Uwelanatsiku. Su sa sai!*"

". . . *Raaaa-dee-oh Freeeeee Eur-opppp* . . ."

Don was moving again, too, scrambling—not higher, but toward the trunk, where he could maybe get purchase to sturdier branches—or possibly make the ground again and escape. That route took him perilously close to the second stone spire, though, and Calvin heard the boy shriek as he brushed it and it oozed out to block his way. The boy was faster, though.

And—thank Brock . . . Kanati . . . the God of Abraham, all—Spearfinger was climbing again, in exactly the direction Calvin wanted. Bracing himself as well as he could, Calvin slowly rose from his limb, hooked a leg around a branch that angled out from the one on which he stood, and once more took aim. He could feel his body relaxing into the stance he had worn a thousand times since he was ten, the one that had accounted for more than a deer or two in its time. He could feel the centers of strength easing into alignment: the tension in his shoulders as he drew the bow, the matching twinges in his biceps, the pain in the fingers he'd curled around the string.

He had it, was squinting down the shaft, then looking beyond, to where Spearfinger was almost in full view. Her song had grown louder, too, and acquired a secondary melody, and Calvin forced himself to ignore the way Brock's tune ended abruptly in a strangled scream.

The ogress was maybe twenty feet from the ground now, with Don perhaps five feet higher and to her left and looking as frightened as Calvin had ever seen a kid look. Now all he had to do was to draw perfect aim on Spearfinger's hideous hand and send an arrow through the very center.

It was a broad-tipped hunting arrow he used, one of the three he had, and there was rust on it from disuse. He wished he'd had time to clean it, to purify it, to mutter spells of accuracy upon it. But the only charm he knew, he slowly whispered.

"*Usinuliyu Selagwutsi Gigagei getsunneliga tsudandagihi aye'liyu, usinuliyu* . . .

"Instantly the red *selagwutsi* strike you in the very center of your soul—*instantly* . . ."

And there was the hand, rising higher as Spearfinger used it to push aside a branch, even as the stone beneath her lifted her another few inches.

Closer . . .

Closer . . .

Calvin released his breath he'd been holding in a shouted "*Yu!*" and loosed the string.

The arrow flew slowly, or so it seemed: too slowly; and in that long instant Calvin felt his heart stop cold.

For the Stoneskin's song had ended abruptly.

And as he gaped incredulously, the arrow buried itself exactly where he had aimed: into the center of Spearfinger's left hand.

The air suddenly rang with a horrible shriek like stones being ripped asunder, and even at this distance, Calvin could see blood gushing out, for the arrow had continued straight through until stopped by the fletchings. Another scream, a sort of incredulous gape as stony black eyes probed straight at him and then the ogress was falling— but she did not tumble off the mound. Rather, it was as if she simply lost her substance and her whole body trickled down the precipitous slope.

A startled exclamation followed quickly by a burst of agitation from the foliage was Don's reaction.

"Stay there!" Calvin shouted. He pitched the bow and remaining arrows to the ground, grabbed the .38 and the scale, and started down the tree. Not as easy as it looked, either: his limb was too high to leap from, and he saw no point in *changing* for that one act. The bark of this particular tree was uncommonly rough, too, yet free of useful projections, so that Calvin's bare chest and thighs bore more than their share of scratches and gouges when he finally let go and leapt the last few feet to the ground.

A quick trot out from under the low-hanging branches showed him poor Brock in the embrace of a low mound of stone that had risen up behind him and prisoned him in much the same way the stones had earlier captured Calvin. The runaway was yelling like a fool, but once he saw

Calvin, his tone changed to one of joy: "Hey, good job, Calvin, m' man! Hey, you done it, you done it!"

Loping across the meadow, Calvin hoped he had.

As he neared the fingerlike projections he unlocked the safety on the revolver, still on guard, though those excrescences too were shrinking, evidently freed by their mistress's demise.

Closer and closer, and then he was standing maybe a yard from the ogress, on the side opposite the wounded hand.

Above him, Don had made his way to the lowest branch, but an upraised finger and a warning shake of Calvin's head kept him from coming any closer.

Calvin stared down at his adversary. She lay flat on the ground amid the knee-high grass, arms outstretched, mouth agape, eyes staring and dull. The arrow still protruded from her palm. She looked dead. *Very* dead, and Calvin suddenly felt his gorge rise because murderer or not, she was also a sentient being and the idea of killing a sentient being repulsed him. For the merest instant this was not a shapechanging monster, but merely a withered old woman, not unlike his own grandmother. Except that he did not dare allow himself to think along those lines. No, this *was* Utlunta Spearfinger, the Stoneskin, and he had laid her low. Above him the falcons circled lazily, their shadows tracing spirals across the ground.

Finger still on the trigger, Calvin nudged the body with his toe. It gave no resistance, though it seemed unusually heavy. But Spearfinger's withered breast neither rose not fell, and the long gray hairs on her chin did not quiver with even the shallowest of breaths.

Finally he lowered the weapon and sidled around her; at a loss as to how to proceed, since none of his schemes had extended beyond this point. It would be another body, he supposed. More grist for the mill that could hang him— which he imagined meant that he'd now have no choice but to make some kind of lightning shapechanged raid on Sandy's house, explain things, and move on, adopt another identity, or maybe simply do what he'd considered a time or two before: become animal and never return.

"Is she dead?" Don whispered nervously from his limb. "Is she, Calvin?"

Another prod of his toe, and Calvin nodded. "I reckon so."

"So what d' we do now?"

"Good question. I guess we—"

But he could not finish, for without warning the dreadful awl-finger stabbed up at him. He had just time to fling himself backward before Spearfinger leapt to her feet and was slashing at him over and over again. He dodged twice, but the third time he felt the edge of her nail scour a line across his belly.

"So you thought to *slay* me, did you, Edahi?" she cackled, as Calvin scooted backward crabstyle, unable to rise because of the way she was looming over him, and unable to shoot because Don was so close above. "So you thought to slay Spearfinger? Well, you trusted too much in white man's wisdom in that, *Calvin,* for if you had thought, you would have known the truth. Spearfinger *was* slain, so how could she live again? She is not like the beasts of Galunlati, gifted with endless lives. She was a woman of this World once, and was slain and rose no more."

"But how . . . ?" Calvin blurted, so full of despair and dread he could barely function.

"*That* Spearfinger was my mother," the ogress shrieked. And then she lunged.

The horrified shouts of two boys and one young man broke the quiet of the meadow, but rising above them all was a maniacal female cackle.

Chapter XXIX:
Gathering at the River

A quick roll sideways was all that saved Calvin, and even then he felt hot agony bounce along his ribs as the terrible fingernail grazed his side. A second, duller pain was the arrow fletching raking his hip raw as the hand continued its arc—and then he was clear: on his back and kicking out at Spearfinger's thin brown ankles. He connected, too, but it was like impacting stone, and more pain shot through his shins. The ogress, however, did not seem to be affected at all. He glimpsed her from the corner of his eye as he rolled once more—and saw just enough to know she was yanking on the arrow that impaled her hand, jerking the shaft inch by agonizing inch through her stony flesh.

And freeing it—to fling it straight at him with uncanny accuracy. He managed to dodge, but his frantic scrambles brought him full into the shadow of the oak, where hard lumps of acorns poked at him from the ground, adding their own tiny bruises to his already bleeding flesh. A ridge of knobby root ended his progress abruptly, and he grunted in dismay, still unable to regain his feet, use the scale, or get off a shot at his adversary—who was now hurling herself at him, oblivious to her obvious wound.

She might have struck him dead on, too, had Don not chosen that moment to drop from his branch onto her shoulders and wrap his arms around her neck in a sprawling clench that was born part in anger, part in panic, and part in abject surprise. The boy was also hollering at the top of his lungs, perhaps to keep himself sane; and Calvin could see the monster flinch as strong boy fingers found her trachea and curled inward. But then fury burned into her coal-lump eyes, and she gave her whole humped body a violent shake that sent Don's legs flying straight out behind her. He held on through two such assaults, but by then Utlunta had snaked her hand to the side, so that the boy's next gyration would impale him upon the finger.

"*Jump!*" Calvin shouted desperately. "Jump, Don, *jump!*"

Don did, coming to rest with an unceremonious thump maybe six feet to the Stoneskin's right. The sudden shift in balance made Spearfinger stagger in the opposite direction—which gave both Don and Calvin time to regain their feet.

"Run!" Calvin motioned Don toward the open field. "Go help Brock, and then get the hell out of here!"

And then Calvin was himself on the move, trying to at least get clear of the tree so he would have more options. The arrow hadn't worked, which probably meant that Spearfinger's heart was not where legend said it should be. But that still left the rest of her body. And he still had the gun—and, finally, a clear target.

Spearfinger was charging him, pounding toward him at a surprising pace, her awl-finger outstretched before her like a lance. It would have been a ludicrous enough image to make him laugh—a bag lady on angel dust—except for the leer of hatred that contorted her gray-brown face.

He aimed by reflex, pulled the trigger, spat six bullets into her chest. Dust erupted in a long line across the rags, and blood was everywhere, but she did not falter.

Calvin clicked the trigger twice more before he realized the .38 was empty.

And Spearfinger was still rushing toward him.

He tensed and turned sideways, gun in his right hand,

scale in the other, hoping to club the back of her skull with the butt of the revolver when they came together. *Next year,* he told himself—hell, next *week*—he'd enroll in one of those martial arts classes he'd been promising himself forever. If there *was* a next week for him.

Closer and closer . . . then impact. The force jarred Calvin so much that he dropped the gun and retained the scale only by gripping it so tightly in his fist it almost brought blood. They grappled together for a moment, locked in an awkward embrace made more so by the pervasive gore and the fact that Calvin did not have full use of both hands. Spearfinger's face was inches from his; he could smell her breath—sweet and sickly like rotting blood and day-old meat; nearly choked on the hot-stone-and-dust odor that billowed out from her rags. Somehow he managed to confine her elbows at the waist, thereby restricting the deadly finger—whereupon he twisted sideways, hoping his superior leverage would hurl her to the ground. Once he got her down, maybe he could hold her until he could regain sufficient presence of mind to *change,* or one of the boys could retrieve the bow—which were the only options he could think of.

Miraculously, his effort succeeded—in part—for he felt Spearfinger's legs leave the ground. Abruptly she seemed much lighter, which shocked Calvin so much that he lost his balance and toppled to earth again, fortunately atop her. He locked his legs around her, prisoning the finger between her thigh and his, and glanced up frantically. "Don! Brock! Get the bow, it's under the tree I was in."

He saw a small, dark-haired shape sprinting that way from the direction of the live oak; while another crouched to one side holding something dark before its face, all but hidden by the tall grass. That last was odd, too: he thought Brock was more reliable than to waste time playing games. But then Calvin had no time for puzzles, because Spearfinger was writhing beneath him, twisting back and forth so vigorously it took every ounce of strength and all his concentration to keep her pinned.

"You cannot defeat me, Edahi," she spat. "When this day ends I will have eaten your liver!"

''The hell you will!'' And Calvin renewed his desperate hold.

An evil grin crossed the Stoneskin's face, and her features wavered: blurring, running, smoothing, and realigning—until Calvin suddenly found himself staring into the china-blue eyes of Allison Scott. ''You wouldn't hurt a little girl, would you?'' Spearfinger cackled. ''Not pretty little Allison Scott! But you already *have*, Edahi. She is dead and you are the one who brought death to her!''

Calvin gasped, sick at what he knew was the truth, but he maintained his grip, not daring to relax in spite of what he saw, for the shape beneath him, though a tiny girl's, was strong as ever.

The features slid and shifted again, became those of a tired-looking woman in her late twenties. ''This one's liver I sampled *first*,'' Spearfinger crowed. ''But it was poisoned, as your kind poison all things including themselves. That is why I would keep you forever from Galunlati!

''But this,'' she added with a triumphant cackle, ''was sheer pleasure to devour: the liver rich with life and joy and strength.'' And she took on the startled, perky features of Don Scott's dead friend, Michael.

''And *this*—ah, *this* liver was tastiest of all!'' With that Calvin looked upon the face of his father. ''You killed me, my son,'' he growled, though it was Spearfinger's mocking tones. ''As sure as you live you brought my death, and that will forever be on your soul!''

''No!'' Calvin shouted, jerking back reflexively, and in that moment Spearfinger made her move, threw her whole unwieldy weight up and over, and Calvin was suddenly trapped beneath her. She was in her right shape now, but fortunately he still held the deadly hand immobile—though that did not seem to concern her.

And *where* were Don and Brock? He couldn't see Brock at all, and Don was fumbling around the base of the tree Calvin had shot from. Which meant he couldn't count on help from that quarter any time soon.

Spearfinger grinned even more gleefully and opened her mouth to sing. It was the alternate tune, the one that called upon the earth, and Calvin felt the ground trembling beneath him as limestone from the depths responded to her summons. Though the monster was astride him now, he could hear her feet keeping time against the ground, sending thrummings all along the meadow. He knew what she was about, too: she'd keep him here until the stone could rise up and engulf him. And then she'd eat his liver. Probably both boys', too: she didn't seem to fear them at all, though Don had something long in his hand now. Brock, for his part, was still missing.

"The arrows!" Calvin yelled again. "Get the arrows! Get the—"

The song shifted abruptly, became the paralysis spell; still mingling with the other. This close it was overpowering, and Calvin could feel the earth heaving at his back, even as his tongue went limp and his muscles began to weaken.

He jerked and twisted desperately, and as he did a glob of spittle flew from his mouth and splattered against Spearfinger's bare arm. To his surprise a thin tendril of steam rose there. She grunted, as if she had been bitten by an insect, but for that instant her song faltered, and Calvin acted. He wrenched a hand free—the left, the one that was not holding off the deadly finger—and smashed it into Spearfinger's mouth. It hurt like hell, and blood erupted from his knuckles, but he managed to work his fingers inside, and actually seize her tongue. It was like grappling with a wet rattlesnake, but he held on desperately, feeling his strength return as the song turned to strangled gaspings.

"Don!" he shouted again. "Any *time*, man!"

But Spearfinger had recovered, and very calmly and defiantly bit down. He felt her teeth tearing into his fingers until they grated against bone, but she was not strong enough to bite through, and he held grimly on, meanwhile trying with all his might to fling her away and get to his feet again.

He almost succeeded, but she dragged him back down as he rose to a crouch; and they rolled over and over on the ground. And then she was once more on top of him, her whole filthy, sticky body pressing down against his. He still had his hand in her mouth, was still being bitten, but the movement had made him lose his grip on her arm. Only then did he realize that he had somehow dropped the scale.

He tried frantically to locate it, but could not, and an instant later, she had him pinned even more thoroughly than before. He saw her left arm, the deadly digit at its end, shoot sideways, then arc around to snake between them. A snarl of glee contorted the hideous features inches from his own. He felt the finger pause above his heart, expected to find it jabbing up under his rib cage to still his live—but it drew back instead, until it was poised directly below his ribs on his right-hand side.

And Calvin could not move, for it was as if all the weight of the world held him down.

And slowly, slowly, he felt a warm wash of pain as the finger pierced his skin, poked through the long smooth muscles of his side, and encountered what they sought. It did not hurt as much as he expected, but the strangeness of it—something wiggling around inside him—made him gag.

Spearfinger cackled—which freed his hand, though there was little he could do with it now except flail ineffectually against her back—and she bent close to whisper in his ear. "I am touching your *liver* now, Calvin Fargo McIntosh. It *feels* like a nice plump one. I hope you enjoy losing it as much as I will enjoy taking it from you!"

Calvin struggled in vain, and gagged again as the finger rubbed against something deep in his gut. Another gag—base reflex—and suddenly something brushed his lips. It was the ogress's ear! Lacking any other options, he bit down hard, felt cartilage part and his teeth meet, sawed them back and forth.

Utlunta howled, but did not release him, though now he could taste blood.

Something stirred in him at that: a fleeting flash of Power, almost exactly like he felt when he *changed!* And with it, unaccountably, came a realization. Spearfinger was a shapeshifter, was as full of Galunlati magic as the uktena was. He had lost the scale, but still tasted her Power now. And he had hunted her as well, which meant . . .

One chance.

He closed his eyes, shut out the probing pain in his side, and prayed he was right—that her blood was as potent a talisman as the scale—and willed the *change.*

It was the hardest one he had ever done, because he had to shut out all outward sensations—the agony in his side, the stench in his nostrils, the awful taste in his mouth—in order to succeed.

But apparently it was working, for strange memories began to mingle with his own, and he felt his body grow at once weaker and stronger than before, felt the probing in his side become more distant and then vanish altogether as Spearfinger found herself embracing a twin as invulnerable as she.

He shoved, she shoved back; but she was the shocked one now and he regained his feet. A glance over his shoulder showed Don finally with arrows, heading his way, though he hesitated every few yards and looked back, as if torn by indecision. He was evidently shouting at someone, too; but Calvin couldn't tell who, or hear what was said above Spearfinger's rasping breathing.

But then he had no more time for him, for the Spearfinger instincts were trying to take over. He let them—dared to let echoes of that other mind touch his own, for maybe, just maybe, if he was careful, he could find out what he wanted.

A deep breath, a withdrawal of self to a deeper level, and the Spearfinger thoughts filled his mind. He prowled among them, searching . . . ? And then . . . pay dirt! Her heart was in her *other* hand—that he should have guessed. But lurking in hidden places behind were those things she most feared:

Fire . . . air . . . and water!

It was as simple as that, for fire could crack rock, or wind and water turn its own sandy children against it and wear it away.

But there was no fire here, and it would be as dangerous to him as to her.

Air, though . . . Spearfinger had seemed lighter during that brief moment when he had held her aloft. He tried that again, filtering his human knowledge of wrestling through sorceress muscles—and had no trouble wrenching his foe from her feet and flinging her over his shoulder. Her weight diminished immediately, and he could feel her stabbing at him with the finger, though it could not pierce his skin, now as hard as hers. It was still an irritant, however, but a shift of his grip to include her bony wrist put an end to that.

Now if only he could get her to water, perhaps he'd have a chance.

The nearest wasn't far, either: a tributary stream to Iodine Creek he'd spotted from the air. In fact, the narrow end of the meadow actually bordered it. He started that way at a slow trudge, for though Spearfinger was lighter than she had been, still she was a considerable weight for an old woman's body to support.

Or did he actually *need* her form now?

But then a disturbing thought struck him: Spearfinger had tasted his blood as surely as he had tasted hers. Why, then, couldn't she shift herself, become *him*, and begin the whole battle all over? And worse, since he had used the monster's blood instead of the scale to empower the *change*, how was he going to return to his rightful form without either biting her again (which would be pretty awkward) or finding the latter? And then a ghost of alien memory answered both questions: the ogress had to have eaten a person's liver to take his shape (she was evidently limited to duplicating humans); but *his* transformations were based on a slightly different system. More to the point, though, as long as her blood was in his body he no longer needed outside assistance to *change*.

So maybe . . .

A pause, a blanking, an application of will, and he was himself once more. Stronger now, he strode onward, until barely fifty paces separated him from his goal.

"I'd stop right there," a voice shouted suddenly, amplified through a megaphone and echoing across the meadow. "Stop right there, Mr. McIntosh, or we'll have to shoot!"

Calvin glanced toward the shout, and glimpsed three men—sheriff's deputies Adams and Moncrief, and Robert the policeman—slowly advancing toward him, the deputies with drawn .38s. The coroner was with them too, though a little behind, waving his arms at them as if to call them back. He was also holding his video camera, and Calvin realized he was the one he'd glimpsed lurking in the tall grass earlier—the one he'd stupidly mistaken for Brock. A further check showed him that Don was there as well, fully equipped with bow and arrow, but no longer advancing.

His heart sank. He was so close, so close, but he knew what the cops must be seeing: a naked guy lugging a struggling old woman toward a creek. But he had no choice.

"Stop, I say!"

Brock's voice interrupted from out of nowhere, cracking up and down the scale with urgency. "No, officers, you don't understand, you don't *understand!*"

"Get away, son!" That was Adams.

Calvin simply kept walking, determined to get as far as he could. Maybe if he was lucky, Don would get his act together and shoot Spearfinger in her vulnerable spot.

Maybe pigs would fly in from China.

"Stop!"

A shot rang out, coupled with a cry of dismay from Brock. But it had been a woman who had shouted, and Calvin turned just enough to see that Brock and Robyn had joined the fray. Brock was hollering at the men indignantly. But Robyn—bless the girl she was holding them at bay with something that looked suspiciously like a pistol, without a doubt the inhabitant of the empty holster he'd spotted earlier. Evidently she'd just fired a warning shot, and *not* at Calvin. An explosion of conversation ensued, which Calvin couldn't hear above the rustle of his legs through the grass and the noise of Spearfinger's grunts and threats and thrashings. But the next thing he knew, Don had slipped away from the furiously taping coroner

and had drawn a bead on the lawmen with the bow, even
as Robyn eased around to impose herself between the deputies and Calvin.

How long *that* standoff would last, Calvin hadn't a clue.
But he tried to move on a little faster.

The wind shifted somewhat, and he found he could hear
more clearly: the sounds of scuffling, of shouts and orders
and counter-orders.

"We've gotta get out there."

"He'll hurt her if we try to take him, though!"

"Let me *go*, goddamn it!" (That was Brock).

And then, "Jesus, damn! The bastard bit me again!"

"Catch him!"

"Don't move a *muscle*, you asshole!" *That* was Robyn.

Calvin wished he could see what was happening. But
Spearfinger was struggling even more violently than heretofore, and he had no choice but to continue his march
toward the stream, with the hapless hag writhing, kicking,
and kneeing him whenever she could. He still held the
deadly hand, though, and she was powerless. And she was
not singing, which he thought strange until he remembered something else from the brief time he had shared
her mind: the earth would aid her only if she stood upon
it—that was why she was so weak now.

More shouts, then; feet thumping on the ground, the
swish of tall grass against clothing; and suddenly there
was someone beside him. Calvin knew from the flash of
blond hair who it was.

"Brock!" he gasped. The boy's hands reached out to
brace him as Spearfinger's thrashings became so vigorous
wild he almost fell.

"That's me, man!"

"Mind tellin' me what the *hell* is goin' on?"

Brock shifted his grip and began. "Well, when you flew
off there wasn't anything I could do but follow, was there?
And when I finally saw there was something I *could* do, I
just did it. Them rocks 'bout got me, though," he added.
"But soon as I got loose I ran for Robyn 'cause I knew
she had a gun. Figured I'd get it for you. Trouble was, the

cops showed up right as we got back—'parently they'd heard your shots, or something.''

"And now they won't dare shoot for fear of hittin' you!''

"Robyn'd shoot *them* if they even tried!''

"There just the four of 'em?''

"Yeah,'' Brock replied. "The stupid skinny one and the stupid fat one and the police-guy—he's on your side, I think. Oh, and that coroner-fellow—he'd have *helped*, 'cept he twisted the shit out of his ankle just as he got here.''

"I'd surrender, if I was you!'' Abner called ineffectually. "We'll get you sooner or later!''

"Later's all I need,'' Calvin shouted back. "Sorry, guys, but I know what I'm doin'.''

"Don't be a *fool*, boy; put that woman down!'' That had been Robert.

Calvin ignored them. The ground had grown mushy and was lowering toward a scrap of sand at the edge of the creek. Spearfinger was almost frantic with terror: shrieking and kicking furiously, but Brock had seized her feet and was dampening her more violent gyrations, though she rained threats on top of threats upon their heads.

And then sand squished up between Calvin's toes, and an instant later, he was wading into the water. It was neither wide nor deep—maybe ten feet across and barely past his waist at the center, where he halted.

"Get back'' he told Brock—whereupon he heaved Spearfinger off his shoulder and plunged her into the stream. He lowered himself, then, grasping her firmly by the elbows while he braced her back across one knee and gradually secured his hold—rather like an old-fashioned baptizing, until Calvin began to force her head down.

The ogress screamed piteously, as if she had been plunged into boiling oil, and Calvin was startled to see steam rising around them, steam that he felt hot against his skin. Utlunta was flailing more than ever, but he clearly had the upper hand and the strength to restrain her. Brock backed away a few more paces and stood with his arms outstretched, shielding Calvin from the bank, but he could hear shouts and the sound of running and knew the cops would not be long in arriving.

A deep breath, a fast decision, and he thrust Utlunta's head beneath the surface. More steam rose, and he could actually feel her weight decreasing, as if she were dissolving, melting away, washing downstream with the water.

A sudden convulsion so startled him that he would have lost her had he not yanked her back by a strip of leather thong that bound part of her garment. Her head broke water, though, and his gorge rose, for the ogress really was partly dissolved: her lips were in tatters and her cheekbones showed through her skin. Their eyes met, but where before those stony black orbs had been filled with hate and arrogance, now there was only fear and pain. And Calvin realized that he truly did not want to do this. Spearfinger was his foe, a monster from his childhood nightmares made manifest. But she was a sentient creature, too: had a brain, feelings, cognizance of her own mortality, and more on her conscience to make her fear death than many. Lord knew he understood how she might feel about *that*, had she any feelings left. *He* had deaths on his conscience, at least four of them. She had many times that number across uncounted years. He wondered if they came back to haunt her as his already were doing not a day old.

Did he want *another* death on his conscience?

"I'll let you go" he gritted. "I'll raise a fog and send you back to Galunlati if you'll give me your word you won't come back to this World."

"They will kill you, boy; you know that."

"Maybe; but that's not your problem, is it? I don't *want* to kill you, Utlunta. I just want you out of this World, I want you where you belong."

"You want to save your friend, that is all."

"Isn't that enough? But you're wrong there; I want to save more than him; I want to save *all* your victims."

"I will have victims in Galunlati!"

"But you're *part* of Galunlati."

"Death is death, and life is life. Do you trade lives here for lives there?"

"I have no choice," Calvin choked. "But there's a thing you should know, and that's that even if you remain here, even if I'm jailed and you go free, others'll still be after you. Maybe Dave'll even bring the folk of Tir-Nan-Og to hunt you, sealed borders or not. And if *our* folk catch you, Utlunta, then you'd *really* better watch out, 'cause they won't imprison you in *chains*, they'll imprison you with *science*. They'll find out that you're not like anything they've ever seen, and then they'll begin to wonder about you and where you come from, and they may find out about Galunlati, and then men from the Lying World will go there in such numbers that everything that makes Galunlati special will cease to be! Do you *want* that, Spearfinger? You came here to save your World. If you don't return you'll destroy it, more surely than the secrets Dave knows ever will."

"You lie!" Spearfinger shrieked. "All men are liars!"

And with that, she broke loose and floundered toward the shore. The force made Calvin fall backward, and when he surfaced again, it was to see Spearfinger almost to the beach. Brock was there, and Don as well, both gaping incredulously. But then two more figures loped into view behind them: Abner and Adamo, both with naked .38s.

They took in the scene in an instant, and though Abner's revolver wavered briefly toward Calvin, it soon shifted toward the ogress. She seemed to be totally insane now, and leapt straight toward the startled deputy.

"*Uwelanatsik—*" she screamed, but as she did twin barrels spat lead into her and she staggered, one leg apparently shattered. But she was not so easily cowed, and somehow found strength to stumble another few steps toward shore before guns blazed again and the other leg collapsed. She fell with her left hand on the bank and her body in the stream. Nor could she rise, though she tried. Calvin splashed over to where she lay, while the boys hung back and the two deputies made their way down the bank, guns still drawn and cocked.

But they were too late: for the water had finally eaten its way through Spearfinger's right wrist, and even as they watched, it separated and swirled away in the tannin-dark waters, and with it went her hidden heart. The pace of her dissolution accelerated then, and Calvin glimpsed three more faces at the top of the bank: Robyn and Robert, who together were supporting an obviously limping coroner. He had a video camera on his shoulder, and with it he taped the final dissolution of Utlunta Spearfinger, the Stoneskin.

When nothing remained but her left hand and her tattered dress, Calvin hauled himself to shore. Robert passed him his black leather jacket, which he tied around his waist by the sleeves before slumping onto a rock, where he stared vacantly at the forest on the other side of the creek. It was over. He had won. But he was in nowise free of either guilt or responsibility.

Robyn flopped down beside him. She took his arm, laid her head against his shoulder, then removed a black and white bandanna from her pocket and began to try to pat him dry.

Someone joined him on the other side: the round-faced coroner. "I reckon we're gonna need to talk to you some," he said. "But I reckon I saw what I saw, and I reckon I've got witnesses, and I reckon this here camera ain't gonna lie."

"What'd you get?" Calvin asked dully. "How'd you know how to find us?"

The man grinned broadly. "Well, first there was that eagle where there shouldn't have been any eagles, and then two Abners in one place was a little more than even *I'm* willin' to take for granted, so I just had to find out what was goin' on. And I'm a little better tracker than some of these folks, so I just followed your trail away from the Scotts' house until it ran out. Lost you for a while there, but then I looked up and saw that eagle again, only this time it was flyin' along with something in its talons and beak that looked a whole lot like a bow and arrow, and I just climbed up in a tree and followed it with my binocs till it dived down behind some timber, and then I guess I just trusted to luck and headed that way."

"He's spry, for an old guy," Robert inserted.

"Not spry enough, though." the coroner laughed back,

though there was a trace of pain in his face was well. "Just about the time I got to where I could see something—you'd just jumped stark naked outta that tree—I tripped and fell. Twisted the *hell* outta my ankle, but by then I wasn't goin' nowhere anyway, not with what *I* was seein' out there in the meadow." He patted his camera like he would a favorite dog. "Fortunately I had me a walkie-talkie, and Robert had seen me leavin' and wanted to ask me something, so he followed. I radioed back for help and got him—and Adams and Moncrief."

"And the camera?" Calvin wondered. "Did you . . . ?"

The coroner grinned broadly. "Not *everything*, but I got that whole fight on tape—got proof that thing could change shape. And I've got proof she washed away. Also," he added, resting a plastic bag carefully on his knee, "I've got her hand here with that finger on it. And I bet it'll match samples we've got off at least four bodies."

"*Four?* So that woman in Jefferson too . . . ?"

" 'Fraid so—but I think we've got enough between 'em to clear you, if you're willin' to make a deposition. And if these kids are willin' to answer some questions as well."

Calvin eyed Don and Robyn and Brock curiously. "Don will, I think; won't you?" he asked, and Don nodded eagerly, but his voice cracked when he spoke.

'For Calvin, and for my sister," the boy said. "And . . . and for Michael." And with that name his eyes misted and he finally gave vent to the last of the anguish he had so long suppressed, burying his face in Robyn's shoulder when she rose to comfort him.

"What about you two?" the coroner inquired. "I 'spect they'd like statements from you as well."

Calvin could see Robyn stiffen. "*That* may be a problem."

"No it won't," Brock interrupted. "We'll tell the truth, and the whole truth. We'll tell it about everything."

"No," Robyn cried again. "Brock, we *can't*. It's too awful."

"What is?" the coroner asked, taking Brock's chin in his hand and forcing the boy's eyes to meet his own.

Robyn looked desolate. "I . . . I'm pregnant!" she

wailed. "My stepdad knocked me up. I tried to tell 'em, but nobody'd believe me. That was the final straw."

"Oh Christ," Calvin groaned. "Why didn't you let me know?"

"Why? Wasn't your fault. Nothin' *you* could do."

"Yeah, but . . . well, maybe I'd have been a little more considerate."

"One person's as important as two," Robyn countered. "And besides, you *were* pretty damned considerate—I just didn't know you were."

"Georgia law allows DNA evidence," the coroner inserted. "A couple of samples, a test or two, and you're home free."

"Not quite," Robyn replied flatly, her hands still patting Don absently.

"Never *home*," Brock appended. "One thing, man: we *ain't* goin' home again."

"Well, *I* certainly can't guarantee that," the coroner replied, somewhat taken aback, "but I kinda imagine they're gonna want you to stick around up here a day or two, anyway. After that, we'll see. And now, if you don't mind, we need to get this circus moving." He cast a glance at Calvin. "You okay, boy? Well as can be expected?"

Calvin nodded wearily and rose, then knotted the jacket sleeves more tightly around his waist and joined the party at the bank. There were more cops there now, but none seemed disposed to harass him, though Abner definitely looked more than a little disappointed.

"You know, this could get to be a real mess," Calvin told Robert confidentially. "This can't go far, or there's no tellin' *what'll* happen."

Robert raised an eyebrow in reply. "It won't go no further than it *has* to, that's for sure! Still, most of what's happened, we can chalk up to some poor old bag lady gone insane. Sheriff's boys had to shoot her. Got physical evidence to link her to the murders' that oughta be enough."

"What about me?" Calvin wondered.

"We'll need you to talk some," the coroner said, joining him on the other side, with Robyn helping him along and Brock proudly lugging the camera. "And then I'll need to find some way to arrange a power outage to destroy the files. I understand your little friend here might be of some use there—hear he's got quite a knack for managing those kinda occurrences." He grinned at Brock and cuffed him. "Not much for Southern hospitality, are we? And if I was *any* of you, I'd think a long time before I come down here again, and longer before I fooled around with magic."

Calvin started at that. "How'd you know?"

"I've read some books," the man chuckled. "And a coupla days ago I was down at Cumberland to tape the storm—that's kinda a hobby of mine—and right in the middle of the worst part I seen a fleet of ships sailin' in the air. That enough for you?"

"It's enough," Calvin agreed, for the man had obviously witnessed the Faery naval battle that had marked the end of his and Dave's previous adventure—the one he had come here to sort out. "Don't ask me any more," he added. And then they started across the meadow.

The sun came out then, and cast Calvin's shadow dark beneath him, but he was not surprised when two more joined it: winged ones, darting in to flank him on either side. And then two more, and then two more, and then dozens.

"Peregrines," somebody exclaimed. "Thought they 'uz gone from here."

"Wrong season anyway," someone else decided.

"Not this time," Calvin told them, and bent over to whisper so that only Brock and Don and Robyn could here. "Not when they're your totem."

Epilogue I: Road Trip

(east of Whidden, Georgia—
Friday, June 20—mid-morning)

It was not, Calvin reflected as he wandered through the oak woods east of Whidden, an optimum day for magic. But that conclusion was not based on any consultation of signs or portents, not on a reading of auguries in sheep entrails or the position of planets and stars. Rather, it was founded on the simple assumption that there was no way on earth that magic could have improved on the world around him that particular morning.

It was warm, but not enough to provoke a sweat. And the humidity was as low as it ever got in Georgia, so that for once he didn't feel sticky when engaging in a moderate amount of exercise.

And there was the land itself. It was as though the whole natural world was thanking him for the destruction of some plague the best way it knew how: with bright light and clear weather, with oak leaves so transparently green they looked too fine to be silk, with palmetto fronds glossier than any wax candles, with tendrils of Spanish moss so delicate that the finest carded wool could never hope to match them. The very sky had a polished look about it, and the air was almost too fresh-smelling to be entirely real. Even the dragonflies flitting above Iodine Creek like tiny jeweled stealth-fighters seemed to sparkle more brightly in the slanting sun. And the animals, too, seemed to have abandoned their usual reserve, for on his trek overland from the hearings in town Calvin had seen three deer, including one with the rare piebald coat; more squirrels and rabbits than he could count; and even a sleek furtive flash of grayish-tan that he was almost certain was a panther, though there were officially none left in Georgia. Certainly he'd never seen cat tracks that large left by anything else.

As for birds, there were red-cockaded woodpeckers and pileated woodpeckers, great blue herons and green-backed herons, snowy egrets and bobwhites, blue jays and redtailed hawks. And peregrine falcons, of course. *Lots* of those.

Yeah, it was a beautiful morning. All that was lacking was Sandy—but Calvin'd be seeing her soon enough; she was already on her way down to pick him up. After all, he still had a wedding to go to in less than twenty-four hours, and there'd be a few more days tying up loose ends down here after that.

Meanwhile, he had to retrieve some things from his campsite. He paused to rest on a fallen log and thought back over all that had transpired since Spearfinger's fall.

As soon as the authorities—mostly Police Lieutenant Robert Richards and coroner William Roach—had gotten affairs in order at the meadow, they had escorted Calvin and the runaways to town and put them up in a motel at county expense. He wasn't certain what had become of Robyn and Brock after that, but *he* had spent the remainder of the afternoon and a good part of the evening matching reasonable questions with unreasonable replies—and without hostility on either side, though what he told the very select number of state *and* federal investigators, some of whom had choppered in all the way from Atlanta, certainly strained their credulity and elicited lots of shrugs and whistles and sighs and upcast eyes. But every time the grilling threatened to get out of hand, good old Bill the coroner would simply run his tape again and inquire, very calmly, if there was any *other* explanation.

There was not.

And fortunately, no one had thought to inquire how Spearfinger had come into this World to start with—apparently the notion that such a being was from Somewhere Else and could actually be summoned (whether by accident or design) was beyond their comprehension. Calvin was just as glad, too, for that would have opened up far too large a Pandora's Box for even him to try closing. Telling the *exact* truth had saved him more than once, but he was tired of being forever on guard.

As for Abner Moncrief, he had been sent packing along with most of the rest of the sheriff's department once proof of the secret interrogation room had surfaced (its usual guests were low-life out-of-towners who'd never heard of either law or lawyers). There was even talk of opening it to the public, for it really had been used by the Underground Railroad two courthouses ago. Sheriff Lexington himself, already scrutinized by the Georgia Bureau of Investigation for nepotism, procedural violations, and general corruption, had been suspended pending further investigation, with Robert Richards swapping uniforms to assume his duties. There were advantages, it seemed, to the fast-moving justice of small rural counties.

But now, this morning, Calvin at last had time on his hands, and chose to spend it by resuming the quest that had brought him to Willacoochee County in the first place: the desire to get his head straight about magic.

Yeah, maybe a couple of hours by Iodine Creek would mellow him out enough that he could focus on the finer points of lycanthropy.

Or perhaps not. For now that he was near enough to see the flash of sunlight on the narrow strip of white sand just south of his campsite, he was sufficiently close to hear the low murmur of voices. He tensed, fearful the authorities had chosen not to trust him again, though they already had David's bow as further evidence of his forays into other Worlds, and he'd finally recovered the scale as well. *He* still had that.

But he need not have been concerned, for it was only Brock and Robyn, both looking clean and energetic and well-fed as a result of *their* twenty-four hours of alternating bed-rest, face-stuffing, and intensive interrogation. Calvin hadn't been permitted to see them during that time, nor Don either—a shame because he'd long since started regarding them as friends.

Brock looked up from cramming a handful of candy wrappers into a plastic garbage bag and grinned wildly. "Calvin!" he shrilled, sprinting straight toward him, only to recover himself at the last minute and finish his approach with the languidly self-conscious nonchalance he doubtless affected with his mall-haunting cronies.

Robyn simply danced over to hug him, and—to his utter amazement—planted a wet one right on his mouth.

"You guys movin' on?" Calvin wondered after they'd caught up on greetings and the happenings of the past day.

"Reckon so," Brock replied sadly. "Mom sent us some money for airfare to England. She's gonna settle things with the lawyers once and for all, then call us back. They've already applied for a restrainin' order, or whatever you call it, on Dad. Seems they think Robyn's . . . problem may finally convince some folks of how serious things are."

"What *about* your . . . problem?" Calvin ventured, looking at Robyn.

She shrugged. "Oh, I'm gonna have the kid, then give it up for adoption in England." Calvin thought she was trying to sound casual, though he suspected that a lot of angst had gone into that decision. "They've got socialized medicine over there, so it'll be cheaper," she added with unnecessary defensiveness.

"But . . ."

"Kid can't help who its father is, Calvin. And neither can Brock and me. Only difference is, we can do something about it."

"What about the DNA test?"

"Gonna have it and split. We'll send taped testimony if we have to."

"Sounds good. I— "

"Calvin?" Brock interrupted, looking very anxious. "Can . . . can I ask you somethin'?"

Calvin ruffled his hair. "Sure guy. You can't *possibly* ask me anything I haven't heard before."

"I . . . would you teach me how to do magic?"

Calvin's face clouded. He took Brock by the shoulders and regarded him seriously. "Are you *sure* you wanta do that? You've seen what it can do. But one thing it *won't* do is make you happy."

"But . . ."

"No, *listen* to me," Calvin went on earnestly. "I know it looks like fun, looks like a way to get your heart's desire—but believe me, it's a lot more trouble than it's worth. For one thing, you have to be *really* responsible 'cause you can't always foresee the outcome of your actions, even when they're well-intended. Like when I opened the gate between here and Galunlati and called the Little Deer, I had nothing but good in mind, yet I let Spearfinger into this World, and that cost four folks their lives and several more major-league psychological trauma, and those are both things I'm gonna have to live with for the rest of my days. Worse, it's gonna cost a lot of folks their peace of mind, 'cause most folks don't believe in other Worlds, only a lot of 'em suddenly have evidence to the contrary, and *that* worries me a lot, 'cause info like that has always been privileged, always been guarded—only all of a sudden it's not guarded anymore. Suddenly me and my friends can't control who knows. And that's just *one* of the problems."

"Yeah, but what about the neat stuff—shapechangin', and all?"

"Yeah, well, there *is* that," Calvin admitted. "But I've been a kid too, Brock, and not that long ago, however old I may look. I know the temptations you guys are under. You wouldn't be able to help showin' off, wouldn't be able to resist hintin' to the guys that pick on you that you could top *them* if you wanted to, that you're somehow special. Except that that'll only get you in more trouble. Trust me, I've been special one way or another all my life, and it's certainly not a picnic."

Brock's eyes misted. "Gee. Cal, I thought at least *you'd* understand."

"Tell you what," Calvin drawled after a pause. "I'll do this much: I'll meet you a year from now at this same place—or any place you choose. And if you still want to do it, I'll show you how to do *one* thing. Meanwhile, I'll try to talk to my teacher about you—I've got a feelin' he's gonna be gettin' in touch with me real soon. If he sounds interested, I'll pass you on to him. That's as much as I ought to do now."

"Yeah, well . . . thanks." Brock smiled tentatively and stuck out his hand, as if to say, "No hard feelings," but Calvin could still see his disappointment.

"Sorry," Calvin whispered, with another muss of his hair. "But remember, I didn't say *no, just maybe later.*"

"Later's a long time for a kid," Robyn noted, but the relief on her face told Calvin that from her point of view, he had made the right decision.

"But a life's too precious to waste chasin' after things that won't make you happy," Calvin replied.

"Yeah, and speaking of that, I can't help but wonder what might have been." She glanced at him with a coy smile.

"Yeah." Calvin grinned. "Like maybe if we'd met two years ago."

"Yeah." Robyn grinned back. "Like that."

"There's better guys in the world for you than me, though," Calvin assured her. "I'd be nothin' but trouble. And you never could tell who you were gonna get for company."

"But it'd be really nice to have you around while we're working through this."

"Got ears, got money, you've got my number, all you need's a telephone."

"Thanks," Robyn sighed wistfully. She took his hand, raised it to her lips, and kissed it, then returned to her packing, rather less energetic than before.

Brock was still hanging around, though, and Calvin realized suddenly that he was really going to miss the kid. That seemed to be a thing with him: he'd just start getting to know somebody and then lose them. That he'd actually managed to make friends with Dave was something of a miracle.

"Well, at least *your* problem's settled," Brock mumbled awkwardly.

Calvin shook his head. "Not hardly! I've still got to go before the grand jury sometime, *and* talk to the district attorney. And somehow I've gotta try to keep this as quiet as I can, and get word to my friends about what's happened so they can be on guard. And I've gotta think about some dead people," he added. "It's a hard thing, Brock, to have people's deaths on your conscience."

"Yeah," Brock said. "I know."

Calvin regarded him curiously. "Yeah," he echoed, "I think you do. Least you know it's not all Saturday mornin' cartoons and RoboCop and Rambo."

"Yeah."

"One thing puzzles me, though."

Brock cocked an eyebrow expectantly.

"Why in the *world* did you choose *that* song to counteract Spearfinger?"

"It's the only one I could think of," Brock admitted. "Scared me too, once I got started, 'cause I sure didn't know all the lyrics."

"I noticed."

"It saved your ass anyway."

"Tisk, tisk, what would Robyn say?"

"She'd say—"

"Yo, Calvin!" a new voice broke in, and Calvin glanced over his shoulder to see Don Scott bouncing down the deer trail that served as a path almost all the way to his house.

"Enough of this foolishness," Calvin told Brock hastily. "I kinda need to have a word alone with Don." And with that he trotted over to meet the new arrival.

"I just wanted to say thanks," Don told him. "Mom says thanks too—more or less. Well, she didn't actually say that, but I think she more or less understands what's goin' on. Robert's been talkin' to her a lot."

"You didn't tell her, did you? Not the *whole* thing?"

Don shook his head. "I let the coroner take care of that.

But she knows you're not guilty. She believed that bag lady stuff, I think.''

"What about Mike's dad?"

"He believes the same thing, don't wanta know more."

"Probably just as well."

"Yeah."

"What about you?"

"I'm fine."

"Tough?"

"Yeah, tough."

Calvin gave him a brotherly hug around the shoulders. "Know something, Don-o?"

"What?"

"I know somebody I bet was just like you at your age—somebody just like you're gonna grow up to be."

"Who?"

"Name's David."

"What about me?" Brock interrupted, rejoining them. "You know anybody like me?"

"Yeah." Calvin grinned. "And *his* name's David too!"

"Brock!" Robyn yelled. "You 'bout ready to go?"

"Yeah," Brock called back. "Just a sec."

"*Go?*" Don cried in horror. "Go where?"

"To town," Calvin told him. "They've gotta stick around here a couple more days."

"You too?"

Calvin shook his head. "Leavin' tonight, comin' back late Sunday—but I'm gonna be hangin' 'round Whidden till then."

"Want some company?"

"If you do."

"Sure."

"You know," Calvin mused, when he and Don had rejoined Robyn and Brock, "I really *could* get into showin' all you folks around the mountains."

"That's real interesting," Robyn laughed. " 'Cause I bet all three of us could sure get into being shown!"

Calvin's reply was to whistle, very softly, the "Werepossum Blues."

Epilogue II: Roadkill

(Enotah County, Georgia—Friday, June 20—late afternoon)

"Hey, Alec, come here—I wanta show you something!" David Sullivan cried with wide-eyed urgency, snagging his best friend by the collar and steering him around the corner of the rambling wooden farmhouse he shared with his parents and brother. It was still an hour before suppertime, but the mountains that rose close behind the Sullivan homestead were already darkening ever so slightly, though the rounded ridges across the hollow still shone luminous green. In a little while David and his buddy would be leaving to attend Gary Hudson's rehearsal dinner. A bachelor party would follow, and tomorrow the first of their high school chums would be married. *They* were to have their first go at being groomsmen, another taste of impending adulthood.

That was scary to think about, too, but for now there was still time for hanging out, time for just being kids.

David had just returned from lugging a bag of particularly odorous garbage to the family burning pit—a chore Alec had understandably elected not to accompany him on, preferring a second helping of Mama Sullivan's Red Velvet Cake.

"What is it *now*, oh Mad One?" Alec chided as he trotted dutifully along behind his friend. "We've gotta get *goin'* in a minute."

"Something strange," David replied ominously. *"Real* strange."

"How strange—David, you're not gettin' mixed up with magic again, are you?"

David shrugged. "I *hope* not. But see for yourself."

They were behind the barn now, right at the edge of the forest. A rock outcrop rose up there, one they'd played cavemen on when the were little. A thousand imaginary dinosaurs had been hurled to their death from the top of that slab of granite.

But it was different now, and when David stepped aside, Alec saw how much it had changed.

For, emerging from the rockface exactly at David's eye level, with its back still imprisoned in solid stone and its face contorted with fear and shock, was the frozen figure of a young man wrought from thousands of pebbles. And it looked exactly like David.

"Weird," Alec ventured.

"Yeah," David agreed. "You could say that."

"All we *need's* another mystery."

David rolled his eyes. "No kiddin'! Hey, maybe—"

But he was not allowed to finish, because his younger brother, Little Billy, came charging up all out of breath. "You've got a call, Davy! It's from Calvin. Says it's urgent."

David and Alec exchanged wary glances. "Wonder when he's gonna be gettin' here," Alec mused as they started back at a jog. "I figured he'd have checked in by now."

"Search me," David yelled over his shoulder as he poured on a burst of speed and raced ahead. "Wonder what he'll say when we tell him we've got *another* blessed magical mystery."

"What indeed?" Alec said to the silence of the mountains.

But if the mountains could answer, they chose not to.

TOM DEITZ grew up in Young Harris, Georgia, and earned bachelor of arts and master of arts degrees from the University of Georgia. His major in medieval English (it was as close as he could get to Tolkien) and his fondness for castles, Celtic art, and costumes led Mr. Deitz to the society for Creative Anachronism, of which he is still a member. A "fair-to-middlin' " artist, Mr. Deitz is also a car nut (he has lately acquired a black '62 Lincoln named Uriel which he hopes to restore someday), has recently taken up horseback riding and hunting (neither with remarkable success), and *still* thinks every now and then about building a castle.

Stoneskin's Revenge is his sixth magical adventure set in Georgia, and the first to focus exclusively on Calvin McIntosh. His previous novels include the tales of David Sullivan: *Windmaster's Bane, Fireshaper's Doom, Darkthunder's Way, and Sunshaker's War,* and an independent fantasy, *The Gryphon King.* All are available from Avon Books.